THE VINE TREE

S. P. DAWES

Copyright © 2020 by S. P. Dawes

All rights reserved.

No part of this book may be reproduced in any form or by any electronic or mechanical means, including information storage and retrieval systems, without written permission from the author, except for the use of brief quotations in a book review.

❦ Created with Vellum

SYNOPSIS

Hayley may have escaped the sect that once held her captive, but that didn't mean life moving forward will be easy. With a new baby, nightmares that haunt her, and the trauma of it all has her falling into a dark place. When an unexpected admirer makes himself known, she only becomes more confused. She has to decide how to handle him along with the failing relationship she and Jesse cannot seem to get right. Will she be able to survive it? Or will all the different forces once again win and pull her back in?

Jesse finally has the family he always wanted. The problem he is facing is that he has no idea how to act after the love of his life has escaped such a horrible sect. Every time he tries to get closer, it ends in an argument that pushes them farther apart. Frustration and a new player in their lives, one who is manipulating this fragile relationship, is not helping. Will he be able to find the proper way to her heart? Or will he give up when he seems to be beating his head against a brick wall?

This family could use a break. They have been through more than most. Does love really conquer all, or is it not strong enough to save this one?

DISCLAIMER & NOTE FROM AUTHOR

Disclaimer

This romantic suspense thriller is a work of fiction. All characters, storylines, events and locations in this novel are a work of fiction.

Note from the Author

This is a dark romance and as such it touches on some dark areas that could be a concern for some readers. Although every care is taken not to cause pain to any reader, this book could cause triggers if you have gone through certain things in your life. So please be cautious if you have experienced domestic violence, miscarriage and /or rape.

I am a big believer in strength and courage whilst facing great adversity. This story is to reflect that and not glamourise abuse in any way.

Trauma does not make you a victim, it makes you a survivor.

Hold your head high.

PROLOGUE

A BOY LAY SHIVERING ON THE FROZEN FLOOR, TEETH CHATTERING relentlessly at first, then drowsy and barely breathing. Naked with his knees curled up to his chin, he welcomed the sudden warmth, as if a sudden afterglow had surrounded him. All he could see was darkness, with the wind cutting into his pale skin, but he couldn't remember how he got here.

WHY HAD it come to this? Looking at the sky it grew even darker, the clouds had disappeared from view, but he knew they were there, because the stars had abandoned him a long while ago.

FEELING HIMSELF GROW WARMER, finally descending into it, his eyelids grew heavy, his head lolled as his body ached and deepened. His head turning into an anchor, heavy and keeping him from floating upwards, as he could only hope he would float upwards. He wasn't an evil person, not really. He'd done things, but he had tried to put them right. He had really tried to be better, hoping it all counted as he let go of his last breath, darkness descended.

CHAPTER 1

Hayley sat on the settee, proudly watching Daniel, who was engrossed in the fuss that was being made of him by his grandparents for his 'naming' party. Refusing to have him christened had caused unrest in the family, and this was her way of smoothing things over with everyone it had upset. Hayley and Jesse, Daniel's father, reconciled that a naming celebration gave everyone a chance to have a party and officially welcome him into their family. Something that needed to happen because of his abrupt and shocking entrance.

Hayley couldn't stomach doing that in a church. She never wanted to go near one ever again. Coupled with the fact she didn't need a priest to deliver him from evil because in her mind she'd already achieved that herself, she didn't need God. He had deserted her a long time ago.

Daniel had been born the day Hayley had escaped captivity from her former ex. He was the head of a religious sect that dabbled in arranged marriages and financial contracts such as drugs and prostitution. After Hayley had escaped the first time, she had thought her life could only get better. But she had become embroiled in a case that Jesse had been investigating. When Hayley had escaped for the second time, to protect Jesse from a hired hit man, she had gone into labour. Everyone at the time had thought the child resulted from the abuse she'd endured at the hands of Demy. But after DNA testing, it had confirmed that her scant time with Jesse before they had abducted her, was enough to father Daniel.

Her abuser was living at her majesties pleasure awaiting trial for his part in sex trafficking and illegal drug distribution as well as abduction, rape and illegal imprisonment. He hadn't seen her since the day he'd left to complete a transaction at the port, and she was in no rush to face him in court. Her testimony was going to be harrowing, and she only wished she wouldn't have to attend. But part of her wanted to see him rot in jail and look him in the eyes when she delivered the last nails to his coffin.

Daniel's arrival into hers and Jesse's life after such a traumatic experience wasn't something, they handed self-help pamphlets out for, and they had struggled. Their relationship had become so strained that eventually Hayley had called time on them, moving out several weeks before the party, and only a week after their first Christmas together.

Jesse's parent's Marie and Michael had welcomed her into their home for the second time. And whilst she knew it disappointed them, they had never made her feel any less part of the family, and she appreciated that. With no one else to rely on for help, their unwavering support was much needed, if undeserved, in her mind.

Daniel's grandparents were more than prepared to show him off and take the limelight. Something else she was thankful for. With so many people she didn't know coming and going through the house all day to drop off presents and request cuddles, she felt even more out of the loop. She kept having to remind herself that this was what family was; she wanted Daniel to have as many people as possible. Knowing how it felt to be alone, she'd never want that for him.

Preferring to be in the shadows, she made her way round the living room to pick up everyone's empty cups so she could escape to the kitchen to replenish everyone's drinks. Being useful felt a lot better than observing everyone around her dote on her son when she didn't feel involved.

Hayley didn't understand what was happening. She felt down all the time, lonely, but didn't want involvement with anything. She wanted to cry so much that it hurt to hold the tears in and any energy she woke up with quickly depleted. While she knew she needed help, asking for it was too remote to comprehend. She was hoping the enormous dark cloud hovering over her would break soon and disappear, but the more it hung around, the more she felt under it. Breaking up with Jesse had only compounded her feelings of worthlessness, he didn't deserve her outbursts and shitty moods, and she'd seen him struggle with her emotions. Jesse, tiptoeing around her, walking on eggshells in his own home, upset her. He'd been nothing but good to her, and she had brought her darkness along for the ride. She felt broken and she couldn't allow Jesse to fix her; he didn't owe her anything, and she needed to keep it that way. In her world, debts always got paid.

Daniel eagerly watched his Nana shake a rattle in front of him. Marie looked at him with love and admiration while Michael looked on with unmistakable pride in his eyes. Lifting him up in the air, above his head making him giggle, Daniel dripped saliva onto Michael's balding head. Grimacing, he lowered him once again, wiping his face on his sleeve. Hayley watched on as Marie lunged forward to take her grandson in her arms as the living room door swung open and Jesse stood watching the excitement unfold.

Turning to Hayley who stood motionless as she watched him breathe heavily from running, saw his expression waver slightly, and it had her heart clamping. Pinning her with his eyes, she could see it hurt him to see her there and a wave of renewed guilt washed over her. She had been his biggest mistake.

A week after Christmas they had gone their separate ways, after finding it impossible to be the people that they each needed. No matter how much they had attempted to stick by each other and help one another through their trials and tribulations, they had fallen short and had ultimately reconciled that they needed space from each other to heal. But with being eternally connected through their only son, they were still learning how to be around each other without being 'together'. His face now proved to her, he hadn't worked out how to do that yet, and maybe she never would.

Walking over to Daniel holding his hands out, Daniel strained his podgy little arms to get to him and Marie passed him over, laughing at how much Daniel must have missed him. Hayley and Jesse understand the hint and looked at each other knowingly but with warmth before Jesse turned back to his son, pulling at his tie.

Michael and Marie had not taken the news that they were giving up well, they were both convinced that they should work at it, but Hayley and Jesse had ultimately decided that maybe they shouldn't have to work so hard to make something that should come naturally, work.

"How are you?" Asked Jesse, leaving the chaos of the living room and closing the door behind him a few minutes later.

Hayley had taken leave as soon as possible. Having Jesse in the same room as her only stirred up emotions that were best left alone. Turning from the kettle, she smiled her fake smile to show he had no effect on her and she could be around him without wanting to cling to him like an infant. "Good. You?" She squeaked, trying to sound brighter than she felt.

Jesse watched her shifting from one foot to the other as if to find a position she didn't feel so vulnerable in. But other than she looked good, happy, and that thought pained him, as he hadn't been able to provide her with that whilst they had been together, to realise she'd found that without him stung. The sudden realisation made him feel useless. How had she become so empowered without him when all he'd tried to do was to protect and take care of her? How had he failed so badly to show her how much she meant to him? Because he'd failed to protect her, and that was the long and short of it, she held him responsible, and she'd be right to. He felt dreadful for how he had treated her before she had gone missing, and even worse that they had taken her at all. It had been his job to protect her, and he'd failed.

"Yep," answered Jesse, running his hand through his hair.

Thinking of asking him what was wrong, she instantly dismissed it. She couldn't be that person anymore, after all they were trying to cut ties, not get closer. All she had to do was to take part in making a stable environment for Daniel, so their contaminated relationship never affected him. That meant stepping back, letting someone else take care of him. That thought alone sent a shiver down her spine and she turned back to the kettle to re-balance.

"Coffee?" Jesse nodded and Hayley took another cup down from the cupboard above her head, trying to control her pounding heart.

When the kettle finished boiling, Hayley made the drinks and Jesse walked over to help her deliver the cups. In doing so, his hand brushed across the top of hers. Both feeling it, they stopped moving and gave each other a second to process what had happened. They weren't together, but that didn't mean that the spark between them had received the memo.

Hayley forced herself not to look up, knowing her lips would be only centimetres from his, scratching her right eyebrow instead. She covered her face from view as Jesse watched her tense. "Do you want to take yours and your dad's in?"

"Sorry?" Asked Jesse absently.

"Drink." Smiled Hayley; embarrassed to be caught daydreaming.

He picked up two cups by the handles, turning away from her as she looked up towards the ceiling, to steady her breathing, and tip the threatening tears back into her eyelids. Christmas had been the last time the family had been together and what should have been a joyous occasion felt oddly sombre, especially with it being the first time the family had all got together since her abduction. The celebration his parents had envisioned hadn't materialised. Feelings were still raw, explanations still hadn't surfaced, and the tension had been so visible you could almost cut through it with a knife. But they had all agreed to meet up for Daniel. Although the brothers and Hayley understood, it was more for their parents' sake.

Later into the Christmas evening, keeping up appearances had been hard to manage in the face of such bombardment, so they had both stepped outside to get some fresh air when Daniel was being force fed angel delight. They hadn't spoken, just leant up beside each other in the cool air, taking in the scent of the icy sugar beet factory that surrounded the old market town. But oddly, it had been the only time of that day they had enjoyed. It had been quiet, still, and they had been close to each other without messing it up and causing more upset or anguish. Something they'd barely been able to manage since she'd given birth to their son.

Thinking back, Hayley remembered it being the only time they hadn't argued. Just stood enjoying the cool air on their faces away from the excitement. Then as quickly as it had happened the spell had broken by his phone and he had disappeared inside to answer it. All she had wanted to do was tell him how sorry she was and wrap her arms around him. Hoping he would pull her into him. She needed to feel his heartbeat under hers, and the security he offered, but then that led to the memories of rejection. He hadn't touched her since she had got back, as though she was spoilt and she hated he saw her abuser every time they got close. It only reminded her of what he'd done to her, and that they broke her.

Hayley leant on the worktop still looking at the ceiling remembering Christmas with sadness weighing heavy in her heart. Whatever feelings she had had all those months ago, she knew they would not disappear overnight, but they were becoming more like sores. One scratch and they seeped, reopened, and got infected, causing more pain than before. If she wasn't careful, they'd never heal.

She'd never heal.

"Where is he?" Shouted Rob, bursting into the kitchen like a wind up jack-in-the-box.

Hayley turned to him, smiling, nodding towards the living room. She watched him repeat the process before swinging Daniel around in the air. It had been remarkable how Daniel being on the scene had helped repair the damage done to Jesse and Rob's relationship. It had taken a little longer with Hayley but they were now on speaking terms and she was sure he believed her version of events, even if he still didn't like to hear about his ex-girlfriend's involvement. But she couldn't blame him for that.

Caitlyn had conspired with Hayley's ex, Demy, to abduct her, resulting in Hayley being beaten, starved and raped. Her involvement had been pivotal in getting Hayley where they needed, and so Jesse's team had thrown the book at her, establishing a guilty sentence lasting five years. Rob had always defended her involvement, saying she hadn't had a choice. They had threatened her, and she was defending and protecting herself. Jesse hadn't taken to his version of events very well, and they'd come to blows frequently.

Twenty minutes later Daniel sat between Jesse's legs on the floor banging on his drum kit with the palm of his hands, enjoying the sound it made and the reactions from his grandparents each time he hit it.

Hayley had handed everyone a drink, and she sat on the arm of the sofa closest to the door whilst watching Daniel belly chuckle at his grandparents. Rob sat in the middle of the sofa quietly watching with a contented look on his face. Hayley couldn't help smiling. Watching Jesse made her realise what a wonderful dad he was. He cared deeply for him, and his eyes always sparkled around him. She just wished those same eyes descended on her, but then she knew her resolve wouldn't stand a chance.

"I hear you're joining us next week?" Asked Rob, glancing to Hayley.

Her smile suddenly dropped as she turned to him, realising immediately he'd said something he shouldn't have. He quickly looked to Jesse. Hayley doing the same saw the shock and horror on his face.

"Sorry, I didn't mean..." apologised Rob after registering Jesse's face.

Hayley shook her head. "No. Don't be daft, I meant to say something, I just forgot with all the excitement," she replied unconvincingly. Having them all turn to her, she felt her face flush and a heat wave sweep her body. Biting her bottom lip, she begged herself to stay cool and not cry. "They said I could have my old job back," she offered, sounding apologetic and child like. The room remained silent even after Daniel had stopped chuckling, and she felt suddenly nervous and unprepared.

"What's happening with Daniel?" Marie asked.

Hayley could tell Marie had only asked what everyone else wanted to know. It was obvious from Jesse's face that he wasn't happy, and she chastised herself for not saying something before now without the audience. "I've found a childminder, she's lovely, and she's flexible so I can work shifts," Hayley wasn't sure why she felt so guilty. Surely, he realised she had to work.

Jesse looked over to his parents before standing up. Walking towards the kitchen, Hayley took her cue to leave when he glowered at her. In the kitchen Jesse stood with his hands on his hips waiting for an explanation.

"I don't know what you want me to say?" Asked Hayley pleadingly.

"Why didn't you say anything?" Jesse had frustration written all over his face.

"You know why," she answered. They were both aware it would have just caused another argument, and she had been attempting to miss that, at least until today was over. She had five more days till she started back at work. Five days to think about how to tell him.

"So what? You just thought you could palm my son off on anyone and I didn't need to know?" Jesse shook his head, looking at the floor as though he couldn't even bear to look at her right now.

Taking a deep breath, "One, he's *our* son. Two, she's fully qualified," Hayley continued to finger count. "Three, how the hell did you think I would survive without a job. Four, you work full time, why the hell can't I? and five, remind me again why I need your bloody permission?" She asked, trying to stand taller, hands on hips braced for the impending argument, she knew she had raised her voice by the end of her point but he was infuriating, he expected everything to just fit into its own space and her feelings meant nothing. He was a damn control freak, and that was the last thing she needed.

Jesse was attempting to control his frustration, but Hayley recognised the signs of an imminent explosion. His carotid artery was pumping, his jaw had stiffened and his nose was flaring. Being fully aware of his family being only a few feet away, he didn't need them to tell him how badly he was handling it, but she got under his skin. He just wanted to grab her and devour her antagonistic lips and drag her back to his house until she submitted to him. Where the hell had that thought come from, he thought, as he lowered his eyes from her blazing sapphires.

"I don't expect you to ask me. But a heads up would have been nice, didn't you think I would want to do my own checks on people before I placed him anywhere and if you were struggling with money, you could have told me," He said steadily, taking a breath he added "I'd have helped."

"I don't want your damn help!" She shouted, cursing herself for losing her temper. "I'm quite capable of standing on my own two feet!" She hissed. Sometimes she wished Daniel was Demy's, at least she wouldn't have to ask his permission. Then the guilt of thinking such a thing hit her in the stomach and made it churn.

"I'm his Dad, if he needs anything, ask me." Why did she find it so damn hard to ask and accept help? Why couldn't she just stop pushing him away? She made the walls she was building around herself of strong and it was getting higher by the day. He hated it, but knew he was also guilty of enabling those bricks; it was as though he had bought her the supplies and hoped she didn't have a clue how to mix them.

"He doesn't, all the money you give me, goes on him," she cursed her voice for breaking. She could ill afford to look weak in front of him. All men took advantage of weakness, she'd learned that long ago. "I need to work to afford a home."

"I thought you were staying here?" he asked, confused, and a little taken aback.

Hayley bit her lip and folded one hand into the other. She felt a lot less confident about this than she'd hoped. "I've seen a two bedroomed flat." she admitted quietly.

"Thought we were on a break?" He asked, exasperated. "I thought this was time to just…?" Realising quickly that it was a lost cause. "didn't think…" Jesse rubbed the back of his neck, looking back down to the floor before gazing back up to her watery eyes. "I didn't realise we were just over."

Shaking his head, he paced the floor, looking anywhere but at Hayley. She could see he was struggling.

"This is so fucking stupid," he said in a breath, barely catching her ears. "I'll give you some extra." He didn't enjoy sending Daniel to someone he didn't know, or having absolutely no say about it. But the thought Hayley saw no future for them gutted him and if he was being honest with himself, he worried about Hayley. She wasn't ready, she liked to portray strength, but she was fragile.

"You will not be keeping me Jesse." Hayley shook her head vehemently. "I'll work and pay for my way."

Jesse stopped pacing, favouring to look at the ceiling as he tried to regain some composure. "When are you going to realise that I just want to look after you?" When she didn't answer him, he looked at her from the corner of his eye, she was wiping a tear from her cheek and he wanted so badly to do that for her. He hated himself for causing her to cry, but he could never seem to find the words to explain himself. She saw everything as an attack. Being always on the defensive made him want to smash through her defences, but it only ever fortified them.

"I'm sorry I didn't tell you. I was going to tell you tonight," she offered, watching him war with himself.

"After you had already organised everything," spat back Jesse, watching her pale.

Hayley felt terrible, she could see the disappointment on his face, she'd let him down. That was all she seemed to be to him anymore, an immense disappointment. She wondered how much better his life would be now if she'd just let Demy kill her. After all, no one needed her, even Daniel would be ok without her. He had his grandparents, his Dad and his uncle. She had no one, and it left a gigantic gaping hole inside of her, that was becoming harder to miss or conceal.

"I didn't do it to hurt you."

"No. You just did it so I couldn't change anything." With his last remark he sauntered past her and returned to his son's party, leaving the door to swing back in his wake.

They had encouraged Hayley at the prospect of starting back to work in the kitchen, but after that conversation she no longer knew if she was doing the right thing, if it would cause an even bigger rift between them, was it worth it? Having wanted to keep things civil between them for Daniel's sake, it seemed she'd fallen at the first hurdle. Walking over to the worktop, Hayley leant against it for support. She no longer wanted to be part of the celebrations. She no longer felt welcome. Glancing at her watch, noting the time, she wondered what would be a reasonable time to put Daniel to bed and crawl under the covers herself. If she could get through another day, she'd have at least achieved something.

She hoped that with each day she'd feel more worthy to walk the planet; right now, the endless sleep called to her. Not waking up seemed such a peaceful way to go. Daniel would be too young to remember her, which caused her to tear up, but on the flip side, would he really feel her loss if he couldn't remember having her? Maybe it would be the perfect time to leave. Jesse would take excellent care of him, hopefully find someone prepared to share her life with their son. Imagining Daniel saying mummy for the first time let the tears finally fall and she bit her wobbly lip trying to compose herself as the fake family she envisioned played out in her mind. She was right, they wouldn't miss her at all. Sure, they'd cry, wonder why, but then they'd get on with their lives and they wouldn't have to put up with her. After all, it was only a matter of time till they got bored with her, anyway.

"So, Jess didn't know?" Asked Rob, walking in the kitchen clanking the empty mugs together, before placing them in the sink.

Hayley just shook her head. There wasn't really anything else to say on the subject. Jesse had been right, the only reason she hadn't told him was because she knew he wouldn't be happy about it.

"I didn't mean to…"

Hayley moved her face away so he couldn't see her crying and tried to wipe her face inconspicuously on her wrist. "I know. It's not your fault, I should have said something before," she cut in apologetically. She had put him in an awkward position and with things still fragile between them, she didn't want to be the one to cause another rift. Feeling the knot loosen in her throat, she swallowed a few times to free it up further.

"Why didn't you?" Turning to her while leaning on the sink with his arms folded across his chest, he waited. She just stared up at him.

She wasn't sure what to say. Jesse was private, and he didn't like people knowing things about him he wasn't ready to divulge himself. Hayley opted for a shrug.

"If you need the money, you've not really got an option, have you?" Hayley shook her head. "I'm sure he'll calm down," he offered, looking at one another with doubtful grimaces on their faces.

They couldn't help but laugh a little. They both knew he wouldn't calm down or change his mind, or at least not for a while. Once he made his mind up, he was hard to convince otherwise.

Rob dropped his glance. They hadn't spent too much time together since she had got back, things had changed since their days in the kitchen together. They had once been wonderful friends once. Bouncing ideas around, helping each other out and jovially throwing around banter like a pair of comedians, but they weren't sure they had it in them anymore. Their relationship had changed.

"I am sorry about what happened." Offered Hayley as though reading his mind. Watching him turn to her, she saw his face soften.

"Thanks." Rob thought back to the prison visits he'd had to endure to see Caitlyn, right until she had told him they were over and not to visit anymore. It had pained him to hear her tell him she no longer loved him and didn't need reminding of life on the outside every time he visited her. He still loved her and missed the life they'd made together.

"I'm pleased you're ok." Offered Rob, watching her lips press together with embarrassment.

"Thanks," Rob stepped up to her and engulfed her in his large arms.

At first, she stiffened, but then she relaxed into him. Kissing her head, he rubbed her back, and she just wanted to break down and cry again. She wanted to be vulnerable, for someone to tell her everything would be OK. She wanted desperately to know she meant something to someone. Holding onto him tighter, she heard his heartbeat under his shirt and closed her eyes. Feeling his arms grow closer around her made her feel safe, as though they wrapped her in a cocoon and she didn't want to come back out. The world was harsh; she just wanted to stay.

"What's going on in here?"

Hayley let go, jumping back as Rob shifted towards Jesse whilst rubbing the back of his head uncomfortably.

"Nothing, just chatting," answered Rob whilst making his way back into the living room. Jesse looked towards Hayley but she just smiled timidly, feeling as though he had caught her in an intimate act.

"I need the name and address of the childminder, I need to do some checks," said Jesse.

Hayley just nodded. Why would he just take it from her she wasn't putting him in the care of a serial killer? "What's going on with you and Rob?"

Hayley raised her gaze from the floor back to him. This time it confused her, unsure what she was reading in his eyes. "Nothing." snapped Hayley.

Jesse just nodded but didn't look all that convinced. "I'll get Daniel to bed soon; he's had a busy day."

Hayley couldn't stop much longer the atmosphere between her and Jesse was unbearable. It would be a much better idea to part before it got worse, and they each said or did something they would regret and couldn't take back.

"If you're tired, just go to bed. I'll take him up."

Hayley stared at him; it was as though he was intentionally trying to get rid of her. Maybe tonight would be the night she could escape. He'd seen death before, he would adjust better than Marie and Michael, he'd understand.

"Maybe I'll grab a bath," she admitted, wanting to get away from him as she walked towards the door to the stairs. "I'll have a long soak."

"Mum and Dad are in their element," smiled Jesse. She understood what he was trying to do; guilt trip her into staying with them longer. "Now that you'll be moving out and working, I don't suppose you'll have much time to just pop in," he added.

Hayley nodded, if what she had planned worked, they'd have all the time they wanted. She'd no longer be a barrier. "I'll get here as often as I can, it means just as much to me to have him know his family."

Jesse nodded, but she wasn't sure he understood how important it was to her. How could he? She had no family. The thought of spending time with them was probably alien to him, but she had needed them once. Just as much as Daniel would soon. The thought tightened her throat again, but she schooled her feature. If he knew what she was planning, he'd stop her.

Marie and Michael had been like surrogates to her, they had been there for her each time she had needed them, even when it meant offering her a bed when she had finally walked out on Jesse and they had never made her feel guilty about it or to coax her into going back. They had allowed her time to make her own decisions and then supported her. No one had ever done that before without expecting something in return. But she couldn't expect them to carry on doing that, she wasn't their problem.

"He'd know them a hell of a lot more if you'd just come home?" Sulked Jesse.

Hayley wasn't sure she had heard him right. All they had achieved since splitting was arguing and feel awkward around one another. The plain sailing, they had promised one another still wasn't something on the horizon so a reconciliation wasn't something she had considered being on the cards and how could it be?

"Jesse, we can't," said Hayley, watching him make his way to her. Standing directly in front of her, she felt penned in, and her heart rate increased. He seemed to notice and took a step back so as not to crowd her. She was still battling with PTSD and so he feared triggering her, but sometimes she just wished he'd do something. This dancing around made her even more anxious. Never knowing what to expect made her over think everything, and she just wanted her head to silence.

"We can, if we try," said Jesse, sincerely.

"We can't fix this," said Hayley, flicking her index finger between them, as she watched regret flicker deeply in his eyes.

"We can if we both want to," added Jesse, stepping forward again, hoping she was ready. It was the closest they had been in six months, maybe longer.

She could hear her own heartbeat speed up as she inhaled his aftershave. Her heart clenched, screaming for her to let him in. But her head was a cacophony of noise warning her to not enter, and she stepped back. The space between them grew and with that, so did the distance between them.

"Daniel needs a family," spoke Jesse sternly, attempting to aim for her weak point. He hated using his son to get her back, but he hated losing her more. Besides visiting his son when he had time, wasn't what he'd envisioned his family to be like when he had children. He wanted to go home and be around them, share meals and nights with Hayley, enjoying their son together. They had spent too much time apart already. He wanted to tuck Daniel in every night and read him a story. Be the Dad he had always craved to be, not a weekend visitor.

He wanted to cuddle up with Hayley every night, smell the coconut scent of her hair and wrap it around his hand as he kissed the delicate porcelain skin below her ear. He yearned to hear her sigh and moan and give up fighting. Since she'd been back, it was as though she had morphed into a crocodile; Thick impenetrable skin and a snappy jaw baring razor like teeth. In her head she was still at war, armed to the hilt and ready for action. He just couldn't get close enough to convince her otherwise, without being bitten.

"So, you think getting Daniel back is what we both need to rebuild our relationship, so what you really want is to get your son back whilst I just get to go along for the ride?" Hayley struggled to keep her temper in check.

She didn't want him to just want their son; she wanted him to want *her*. Their son had arrived unexpectedly; neither had had time to adjust to the idea. There had been no scans, no talk of names before the arrival, no enjoyment of watching her stomach grow. For them it had been instant. He was there, all ready and raring to go. That's what her abduction had taken away from them, the enjoyment of becoming a family. The excitement of getting ready, and she felt cheated because when she had given birth, she couldn't look at him.

She had told herself that he was Demy's and no good would come of it. She had felt immense relief when she had received the news that Demy wasn't his father, but that had brought its own drama. Jesse was tied to her for life, whether he wanted her or not. Hayley knew he felt responsible, that he would take his responsibilities seriously, but that meant they took away a choice from them. She was no longer sure he would choose her or walk away if it wasn't for Daniel. She didn't want to be someone's responsibility, someone's chore, someone's consolation prize. Hayley knew he'd always envisioned a nuclear family, and all she had ever wanted was someone to love her unconditionally, but she didn't know what that looked like.

"I didn't mean it like that," said Jesse, stepping back, realising she was defensive once again.

Silently warring with himself, he thought about kissing her, forcing her to admit her feelings for him. He knew she'd give in to them, but he didn't want to force himself on her. She had to choose him. She had to feel in charge, otherwise he'd just be another man to put pressure on her, and he had to show her he was different, that he was worth letting in. But it seemed every time he spoke to Hayley, he said the opposite of what he felt, and just dug a deeper trench between them. He was wondering when he'd need a new shovel; he was undoubtedly over using this one.

"No, course you didn't," said Hayley sarcastically under her breath.

It cut deep that she was comparing him to every other man in her life, but then could he really blame her, when no one had ever just loved her?

"What's that supposed to mean?" Jesse's voice rose, and she glanced at the door in a way to remind him they had company.

"Have you forgotten why we split up?" She asked genuinely. Taking a step closer to him so she didn't have to raise her voice, she reminded him, "You couldn't bear to be near me, how's that changed?"

Jesse dropped his head. He knew he had been distant with her. After watching her nurse Daniel, and with the impending trial, Jesse had removed himself from being Hayley's shoulder, confident and lover.

He still didn't properly understand why he had himself, but he just knew he had. That was undeniable. He couldn't listen to her describe the things she'd endured. He wanted to punch something every time she opened up, and the adrenalin that caused through his veins made him pace, flinch and sometimes hit out. That was when he would leave her to beat the shit out of a punch bag back in the police station's gym. The nightmares made him feel helpless and watching her lie her way through explaining them was heartbreaking as she stopped trusting him with them. He'd messed up, but the whole thing had been disturbing and had made him feel physically sick to think about all the things Hayley had been through, and on the times he was honest with himself, he felt guilty, guilty that he had let her down. She had needed him to protect her, and instead he'd hauled her into the cop shop to grill her about the brand Demy had burnt onto her back. The same symbol they had printed on cocaine bags.

They had needed to know where the logo came from, but he had known the last thing Hayley would want to do was recount the story of how she had got it. So, he'd betrayed her and forced her to go on tape, only to find out later that day, she was under the illusion she was visiting him in hospital after being involved in an accident. Realising there had been no accident and Hayley had disappeared off the face of the earth for six months. The longest six months of his damn life. Six months he would never get back. Six months he could never re write and six months where the beautiful girl he knew was being brutalised and turned into a spitting cobra. She was frightened and trying to disguise it with an attitude she didn't really possess, but it was enough to keep them separate and so was a barrier he'd have to deal with if he would ever see the girl underneath again, but it was unrelenting, and exhausting.

"I just needed time," explained Jesse, hoping she'd understand.

Hayley wasn't so sure that it was time that was the issue. He could no longer see *her*, all he saw was what she had been through, and she couldn't deal with that. Being reminded you were a victim every day, did not build self-worth, it just reinstated the idea that she'd never be unblemished. "There can't be an us, when he may as well be in bed with us." she answered, swiping a lone tear from her cheek, before turning back towards the door so she could run that much-needed bath.

Thinking quickly that she didn't want this to be the last conversation he had with her, she turned back to him. "Jesse." When he met her eyes, she sighed to see the hurt she'd put there. "I'll always love you." Before he could respond, she rushed from the room.

∼

Hayley filled the bath, running bath liquid into the flow from the tap, watching the bubbles they created at the bottom as they mixed. Grabbing her cheap razor, she examined it to check it was clean, then laughed at herself. Infection would not be an issue for her, not if it worked anyway.

Slipping out from under her clothes, she folded them up, placing them on the toilet lid. No reason to make Marie do any more work. Stepping in, it comforted once the warm water enveloped her, sinking into the warmth as her muscles relaxed and the tension in her neck dissipated. Taking the razor, she cracked the side open, removing the blades carefully. Twisting them around in her fingers, they glinted as the light above her caught them. Suddenly feeling anxious, she held the blade to her left wrist and closed her eyes. Breathing deeply, she felt the blade cut through her skin, sending a sting up her arm.

A tear rolled down her cheek, and she shakily breathed in again. She could do this, she just had to persist. The pain in her heart would stop. Sounds in her head would seize. The sick feeling in her stomach would be no more. Visions of Jesse and Daniel ran through her mind on a film reel, laughing, singing and kissing. Breathing deeply, she forced the blade in, but no amount of breathing was helping her move the blade, and she crumpled into a soggy, tearful spasm. Dropping the blade down the side of the bath from her shaky hands, she pulled her legs up to her chin and sobbed. She couldn't even do that right, she thought, watching blood stream down her legs and turn the water pink.

CHAPTER 2

DS Martin Wells walked past Jesse's open office, stopping. He leaned back to see Jesse flicking his biro on the table. He had that distressed expression on his face, which usually only existed when a fresh case had fallen on his lap and he hadn't quite made sense of it. Walking through he sat down before Jesse had even registered, he was no longer alone.

"What is it?" Asked Martin.

Jesse looked at him, confusion written all over his face.

"Well, you look like you've lost a stripper a found a corpse." Jesse smiled; he could always rely on Martin for some much-needed humour. "So, did you?"

"No, just waiting to hear from the CPS. That case is so tightly bound, Houdini would struggle to get out of it," answered Jesse.

"So why the long face?" Asked Martin, walking over to the door to close it. If it wasn't work related that made it personal, and they'd need privacy.

Jesse resigned himself to answering and waited till Martin had returned to his seat. "We had another fight," Jesse sighed, sitting back in his chair, closing his eyes. They were heavy from lack of sleep and his head was banging from dehydration. After getting home on his own last night, he'd struggled to get Hayley off his mind and so had resorted to desperate measures, when the alcohol had enabled him to pass out, he'd regretted it the second his eyelids had opened to the sound of his alarm.

"Serious?" Asked Martin, instantly regretting the question because if it hadn't been, his boss wouldn't be contemplating whatever it was he was contemplating.

"She's going back to work." This time he sat forward and leant on the desk for support, eyes fully open. Martin flashed him a look that told him he didn't see the big-deal. "She's going back full time, and she's moving out of Mum and Dad's. I kind of ripped her head off about it, last night."

Now Martin understood the face, he was feeling guilty; he'd acted irrationally and was now viewing the argument from Hayley's perspective.

"So, apologise for being a dick, it's what us men do, isn't it?" Asked Martin "I regularly apologise to my wife, whether I mean it or not. It keeps the house in order and a roof over my head. After a crap day at work, I needed the peace and quiet to be quite honest."

"Not that simple," stated Jesse solemnly.

"Never is mate, wait till you're married as long as me." Martin stretched his back out before standing back up from his chair, but Jesse's face had glassed over again and he realised it was no ordinary argument, whatever it was, it was eating him up. "Seriously, if you've said something you regret, tell her. You two are so fucked up, you make the rest of us look like the Walton's," watching Jesse nod glumly he added "tell her how you feel and stop being a stubborn bastard."

"Yeah, thanks for the advice, Jim Bob," said Jesse, unable to stop the slight smile, whilst simultaneously stopping the conversation.

Martin grabbed the door and left, only turning a split second later to see Jesse holding his head in his hands. Jesse was his own worst enemy, and he contemplated donning a wedding hat just to achieve the power of Cilla to get them two in a room together to sort their shit out.

∽

MARTIN WAS SCANNING the computer in front of him, looking for a vehicle registration number and its owner. He needed to catch up with someone regarding the car seen near a suspicious death. Glancing up, he watched Jesse through the blinds on a telephone call; hoping it was the CPS giving them the all clear. They'd worked for months on that case, and they needed it off their desks so they could continue with the suspicious murder unburdened. Tapping away, he continued to scroll the page before looking back up.

Jesse was looking rough, thought Martin. Wondering what could have happened the night before to put paid to their amicable split. He decided to call Hayley later, use the excuse that he was checking in on his namesake. That kid had a special place in his heart, and not least because they'd given him his name. Suddenly remembering it had been Daniel's naming party yesterday, he'd use that as an opening, that was sure to have opened old wounds, and was probably why Jesse looked so downtrodden. Maybe that's all it was, he wasn't sure how his friend had dealt with the last six months but he admired him for getting back to work after being set up for kidnapping and murdering his girlfriend, that was no easy thing to come back from and he was sure he hadn't come out of it unscathed. In fact, he was certain Jesse's zest for life had faded away along with his colouring and his bulk, and he was looking paler and thinner by the day.

He made a mental note to ask Jesse out for a beer too; it seemed like an age ago since they had shared a drink and spoken about their woes. In fact, he was sure the last time they had had been just after him and Hayley had broken up. That conversation had been heavy and fraught with emotion, he held his hands up to any counsellor who could listen to other people without becoming emotionally attached because he'd been thoroughly drained. Jesse had been in deep depression and he hadn't even been sure whether he'd be seeing him on a mortuary slab the next day, it was a relief when he had gone down there and been told a young woman was the interest of the day and until then he had never believed someone else's death would fill him with such relief, but Jesse had been the worst he had ever seen anyone. That was when he knew he had to speak to the super, the one and only time he had ever gone around him, but he had needed professional help. He just wondered if he was still receiving it? Finally, seeing what he was looking for, he copied the information down before logging off.

∽

Back at home, Jesse answered the door in his jeans and t-shirt, seeing Rob holding a four pack, with a smile on his face whilst swinging the beers to gain an invitation. Jesse smirked and let the door go, grabbing it before it swung back Rob walked in. His eyes widened as he surveyed the room.

"Shit! You've been burgled!"

Jesse turned to him and grabbed a can, slipping it from its seal, before falling onto the sofa. Pulling the ring pull off, he took a long sip.

"Wow, bad day?" Asked Rob, dropping in the chair watching his brother drink in the relief that the can offered, whilst he covertly surveyed the mess around the room. Clothes discarded into piles, food cartons scattered. If he'd not known Jesse owned the house, he'd have been forgiven for thinking he'd just walked into a squat.

"Could say that," said Jesse finally. "Although I can only strictly have one, I'm still on call," he said, holding the beer in front of him, before letting out a belch.

"How come you're not at Hayley's?" Jesse looked at him as if to warn him off. "Just thought you'd be making more of an effort. What with Hayley starting back at work soon?" Jesse stared at him, wondering why he was so interested in his love life or lack of suddenly. "You didn't seem overly happy about her starting back."

"What did she say?" Asked Jesse, feeling the hairs go up on his neck.

Rob shrugged. "Nothing, she won't will she, too petrified you'd rip her head off I assume."

Jesse knew it was a dig from how he'd reacted the other night but ignored it, deciding to take another sip of beer to dissipate his anxiety.

"What's the crack with you two, anyway?"

"Back off," warned Jesse, holding his finger up from his can.

"She was abducted, had your kid, then nearly a year later, you've split. What's the crack?" Rob watched pain flush over Jesse as the muscle in his jaw ticked. It was like watching a grim shadow descended on him.

"There's just stuff you don't know about. It's not that easy. We're not in a Disney happy ever after kind of world, are we?" Snarled Jesse before tipping the can to his lips again.

"Not compatible in the bedroom anymore?"

"Rob, just shut the fuck up," snapped Jesse. He wasn't in the mood to have his failed relationship picked over like some science experiment. There would always be things that only he and Hayley could share with each other, and he wasn't about to open up old wounds with Rob.

"Well, Mr Family man backing down from a challenge, never thought I'd see the day," goaded Rob, shaking his head in faux disbelief whilst sitting back in the chair.

Jesse looked across to him, waiting for the explanation for his outburst.

"Bags a girl, puts a bun in the oven and then leaves her!" Rob laughs. "Even Dad didn't see that one coming, I genuinely think you may have slipped from that great big fucking pedestal they have you on."

"No one has me on a pedestal."

"Like hell they don't!" said Rob. "Golden balls, walking away from his family, you've definitely come down in their estimation," mocked Rob.

Jesse took another drink, but it was tasting sour. He wasn't sure if it was the company or the beer. "Did you just come round to put the boot in?" Asked Jesse, wondering why his brother had descended on his home to state the bleeding obvious.

"Just thought I'd bring my big bro a beer," answered Rob with a smile as though there was nothing else to it, but Jesse looked at him unconvinced. "And find out where the land lies with Hales."

"Why? What's she got to do with you?" Jesse tensed. He didn't trust many people, but if he had to make a list, Rob would be closer to the bottom than the top.

"Nothing. Just we'll be working together again soon, don't want to say anything that may hit a nerve, you know cause a problem," he said jokingly.

"Like what?" Asked Jesse. His hackles had gone up and Rob couldn't help but play with him. Jesse cursed himself for making it so easy.

"You know," shrugged Rob, "people gossip in the kitchen, talk about their lives. Just didn't want to put my foot in it," Rob drank some beer and watched Jesse staring at him. "She's a splendid-looking girl."

"Stay away from her," warned Jesse.

Rob lifted his hands in the air as if to surrender. "Not me! I'm talking about the other chefs, the maintenance guys, the delivery drivers…" Rob couldn't help smirk at the look of hatred on his brother's face. "Just saying, there's a lot of men come by the kitchen and she's not a terrible-looking girl."

"Stay away from her," warned Jesse. "I mean it Rob, stop fucking about and keep a lookout for her, she's not ready for this, but she won't listen to a word I say." Jesse took another sip of beer then muttered, "It's like she does the fucking opposite just to piss me off."

"Wonder why that might be?" Asked Rob sarcastically, pulling the ring pull off the top of his own beer.

～

Hayley opened the door to see Martin on her doorstep, instantly smiling she pulled the door back to let him in. "How are you?" Asked Hayley, grabbing the kettle to fill it up at the tap.

"Good, you?" Martin looked around the kitchen as he followed her. It was obvious they'd had dinner, as the neatly stacked pots sat on the drainer, sparkling. Plus, there was the hint of lime and antiseptic in the air along with something rich and fragrant.

"Not bad, Daniel should be up soon. He went down about an hour ago, but he'll be wanting his tea soon," said Hayley, flicking the kettle on.

"Smells amazing in here," he said, sniffing the air.

"Lasagna, it's a firm favourite," she laughed, grabbing two mugs from the drainer. "There's some left if you want some heating-up?"

Martin rubbed his stomach and thought about how much trouble he'd be in if his wife knew he'd already eaten. Claire was many things, but a decent cook wasn't one of them.

"I won't tell," she said as if reading his mind.

Chuckling, he nodded. "Go on then, you've twisted my arm, but make it a small piece or she'll know."

Laughing again, Hayley walked to the fridge and pulled out the ceramic dish she'd covered in cling film.

Taking a seat out from the round table he sat down watching Hayley cut a slice up from the dish before placing it on a plate and putting it in the microwave with a lid on. "How is the Daniel Martin?"

"Good. He's getting there, you know." Folding her arms across her chest, Martin realised she wasn't telling the whole truth. She was trying to hide how difficult she was finding it. Probably because she saw it as a weakness, and she didn't want to be viewed as incapable.

"Heard you're going back to work," said Martin brightly. He didn't miss her roll her eyes before she turned back to the kettle. Spooning coffee from a flowery terracotta canister, she replaced the lid. "I'm not here to criticise."

"But?" She said, waiting, as she dropped the teaspoon in one cup. When he didn't reply, she turned back round to face him.

"I'm not here to criticise." he repeated genuinely. "Just wanted to check you're OK."

"What did he say, Martin?" Hayley couldn't hide how frustrated she was that he'd gone to Martin to complain about her.

"Just that you were going back to Eden."

Hayley waited for more, but when none came, she turned back to the cups to finish making their coffees. Handing Martin his drink, she pulled out a chair for herself and sat down.

"Are you ready?" asked Martin as she sipped her drink carefully.

"Yep, I think so," answered Hayley, realising he was just genuinely concerned, and not there as a spy. "As I'll ever be."

"What happened?" Asked Martin, flicking his index finger to the bandage wrapped round her wrist.

"Oh, I burnt it. It's nothing," answered Hayley, quickly placing it under the table. Martin watched her shift her gaze around the kitchen and wondered what she was hiding underneath that bandage.

"He'll come round," said Martin, placing his drink on the table. "He doesn't really have a choice."

Hayley quickly looked back at him to gage his feelings, but relaxed when his face said he was just stating a fact. "I still care about him," said Hayley, hoping she wasn't saying something inappropriate. But it felt good to admit it. She couldn't say that to anyone else because they'd get too far ahead of themselves. She knew Martin would take it for what it was; simple, unadulterated truth.

"I know. He does too," answered Martin, watching her face fill with sorrow. "When was the last time you went out?" Asked Martin, changing the subject and hoping to dissipate the awkward atmosphere.

"Erm... I don't know, I can't remember," lied Hayley. "Long time."

Remembering exactly when it was, her cheeks reddened. It had been Jesse's works Christmas party, and the station had hired a hall for drinks and a dance. The minute she had walked in on Jesse's arm, she could have sworn the music had stopped and everyone had turned to stare at her. She had just wanted the ground to swallow her up. It wasn't an experience she wanted to repeat.

"Right, well, you're coming out with us. We can go to a Chinese or

Indian and have a meal and a laugh. See if Marie and Michael will babysit?"

"Who's we?" Asked Hayley suspiciously.

"You, Me, Claire and Jesse."

Hayley pulled a face as he said Jesse's name. "I'm not trying to set you up, we can all just go out as friends." said Martin, watching Hayley intently to gage her response.

"I don't think that would be a very good idea," she admitted, taking a sip of her drink.

"Why?"

"We're not getting on very well at the moment. Five minutes in and we'd be arguing, we'll ruin yours and Claire's night, it wouldn't be fair."

"I'll pre-warn Claire to bring her referee whistle," Martin chuckled. "Seriously, you've not been out yet. You're starting back at work soon, and you've no idea how you will cope with that. I think you'd be naïve to think you're just going to fit back in. So, I'm suggesting we go out, all as friends, and help you enjoy being out of the house in a relaxed atmosphere with people who care."

Hayley couldn't help smile at his empathy, but if he thought she was entirely buying into the no set up thing, he was kidding himself. Just then the microwave dinged, and she stood to retrieve his plate.

"Marvellous idea, but I still don't think we'll manage it. I'd love to spend some time with all of you and enjoy a meal, but we're like a ticking time bomb. I'd get nervous just waiting for it to go wrong," answered Hayley. "And it inevitably will."

"Trust me with this," pleaded Martin. "When have I ever let you down?" He gave her the eyes that were no doubt meant to convince her.

"Eat your Lasagna," answered Hayley, trying not to laugh.

CHAPTER 3

Hayley entered the kitchen at the Garden of Eden almost a year after.

All her anxiety instantly vanished on hearing Ash bellow at one waitress for mixing up an order. The familiarity making her smile. She rounded the corner to the main room as all her old colleagues turned to welcome her. A feeling of arriving home overwhelmed her as they cheered.

Laughing, she accepted Sam's offered hug. "Nice to have you back, sweetheart."

"It's good to be back," said Hayley, being tugged from Sam to hug Ben. When he finally let go, she saw Steve wipe his eyes on a tea towel. She knew what he was thinking. Swallowing the past, she meekly smiled to say she was OK, before acknowledging Ashley who had been staring at her. Nodding reservedly, she did the same before he thrust a menu in her hands from the nearby table.

"There's a delivery in at eleven, can you get started on the desserts?" Nodding she watched him linger on her as if he was fighting with himself to say something. Deciding to let him off the hook she thanked him and gave a smile she hoped portrayed she understood, so they could just carry on, but before Ash passed, he squeezed her shoulder, Steve caught the action and smiled wryly.

～

Downstairs in the locker/stock room, Hayley placed the ingredients she needed into an enormous stock pot. Balancing it on her knee, she stretched to reach the vanilla pods at the top of the racking.

"What's it like to be back?" Turning, she spotted Rob entering the locker room, flicking his car keys between his fingers.

Hayley laughed. "Good."

Watching her struggle to reach the plastic container, he moved towards her. "What?"

"I'll get it Shorty." Lifting, he grabbed the container before handing it to Hayley. "It's good to have you back."

"Thanks," smiled Hayley.

"Besides, those bloody brulee's are killing me," he answered, shaking his head.

"Still burning them?" She laughed, remembering how many times he'd put them under the grill only to forget they were there until the smell of burnt sugar took over the kitchen.

"I swear he only puts them on the menu to watch me fail," he added, knowing Ash found it amusing to see him rush around panicking.

"I'm sure he doesn't." She tried to assure him, but the skeptical look they both gave each other confirmed they knew differently.

～

"Martin, grab your coat!" Jesse called out from the main office; Martin instantly turned, grabbing it from the back of his chair, before rushing over to follow Jesse into his own office. "There's been a murder."

"Very Taggart," Martin smirked, watching Jesse grab his keys, warrant card and mobile from the desk. "Where?"

"Boy found near Balderton Lake, suspicious, I've just rang through to get the pathologist, we'll no doubt meet him there." Rushing from the police station, Jesse threw Martin the keys as they neared his car, "You drive and I'll make the calls."

When they arrived, a white tent had been erected and police tape was securing the scene to deter anyone from wading through forensic evidence. Having been handed paper suits as they flashed their ID's they carefully made their way over to the body.

"I've only just got here myself so hold fire with the questioning," said Mike Harvard, the pathologist.

Jesse nodded, taking in the scene before him.

Jesse and Martin looked down at the boy, resembling a fallen angel. His lips were deep blue with a hint of purple, and his skin looked almost translucent. His eyes were closed as though he was just catching forty winks, but the white wings attached to his back were the alarming part.

"He looks no older than seven," said Martin quietly; it didn't seem respectful somehow to raise your voice around a child. "Poor kid."

"You OK?" Asked Jesse, thinking of Martin's own children no doubt on their way to school.

Martin nodded, he'd seen his fair share of dead bodies, but kids were always the worst. It was always better to filter out the emotions and survey the evidence as any other case, but it was easier said than done sometimes. "Looks like he just went to sleep."

The boy was curled up in the fetal position. No obvious signs of injury apart from the wings, but he was naked, and that alone would put accidental death out of the question.

The pathologist stood up, placing his hands on his hips. "Ok, well I can't give you a full report until we get back, but it resembles hypothermia to me. I'd guestimate him being here for at least a day, but like I said, I'll know more back in the lab, questions?" He looked from one detective to the other. They both appeared pale, and he didn't think either of them would take a bacon sandwich back to the station as he'd seen them do many times before.

"What the hell's he doing out here?" Asked Martin, scanning the lake area, surrounded by trees, blocking out the housing estate just behind them.

The pathologist put his hands up in surrender. "Fraid, that's your job."

"Sexual assault?"

The pathologist shook his head, but then reiterated he'd know more after the tests.

"Well, I hope that case got through, cus it looks like we've got another," said Martin, walking back to the car.

"Yeah, and I don't like the look of this one at all," remarked Jesse, biting his bottom lip.

"I best grab us some coffees, I think we might be out here a while," said Martin, rubbing his hands together and hopping from one foot to the other to ward off frostbite. The ground was still crisp from the overnight frost.

Jesse nodded turning around to look for anything obvious, it wouldn't have taken long before the boy had lost consciousness, but that didn't answer the question of why he was out there in the first place, where his clothes were or why wings were tied to his back? A sick feeling swirled round in his gut.

∾

DANIEL HAD CRIED that morning after being left with Kerrie the Childminder, and it was him she was thinking of as she stripped out of her chef whites. Hoping he had cheered up and enjoyed his day, she threw her shoes in the bottom of her locker.

Rob walked in and took off his chef's whites. "Need a lift?"

Hayley turned to check he was talking to her. "Sure, if you don't mind?" She smiled. "I need to pick Daniel up from the minders though."

"Where do you pick him up from?" Asked Rob.

"Near your Mum and Dad's, it's literally round the corner." Hayley watched him pull his jumper over his head before slamming the door to the locker shut. "Thanks for this; I've missed him more than I thought I would."

"No problem, besides I can stop awhile and get my cuddles," he laughed.

"I'm sure he'll love that," smiled Hayley.

"Who said I was talking about him?" Rob winked.

∼

"You look deep in thought," acknowledged Martin walking into Jesse's office, seeing him hunched over his desk.

Jesse looked up, seeing Martin with a bundle of papers in his hands. "What are those?" He asked suspiciously. He did not need a fresh case on top of what they had found this morning.

"Path reports," explained Martin handing them over to him.

"Thank god for that." Jesse took them, before flipping through.

"What's on your mind?" Martin, eyed his friend's depressed face.

"You mean besides from the obvious?" He asked, lifting the file.

"Yep. Whatever it is, has distracted you all day, what's up?" Martin stepped back to close the door behind him so they had some privacy. Then he grabbed a chair out, making himself comfortable. "Problem shared and all that?" Offered Martin, watching his friend staring at a computer screen he wasn't privy to.

"It's not really a problem, just something Rob said,"

Martin raised his eyebrow to wait for more. He never had liked Rob, there was something about him he could never put his finger on, but he was Jesse's brother and he kept out of family drama.

Jesse sighed and sat back in his chair. "He came round the other night asking about Hayley."

"What about her?" Asked Martin warily.

He knew more about Hayley's ordeal than most, and he wasn't entirely comfortable about it. He'd had to keep things from his friend, to protect him. He'd seen things you'd never want to see of a friend's girl, and he was more than aware of how Jesse felt about her and how badly he had taken her disappearance.

"Nothing really, but I don't know… I'm probably making a something out of nothing." Jesse sat back up and clicked some keys on the computer.

"Why don't you ask her?" Martin felt like he had repeated that same question over and over to Jesse, only for him to ignore it each time in pursuit of a peaceful life. "She's started working with him again, hasn't she? If you're worried about him, ask her if he's OK with her."

Jesse chewed the inside of his mouth and nodded slightly.

"I wish you two would get your acts together," sighed Martin. It was excruciating. "It's so bleeding obvious you're still in love with her."

"Any decent information in the path report?" Asked Jesse, wanting to change the subject quickly even though he knew what they held, as he'd just skimmed them.

Martin took the hint. "Only what we already know, cause of death asphyxiation. The wings belonged to a swan, plenty of them around the lake, and they laced it into his back with garden twine. Nothing extraordinary, and thankfully post-mortem. Time of death is within forty-eight hours the rest I'll let you read, I'm going to grab a couple of plods and ask them to take another look at the scene and then make some more house-to-house enquiries."

Jesse nodded thoughtfully.

"Someone's got to have seen something right?"

"Do we have an ID for the boy yet?" Asked Jesse.

"Nothing yet, Still waiting on dental records, but he's made it a priority."

Jesse nodded again and watched Martin leave his office. Picking up the wooden frame on his desk, he smiled at the photo of Hayley and Daniel. Hayley had flour in her hair from making mince pies earlier in the day. He remembered the photo being taken by his mum; it had been just after Hayley had opened her present from him; he had bought her a new camera; hers had gone missing whilst she was captive, and he had known how much she enjoyed taking photos so he had gone out and bought one most like the one she had had before, she had been over the moon with it and had without thinking grabbed him to hug, they'd both felt it, that slight sizzle of electricity, but she had pulled away embarrassed. Then his mother had taken it and asked to get some photos of Daniel. This was the first one on it, and Hayley had given him it to say thank you. It had Daniel's scribble on the back, as if to show it was only from him.

"Hey, fancy grabbing a pint tonight?" Martin asked, popping his head back round the door, whilst he zipped up his heavily insulated coat.

"Sure, where are you thinking?" Asked Jesse.

"Not fussed, we can go out, or I can come round yours, I'm easy," replied Martin.

"That's what Claire said," laughed Jesse.

∼

MAKING their way to Rob's car, they quickly realised it was raining. Rushing, they jumped in. "So, what's going on with you and Jess?" asked Rob.

Hayley watched him pull his keys from his pocket and push them in the ignition before answering. "Why?" She asked.

"Just making conversation," he shrugged before bringing the car to life. "Just wondered if there's any chance of you two getting back together?"

Hayley shook her head. She could have sworn she saw him smile, but he turned away to watch for traffic at the exit.

"What happened? You two not like living with each other?"

"I'm not sure I should really discuss your brother." Hayley wished he'd just drop the conversation. There was plenty wrong with them, but she neither wanted to put it into words or tell his only brother how she felt about their demise.

"I won't tell him," insisted Rob with a flash of a smile.

"That's not the point," responded Hayley as Rob looked across to her whilst scanning the junction.

"Sorry, I didn't mean to pry."

"Yes, you did," laughed Hayley.

Rob shrugged and then smiled in a way that made her laugh again.

"There's not a lot to tell, we just didn't work out, so we're moving on."

Rob pulled across the road and drove along the A46. They said nothing else. He could tell Hayley just wanted to watch the fields go past her window while listening to the music on the radio, so he let her;

she must be shattered, he thought. It had been a long and busy day back.

Pulling up outside the Childminder's. Rob watched as Hayley rang the doorbell. A few minutes later she exited with a car seat and a pushchair. Rob got out, taking the pushchair from her as she fixed the car seat into the back. Shuffling items around in the boot to fit the umbrella pushchair in, Hayley went back to the door to retrieve Daniel. Saying her goodbyes to the minder, she fastened Daniel in his seat.

When they were all inside the car, Rob drove off. By the time they had made it to his Mum and Dad's around the corner, Daniel was already fast asleep in the car seat. Rob said he'd get the push chair and car seat while Hayley settled him inside. Taking him straight to his cot upstairs in Jesse's old room, she laid him down, barely stirring; she pulled the blankets up around him, tucking them in before kissing him on the forehead and leaving.

Rob was in the kitchen, putting the kettle on.

"That's music to my ears," said Hayley jovially as she noticed him searching for cups. "I'd forgotten how tiring the kitchen is," she said, pointing to the cupboard in the corner on the wall where all the spare cups were when the usual ones were dirty.

"He sparko?" asked Rob, raising a brow.

Hayley smiled, nodding as he handed her a drink. "Yep. Sorry about cuddle time," Hayley took a sip and made her way to the sofa in the front room, curling her fingers around the mug for warmth. She needed to put her feet up, she'd been on them all day and they ached.

"Wasn't him I was talking about."

Hayley looked up at him as he entered the living room, wondering what he meant. Then remembered how she'd clung to him the night of the naming party and flushed with embarrassment. "Sorry about that, was a tough day," said Hayley ashamedly.

Rob shrugged as though he didn't really mind, before winking at her. "Will he wake up again then?" Asked Rob, sitting down next to her on the settee.

"Depends how hungry he gets," she answered, sitting back carefully so as not to spill her drink as she watched Rob sip his own coffee like it was amber nectar. "That good?"

"Yep," he laughed, placing his cup on the coffee table, before leaning back.

"How are things?" She finally asked, wanting something to fill the awkward silence that had descended.

"You mean since the incarceration of my girlfriend?" He asked, raising his eyebrow.

"Sorry, I didn't mean to bring it up," she apologised, realising they were on sticky ground. As far as she was aware, he still resented her for that.

Rob blew out a long, heavy breath before answering. "I know it wasn't your fault," he said finally, watching how she'd take the news that he no longer blamed her.

Tightening her smile, she nodded, diverting her eyes from him to the black screen of the television.

"I know that we're not together anymore, and that won't change."

Hayley couldn't help but empathise with his anguish. He had been happily engaged until things beyond his control had put Caitlyn behind bars and ultimately led to their relationships down fall.

"But I just miss her."

Hayley leant forward, placing her mug on the coffee table in front of them. "It's only natural, you'd been together a long time, were building a future."

He laughed, but it wasn't with humour.

"I'm sure if Jesse could have kept her out of it, he would have, but he- "

"No, he wouldn't, he's been trying to find something to get me back for years now," said Rob dismissively.

Hayley bit her tongue. If she wasn't careful, they would get into an argument, and she had only just got him back as a friend.

"You don't need to know, just don't go thinking my brother's some bleeding saint, 'cus he aint."

"I don't think that, but I know he tried to do everything he could to find me," she admitted timidly.

"Yeah, well, we'll just agree to disagree on that one," said Rob before sipping his drink again. "Look, forget it, whatever our issue is, it doesn't concern you." He rubbed his hand on her knee and she instantly tensed. "He's always been the one to come in like a knight in shining armour, save the day, and if he made me look like a fool in the meantime, bonus!" He raised his cup in the air in a mock salutation.

"I'm sure it's not like that," she answered, staring at his hand.

"You not noticed how he likes to be in charge of everything and still come out like he 'had to help' us mere mortals?" Taking another sip. "You know, like it's not engineered to make him look good, holier than bloody thou."

Hayley hadn't realised how much resentment Rob held for Jesse, but his face was showing it now and she wasn't sure how to feel about it, she'd thought they'd made peace. "Anyone else would think you're a little jealous," laughed Hayley trying to lighten the tense atmosphere, before taking a sip of her drink for courage. He obviously needed to get something off his chest, but she wasn't sure she was the right person to do that with.

"There's only one thing I was jealous of," said Rob, turning to her with a weird look in his eyes. Her eyes widened, and she hoped she was reading him wrong. "Doesn't matter though, he's not got it anymore."

Hayley took a large gulp of coffee before standing up.

Rob tipped his head back to follow the swirls of Artex on the ceiling, before hearing Hayley move around in the kitchen. Following her into the kitchen, he watched her pop some bread into the toaster before pulling the lever down and taking the butter from the fridge.

"That all you're having?" Asked Rob, walking towards her.

"I might grab something else later," she smiled thinly, hoping she was convincing him. Reality was her appetite was fairly none existent. She was eager for something to do as Rob was making her feel uncomfortable, she hoped he was getting the hint she was ready for him to leave, but with it being his parent's home she couldn't really ask him to do that without being rude.

"You've lost weight," observed Rob scanning her body in skinny jeans and a white vest top.

"A little," she admitted, feeling vulnerable under his gaze. Why was he being weird? The hairs on the back of her neck were spiking, and she didn't like it, she'd never felt like that around him before. What was wrong with her?

"You look good for it," he nodded, looking up to her enormous doe eyes.

"Not sure how I should take that," she laughed awkwardly, turning to the butter dish and grabbing a knife from the cutlery drawer.

"As a compliment, it's how I meant it," sensing Rob move closer to her, she shuddered.

"Excuse me," she croaked as she sidled past him to retrieve a plate.

Why was he acting weird? Was she being overly sensitive?

"Do I make you uncomfortable?"

Turning back to the toaster, she tapped her fingernails on the worktop, biting her bottom lip. "Is that what you're trying to do?" She asked hoping she sounded more confident than she felt, she knew he was probably about to land a prank on her, but she felt uncomfortable, and she hated that what she had been through always made her think the worst about people, and she knew Rob, right?

"No, of course not." He stood next to her and leant up against the worktop to face her.

Hearing the toaster pop, she quickly took the toast out, dropping them on the breadboard, before singeing her finger tips. Rob watched her butter the toast before cutting them into triangles, observing her shaky hands as she placed them on a clean plate. Following her back to the living room sofa, he sat down beside her.

"Jesse should be here soon," she said, hoping he would take the hint to leave. Biting her toast, she cursed how loud it sounded as her throat tightened, making it near impossible to swallow. He had said nothing for so long she wondered what he was expecting. Hayley cleared her throat. "Any way, it's getting late."

When she looked back at him, he had looked away and was standing, feeling her muscles relax a little, and realising he probably just didn't get hints that well she placed her plate on the coffee table before walking over to the door.

"Jesse's a damn fool for letting you go," said Rob.

Hayley stood in shock, while Rob stepped closer to her, placing his fingers on her jaw. Noticing she was staring at him, she glanced down anywhere but at him.

Rob smoothed the skin on her jaw. He could feel her jaw tense, but when she refused to look up, he let go and left.

Pushing the door shut, she turned around to lean up against it, before letting out the breath she'd been holding. Inhaling deeply sent her head swirling round like a waltz from a fairground. Hayley held her trembling hands over her face. Where the hell had that come from? And why the hell hadn't she moved away?

∼

"I BRING PIZZA!" Cheered Martin as Jesse opened the door to him. "and Laphoaig."

"You in it for the long haul or just trying to get pissed quicker?" Asked Jesse, taking the whiskey from him as he walked into the front room. Rolling it round in his hands, he observed the label. "Nice."

"Thought we deserved it, works been fucking dreadful," answered Martin, throwing the top of the pizza box open and smelling the aroma as though it was his last meal on death row.

"You're not wrong," said Jesse, walking over to the cabinet before pulling out two heavyweight whiskey glasses. Filling them from the bottle, he joined Martin on the sofa. "What pizza did you get?"

"Meat feast, of course. Man's pizza."

Jesse laughed and passed him his drink, before grabbing a slice.

"What you watching?"

"Nothing been flicking around." Jesse picked up the control and scrolled down the movies on 'on demand', deciding on the 'hangover' he flopped the control carelessly back on the sofa. "So, how's life?"

"Good." Martin swallowed hard on the big bite he'd just taken. "Claire's pulling her hair out, kids are sending us both up the wall, and her mum's stopping."

"Sheeeesh," said Jesse, realising why his friend direly needed a night off. No wonder he had asked Jesse for a drink.

"Yeah, my life's about as fun as it sounds," said Martin, scratching the back of his neck, before swallowing a large gulp of whiskey and hissing as it burned his throat.

"How come the mother-in-laws stopping?" Asked Jesse.

"Claire's been giving it all that," he said signally, a mouth moving with his hand. "About how she's on her own while I'm at work, so she's come to 'help'; now I've got Claire in one ear." again with the hand signal, "and her mother in the other."

Jesse couldn't help but laugh, he felt his pain. He'd never really got on very well with his ex-wife's parents, but he'd never had to endure them stopping over. He could only imagine how bad that would have been, and Hayley's parents were both dead.

"Anyway, enough about me, how's you?" Martin took another bite of pizza and waited for the answer.

"Same, not much happening," answered Jesse, watching the screen, as Bradley Cooper stood talking on the phone alongside a car.

"Tell me to fuck off if you want, but you look at the photo in your office an awful lot, not to be doing something about it."

Jesse sighed heavily. "We called it a day, remember, I get to drop in and see Daniel whenever I like. She's cool with that, but as for us, she seems happier on her own," sulked Jesse.

"Yeah, but how long's that going to last?"

Jesse just shrugged and took another mouthful of whiskey, making a grimace as the liquor burnt the back of his throat.

"I've no idea how, but you need to fix it, cus you're nowhere near ready to see her date someone else."

"She's not dating anyone," said Jesse defensively, hoping he was right.

"He doth protest too much," said Martin dramatically, waving his pizza in the air.

"It's up to her anyway, I can't tell her what to do," said Jesse, wishing he could.

"Yeah, OK," Martin nodded before taking another slice of pizza from the box. He knew not to push it, but then that's why he'd brought the drink. He needed to loosen him up, so he'd off load all the crap he was carrying around on his shoulders. They'd get there.

Two hours in and a bottle of whiskey an inch away from being empty. Pizza box open and thrown on the floor. Jesse was slumped in the settee in one corner and Martin in the other, legs outstretched and crossed at the ankles.

"I just don't know what the fuck to do," admitted Jesse, swirling the liquor round in the glass.

"Talk to her." Martin was getting pissed off with himself for repeating the same thing, but Jesse just wouldn't listen. "For fuck's sake."

"She won't listen. Just walks away, refooses to have a consersation, combershate, confersesation," slurred Jesse before giving up. "You know what I mean."

"Book a table. Buy some flowers, chocolates, get a babysitter and gaffer tape her to the fucking chair if you have to," advised Martin, realising his head would kill in the morning. He hoped his superior was grateful for this selfless act tomorrow.

"Yeah, you might be right," giggled Jesse. "I think that's what it would fucking take too."

"Grand gesture! Women love that shit," said Martin, feeling a little woozy.

"Not Hayley," answered Jesse. "No grand chesters for her," announced Jesse, pointing his finger at Martin knowingly.

Martin wondered how much of the bottle he'd dropped? Tomorrow would be an interesting day, thought Martin as he watched Jesse slump back on the settee. He was rat arsed.

"I asked Hayley to come out with you, me and Claire," admitted Martin, thinking it was best to tell him while still under the influence.

"Why?" Asked Jesse, exasperated.

"Because I could do with an enjoyable meal now and then. And if I take the missus out, she thinks it's a treat for her."

Jesse just looked at him, eyeballing him to admit that wasn't what he had meant.

"OK, OK, I thought you could both do with… neutral ground without a certain little man in the mix," slurred Martin.

"Mart! What the fuck!" Standing up abruptly sent him off balance and he fell back on the sofa with a whoosh. "She won't come," said Jesse. "She can barely stay in the same woom wiv me."

"We'll see."

"She finks I'm to blame, she finks I didn't find her because I dint care enuff," said Jesse aggressively, his dialect coming more pronounced the more the alcohol took effect.

"Yeah, well, I think you're a stubborn arsehole who needs a bloody good shove in the right direction."

"Can't believe you went against bro code," said Jesse, shaking his head, defeated.

"Bro code? Who are you, Diddy from the hood?" Asked Martin, laughing at Jesse's inebriated state. "You need your bloody heads banging together."

"You know nothin' mate," sighed Jesse, rubbing his temple.

"I have eyes and ears."

"And a big fucking mouth by the sounds of it," argued Jesse.

"You're just jealous because she said yes to me," Martin smirked childishly.

"You know I think I need you to go over some CCTV tomorrow," said Jesse, rubbing his eyes.

"What CCTV?" Asked Martin; he was about sick of CCTV. It seemed all he'd done lately was scan for information from a black-and-white screen; he was sure he'd watched more than was necessary already.

"Don't know, I'll find you some," smirked Jesse, watching Martin realise he was pulling his leg.

"You know it's a good job you're pissed or I might take action."

"What action would that be? I've seen you in the gym, remember; you couldn't knock the skin of a rice pudding," laughed Jesse, knowing he was winding him up about the amateur boxing match he'd fought in for charity last year, when he'd been knocked out in the first round by someone resembling the jolly green giant.

"Bollox, that bloke was Ivan Drago's reincarnation."

"He's not dead," said Jesse, laughing.

"Sure, he is. Rocky kicked his arse in that film," answered Martin.

"He still didn't die," stated Jesse.

Martin shrugged nonchalantly. "So, you going to tell me what's going on with you and Hayley?" Asked Martin seriously, hoping it was the right time.

Jesse sighed heavily before launching his head back to rest on the sofa as he looked to the ceiling for help. "Things just aren't the same."

"No shit, were you expecting them to?" Martin sat forward.

"No," answered Jesse, shaking his head along the sofa. "But I had hoped she'd let me help her."

"Why?"

"What do you mean why?" Jesse was sitting back up to face Martin.

"Why do you expect her to open up to you?"

"Because… because." Scratching his head, he tried to work out what he was trying to say without coming across as an idiot. "Because, I'd help her."

"Why would she think that?" asked Martin, watching Jesse look at him as though he was expecting him to recite the definition.

"Think about it from her point of view. Hayley tried to protect her sister, and then her sister tries to get you charged with Hayley's murder and her own ABH. She asks her Dad to help and then an hour or two later he's dead, or presumed dead. She was told by Caitlyn you were in hospital only to arrive at a warehouse and abducted, she was told to get a DNA test to prove Daniel's parentage only to find out he was conceived before she was under Demy's roof, and then you two split up. When she got back, she not only has a child in toe but she also spent the best half of a year with a psychopath who abused her daily just for kicks. Who would you trust?"

Jesse felt as though he'd been throat punched.

"She doesn't know which way is up right now, and she's trying to grasp onto the things she knew gave her peace before, like a home and her job. The only missing piece is you, but you're so all up in her face about not opening up that she shuts down even further and no doubt putting a deadbolt onto her emotions. That girl has been through hell ever since her mum died, and she's had no one to rely on. Why would she suddenly believe you can be trusted?"

Jesse watched and felt every word that came from Martin's lips as they landed with full force.

"If you want her to open up, first, she's got to trust you. Trust you that when she says something you listen, that you take what she's saying on board and you respect her decision. She knows she's not handling this well, but she equally doesn't need someone to tell her that. She requires encouragement. When she knows she can trust you and that you see her as your equal, she'll see you for you, at the minute you're just someone else trying to take something from her."

"I'm not trying to take anything from her," argued Jesse defensively.

"You got in a strop about her getting a home. Didn't like that she was going back to work. Didn't like her decision about a childminder, and you've made her feel worthless," spoke Martin honestly.

"I hadn't realised we were over for good. She's not ready to go back to work. He's my son too, she should have at least spoken to me about it. And I've never tried to make her feel worthless," answered Jesse, hoping that wasn't how she felt.

"She has never been in a relationship, Jesse, ever. Not even a bog-standard parent daughter relationship. Hayley doesn't understand how they work. She doesn't understand unconditional love because she's never had it. All she knows is that people only want her when they want something from her. She's judged what you want."

CHAPTER 4

THE NEXT DAY HAYLEY WASN'T SURE HOW TO HANDLE THINGS WITH Rob. He seemed to be just getting on as normal, but something made her feel weary. She was unsure how she felt or what to think, as far as she could tell he had made his feelings clear to her, but knowing that her ex was his brother, was beyond complicated. It was a disaster waiting to happen and she wasn't going there, besides she didn't have any romantic thoughts about him, she saw him much like a brother.

In the locker room, Hayley checked her phone. Seeing a message from Jesse, she eagerly tapped on it. Reading that he wouldn't be popping by tonight to see Daniel as work had just got heavy, and he didn't think he'd get away at a decent hour. It hit her with a sudden wave of disappointment. She'd been looking forward to seeing him, especially with what had happened with Rob the previous evening. Something made her want to be around him, and that was confusing, since all she'd done was pushing him away. She'd spent almost every day since they'd broken up, hoping not to spend time with him, but one sudden knock to her confidence and she just wanted to crawl into his arms and feel safe.

"Lift?"

Hayley jumped. Realising she'd been daydreaming as Rob

approached her from the kitchen. "No, thanks, I'm fine honestly," she smiled, hoping she was coming across as genuine.

"Don't be daft. I'll give you a lift, it's pissing it down out there, you'll get soaked."

Deciding she had no proper choice unless she wanted to appear rude, she nodded before thanking him.

"Not that I wouldn't like to see you in a wet T-shirt contest," murmured Rob.

Hayley tensed before looking down at the floor.

Why was Rob suddenly making her feel uncomfortable? Why did she feel like she'd suddenly turned into his prey and he was circling her, waiting for vulnerability? Was she just seeing things that weren't there? Was she so badly traumatised that her mind considered everything a risk or a threat?

Taking a deep breath, she told herself to stop being so stupid. Over-sensitivity was going to catch her out and make everyone think she was insane. Hayley had to control it. She couldn't let other people see how broken she felt. She was barely recovering as it was.

Walking to the car felt awkward. Getting in, she fastened the seat belt across herself. Rob started the engine and pulled out onto the A46. Taking her phone from her pocket, she scanned through her photographs of Daniel, giving her something to do other than sit in the awkward silence, or try to start a conversation with the confusing man beside her.

Rob turned the radio on after a few minutes, humming along to a George Ezra song. Hayley looked into Jesse's blue eyes on her phone. He was holding Daniel with love in his eyes. It was the day they'd walked around Newark Castle, when the riverside festival was on. It had been a lovely day, and it made her smile, remembering it. She'd do anything to go back to that day.

Daniel had been only a few months old. They'd taken him out to show him the castle, the river and listen to the music being played. Daniel would have been happy anywhere as long as they fed and changed him. Hayley had really enjoyed being around people. She thought she would find it overwhelming, but it hadn't been overly crowded and Jesse had waited in queues to get drinks and food etc so she didn't feel penned in. He'd accommodated her anxieties, and he somehow helped soothe her and allowed her to enjoy the warm sunny day.

The memories made her smile. It had been an enjoyable day, and maybe she'd been too harsh or too quick to pass judgement on their relationship? There had always been a connection between them, but she just couldn't bear to see the regret on his face every time he looked at her. He deserved better, so much better.

Pulling up outside Kerrie's; Hayley rushed out, closing the door after saying goodbye and thanking him. But when she left Kerrie's with Daniel in the pushchair, with the rain cover pulled down, he was outside waiting. Feeling her stomach twist, she walked towards the gate and reluctantly opened it. When she was through, Rob got out the car.

"It's OK, we can walk. He's all strapped in now, anyway," she smiled, hopefully.

"Don't be silly, where's his car seat?"

"I didn't bring it this morning; he only has it when Jesse drops him off."

Rob scratched his neck, thinking. "Ok, just hold him; it's only round the corner."

"No!" She said more forcefully than she intended. Putting her best smile on, she readjusted her voice so as not to antagonise him. "I mean, it's fine, we can walk, it'll take us five minutes, and you've already helped me by dropping me off." He was watching her, hoping her face didn't betray her until she smiled wider.

"OK, if you're sure?" He said finally, stepping away from the front of the pushchair so she could get by.

"Thanks Rob, see you tomorrow," she called back, hoping the lift in her voice was believable.

Realising he was out of sight, she rushed the extra few minutes and arrived home, locking the door behind her and attaching the chain. Standing behind the door, she noticed her breathing was jagged and her heart was beating out of her chest. Why was she reacting like this?

It was just Rob; he was harmless. Was this a side effect of being taken hostage, was she never going to trust anyone? Shaking her thoughts away, she lifted Daniel's rain cover and looked down at her sleeping son. Crouching down, she watched him breathe, his chest rising and falling at a steady pace.

"OK Tiger, I'll let you sleep." Kissing him on the forehead, she walked into the living room to see Michael and Marie.

∼

JESSE ROLLED HIS EYES, "Yes sir…. yep, I know, we're holding a meeting in five, of course…."

Martin watched Jesse angling to get off the phone while his superior gave him an ear bashing. Finally, he hung up and nodded towards Martin.

"What's up?" Asked Martin, sitting on the chair across from him holding a stack of paperwork on his knee, that they'd dedicated time to trawl through together.

"Super's just wanting results. The media's got hold of it, so bang goes our low key," said Jesse, throwing the pen across the room after he'd been flicking it between his fingers.

"Was always going to happen," noted Martin.

Jesse nodded sombrely.

"OK, tell me what we've got, before I set the cat amongst the pigeons," asked Jesse, sitting back.

Martin explained that the man found asphyxiated in his garage had done so apparently of his own free will. Even though everyone around him thought it was out of character. When he'd finished relaying what they had learned and suspected, he closed his book and looked at Jesse expectantly.

"So, it could be payback?" Offered Jesse.

Martin nodded as though it had crossed his mind too.

"Why did no one report it?"

"It's the Devon. Some families have close links to the gypsies in town, you know what they're like. They sort things out themselves," answered Martin.

"So, when did the alleged assault take place?"

"A couple of months ago."

"And it's taken this long to seek justice?" Asked Jesse with a heavy dose of skepticism. "They're not known for hanging around."

"According to a neighbour, he's only just come back."

Jesse nodded, that made sense.

"Mexico."

"Ok, let's get this done," Jesse said standing up, taking his coffee mug from the desk. "How's the head?" He asked, whilst holding the door open.

"Like someone's thrown a brick at it," answered Martin "You?"

"Like someone invited the Irish to river dance on my frontal lobe."

Martin scoffed beside him as they watched their DCI walk in to the incident room ahead of them.

"And there's the Philharmonic orchestra."

CHAPTER 5

Jesse glanced down at the child curled up in the fetal position on the frozen grass. With height and colouring, he couldn't help see the resemblance to his own son. On first appearance it looked as though he had fallen asleep, but he hadn't or Jesse and Martin wouldn't be there. Looking at one another they silently shared their own thoughts of their own children and thanked the universe they weren't in this boy's parents' position.

"How long's he been out here?" asked Martin, sensing Jesse was finding this more difficult than before. It was times like these Martin was thankful his children were older, but he could see Jesse was making the connection between the boy's demise and his own child. Daniel might have come as a shock, but it didn't stop him from being the centre of his world.

"I'd say he's been here for a few days. I can get a closer time frame once we get him back," explained Mike Harvard the pathologist. He had only recently moved to the area, but he was well-liked and efficient, in his late fifties with greying to white hair. He carried an air of authority and experience, he was the welcome calm needed on such sights. "I'd hazard a guess at hypothermia." He continued as he surveyed the body.

"Poor bastard," said Martin sympathetically.

"Yeah, the poor lad is showing extensive bruising under the colouring; I'd say he was better off out here." Mike looked up at the detectives sadly, as though he'd never normally wish anything so awful on a poor innocent kid.

Jesse couldn't take his eyes from the child, he looked so much like Daniel. He just wanted to wrap him up in a blanket and tell him everything would be ok, but it wouldn't. They were too late; no help had come. He had died believing the world was a brutal and lonely place, and for him it had been.

"Ok, can you get the report back to me as soon as possible on this; we need to find the bastard who left him out here." Jesse turned, trying to swallow the bile that had risen from his stomach.

Martin nodded his thanks to the pathologist and followed Jesse back to the car in silence. "You ok?" he asked as they sat next to each other, looking out of the front windscreen in a daze.

"Not really," admitted Jesse.

"Daniel?" Offered Martin. Jesse just nodded. "Just give him a hug when you see him, that's all you can do, mate."

"And find the bastard who did that," answered Jesse.

Nodding, Martin watched the pathologist move around the scene, taking great care with each step. "How's the head now?" asked Martin, feeling his own headache easing off.

"I'm less concerned about my head than I am the fact I'm still probably over the bleeding limit." answered Jesse.

"Well, don't say I didn't offer to get one of the bobbies to drive us here." sing-songed Martin.

"Yeah, because the DCI would be over the moon to hear his DI was having to be chauffeur driven at his expense."

"Better than failing a breathalyser," shrugged Martin.

"Just grab the bloody coffee's before I suspend you for insubordination," said Jesse pointing to the café over the road, as the owner pulled the cord on the blinds and flipped the sign over.

Laughing, Martin rushed over the empty road while Jesse rested his pounding head on the steering wheel. After the meeting that had been more bad news than results, a pounding head and now the image of his son dead on the ground he needed to take a breath before he lost it, and Martin had been dancing on his last nerve since revealing his plan to have him and Hayley in the same room on a night out, that would never be productive.

∼

HAYLEY WAS RUNNING LATE. If she didn't get a move on, she would not make the bus in time. Daniel had thrown a tantrum this morning, resulting in him and her being covered in Ready Brek. A quick shower and an even quicker breakfast, they rushed out of the house and round the block to Kerrie's house.

"Hi, I'm so sorry we're late. Had a mishap with the porridge. He's barely eaten breakfast, but I've put a yoghurt in and some rusks. I'm really sorry but I have to get off, I'll see you later."

Shutting the door behind her, she ran to the gate before realising she still had the baby change bag over her shoulder. Turning back, she made for the door just as Kerrie was opening it. After sharing a knowing smile, she was on her way.

Running round the corner, she watched the bus pulling away.

"Shit!"

Stopping her run, she bent over at the waist, taking in cool breaths to replenish her oxygen levels. Standing back up, she watched the bus turn round the bend at the top of the road. Tears in her eyes, she walked over to the bus stop shelter. Sitting on the bevelled seat, she pulled out her mobile. Looking through her contacts, she contemplated calling Jesse. But he was at work, and he'd already explained how busy he was. Not wanting to be a burden to anyone else, she checked her wallet. She had ten pounds. Not being sure whether that would even get her there in a taxi, she slumped back in the shelter, about ready to give up and call it a day.

Beeping made her look up. "Want a lift?" said Rob after winding down the window.

THE VINE TREE

"Please, you'd be saving my life, I missed the bloody bus." She admitted furiously.

"Get in." grabbing the handle, she pulled the door open and sat down. "Thanks for this, I thought Ash was going to kill me if I had to ring in and tell him I was waiting for the next bus."

"Why didn't you phone me?" asked Rob, pulling away from the bus stop.

"I didn't think, and Daniel had a paddy this morning, after I got cleaned up and out the door I was already running behind."

"What was he having a tantrum about?" asked Rob, making his way round the roundabout to get on the A46.

"He didn't want his porridge, so he decided to re-decorate the house." Rob laughed. "Yeah, I wasn't laughing when I was trying to get it out my hair in the shower, and while I love your Mum to bits, when Daniel's in one of his moods, I swear she makes it ten times worse by trying to pacify him."

"Like I said you should have called." said Rob laughing as she vented her frustration at him, Hayley looked at him, he sounded like he was just offering help but after her comment about being in the shower she wasn't sure how he meant it.

∼

AFTER GETTING CHANGED they made their way upstairs into the kitchen, starting on the desserts Hayley went in search of the drain pipes they used for the raspberry cheesecakes, while Rob threw a box of oranges on the table to fill the juice machine back up with. Four hours later service was about to start when the kitchen phone rang, thinking it was a group order Hayley picked it up ready with a notepad and pen in hand. "Hello, Kitchen."

"Hi, is that you, Hayley?"

"Yes?" asked Hayley, unable to place the voice, even though it sounded familiar.

"It's Kerrie, I'm sorry to bother you at work but I'm worried about

Daniel. He's got really warm. I think he might be coming down with something. Would there be anyone who could pick him up, please?"

"Oh crap, that's why he was kicking off this morning." said Hayley realising she'd missed the signs. "Yes, of course, I'll arrange something. Can you hold on a sec?" After holding her hand over the receiver, she called Ash over, who was trying to sear lamb cutlets. "Daniel's unwell, is there any chance I can leave?" just as she finished asking him, Rob sauntered past with a tray of eggs.

"What's wrong with him?"

"Fever." answered Hayley.

"I can take him to Mum and Dad's. They'll have him. I can be back in an hour," offered Rob, looking from Hayley to Ash.

Hayley appreciated his offer to help, but she wanted to be with Daniel. Especially now she knew he was poorly. But before she could say anything Ash nodded, confirming that was fine and Rob ran out the kitchen. Deflated Hayley removed her hand and explained to Kerrie what was going on.

∾

THE DAY DRAGGED BY. Even when Rob got back and could confirm he was ok and being fussed over, she still couldn't shake off the feeling of being a terrible parent. With her mind elsewhere, she wasn't concentrating enough and making silly mistakes, so when four-thirty finally arrived she could have cried. Rushing downstairs, she threw off her jacket and slipped out of her steel toe cap boots. Throwing her skull cap in her locker, she turned to see Rob.

"Give me five seconds and I'll give you a lift, bet you're dying to see him, aren't you?"

"Like you wouldn't believe." she answered.

∾

WHEN THEY ARRIVED HOME, Hayley rushed into the front room to see Daniel sleeping peacefully on Marie's lap. Smiling, Marie gently handed him over to Hayley so she could hold him. She snuggled him in to her gently; taking in his familiar scent. Realising how worried she'd been about him, tears slid down her cheeks.

"Hey, hey, he's fine. Just a little temperature. He's probably just teething," assured Marie, rubbing Hayley's back.

"I'm sorry," she croaked, trying to wipe away the tears, feeling foolish.

"Don't be daft, you worry about them, you never stop, whether they're two or twenty-eight." said Marie smiling empathetically.

Hayley nodded, then saw Rob watching her from the doorway. He had that funny look on his face again, but once he realised she was staring, he turned back to the kitchen. "I'll make you a drink; you stay here and take your cuddles while you can."

"Thanks for looking after him today." said Hayley before Marie walked into the kitchen.

"Not a problem at all, he's an angel."

After a few minutes Hayley realised that not only was Daniel safe but he was nowhere near close to waking up, so she slid him into the travel cot they had set up in the front room before making her way into the kitchen to help Marie with the tea.

"Oh, where's Marie?" asked Hayley, closing the door behind her gently.

"Shop, we've run out of milk." answered Rob.

"Oh, I'd have gone if she'd have asked." said Hayley guiltily.

"I offered, but she insisted," answered Rob, taking a sip of black coffee, watching her over the rim of his cup.

Feeling on edge again, she moved away from him and sat at the table. "Well, I can't say it's not much needed." she said, flipping the pages of the magazine that rested on the table. "Today feels like it's lasted forever." she exclaimed, scanning the articles. Just then she felt hands snake around her shoulders and she spun round to see Rob looking down at her. "Rob, what are you doing?"

"I'd say that was obvious." He said pushing her down in the chair, whilst lowering his head.

When she could almost feel his lips on hers, her head screamed to put the brakes on. She screwed her eyes up tight, begging him in her head to stop. Suddenly frozen, but with the feeling of fire raging through her veins, a tear fell from her eye and ran hot down her face. "Please don't do this." she pleaded.

Still feeling his breath on her face, she slowly opened her eyes to see him staring at her, watching her chest rise and plummet.

"I didn't mean to scare you." He said meeting her eyes, but still leaning in. "I've just thought about kissing you for so long."

Hayley's eyes grew in size, the shock clear on her face, which just made him smile.

"You're all I've been thinking about all day."

Hayley shimmied out from under him and stood away from his leaning, still holding onto the magazine.

"Hayley, I think you know what you've been doing to me."

She could feel goose bumps rise on her neck and arms, and they weren't the good kind. Without warning, he took a step forward, tipping her jaw up. He captured her lips with his and forced her mouth open, delving his tongue in to taste her. A few seconds before she burst free and pushed him away. Feeling embarrassed, she walked away, rushing upstairs to the toilet to throw up.

∼

AFTER A FEW MINUTES of leaning over the sink and looking at her reflection in the mirror, she decided that she'd eventually have to leave the bathroom and face Rob. She might as well get it over with; taking a hand towel, she dried her wet face before pulling the door open. Gingerly she walked downstairs towards the kitchen.

As she drew closer, she heard voices and breathed a sigh of relief to hear Marie's. Entering the kitchen, she ignored Rob and smiled at Marie.

"You ok, you look peaky?" asked Marie, scanning Hayley's face.

Hayley couldn't stop her eyes from darting to Rob, who was trying to hide a smirk behind his cup. "Fine. Just tired." Lied Hayley, taking the cup Marie offered her, which evidently now had milk involved.

"Well, you two go in the living room, and I'll sort tea, you must be starving."

Following Rob into the living room, she turned to him as soon as she was sure Marie wouldn't hear. "Rob, I think I might have given you the wrong impression."

Looking up at her from the sofa he'd sat down on, he snatched her wrist, trying to take it out of his grasp. He tugged on it harder until she fell on his knee.

"There's no need to rush, we'll take our time." He whispered in her ear, making her shiver.

"Rob, you don't understand-" before she could finish, he placed his finger on her lips to stop her from speaking.

"I'll be here when you're ready."

Deciding to nod as it was easier than arguing, she allowed him to move her off his knee before walking to the door and going back into his Mum. Shaking, she glanced to Daniel, sleeping with puffy red cheeks and hair that stood up from sweat. Maybe she was coming down with something too?

CHAPTER 6

JESSE AND MARTIN STARED DESPONDENTLY AT THE GREY BOY ON THE mortuary slab. The chill in the air wasn't just from the refrigeration unit, but from the heartbreaking scene in front of them. "Please tell me you have something new for us to work with," said Jesse, looking towards Mike.

"I'd like to give you coordinates to the perp's house, but unfortunately I've only got the basics. This boy died because of his internal organs failing. Someone has poisoned him over a generous amount of time, probably via his food and water, though his stomach was empty at the time of death. He died around a week ago, but I've reason to believe they have kept him in a cool area for a suitable length of time. I don't think he's been outside, for the amount of interference we'd normally see, so someone's moved him. They broke his back in several places; some injuries are consistent with a fall from a significant height whilst others are consistent with blunt force trauma, a baseball bat, rolling pin, something of that type. I noticed a scar on his back that I thought would interest you both," he said, looking at them as though asking for permission to continue. Nodding, he turned to the screen behind them, flicking it on via the remote an image stared back at them.

"Is that what I think it is?" Asked Martin in disbelief. Moving closer to the monitor, Jesse stared at the enlarged scar.

"This can't be happening," whispered Jesse, turning to Martin, horrified. "How old is that scar?" Asked Jesse, pointing towards the screen.

"It's not old, it's fairly recent," explained Mike sadly, "maybe a week before death. It would have caused immense pain, and it doesn't look as though it was well-managed afterwards either. He'd have had a distinguishable scar had he survived," continued the pathologist, unaware of the screaming going on in Jesse's head. "And infection."

"It doesn't mean he's getting out," said Martin, watching Jesse visibly pale.

"No, but it means one of his cronies is continuing his work," explained Jesse. "I thought we had dismantled the fucking thing." Turning around on the spot, he furiously ran his hand through his hair, thinking about how he would ensure they would be.

"Is there something more I should know?" Asked Mike, flicking his gaze from each detective.

"Hayley has that scar," explained Martin, calmly.

"Hayley?" Asked Mike, confused.

"My-" faltering, Jesse wasn't sure what to call her anymore.

"His girlfriend. She was the one they kidnapped last year," explained Martin, hoping he wasn't saying anything untoward, but it was significant to their case once again. "She has that symbol on her back too."

"Oh, I'm sorry, Jesse. I wouldn't have just dropped that on you like that had I known," said Mike sympathetically.

Waving his sympathy away, Jesse made for the door. He needed some fresh air before he threw up and embarrassed himself.

"Don't worry about it," said Martin after Jesse had left. "Do we have anything else?"

"There's plenty in my notes, but I'll let you read at your leisure," answered Mike, still eyeing the door as though Jesse might rush back in. "Should he be on this case?" He asked, turning to Martin as he flipped through the reports from the side table nearest the screen.

"No, and this was the first thing that's come up to suggest we connect the two cases. It's like déjà fucking vu," sighed Martin reading the toxicology report. "Would you be able to confirm whether the same hand did the brand?"

"It's not out of the question, but it might be inconclusive. It's much easier to see how a knife's used, by which hand and at what angle. With a brand, it would more than likely be from above and with force. Then the skin's thickness would have to be considered and the strength of the perpetrator. The results might not give you any more than you have now, but I'll certainly cast my eye over them and look for any anomalies."

"Thanks Mike, right I'll take these and be in contact."

Mike nodded as he watched Martin step heavily from the room.

∽

Jesse walked in to Hayley, Marie and Michael eating apple pie and custard.

"Hi, didn't know you were calling in, I'd have saved you some custard if I'd have known." said Marie, getting up from her chair to cut Jesse a piece from the dish left out on the side.

"Yeah, I wasn't going to come, but I need to speak to Hayley." At the mention of her name, she caught the look in his eye and knew that he was here to tell her grievous news.

"What is it? Is he being released?" She panicked, dropping her spoon, sending it clattering into her bowl.

"No, no, of course not, but can we talk in the living room?" Gazing towards Marie and Michael, who both nodded their understanding to leave them alone for a few minutes, they made their way into the living room. Jesse looked towards the travel cot and raised an eyebrow.

"He's been unwell today. Your mum's been looking after him," answered Hayley.

"What's wrong with him?" Asked Jesse, alarmed.

"Nothing, teeth," answered Hayley. Nodding, he held out his hand for her to sit down. "What's going on?"

When she had taken a seat, he perched on his Dad's armchair so he was close to her. "We've found a body recently, and it bares the same brand you have."

Hayley's stomach dropped, and her throat instantly dried at the reminder of the night her betrothed pinned her down on the altar before pushing a red-hot branding iron into her lower back. The pain had been excruciating and led to her passing out, but not before the stench of burnt skin had filled her nostrils, and the tears had stained her face.

"Hayley! Hayley!" Sensing Jesse holding onto her arms, she realised her body was shaking.

Hearing the commotion, Marie and Michael rushed in to see Hayley amid a panic attack.

"Mum, grab me a paper bag!" Shouted Jesse, knowing his Mum kept all kinds of rubbish in the top drawer of the kitchen. Jesse tried to calm Hayley down with reassuring words and gentle strokes along her shoulders, while he waited and his Dad cast him inquiring glances, he'd answer the obvious questions later.

Passing the bag over. Jesse helped Hayley hold it over her mouth and nose, telling her to breathe in slowly and breathe out slowly. After a manic few minutes, she was taking in oxygen steadily, so Jesse removed the bag. Nodding to his mum and dad to reassure them she was OK. Watching them leave, he moved to sit next to her.

Taking her hands in his, he could feel how cold and clammy they were. "Hayley, can you think of anyone else who might use that brand?"

Hayley absently shook her head, tears in her eyes as she stared at the mantlepiece with a picture of Daniel on.

"Hey, he's fine," said Jesse, seeing where her thoughts were going.

"Who did they kill?" asked Hayley calmly, turning to him.

Jesse thought about telling her and the need for confidentiality, but if she knew anything, he first needed to show he trusted her. "A boy."

Hayley screwed her eyes up as they squeezed tears out. "How old?" She croaked, willing it not to be true.

"Hayley, I -" started Jesse. He couldn't reveal too much.

"How old?" She asked again, this time sterner with a hint of fear.

"We don't know yet, but young," answered Jesse truthfully. She didn't need it confirming that the child was close to Daniel's age. "Hayley, are you sure that we got everyone involved?"

"No," said Hayley, shaking her head. "No, I don't. How could I? He never allowed me to be around his dealings, especially after grassing him up the first time. I thought Darren gave you everything you needed?" Said Hayley desperately.

Darren was Hayley's brother and a tech wizard. He'd got enough on file that he could plant it and make it look like the police discovered a goldmine of information. But he was someone they couldn't find, and Martin had made a deal not to go after him or release his name, to save both Hayley and Jesse's lives. To the team he was a ghost, but there was always the risk that he had more to do with the sect than he had led them to believe.

"Seems, he may have left someone off the list," said Jesse quietly.

"Are we safe?" Asked Hayley, watching Jesse's face for any sign of an answer he might not want to divulge.

"Honestly, I've no idea," answered Jesse, shaking his head and running his hand through his gelled hair without meeting her eyes that were blazing into the side of his head.

Stealing courage, she knew she didn't possess, she swallowed hard and looked Jesse in the eye. "I had a call earlier about a flat I looked at, it's vacant and they're ready for me to move in," said Hayley quietly.

"You can't be serious?" Asked Jesse, horrified. "You're moving, after this?"

"I can't just put my life on hold. We don't even know if there's a threat. Besides, the flat has CCTV and an alarm system. I checked," said Hayley.

Whilst being on her own was scary, especially after what Jesse had just told her. She needed space. She didn't need an audience, especially when they came in the form of his Mum and Dad.

"I don't give a shit if her majesties regiments are on guard outside, you're not moving out on your own with Daniel while this is going on," argued Jesse sternly.

Hayley jumped up. "Are you kidding me, you're telling me what I can and can't do?!" She shouted.

"I'm *advising* you. That it's just too dangerous at the minute," pleaded Jesse.

"Well, I'll take your advice and then do what I think," said Hayley, crossing her arms, as Jesse stood up.

"No, you won't, you'll just do the bloody opposite just to prove a point!" Shouted Jesse.

"And what point would that be?" She snarled.

"The one where you get to put two fingers up at me."

Hayley huffed. She was unsure what to say to that and just as her shoulders relaxed, realising he was probably right.

"And he's my kid too, why the hell would I want you to put him at risk?"

"Put him at risk?!" She shouted. "I would never put him at risk!"

"Doesn't sound like it, if you're so bloody mumsy why the hell was my mum looking after him today, when he needed you?" The second the words left his mouth he instantly regretted it and the look on Hayley's face made him want to kick himself in the balls. But before he could apologise, she rushed from the room.

He listened to her running up the stairs, before slamming a door and hearing a scream, undoubtedly because she'd just scared the living hell out of Daniel. Looking at the doorway, he saw two faces peaking behind the door at him; he'd have laughed had he been in the mood.

"Your apple pie's ready," said Marie timidly.

〜

THE ATMOSPHERE WAS as icier than the weather outside. Rob had hardly spoken to her all day and when he had, it had only been to pass on information or give orders. She couldn't help feeling responsible for his advances, and she sure as hell knew she should have pushed him away sooner. Made it clearer sooner, and she couldn't understand why she hadn't, she'd just felt paralysed. It was as though her body no longer knew how to process danger except to let it happen and hope for the best. After all, fighting had never got her anywhere, apart from more pain.

Glancing towards Rob over the dining table, while flicking her salad around the plate. She watched him play with the innards of his jacket potato, as though expecting some kind of answer within it.

"I think we need to talk," she said finally.

"*Now* you want to talk?" Asked Rob sarcastically, without looking up.

"Last night was a mistake," she said, watching him stare at his lunch. "But I don't want this to come between us. I don't want this awkwardness."

"He doesn't want you, you know." Rob finally looking up to watch the hurt flash across her face. "He's moved on, got a new girl. Rachel, I think. Works with him, apparently."

Hayley swallowed at the revelation. She couldn't help feeling jealous. It didn't matter that they weren't together. She'd always love him. Knowing he'd replaced her did nothing to stop the pain from losing him. It only went to prove that she was the problem. They damaged her, broken her beyond repair, and had left her unable to maintain a healthy relationship. It should please her he was with someone who could make him happy, but it didn't.

"I didn't mean that to come out so harshly, I'm sorry," said Rob softly as he pushed his hand across the table, rubbing her knuckles with his thumb.

"Sorry," she croaked, moving her hand away. Sniffing and wiping her watery eyes. "I'm an idiot," she laughed.

"No, you're not; he didn't know what a good thing he had."

Hayley tried to smile at his kindness, but she just wanted to curl up and sob.

Staring at her, he watched her trying to pull herself together. "Hey, it's OK. Everything will be alright," soothed Rob. "You'll always have me."

"Oh God, what a mess," she laughed, trying to make light of her embarrassment. "I'm going to get cleaned up; I'll meet you up there, OK?"

Rob nodded, watching her leave the dining room.

∼

"OK, we need to pull everything together." Jesse stood in front of the whiteboard, looking over to his team. "Adam, what do you have?"

"Well, I've spoken to neighbours, and they said the family were volatile, they had spoken to social a few times but nothing came of it. Social has confirmed that there were two calls six months apart. The last one was four months ago, but when they went round, there was nothing overly concerning, so they left. Parents said neighbours were nosy parkers, social seemed to take it at face value, Mum's a teacher and Dad works in an office in town, something to do with web design."

"And what, neither realised their seven-year-old wasn't in his bed?" Asked Jesse skeptically.

"Mum said she put him to bed as usual, but when she checked that morning to get him up, the window was wide open," explained Adam.

"What?!" asked Martin, dumbfounded. "Why didn't they report him missing?"

"They thought he was staying with friends," shrugged Adam. "Apparently he regularly disappears."

"What, out his window at night?" Asked Rosa in disbelief. "And they didn't bother checking?"

Adam just shrugged as though it was the only answer he was getting.

"And Dad?" Asked Jesse, exasperated. They were clearly being lied to.

"Wasn't there that night, he was at work late, apparently?" Adam looked at his notes suspiciously. "Mum told him he was staying with friends."

"Did Dad really not know? And how late?" asked Jesse, watching Adam flick through his notepad.

"He looked genuine to me. I think Mum fed him crap, and he ate it up. She looked shifty about the entire thing, if you ask me. He was late home by two hours, said he had stuff to finish on a design that couldn't wait," answered Adam.

"So, we're looking at an affair," announced Martin. "Get back at Dad."

Everyone turned to him, but he just looked straight at Jesse while he processed what he had said.

"It's a possibility, but what's the significance of the wings?" Asked Rosa. "Looks more premeditated than a simple woman scorned. I'm not saying it's not possible but to poison her son for a week, kill him and then tie wings to his back?" Ended Rosa looking less than convinced. "Unless she's a nut job."

"Maybe she put him to bed, and he just didn't wake up. She panicked," answered Martin. "Maybe she didn't mean to poison him."

"And the wings?" Asked Rosa.

"Maybe they mean something to her," he shrugged, while Jesse's eyes seemed to glaze over.

Realising the team had lost him for a few seconds, Martin continued so the team wouldn't pick up on it. "Maybe she's some religious nut and thought she could give him wings so he could travel to heaven. Weirder things have happened."

"Should have just given him a red bull," said Adam, trying to lighten the tone, but the joke fell flat and the team just looked at him with disdain. So, he hung his head in shame, shuffling papers that didn't require shuffling.

"Was there anything in the house that would lead you to believe there was any religious allegiance?" Asked Jesse.

Adam and Rosa shook their heads.

"No crosses, or figures, or anything. But that doesn't mean they're not. Do you want me to ask?" Asked Rosa.

"No, not yet. If it has any significance, then they'll just lie. Let's just keep our ears to the ground though, if it comes up then see what you can find out." Rosa nodded. "Check social media too."

"I spoke to Mike, and he's pretty sure some bruising on him has been there for months. He said the words 'systematic abuse'." Rosa raised her eyebrow, letting the words seep into everyone's minds.

"OK, so we need to lean on these parents. One or both of them is lying through their teeth," confirmed Jesse. "We just need to find out which one and about what exactly."

"Sir, are we working under the belief that these boys are connected?" Asked Rosa, checking they were all on the same page.

"We're certainly not ruling it out. But the lad with the swan's wings seems a little different, and we had a revelation about the latest boy, when we went to visit him in the mortuary," said Jesse, watching the room grow quiet.

Waiting with bated breath, he glanced to Martin before continuing. "It seems he has a mark on his back, resembling that of the brand on Dmitri Richard's victims."

Watching everyone's eyes grow wide and absorb the news he hadn't wanted to divulge. He took a breath remembering the brand on Hayley's back that had they'd imposed on her as a child as punishment for refusing to marry Dmitri Richards by the Sect's orders. Not only had the wedding gone ahead without her consent. But he had then imprisoned her and systematically abused her. Which had led to her first pregnancy and subsequent miscarriage.

Hayley had laid foundations to escape. Barely managing it, after providing the police with an anonymous tip and slugging Dmitri unconscious with a plank of wood from their back garden. Before hopping over their fence and disappearing. Hayley had escaped and hidden at an old school friend's house after slipping on a bus. When she had become of age, she'd changed her last name to ensure her safety, and then started working in a local supermarket.

Hayley had changed her hair and wore makeup to disguise herself just in case anyone would ever pass by her. She was out but not a million miles away, as her meager funds had only provided a bus ticket and a few meals and clothes before it had run out. Before then, she had solely relied on her friend's family to support her. Thankfully, they had owned a restaurant, so she had worked off her board and lodgings without having to provide her details or much of an explanation.

When Jesse had brought her into the station to interview her about how she had come by the brand. He had done so by blind siding her and making her vulnerable. The same day he'd betrayed her she had gone missing, having trusted his brother's fiancé when she had told her Jesse had been in an accident. She had put their differences aside and rushed to be by his side, only to have been tricked and held captive for over six months. He wasn't sure he'd ever get over the feeling of guilt associated with her disappearance and ultimately the abuse she had suffered at the hands of the man he had been investigating at the time for drugs and human trafficking.

"Sir?" Jesse shot his head up. "I said I'm visiting the nursery this afternoon. See if they can shed any light onto his family life and anyone that may have been in contact with him. Should I ask them about the mark?"

"You can, but Mike thinks they inflicted this fairly recently," answered Jesse. "Same M.O in that someone poisoned him, just minus the wings."

Rosa nodded.

"Although, they physically assaulted him too. There was blunt force trauma, and he may have been dropped and beaten." He heard the room take in a deep breath and watched as their faces reacted to the news. No one was lucky to be on this case, but he knew they all wanted to find the people who had hurt these children more.

Looking at the board he saw the faces of Alex James Cartwright aged seven and Robert Marlow aged two, silently telling them he would bring them justice. He looked back to the team, who were scribbling notes down.

"OK, I'm popping out for an hour, but if you need me call," said Jesse. "Does everyone have something to keep them busy?"

Murmurs went throughout the room and when he was sure no

one needed a job, he grabbed his blazer from the back of a computer chair near the door.

"You going to see Hayley?" Asked Martin, keeping his voice low.

"I don't think I've got a choice. She could know something," answered Jesse.

"Do you think that's wise, considering Daniel?"

"What do you suggest? The last time I didn't tell her, it blew up in my face," argued Jesse, shouldering his blazer on. "Anyway, I already told her last night."

"Oh, and how did that go?" Asked Martin, watching Jesse's face change to a visible 'how do you think?'

"I'm going to go see her. Since she's had a night to think on it, she might have remembered something," he said firmly.

Martin nodded, understanding Jesse was between a rock and a hard place.

"If this comes back to Daniel and I've kept shit to myself, she'll never forgive me."

"We don't know for sure yet, Jesse. This could all just be a cosmic coincidence."

Jesse looked at him to say he wasn't fooling anyone.

"Let's just hope we find this maniac before anyone else dies," spoke Jesse, glancing to his team behind Martin.

"You been to the DCI yet?"

"No, I tried earlier, but he's leading another case and it wasn't the right time."

This time it was Martin's turn to look at him disbelievingly.

"I'll do it," he assured him before leaving.

～

HAYLEY RUSHED downstairs after getting the call that someone was waiting in reception for her. Turning the corner towards the reception desk, she eyed Jesse scanning the prints on the wall with his hands in his back pockets. Walking towards him he turned, on seeing her he smiled, and she smiled back nervously. They had left things badly last night, and neither of them wanted a continuation.

"I didn't mean to interrupt you at work, but I need to speak to you. Is there anywhere we can talk privately?" Hearing him all professional put her instantly on edge, and she showed him through to the locker area at the back.

"Sorry, I'm not sure if we can use anywhere else. You'll have to put up with the stockroom." she laughed lightly, closing the door. She needed to show him she wasn't harbouring any ill feeling.

"It's fine, do you want to sit down?" He asked, seeing the benches in the middle.

Looking at him trying to decipher what was going on, she backed up to the bench and sat down. Jesse followed, taking her hand in his, which only alarmed her more. What had happened? "I handled last night really badly."

"Jesse, if this is personal, we need to leave this till later," said Hayley, realising she did not have time for this kind of conversation at work. "I'm in the middle of making cheesecakes."

"It's not just that. I need to ask you if you had thought of anything over night that might help our investigation?" Hayley continued to stare at him. "It seems it might have been bigger than we thought. I mean we're uncertain it's the same people, but- "

"If you weren't concerned, you wouldn't be telling me," confirmed Hayley. Stopping him from trying to coddle her.

Jesse nodded.

"Should we be worried about Daniel? You said it was a boy's death."

"I've no idea, and I'm probably totally off base, but I'd rather us be over prepared. I didn't want to make the same mistake as last time. I want you to know." When he squeezed her hand, her heart filled, and she inwardly thanked him for thinking about her.

Last time he had kept things from her they had disintegrated. Jesse took her in his arms and squeezed her to him, nuzzling into her neck. "You mean too much to me, I just want you and Daniel to be safe, OK?"

Nodding, she took in his warmth and felt herself relax.

"What are you doing here?"

Jumping back from Jesse; Hayley glanced up at Rob, whose face was thunderous. Rob looked down at their entwined hands and glared at Hayley. Looking away, she gently slipped her hand out from Jesse's, which didn't go unnoticed by either brother.

"He was just leaving," said Hayley, standing up.

"Not what I asked," snapped Rob.

"Hey!" Shouted Jesse, standing.

Rob looked to him and felt instantly chastised. Realising he was coming over as possessive, he tried to shrug off his mood by realigning his shoulders. "They need oil," said Rob, before lifting a tin from the top of the lockers. "I'll see you when you get back up there," he confirmed to Hayley before leaving the locker room.

"He always like that?" Asked Jesse, thumbing towards the door, whilst looking at Hayley.

"I think he's got stuff on his mind," she answered, not wanting to pour fuel onto the fire.

She wasn't sure what was happening with Rob, something felt wrong, but she didn't want to alarm Jesse either. Their relationship was strenuous enough.

"He'll have my fist on it if I catch him talking to you like that again." Smiling at his protectiveness, she laid her hand on his shoulder. The urge to pull herself into him was huge, but she restrained.

"Thank you for being honest with me. I know that must have been difficult," she said earnestly.

"Not as difficult as letting something happen," he answered, watching her blue eyes shine back. "Look, I best get back. Mid case and all that, but I'll pop round tonight, if that's OK?"

"Yeah, of course, Daniel will love it," she said without thinking.

"Do you fancy Chinese; I can pick it up on the way?" He asked, stepping back to the door.

Feeling on edge again, she watched Jesse intently. "That would be lovely, but can we maybe do it tomorrow?" She asked tightly, remembering she had plans later.

Furrowing his brows, she realised he required an explanation. Deciding he deserved one, she took in a deep breath for courage. "The flat I told you about, we're moving in after work today." Watching Jesse's shoulders tense, she got ready for the imminent argument, but something filtered across his face and instead he took her in his arms. Hugging her to his chest. She tensed, expecting a fight, not a cuddle.

"OK, send me your address I'll bring Chinese tonight." Shocked and overwhelmed, she just nodded dumbly as he walked away.

CHAPTER 7

Hayley opened the door on the second knock. "Sorry I was just bathing Dan-." Instantly stopping at the sight of Rob on her doorstep, she looked at him puzzled.

"Thought we could share a bottle of wine," he said shaking the bottle and making his way inside. "Celebrate you moving out."

Unsure how to take that, she watched him walk in, uninvited. "Rob, Jesse's on his way, he's just picking up a Chinese." explained Hayley panicking.

"Oh right, I've not had Chinese in ages. Hope he's bringing enough?"

Open-mouthed, Hayley stared back at him, while his back faced her as he tried to find wine glasses from her cupboard. "Rob, he's not seen Daniel in a couple of days, I think he's hoping to spend some alone time with him."

"OK," shrugged Rob. "I'm sure I can keep you entertained while he visits his son."

Still holding onto the open door, she bit her bottom lip, and rolled her eyes. This was not the evening she was hoping for. Having put on clean jeans and a fairly new blouse, she'd graced her face with a touch of light make up after indulging in a long soak which involved a thorough shave, OK she wasn't expecting it to go that far, but it made her feel better so she'd pampered herself, especially after moving all her belongings into a new home and trying to set it up so it resembled one. It wasn't as if she had much stuff and thankfully the apartment had come fully furnished so while it wasn't to her exact taste, beggars couldn't be choosers. It was clean and well maintained. That was all she required. There would be plenty of time to put her mark on it.

"You trying to let out all the warm air?" Asked Rob, eyeing the door.

"No," she answered swinging it shut before going back to Daniel who sat in his cot playing with his towel still wrapped round him. Taking him out, she patted him dry and then massaged lavender baby oil into his skin. Not only did it help him sleep when he'd already napped, it helped stop his skin drying out too much in the winter.

Grabbing his babygrow, she wrapped him in it and pressed the studs together before holding him up to her face as she blew raspberries on his belly, forcing out chuckles. She loved the sound of him laughing, it always cheered her up.

"He sounds awake," commented Rob, watching her from the doorway.

Suddenly feeling self-conscious, she stopped and stood up, carrying him into the living room. Glancing at the clock, she noticed it was ten to seven.

"Did he nap today?" Asked Rob, following her as she placed Daniel on the floor with his cars.

"Yep, but he should have another hour in him to see his Dad," she answered.

"You might want to start knocking the nap on the head; he looks like he'll be up all night to me."

Hayley bit her tongue and made her way to the kitchen to pick up the glass of wine he'd poured earlier. Why was he trying to imprint himself in her life?

Suddenly, with her back to him, she felt arms slide around her waist and then he dropped a kiss on her shoulder. "I've wanted to do that all day," whispered Rob.

Pulling his arms away, she stepped away from him. Rounding him to go back and sit with Daniel.

"What was that?" asked Rob, holding his hands out.

Hayley sat stroking Daniel's hair as she sat him between her legs on the floor. She didn't want Rob there. She didn't want him thinking he had any right to cuddle up to her, and she didn't want him kissing her. But she wasn't sure how to handle it, so she just kept Daniel close, hoping he'd leave.

"Have I done something wrong?" asked Rob, mystified.

"No, I just… Jesse's on his way," she answered meekly. "And Daniel needs watching."

Rob shook his head as if in disbelief. Walking back to the kitchen she watched him grab the bottle off the side, walking back up to her he shoved it in her face. "I bought this so we could talk, sort things out, I thought that was what you wanted."

Seeing the bottle so dangerously close to her face made her anxious, if there was anything she could spot, it was danger and he was gearing up for a fight. "I'm sorry, it's just that Daniel is crawling everywhere now, I have to watch him like a hawk. Bring the drinks over here," she offered, hoping she was coming across as accommodating and not fearful.

Reading her for a second he decided she was genuine, as she watched him walk to the kitchen to retrieve her glass. Pouring more wine into the already fairly full glass he handed it to her.

"Thanks." she said, taking it and having a sip, before placing it on the coffee table in front of Daniel.

Glancing at the clock, it was now five to seven. Willing Jesse to knock, she took her time playing with Daniel as Rob slumped on the sofa drinking his wine.

Why did she suddenly feel trapped? He was watching her, and she felt like Daniel was becoming her guard dog, praying he wouldn't grow tired too quickly as she played with him.

"It wouldn't surprise me if he didn't turn up," said Rob at seven o'clock.

Hayley wanted to cry, but she just kissed Daniel's head, breathing in his scent.

"Work always comes first."

Grinding her teeth, she looked towards her phone on the top of the microwave, willing it to ring so she could get it without making it into a big thing.

"He doesn't deserve you." He said finally looking from her phone to her, "I don't know if Rachel was working tonight, he might have stopped home if she was off shift."

Hayley felt her stomach tighten. How had she forgotten he was seeing someone? Feeling foolish, she kissed Daniel again before covertly removing a tear from her cheek.

"How long are you going to leave it before you put him to bed?" He asked, agitated.

Hayley felt anger rush through her, if she bit any harder on her lip, she would chew through it. Realising she was letting him get to her she reached for the television control and switched it on. Anything to take her mind of the man on her sofa and dissipate the building tension.

∼

Seven-thirty came round and Daniel was flagging, cradling him in her arms, she gently swayed him. Rob picked up the almost empty bottle and showed her it, in offering. Hayley shook her head, so she didn't have to speak. Her voice would only disturb Daniel.

"Mind if I finish it?" asked Rob.

"No, help yourself," she whispered, realising he really wasn't good with hints.

"Is that invitation transferable?"

Hayley ignored him and looked back to the clock. Daniel was a dead wait, so she eased herself up and carried him to his bedroom. Making sure she tucked him in, and was content, she closed the door enough to darken the room whilst allowing a little light to show so as not to scare him if he woke in the middle of the night.

Feeling alone and vulnerable, she rubbed her arms whilst making her way to the kitchen. She cleared up the odd things she hadn't already washed, mainly from Daniel's meal and snack earlier. Knowing he was still sat on her sofa undoubtedly watching her, she constructed scenarios in her head, in which she could get him to leave amicably.

Hearing her phone ding, she grabbed it, hoping Jesse was just saying he was round the corner. **Sorry I've just left. Are you still on for Chinese? I can be there in an hour.**

Hayley wanted to cry. She needed him here now, not in an hour. Typing back, she wrote, **already ordered, it's on way, please hurry x** Clicking on the internet explorer symbol she found a Chinese and quickly ordered a set meal before clicking pay-on-delivery. Satisfied she'd saved the day she placed her phone back down and carried on drying Daniel's drinking cup.

Hearing her phone again she picked it up to see Jesse had replied **OK, sorry, on way x** Breathing out a sigh of relief she placed her phone back down.

"That Jesse?" Asked Rob from the sofa.

"Yep, he's on his way," she called over her shoulder.

"He'll be awhile yet, if he's getting food," answered Rob walking toward her.

"No. He asked me to order, he's coming straight here," she said without turning, hoping she sounded normal when in reality her nerves were firing on all cylinders.

"Hardly much point now Daniel's asleep."

Hayley wanted to scream. His attitude towards her was putting on her edge and she hated it. Reminding her of being with Demy and how easily he'd fly off the handle, resulting in her being hit or tormented.

"Right, well I'll get off then, it's late," said Rob finally, standing up he made his way to the door. Realising he must be over the limit, she thought about telling him to get a taxi but then that would mean he was in her home for longer, so she let him leave.

Once the door closed, her whole body sagged and the tears fell easily. Dropping to her knees, she hadn't realised how stressed and upset he'd made her. Why was she letting him make her feel so weak? After letting it all out, she wiped her wet face and rushed to the toilet to wash her face. The last thing she wanted was Jesse asking questions about why she was so upset.

∼

THE KNOCK on the door had her running. Opening it, she smiled to see Jesse looking indecisive. "I'm so sorry; I meant to be here earlier," he explained. "Work's been a nightmare."

Hayley stared at him. After the night she'd had, she just wanted him, she needed him, and she would make damn sure she had him, if only for tonight. Grabbing his tie, she pulled him towards her, till her mouth smashed against his. It took all of a second for Jesse to realise what was going on, as he picked her up, and she wrapped her legs around his waist, whilst attached to his lips, kicking the door shut he made his way to the sofa.

"Don't speak," she whispered in his ear as she dropped to the sofa with him on top of her. Looking down at her, he momentarily wondered what had made her so amorous, as she fumbled with his belt and top button.

"Hayley, what's-" but before he could finish, she reached up and forced her lips on his. His body reacted in a way he'd only dreamed of, but this wasn't right and his head was telling him to slam the breaks on.

Pushing her arms back down on the sofa, he looked down on her, cheeks flushed but with eyes that were betraying her actions. She was in pain. Getting off her, he moved away to create some space.

"What the hell's going on?" Asked Jesse, annoyed.

Embarrassment, then disappointment, overshadowed by anger as it swept through her body like a wildfire. Why couldn't a woman just take what she needed? Why did she have to answer a bloody questionnaire first? Swinging her legs down from the sofa, she sat up. "You can just say no," she sulked, holding her head in her hands.

"What… why… what-" Jesse didn't know where to start, or even what to say. She had taken him completely by surprise. Taking in a deep breath before running his hand through his hair, he sat down next to her on the sofa. Him being above her would not work.

"Hayley, you took me by surprise, that's all," he answered after a few more uncomfortable minutes of silence. "I thought we were calling it a day."

"We are. I'm sorry," said Hayley shakily.

Jesse remained sitting next to her. He could see she was shaking, but he did not understand what was going through her head. Part of him wondered why he'd put a stop to it at all but the other part knew something was wrong. Something had happened to her, frightened her, and she'd craved security or love or just a hard fuck, he couldn't tell.

Had she really come to him for comfort and then he'd pushed her away. God he was an idiot. Running his hand back through his hair, he glanced to her. She wore tinted brown eye shadow and shiny pink lipstick. Had she got dressed up for him? Was she trying to make a go of them again? His head felt as though it was about to explode. He'd only been expecting to see Daniel and have some takeaway. Now it seemed he'd walked in on an ambush.

"Where's Daniel?" Croaked Jesse, realising his throat had dried out.

"Bed," answered Hayley; back under some control. "He was tired out."

"How's he finding childcare?" Asked Jesse, feeling on much safer ground.

"Good, he likes it," answered Hayley. "Kerrie says he's fitting in well."

"Good," nodded Jesse.

"I ordered the Chinese," remarked Hayley.

"Forty-five minutes," they both chorused.

Smiling, they looked at each other, both getting the joke that no matter what time or who they phoned it was always a forty-five-minute wait for takeaway. Taking her hand in his, he kissed the top of it, watching him, she wished he'd just take her.

"It's not that I don't want to," he said watching her eyes on him. "It was just…" Jesse wasn't sure how to word it. "You were adamant the other day that there's nothing left between us and then tonight you're…?"

"Can't a girl just want to have an enjoyable time?" Answered Hayley, shrugging his hand away and standing up to move away from him. She was useless at lying, and she didn't need him finding out what had really occurred. She'd made a mistake thinking he wanted her, she'd been foolish and embarrassed herself.

"But this is you, Hayley," answered Jesse, watching her back.

"What the hell's that supposed to mean?!" Asked Hayley, spinning round to face him with her hands on her hips. Watching Jesse swallow made her stomach lurch. "What I'm too damaged to want to feel affection ever again?"

"No, of course not," argued Jesse, standing.

"Do you not think it's hard enough for me to think about being with someone without you making me feel dirty and broken? What the hell is it with men? They think they can just have whatever they want and fuck the consequences. But if a woman decides she needs something suddenly the universe stops. I thought we lived in the twenty-first century, and women could have sex if they wanted without being called a slut, but clearly not. Clearly, it means something's wrong. Something must be wrong for a woman like me to want to have sex, there's no way someone like me can want to feel again." Freely venting made her shoulders sag. Once it occurred to her what she had just divulged to Jesse she felt sick, and the pity in his eyes was unbearable.

"Have I ever made you feel like that?" Asked Jesse calmly.

"Like what?" Asked Hayley, wondering which part of her tirade was bothering him the most.

"Like a slut?"

Hayley swallowed down the bile that threatened mass projection and felt her eyes suddenly burn.

Walking towards her, he took both her hands. "Hayley, have I ever treated you in a way that made you think I just wanted you just for sex?"

As the tears spilled, she shook her head, watching how his feet became blurry.

"Well, that's exactly how you've just made me feel."

Looking up to his eyes, she could see the pain there. She'd hurt him, she'd done everything to him, that she had received in the past. She'd taken what she had learned and used it against the only man who'd ever treated her with respect. He'd never once forced or coerced her, never once taken advantage of her, and yet she'd repaid him by wanting to use him to make herself feel better, just like Demy had her.

Watching the guilt written all over her face ripped his heart out. He didn't want to hurt her, but she needed to understand what she was doing. If she needed him, she needed to tell him, not use him.

"I'm so sorry," she whispered as she gasped in gulps of air, trying to hold back the mammoth sobs that were threatening to fly out of her chest. Bending over, she tried to stop the sharp pains in her stomach, as her legs quivered and her chest constricted.

After a few minutes of her falling apart and Jesse doing his best to comfort and calm her down, they were finally sat cuddled up on the sofa. Hayley leaning into his side while his arm hung over her shoulders with her legs pulled up behind her.

~

JESSE SAT in his office with the door shut. He could hear the milling around in the incident room next door, but he was taking a few minutes to gather his thoughts and plan his next move. He needed to know more about the boys lives to see if anything crossed over. Everything suggested they weren't random killing but nothing held up to connect them. The only visible similarity was they were both boys under the age of eight, which wasn't much to go on, and nothing to protect another innocent from the same fate.

Glancing over at the photo, he ran his fingers down his son's face.

It was beyond his comprehension how could anyone hurt a kid, he'd lay down his life for Daniel.

Looking at Hayley he thought about last night. How wonderful it had been that something had changed between them. She had finally opened up to him in. They had shared a takeaway, and he had finally sat back and listened to her side of her ordeal at the hands of Demy. Although the subject had made his stomach heave and his jaw and fists clench, he revelled at the fact Hayley could speak so easily to him. He'd never been able to listen before. The very idea of that conversation made him want to punch something, but he hadn't acknowledged how much she had needed him to do that. He'd been short-sighted, believing that if he kept her mind off it, it would somehow repair itself. But he had been wrong and only enabled the mould to fester unsupervised. It had looked like last night Hayley had been suffocating.

How had he let her slip through his fingers? Treating her with kid gloves had been the wrong thing to do, he could see that now. All he'd achieved was to reinforce her belief that they damaged her. But last night she had needed him in a way she'd never shown before. She'd needed him to love her and take care of her, letting her walls of steel slip. But something still wasn't right, he'd noticed her red puffy eyes as she'd opened the door. That anguished look before need had taken over, something had happened, but she'd not confided in him as to what. Turning back to the lab results he put Hayley to the back of his mind, he'd talk to her later.

Hearing the knock on the door, he looked up to see Martin hovering.

"Jesse. Lab's just rang up; you will want to see this." Jesse grabbed his jacket and followed Martin to the pathologist's office in the basement.

∼

Hayley woke up to an empty bed and sighed disappointedly. Moving over to his side she could feel it was cold, so she brought his pillow to her nose and sniffed him in. Feeling silly for being so childish she laughed before laying back on her side of the bed and staring at the ceiling. The joyful feeling she'd woken up with soon dissipated when she remembered how Rob was with her last night. She would have to deal with that, but right now she wanted to remember Jesse being in her bed.

Smiling again, she wriggled under the covers as if that would somehow take her back to being in his arms. Unsurprisingly in didn't, so she cocooned herself in the quilt, wrapping everything they'd shared up with her. Hearing Daniel shout, she sighed. Dragging herself from the bed and grabbing her dressing gown from the back of her door, slipping it on as she padded across to his room on bare feet.

"Hey, munchkin, ready for some breakfast?" Bouncing up and down excitedly, she grabbed him, sitting him on her hip as she carried him to the kitchen to flick the kettle on. Looking down at a note, she read. *Didn't want to wake you, love you x. Smiling* to herself, she kissed Daniel's cheek.

Maybe they would get their second chance, after all. "What do you want for breakfast, we've got toast, cereal, porridge or fruit?" Waiting for an answer she knew she wouldn't get, she scrunched up her nose looking at him and decided "toast it is." Taking the bread, she unwrapped it, placing two slices in the toaster then filled his clean bottle from the drainer with milk. Turning round to sit him on the floor in the living room, she froze.

"He stopped then?" Asked Rob nonchalantly, sitting in the armchair facing her, with his right ankle resting on his left knee. Swallowing, she glanced to the door. "Spare key, remember. You left one with Mum."

"What are you doing here?" She asked, holding Daniel close, for comfort or protection, she wasn't sure.

"I saw you had the day off, so I switched shifts. Thought we could spend it together."

Hayley didn't move. The last thing she wanted to do was spend any more time with him.

"But I see you whored yourself out to Jesse while I wasn't here, if that's what pays the bills?" He mocked.

"I think you should go," she said as firmly as she dare.

"Truth hurt?"

Feeling her body tense up, she shook. Not wanting him to notice, she escaped back to Daniel's room.

"I didn't mean that I'm sorry," he called out before she disappeared into the room. "Hayley, I'm sorry, I lashed out."

Hayley could hear him enter Daniel's bedroom and with the space being even more confined than in the living room, she cursed herself for having used it to get out of his way.

"I don't like to think of you being used," he whispered at the back of her neck.

Placing Daniel inside his cot, she spun round and pushed him away from her. "You need to go now," she said again, firmer this time. Seeing her hand shake she looked up to see Rob had noticed it too, so quickly snatching it back she held her hands together.

Stepping forward, he grabbed the back of her neck and pulled her towards him, but the motion triggered a memory and she freaked. The rage built up so quickly, she punched Rob in the nose before even processing it. Covered in blood, she froze with her hands over her mouth and nose. It wasn't Demy she'd just smashed in the nose for forcing her, it was Rob.

"What the fuck!" Shouted Rob, blinking profusely whilst holding his hands over his now bust up nose. "You fucking bitch!"

"Get out!" She shouted, unable to stop the tremors in her body or her voice.

Watching him turn, she stood at the bedroom door waiting until he disappeared out the front door. Once she was sure he'd gone, she grabbed a now crying Daniel and rushed to the front door to lock it, securing the chain.

"Shh shh." She soothed Daniel, bouncing him up and down. "It's OK, everything's going to be OK," she told him, more to convince herself than anyone else.

"This is definite?" Asked Jesse, looking at the printout that Mike had just handed him.

"Yes, they're cousins. After our last talk I ran DNA tests between them, I remembered some parts of your old case and wondered if the children were connected to that somehow. What with the brand, I know the boy with wings didn't have one, but I got a rush on it through an old friend," explained Mike.

"So, this is a family thing?" Asked Jesse, feeling a little more relieved.

"Well, it's a connection," confirmed Mike. "They're maternally related."

"This doesn't confirm the reason behind their deaths was their relationship, though," said Martin.

"No, of course not, but it adds another layer," said Jesse. "The parents have said nothing," he pointed out. "You'd think if the sisters had both had children killed around the same time, they'd both know about it."

"And if they do, why haven't they mentioned it?" Wondered Martin.

"I suggest we find out," said Jesse. "Thanks Mike." Taking the door from Martin's hand. "I appreciate this," he said waving the results up.

"You realise this still doesn't exonerate the sect, don't you?" Asked Martin in the corridor.

"Yes, of course I do, I'm not a bloody moron Mart," snapped Jesse.

"Just checking," sang Martin as he pulled the door open to the car park, while Jesse glared at him.

"Right, let's get on to these parents and find out if there are any more children who could be at risk, and find out who's got it in for this family," said Jesse flicking through the contacts on his phone to call Rosa once he sat in the passenger seat.

PULLING up outside Alex Cartwright's house, they made their way up the garden path. The front garden had seen better days. The metallic paint chipped gate hung on by a coil showcasing a slab pathway, uneven and broken parting the grass that hadn't seen the right side of a lawn mower in some time, while a mass of dandelions stood proudly. A broken fridge stood near the front entrance missing a door, and Jesse suspected some kind of animal sheltered there when required. An old bicycle under the window had a front wheel missing and a nest as a seat.

"As shit hole's go, this is up there," remarked Martin under his breath. "How do you reckon they paid for it? With buttons or stamps?"

Jesse gave him a look to shut up, but couldn't hide the smirk as he tapped on the door. Waiting for the door to open, they turned to look at the street. The houses down this street were very similar, all fairly dilapidated and unwelcoming. The fact the net curtains twitched over the road told them a lot about the area. So how they didn't have more information on Alex was beyond him.

The door creaked open and a youthful woman stood there, with red-rimmed eyes and a tea towel clutched to her ample chest.

"Hi, this is DS Wells and I'm D.I Hallam," said Jesse as they lifted their I.D for her to scan. The lady nodded without looking and let them in. "Can I ask who you are, please?"

"I'm Anna, Judy's sister." Jesse and Martin shared a look before entering the living room, where Judy sat curled up on the sofa, knees pressed to her chest with a cuddly toy held to her nose.

"Hi Mrs Cartwright, I'm D.I Hallam and this is D.S Wells, we're leading the investigation into your son's murder." Nodding, she barely glanced their way. "We need to talk to you about the last time you saw Alex."

"A.J," reprimanded Mrs Cartwright. "His name was A.J."

Both nodding, they took unoffered seats.

"Would it be possible to get a drink, Anna?" Asked Martin, smiling her way as she hung around the door they'd entered, looking despondent. Quickly nodding and pleased to be doing something useful, she shuffled off, closing the door behind her.

"Can you tell us about the time you realised A.J was missing, please?" Asked Jesse, taking out his notebook.

"I've already told your lot all this," she snapped.

"It's just routine. We need to make sure we have everything, and it's quite possible you'll remember something after some time has passed," responded Jesse undeterred.

After a huff, she placed her feet back on the floor and threw the toy she was holding across the room. Martin glanced Jesse's way, but he hadn't taken his eyes off her yet. Shuffling forward on the sunken sofa, she rested her hands between her knees before looking back up to Jesse.

"I put him to bed as usual, read him a story."

"What story?" Asked Jesse.

She looked annoyed at being interrupted but answered. "Three little pigs," she answered as if she didn't even have to remember. "Can I continue now?" She snapped.

Jesse pursed his lips and nodded. It was taking all his strength not to wring her neck, and she was giving him a bad vibe.

"Any way, like I said, I put him to bed, read a book, gave him a kiss, tucked him in and closed the door, I didn't hear a peep out of him all night, then when I went in, in the morning, he was gone, the bed was made, and the window was open, letting all the cold air in, the room was like a bleeding fridge."

"What time did you go in, in the morning?" Asked Martin.

"Be about eight, to get him ready for school."

"So, what did you do when you found his bed empty?" Asked Jesse.

"I got ready for work. I needed to be there for nine, haven't got time for his bloody antics."

"So, you thought he had what?" Asked Martin, not wanting to give her any ideas or lead her answers.

"Gone to his mates, he's always buggering off, I've already told your lot this," she said looking at both of their faces for the judgement she knew she would find there. But they remained neutral.

"You're a teacher?" Asked Jesse.

"Yes, at the local school round the corner." She nodded.

"I assume you've taken safeguarding training?" He asked.

"Yes, of course, but you don't understand, kids round here are little buggers. Mine's no different, certainly never thought he would end up dead."

"Mrs Cartwright, your son's autopsy reports have come back. Toxicology reports state that your son ingested significant amounts of poison over an extended period which we believe led to the failure of his organs and ultimately his death."

Judy took in a few deep breaths before setting her face back to neutral.

"Would you know how he might have ingested anything the week before he went missing?"

Judy looked around the room uncomfortably before looking back to Jesse. "I have no idea."

"Mrs Cartwright, can you confirm the day your son *went* missing?"

"I've already told you, I put him to bed Friday night, and that was the last I saw of him," she said, raising her voice as she stood and walked to look out of the window.

"Thing is, you also said you went to get him ready for school, but unless school's started opening on a Saturday then that's not the case, is it?" Watching her drop her head and slump her shoulders he waited for her to turn around and explain herself.

Just then Anna came back in with two mugs of coffee; she placed them on top of the wooden fireplace and then exited just as quickly. When they were on their own again and Martin and Jesse had shared many looks of 'what the hell was going on' between them. She finally turned round with tears in her eyes.

"Mrs Cartwright, do you have something you need to tell us?" Asked Jesse, seeing the difference in her demeanour. She had dropped the attitude of uncaring to being heartbroken, and he couldn't be sure which one was the guise.

"You won't understand," she snivelled, looking from one detective to the other.

CHAPTER 8

WALKING INTO HIS MUM AND DAD'S KITCHEN, JESSE NOTICED ROB first as he sat at the dining table facing the door. "What happened to you?"

"He won't say," answered his dad dispassionately.

"Cracked it on the door," answered Rob.

Jesse moved towards him, as if inspecting the injury.

"Well, whoever she was, she's got a mean right hook," answered Jesse.

Michael laughed, while Rob scowled at them both before taking a sip of his tea.

"To what do we owe the pleasure?" Asked Marie sarcastically, noticing him whilst coming through with a basket full of laundry from upstairs.

"Sorry Mum, it's been manic at work. But I took time out of my heavy schedule to make sure you still knew how to make a brew, so here I am." He smiled, holding out his arms expectantly.

"Make your own damn brew," she said grumpily.

"What's up with you?" Asked Jesse. His Mum hardly ever snapped at him.

"Christ, don't get her started-" warned Michael, but before he could finish, she started.

"I've not seen that little boy since she moved out," she sulked.

"Christ Mum, she's only been gone a day. I think Hayley's been working today. She said she'd pop in and she will," explained Jesse.

"That's just what I told her," said Michael, flapping his newspaper open.

"I used to see him every day," she continued. "Now I don't get so much as a phone call."

"You'll see him again. It's not as if she's running away with him, is it?" Said Michael, peering at his paper.

The thought sent a shiver down Jesse's back. "I think the naming party took it out of her, and then she started work. Not to mention she's only just moved out, I can't imagine she'd finding it easy at the moment," confided Jesse to his Mum as he watched her fill the washing machine.

"Even more reason to bring him round. She can get on with whatever she needs to do, and I get to have cuddles while he's still young enough to enjoy them."

"Woman, will you hark at yourself, give her a break" snapped Michael.

Jesse couldn't help stifling a laugh at his Dad, who'd had clearly been getting hen pecked. "Why don't you ask Rob to drop her off one night? He's been giving her lifts back from work. He can pick Daniel up and bob's your uncle," clarified Jesse, eyeing the kettle.

"You didn't tell us you'd been dropping her off," admonished Marie, glaring at Rob.

"Err... didn't think about it," answered Rob, touching his nose gently.

"Didn't think about it?" Questioned Michael "She's been banging on about her all afternoon."

"You should go to the hospital?" Interrupted Jesse. "Cus that looks broken."

"I might pop later," he resigned.

"The longer you leave it, the worst it'll get," warned Marie.

Rob glared at his brother whilst Jesse smiled foolishly at him.

"Come on Mum, I've got ten minutes before I have to get back. That kettle's not going to pour itself," said Jesse rushing from her as she went to swipe him with a dirty tea towel.

"You cheeky sod," she laughed.

"She's got scones in the bread bin," pointed out Michael, catching her glare at him.

"Oh, Mum, you holding out on me?" He remarked, sitting himself at the dining table, knowing full well she'd make him a cup of tea and butter him a scone. "Got any cheese?" he asked questioningly, as she delivered his scone. But he wasn't quick enough to miss the slap she delivered across the back of his head. "You best wrap Martin one up too, he's in the car."

"Why you left him in the car?" Asked Marie critically.

"I'm joking. I've just dropped him off at home, going to pick him back up in a minute. Apparently, Claire's in the middle of a crisis."

"What kind of crisis?" Asked Marie, with her hands on her hips.

"Washers bust, it's flooded the floor, and he's on damage control for ten minutes before we go back to the station."

"Well, tell them to bring their stuff round here if they need to, I don't mind," offered Marie, pouring boiled water into a cup.

"I'll tell him," replied Jesse through a mouthful of scone.

"You still planning on taking Hayley and Daniel on Saturday?" Asked Michael.

Jesse nodded whilst chewing the mouthful of scone he'd just bitten off. "I'll send her a text to remind her, just in case," offered Jesse.

"I hope she's booked it off," admitted Marie. "I gave her the invite ages ago, so she could book it."

"Then I'm sure she has," answered Jesse. "You've seen the Rota, she working or not?" He asked, turning to Rob.

"How the bloody hell should I know?" Answered Rob before leaving the table and walking into the living room.

"What's up with him?" Asked Jesse.

"Probably the same thing that's up his nose," answered Michael. "Girl trouble."

"Didn't know he was seeing anyone," Jesse mused, taking another bite.

"Maybe that's what his nose is about," smiled Michael. "Neither did her fella."

They both laughed.

"Behave you two, you know nothing of the sort," chastised Marie.

Jesse and Michael just shared a look, making them both stifle laughs.

∼

Hayley opened the door to Sam, "Hey, I wasn't expecting to see you today," she said surprised.

"No, I just finished work, thought I'd pop in and see how you are."

"I'm good. Why?" Asked Hayley, concerned.

"Dunno," shrugged Sam. "You looked a little off yesterday, just wanted to check on you and see your bambino, of course."

Laughing, Hayley let her in, showing her to Daniel who was bashing his cars into mega block towers.

"So?" asked Sam, taking a seat on the sofa while Hayley made them a cup of tea.

"I'm fine," shrugged Hayley, "maybe a little tired, but other than I'm all good." She smiled before taking a sip of her drink. "How was work?"

"Usual," answered Sam crouching over to re build Daniel's towers.

A couple of hours later Hayley and Sam were delving into chilli con carne. They'd been laughing about things at work, and Sam had spoken about her husband and her wish to have children. Hayley felt kind of guilty having found herself pregnant with Daniel without even trying. It seemed other people didn't have as much luck. She enjoyed talking to her, finding things out about her she hadn't had time to when working in the busy kitchen. It felt nice to take some time out and get to know one another, especially with things with Rob being so difficult. It would be nice to have another ally.

After a while they got to talking about Jesse and Hayley's relationship. Sam had known that Jesse was Rob's brother, but she didn't know he was a detective or anything else as Rob had never spoken about him.

"So how come you split up?" Asked Sam compassionately.

"Crikey, that's not a simple question to answer," answered Hayley relaxing back into the sofa and breathing out a heavy breath as she thought. "He couldn't forget about what happened," she answered finally. Glancing at Sam, she saw only empathy and no judgement, it what was an agreeable feeling. "I felt like spoiled goods." Hayley swiped the tear that ran down her cheek. "Sorry, I shouldn't be telling you this," she apologised, wondering why she'd suddenly opened up to her.

"Don't be silly, sounds like you need to tell someone," she smiled sympathetically.

Hayley couldn't remember much of her mother, as she had died when she was so young. But Sam had a motherly character that Hayley saw in Marie and craved for herself. She had always wanted to open up to Marie, but with her loyalties naturally lying with Jesse, it never felt appropriate.

"It wasn't all his fault. I was a total bitch to him. I was snappy, aggressive, depressed and then every time he'd come near me or I heard something, I'd jump out of my skin. I don't think he knew what to do for the best. So, he gave me space, but then the space became a crater. I think the nightmares scared him the most, sometimes he struggled to wake me up and once I hit him, caused him a black eye."

"Didn't he try to get you help?" She asked.

"He did, but..." Hayley looked away, feeling foolish.

"Wouldn't go?" Hayley shook her head and then looked at her hands. "Are you're still having them?"

"Yeah, every night," admitted Hayley, taking comfort from her third coffee of the day.

"Maybe you *should* speak with someone," warned Sam.

"Except I didn't have one last night," said Hayley cheerfully, unable to stop the smile creeping along her face.

"Well, that's good," admitted Sam "Did you do something different?"

"He came by last night, and we kind of made some head away."

"So, you're back together?"

"I don't know. He's been at work all day. He left me a note with 'love you' written on this morning though," she said, sounding as hopeful as a child on Christmas morning.

"Sounds like an excellent start," remarked Sam, giving her a wink. "Don't let him slip away, because you don't think you're worthy. That's his decision to make, and I'd say he made it a long time ago."

~

"THIS IS GETTING BEYOND A JOKE!" Shouted Jesse.

Martin dropped his head; he had known he would take the news badly, hence why he had closed the door to his office when he delivered the news. Jesse realised his outburst, although warranted, probably wasn't that helpful, so sat back down and tried to compose himself.

"So, just so I have this straight. The guy we found first, this Eric Hardwick, who we've been told was possibly a nonce, who we have no prior record for has his DNA all over Alex, and the family his mum thought was looking after him were also friends with Roberts parents, and decided not to tell us. They allowed him to take him out the night he died, something that might have been fucking useful then!"

"It still doesn't answer who killed him," said Martin.

"Not unless someone saw him murder the boy and then got their own back," said Jesse.

"By forcing him to commit suicide?"

"Why not? Makes it a victimless crime, cause no one will give a shit about nonce's death, will they?" Jesse knew too well there would be a lengthy line of suspects, which made the job of finding the offender that much more difficult, and a lot less likely for a witness to come forward. But without the perpetrator of the man's death, they couldn't confirm whether the same man was responsible for the boy's death, at least not without a confession, and with evidence in short supply he wasn't holding his breath.

"I don't suppose we'll find anything out until the parents tell the complete truth," remarked Martin.

"You mean her shitty excuse didn't convince you?" Asked Jesse. Having vented his frustration, he needed to compose himself again, through gritted teeth he added, "By which point it'll be too fucking late."

He hated cases like this. But coming away from it was worse. He had a duty to the boys to see it through, and if it hadn't been the man in the garage who'd killed them, then that meant he was still out there and someone out there was trying to lay the blame at someone else's door so as not to be discovered. Neither scenario sat comfortably in his stomach.

∽

MARTIN WASN'T sure about tonight. But he'd worked on Jesse all week and he'd finally relented, so retreating now wouldn't be a good idea. Claire had been over the moon to find out they were going out for dinner, so he was scoring brownie points with her too. The case at work was hovering around him like a dark cloud though, and he couldn't fully comprehend why, which was irritating enough.

"You nearly ready?" Called Claire from downstairs. Tightening his belt, he slipped it into the hooks on his trousers. "Martin?.."

"Yep, I'm coming!" He shouted, before checking the room one last time for anything he might need, and closing the door behind him.

"Ah, you're ready. Thought it was us women who were supposed to take forever?" Quipped Claire.

Martin didn't go into the fact that it had indeed taken Claire two hours to get ready, meaning he was on child care duty until her mother graced him with her presence. At which point he'd ran upstairs to find Claire hogging the entire bathroom with cosmetics and hair curlers and more sprays than he'd seen at the Debenhams counter. When he'd finally muscled his way in, she was slipping on her heels and picking out jewellery.

"Be good," warned Martin as his three kids stared up at him expectantly. "There're sweets in the cupboard and a can of pop each, bed by nine."

Kids groaning, he winked at his mother-in-law as if to say he was doing it for her benefit. "Right. See you later; ring us if you need anything."

Jean nodded, she was a good woman, if not a little obnoxious.

Claire kissed the air so as not to get lipstick on their cheeks, and they left after Martin ruffled their hairs to the sound of their disgruntled grumbles.

Walking into the restaurant, Martin saw Jesse and held his arms up to ask where Hayley was.

"She's in the toilet," offered Jesse.

Taking their seats, they all scanned the menu while talking about Martin and Claire's kids rioting about which movie to watch. When Hayley approached, they all smiled and she sat down nodding to Claire who she hadn't met before.

"I can't believe we've not met before, especially after how you guys met," said Claire.

Hayley immediately looked at Martin, who gently shook his head. "I hear Jesse saved you from a madman?"

Unsure what to say, Hayley felt her cheeks colour and warm.

"What Claire means is when Jesse dived in front of the car to stop some idiot, joy rider ploughing into you." laughed Martin, looking warily between Jesse and Hayley.

"Yeah, well, anyone would have done the same," coughed Jesse into his hand before lifting his glass of coke to his lips to hide his smirk at his friend's chick flick version of events.

"Yep, those damn joy riders," said Hayley unconvincingly.

"Am I missing something?" Asked Claire, looking from one to the other.

"I'm not sure who's blushes he's trying to save, but Martin and I met through an abduction. He saved me from being killed. I knew

Jesse around the same time his investigation involving the man who took me started," answered Hayley.

Claire looked again at the other occupants at the table, one by one, then laughed out loud. "Jeez, you nearly had me there!" she chuckled. "Christ, look at your faces! I should nominate you should all for the Oscars."

Hayley, Jesse and Martin all shared a look and then laughed too. Suddenly the air didn't feel so tense, and Hayley didn't feel so alienated. Claire had taken her story as just that, and Hayley didn't have to put up with sympathetic glances.

The evening went smoothly. They laughed and chatted about work, friends and family. Jesse looked far more relaxed than she'd seen him in months, and it was rubbing off on her. Claire was funny, in a no-nonsense kind of way. She even whipped Martin into shape when he told crude jokes. Hayley really liked her. She seemed to have no ulterior motive, and it was comforting. Martin loved her, even though he told jokes at her expense, but they were never cutting and she always took them as they intended, often adding one in about Martin to re-balance the conversation. As the night drew on, Martin and Claire made their excuses about the children's grandma getting tired and being let off guard duty, finally leaving Hayley and Jesse at the bar in the restaurant.

"Claire's really nice," admitted Hayley.

"Yeah, she is, Martin's got a diamond there. Few women could put up with a copper's life."

Hayley took a sip of her cocktail. It was sweet but strong.

"She'd also burn all his clothes if he ever did anything to hurt her," he laughed. "And probably bill him for the matches."

"I get that impression," laughed Hayley. "But they're good together."

"Yeah, they are," smiled Jesse. "So…"

Hayley took another sip, waiting for him to finish whatever question was burning away on his tongue.

"We haven't really spoken since the other night, and whilst I don't want to take two steps back after what feels like a good place, I'm worried."

Hayley nodded, she had been waiting for the inevitable talk, but had been lulled into a false sense of security with how the rest of the evening had progressed.

"You were really upset the other night and acted out of character. I can't help thinking something spurred that on…?"

Hayley watched him watch her and tried to neutralise her face so she gave nothing away. He knew all her tells as she did his.

"I'm not sure…"

"Hayley, don't lie to me, please."

Taking in another deep breath, she scanned the room. The place hadn't been overly busy for the entire time they had been there, but there was a couple close to the window and one near the huge, gold eagle proudly standing in the middle of the room on a plinth.

"I don't want to lie, but what if I told you something, I know you'd blow up about?" Jesse's jaw clenched and he looked to the barman who was filling the glass cabinet behind the bar. "I'll tell you, but not tonight. Leave it be."

"Are you seeing someone?" Asked Jesse, looking back as her eyes widened.

"No," answered Hayley, putting her glass back down on the bar. "Are you?"

Jesse shook his head.

"What about Rachel?"

At the mention of her name, he rubbed the back of his neck before turning to put his legs under the bar and lifting his half empty pint to the barman. "So, Rob's been running his mouth off then?" Asked Jesse, watching her finish her drink. Shrugging, she placed it back on the bar, pushing it toward the barman. "I meant to tell you, Hayley."

"Don't worry about it. We're single. It was always going to happen to one of us," she smiled, though he could see the hurt written all over her face.

"It's not like that. We got together once, that was it," answered Jesse. "It was a mistake."

"It's nothing to do with me," said Hayley, pasting on another fake smile.

"If I was ever serious about anyone, you'd be the first to know," he said, passing a twenty-pound note over to the barman. "Have you heard anything from Darren?"

Hayley shook her head, confused with the sudden jump in topic. "Why do you ask?"

Jesse shrugged, he didn't want her to know anything that might cause her any more pain, but he couldn't completely shrug of the feeling that the boy's deaths had something to do with the sect, and if he could have got in contact with Darren, he might have been able to shed some light on it.

"I've not seen him since before I had Daniel." Jesse nodded. "Have they found Lynnie yet?"

"No. She disappeared soon after telling them I tried to kill her," answered Jesse sharply.

"I'm sure they coerced her into doing that. I can't think of a single reason she'd have done it otherwise," admitted Hayley. "She was just a kid when I got out, there's no telling what they threatened her with."

Jesse just nodded, he'd heard her tale of events before, but it just didn't sit right in his stomach. There had to have been ample opportunities to get a message to a nurse or police officer to tell the truth, but she'd fled. He just couldn't work out why.

"You never speak about your Dad," stated Jesse.

"Not much to say, especially now he's dead," shrugged Hayley.

"Presumed dead, we never found a body," he warned.

"But they said the amount of blood they found was fatal?"

"Yeah, I know, but I wouldn't put anything past that lot."

"Do you think he's still alive?"

"Honestly, I haven't got a clue." Jesse shook his head before finishing his last beer.

Now was not the time to tell her he wasn't her father, but the knowledge stuck out in his mind like a thorn. "What was he like?"

"He was a drunk. He had a harsh temper when he had had too many and lost all his money at gambling. What do you want to know?" Asked Hayley, wondering where he was going with the questions.

"What was he like before your mum died?"

"He was normal, I suppose. He still drank, and he still had a temper, but I can't remember him ever losing it like the night I saw him kill her. It didn't seem real before that, we'd just been normal, I suppose. He was never hugely affectionate, but I didn't feel like I was missing out or anything."

"What was the argument about?"

"I don't know. I only caught sounds and noises. I couldn't hear what they were arguing about, and I can't really remember much about it other than me hiding my brother and sister under the quilt to cover their ears." Watching him process what she was saying, she took a sip of her new cocktail. "Why are you asking?"

"No reason really, just talking," he answered with a tight smile.

CHAPTER 9

Hayley watched as Rob's car crossed over the junction and came towards her at the bus stop. The rain was thrashing down, and she was sodden and shivery. The car exhaust fumes and the dampness of the fields rose in the air, giving off a scent of damp soil and burning.

"Get in!" Shouted Rob from the driver's side.

Hayley looked around to see if she recognised any of the cars.

"Hurry up, it's pissing it down and I'll be holding traffic up in a minute," he shouted, looking through his rear-view mirror.

Hayley jumped in and slid the belt across, clipping it in as Rob pulled away.

"What's with the hesitation?"

"I don't think you picking me up is a very good idea," she said, looking around.

"Why? Because you broke my nose?" Asked Rob.

Hayley chose not to answer. She'd spent all day with him and he'd barely spoken to her. Everyone had asked about his nose and he kept to the same story; he'd been walking without paying attention and walked into a door. It was about as cliché as he could get, but she didn't need to offer the real explanation, it would only cause more questions.

"I wanted to apologise," said Rob quietly.

"What for *me* breaking *your* nose?" Asked Hayley, facetiously.

"No smart arse, for letting myself into your house and acting like a twat."

"Oh, that."

"I'm trying to apologise," he said, watching her soften.

"Yeah, well, you did, congratulations," she really wasn't in the mood for his whiplash inducing character changes.

The conversation with Jesse last night had left her reeling, after going to bed with more questions than answers she'd barely slept and so her patience was between thin and none existent.

After a few minutes of silence, Rob looked to her a few times before clearing his throat. "Mum wants to see Daniel."

"She saw him last night when she baby-sat for me," answered Hayley, cringing with the information she'd just voluntarily given him.

"Oh. Where did you go?" Asked Rob, shocked.

"Out." She had no intention of letting him on her life that he was attempting to encroach on.

~

"OK," said Jesse, standing in front of the whiteboard. "We now have a connection between these boys, they're both under the age of eight, they both belong to the same family, and they were living with family or illegally adopted. That said, we've reason to believe they also have connections with the Sect investigated last year. We now need to dreg up all the information on file so we can start cross referencing and marking things off. It's more than possible we'll find an answer in there, but in the meantime, we need to understand why the children were targeted? These kids didn't go to church or have any connection with any groups that could tie them together. They went to separate education facilities and didn't know each other, although there seems to be one family who knew both. The Rochester's; Karl and Emily, have two children called Evie and Ben, but so far, they look undesirable for this. The children, although dumped around the same time, weren't abducted at the same time.

"So why the exploration date? Only one had wings tied to his back with wire, why? Why was he treated differently? These are all questions we need answers to. Robert's parents seem to be a lot more cut up, and from what I've been able to determine, they took the child in for his sister. It seems they were looking out for the child's interests at least, so we might find more answers from them. Especially if they get in contact with the sister. The first victim's parents are waiting in an interview room, so we'll see what those two clowns cough up. In the meantime, work with what we have. We now have equivocal connections, let's see where they lead us."

"Sir, with this sect having something to do with your girlfriend, will someone else be coming in to head up the case?" Asked Adam, with the room suddenly going quiet, he looked around to see all eyes on him and visibly shrank into his chair.

"I think as long as our case has no bearing on the one going though court, we can continue as usual," explained Jesse.

"But that will be unlikely, won't it? With the brand coming up again. I mean, it could show that Demy Richards is innocent." Adam wasn't letting this go.

Martin made a throat noise, suggesting Adam should give up with the shovel before they battered him with it.

"The one thing Demy Richards isn't, is innocent," answered Jesse firmly, and with a heavy hint of annoyance.

"Sorry sir, I didn't mean it like that. I just mean from an evidence perspective."

"Let me worry about the case, you just do your job, OK?"

Turning to the team, he looked them all over and resigned himself to making a speech. "Look, Adam has made a valid point. I stepped down from the case last time when it became obvious, they were involving Hayley. I did so for the good of the case and because I respect you all too much to have made any mistakes with its handling.

You're a solid team, so when I say do your job, I mean it with the utmost respect. I know you are all more than capable of securing an arrest, but if this turns out to be a splinter group from the Vine Cross sect, then we need to make sure we destroy it this time. These men use religion to abuse and murder vulnerable people. They're dangerous and ruthless, so I'll be making sure that I and this team does everything in its power to convict these sick bastards. And should that mean I have to step down or get people to check through my evaluations, then so be it. Because this case is too important to fuck up. I'll do you the courtesy of keeping you in the loop as long as you do me the courtesy of leaving no stone unturned." Turning from his team to exit the boardroom, he heard the murmurs of chatter as they all continued to work.

"Churchill would have been proud," said Martin, quietly stepping up behind him.

"Do you mean the dog or the PM?" Asked Jesse in jest.

"Oh Yes," Martin answered, mimicking the dog from the insurance advert. Jesse shook his head smirking. Martin always lightened his mood. "Oh, no no no no no."

∼

Later, Martin hunched over a screen, clicking and taking notes.

"Anything I need to know?" Asked Jesse, slapping Martin on the back as he studiously watched CCTV on the screen in front of him.

Martin paused it before turning to him, shaking his head. "No, you off?" He nodded towards the briefcase in Jesse's hand.

"Yep, taking some paperwork home, but I'm popping round to Hayley's first."

"Wow, you look rather smug to say you're visiting your ex," said Martin, prying as he flashed Jesse a look.

Jesse let out a slight laugh as the smile took over his face.

"Wow, does that smile mean what I think it does?" Martin watched Jesse turn sheepish, and for anything else he would have ribbed him for it, but he was too bloody pleased to threaten a gibe.

"I don't know what it means right now," shrugged Jesse. "We're taking three steps forward and one back at the moment."

"Well, I couldn't be happier for you, or Hayley."

"Thanks."

"Just as long as you don't forget, it was my bright idea to have a meal out."

After squeezing Martin's shoulder, he exited the building, eager to get away in his car. Although things hadn't ended on a high, they'd both had time to think on what they'd discussed and he was hoping she was up to a visit tonight to straighten things out and move forward.

∼

Hayley opened the door to Jesse, bearing a bottle of wine and a takeaway. Holding them out, he looked at her expectantly with a wry grin.

"I'm only letting you in because I'm hungry, hope you know that," she laughed.

"If it gets me over the threshold, I'll take it," said Jesse, handing her the wine. Jesse walked into the kitchen, taking out plates before opening up the foil containers.

"Oh, my God, that smells so good," Hayley sniffed the garlic and onion aroma wafting from them. "I could eat a rabid dog right now."

Jesse laughed, pouring a little curry and rice onto eat dish before tossing Bhaji's and Samosas on top. Hayley sounded in good spirits. He hadn't been sure what kind of welcome he'd receive, and she was a woman after his own heart, food. Sitting on the sofa, Jesse passed her cutlery before opening the wine and pouring into the glasses she'd placed on the coffee table. Handing her a filled glass first, he poured his own. Clinking his glass to hers, they said cheers, before both taking a drink.

"So how was work?" Asked Hayley, taking a bite of her Samosa, feeling the need to make amends. She could see how tired he looked.

"Good, well not good. But the usual, you know," he answered. "What about you?" He asked, looking at her. Those deep blue eyes shot something down his spine, and he shivered.

"Yeah, it's the same as it was before I left. It's been nice just fitting back in," she answered. Jesse nodded and then looked as though something had crossed his mind. "How's Rob with you?"

"He's good," she gulped, taking another sip of wine. "Just regular Rob, you know."

Jesse nodded.

"Doesn't change." She hoped he wasn't picking up on any change in her voice.

"As long as he's dropped the attitude?"

Hayley nodded, it hadn't been the only thing he had dropped.

"I was thinking we need to come up with some sort of plan, regarding Daniel. I know I pop by and take him out, but I think I need to have him over night sometimes too."

Hayley nodded, she was struggling to hear once again their son was the only reason for his extended visit.

"Only trouble is I can get called out late at night and with no one else there, I won't be able to get where I need to quick enough."

Hayley nodded again, knowing his job took him out at silly hours sometimes. "So, what you thinking?" asked Hayley, taking a sip of wine, dislodging the ball of anxiety in her throat.

"Maybe you could stay with him." Jesse saw Hayley's expression change. He had shocked her. "You take the bed the nights he stops, and I'll take the settee," offered Jesse, glancing to her to read her expression.

For one split second she had allowed herself to think the unthinkable. How could she be so stupid? Once again, she swallowed the ball of emotions in her throat. Did he not realise how difficult she would find that, having him under the same roof and knowing he didn't want her beside him.

The night he had stopped at hers seemed to have slipped from his mind. Although they hadn't been intimate, he had held her all night, and his warmth next to her had soothed her. But she'd hoped it was the start of something. It seemed it was just another day, as though he had just been doing her a favour as a friend. She had needed the support, and he'd given her his. But now he was drawing those lines in the sand again.

"What's the point?" Hayley watched his face blanch. "Sorry, I didn't mean it like that. That came out wrong. Just, if we're together, he's not really getting to understand Mummy and Daddy's place, is he? Just that we seem to live in two houses. Why don't you just do it when you know you're not on duty the next day? I know that can change but I don't mind what nights you have him, it's not like he has school or anything is it?"

Jesse took a breath to process what she had said. He had hoped she would jump at the chance to spend some time with him, give them a chance at reconciliation further down the line, but it seemed she wanted nothing of the sort. She'd had a weak moment, and he'd been there. That was that.

Hayley hoped she had papered over the cracks enough to fool him, but there was no way she could stay a whole night in the same house as him and not do something stupid. Hayley could barely think straight with him on her own now. She'd always been attracted to him, ever since she'd walked through Rob's front door at that fateful party. She couldn't see that ever changing. But she had learnt her emotions weren't reliable, and whenever she had let her heart rule her head, it had deceived her. She had to be stronger, especially since she'd already thrown herself at him once and humiliated herself.

"Thought maybe you'd want to," he added, chasing a piece of chicken round his plate.

Hayley wasn't sure what she should read in his expression, but she had to remain strong. She wouldn't make the same mistake twice. "Why?" Asked Hayley. "Jesse, things are good as they are at the minute. We try to play happy families for a couple of days a week and it will get-"

"I'm just saying I think we should try to re-build before we completely demolish."

Hayley sighed and put the glass on the table. She didn't need this.

He was sending mixed messages again, and she was getting a headache. It was like a continuous game of ping pong with him. Did he not realise the more rope he gave her, the more tied up she became. Was he actually trying to hang her? She wanted nothing more than to run into his arm, but she couldn't do that, because all he did was walk backwards and put more space between them. It was humiliating being the one in need. Knowing you would just end up alone again. She wasn't sure; she had much left to give, anyway.

"Jesse, we're not together. We never will be, we just don't work…" Hayley took a long deep breath, to calm her own words. She could feel the threat of tears behind her eyes, and she would need to pick her words carefully or risk falling apart. "What happened destroyed us, and we sat back and watched it happen. It was horrible, neither of us were happy." She didn't want to be saying it, but she was as much to blame as him. They were like magnets, sometimes pulling each other in and other times forcing each other out, and it was confusing and damaging.

"So, I was right, the other night it was just an itch," said Jesse solemnly.

Hayley took a bite of her own chicken; if her mouth was full, she was less likely to start an argument by biting his head off. "I think with the stress we're both under, we just reacted badly." She answered Jesse as if sensing her prickliness.

He had been listening to his counsellor, and what he had said made sense. Jesse had been through a trauma, and he had decided that the only way he could protect the one person he loved was to stay away from her. He had believed for a long time that he was responsible for everything that she had been through, because he hadn't been able to put a stop to it or find her. He had left her vulnerable with a child because he had allowed his urges to take over what he knew was the right thing to do, and he was more than aware that his stupidity could have had dire consequences for her and his son. But when he had finally got her back, she was different. Broken. Her pain only emphasised his involvement or lack of. He had taken all her pain on and felt responsible. Guilt had eaten away at him and infected their relationship, and like a plant without the proper care and attention, it had wilted and died. His hopes that he could suddenly bring it back to life were dwindling, but his heart was beating strongly, telling him not to give up.

"I'm still the stupid girl who got abducted, the girl who thought she could live under surveillance and all would be OK. I'm still the girl that can't look Martin in the eyes properly because of what he's seen, and probably half of your colleagues. I'm a disaster. The broken victim who had to take all the pitiful looks every day, feeling violated like they knew something they'd rather not, and knowing they probably bloody well did. I had to watch you shrink under that pressure and know that you couldn't display your girlfriend on your arm. Where they'd slap you on the back or smile as though you'd won a prize. I was a prize no one wanted, and you soon realised you didn't. But instead of giving up, you tried to carry on as though everything was OK, when we knew it wasn't."

Jesse felt like a sledgehammer had just entered his diaphragm. He felt guilty as hell. What she said made sense, it was how she felt; it was how she saw it. Her perspective.

Hayley cursed herself for losing her temper once again. But the look on his face told her everything she feared she already knew, and that was the truth. He was ashamed of her, and she'd just called him out on it.

They sat with what she said ringing in their ears. Suddenly the radio filled the room in the absence of any other noise and 'Perfect' came on by Ed Sheeran. They both sat listening, the words perfectly fitting their mood. After the first few lines, Jesse held out his hand, and she looked at it. He looked at her to take it, so she did wearily and he pulled her up. She laid her head on his chest whilst he wrapped his arms around her. They swayed, listening to the lyrics. It seemed to say everything neither of them could, and maybe for the first time in a long time how they both felt. They wanted to be with each other, they just didn't know how.

"Do you remember that time at Mum and Dad's?" Asked Jesse

softly once the song had finished. Fingering her hair away from her face.

"The BBQ," answered Hayley still resting her head on his chest. She could smell his aftershave, and it always had made her feel safe.

Jesse smiled at the memory.

"Do you remember the song?" she asked, hopefully.

"It was a John Legend song, wasn't it?"

She nodded, smiling happily for him, remembering it too. She had felt so safe, like she did now. Closing her eyes, she wanted the feeling to last as long as possible. She didn't want to let go. He was her home, her sanctuary, her safe space.

"That was the night I spilled the beans about us," added Jesse.

Hayley laughed, she had been so embarrassed. Then, as most other memories from their past together did, it tinged with sadness. They had been ripped apart soon after. Realising they'd never get the chance to explore their relationship. They lived within a nightmare, and things had never been the same after that. Tears sprang from her eyes and she held her lids tightly closed, undaring to let go.

"I love you," he said finally.

"I know you do." She stifled a sob. "It's just not enough," said Hayley, allowing the tears to fall silently and dampen his shirt.

A few minutes passed by until the music changed and Jesse pulled her jaw up to meet his gaze. "I love you, Hayley. I always have, and I always will. My heart has belonged to you for so long and yet you won't let me in yours."

"I'm scared. I'm so scared."

"I know. I am too. But I'm more scared about losing you forever."

As a tear slid from Hayley's eye, Jesse wiped it away with his thumb while holding her gaze. "Don't throw us away because of fear."

As Hayley nodded, Jesse lowered his lips to meet hers.

As tears streamed down her face, she let Jesse in, into her mouth, into her heart and into her soul. Realising she was crying with relief, fear, excitement and emotion, a memory struck her of Demy telling her off for crying while he raped her. Saying she was spoiling the mood and Hayley pulled away quickly. No matter how hard she tried, he was in her head. Taking her away from what she so desperately wanted. To feel normal and loved and whole.

"What's wrong?"

Hayley shook her head. How could she possibly tell him she'd been thinking of another man?

"No, stop doing this. Let me in, tell me."

"I can't."

"Why?" When she didn't answer him, he lowered himself so that he could see her eyes. "Talk to me, trust me."

"I do."

"Then tell me. I won't be cross. Just speak to me," pleaded Jesse, watching confliction play out on her face.

"He's in my head. Everything takes me back. Sounds, smells, me crying."

"What about you crying?"

"He said I made him feel worthless because I cried when we had sex," whispered Hayley, still not quite meeting his gaze.

"Hayley, you cried because he raped you." Hayley had never found those words easy to hear and broke down.

Grabbing a hold of her, Jesse pulled her in and wrapped his arms around her, holding her head to his heart. "I never want to make you cry. I hope I never do, but if I ever do, you need to tell me and we'll deal with it, OK?"

Hayley nodded while secure in his arms.

"I don't expect you to not have moments that take you back, I don't expect you to forget. I just want you to know, you don't have to worry anymore. I've got you. You're safe, you're alive, and I love you."

"I don't like needing you," whispered Hayley.

Holding her head in his hands, he lifted it toward him, so he could see her beautiful eyes. The eyes that speared his heart each time they were upon him. "I need you just as much."

Hayley's broken heart pumped full of blood and she couldn't help the tears that formed in her eyes as she stared up at him.

As Jesse lowered his head, Hayley closed her eyes. The moment their lips touched, Hayley's body flushed with need. She couldn't decide if she wanted to cry, scream or crush him in her grasp.

Kissing each other like they had never kissed each other before, passionately and without restraint, Jesse lifted her up until she curled her legs around his hips. Letting go of his lips for just a second to take in the oxygen she desperately needed, she opened her eyes and saw how dark his eyes were. The knowledge that he still wanted her, still wanted to be consumed by her, gave her all the confidence she needed. All she had ever wanted to witness on his face was the pure unadulterated lust she'd seen that first time they'd made love. It had been missing, replaced with regret and pain, but now all she saw was need, love and lust.

"Jesse, make love to me."

No sooner were the words out that Jesse's lips came back crashing down on hers. Finding their way blindly to her bedroom, they barrelled in and landed on the bed. Squashed between the bed and Jesse, Hayley couldn't remember a more secure place.

Without letting go of her, he rapidly stripped her as she fought with his clothes, wrestling them from his body as she tried to control her urges long enough to succeed in undressing him.

Once naked, Jesse shuffled her up the bed and parted her thighs, that quivered just from him being so near. Resting between her thighs and gently tracing her hairline, she watched Jesse look at her in awe. "You're beautiful."

Hayley's heart bloomed with the sentiment. After everything that had happened, she rarely felt anything more than damaged. To see him look at her as though she was something special, something to be handled with care, made every nerve inside her tingle as she waited for them to come together and mend each other's broken hearts.

"Jesse, show me. Show me what you need," whispered Hayley.

When Jesse's eyes trailed back up from her body to her eyes, he lowered himself and took one of her breasts in his hands, eliciting a moan as their tongues collided. Hayley's skin felt like it was on fire and her sex pulsed, eager to be filled by the man she craved more than life itself.

"Oh, God, Jesse, please," whimpered Hayley as she trailed her fingertips down his back, trying not to dig them in, just to provide some much-needed friction, connection and relief. Panting heavily while he tormented her body until she was bound up like a coil, he finally rammed home. Gasping at the intrusion and the relief all in one, tears slid down her cheek and Jesse stilled instantly.

"Hayley, Hayley, are you Ok? I can stop."

Hayley panicked, instantly securing him in place between her thighs, so he couldn't move. "Don't stop, please."

"Why are you crying?"

"Because I love you and I need this, I need us so much. It feels like coming home."

As she felt Jesse relax, she too relaxed and allowed her thighs to drop, no longer holding him like a vice. When she heard him chuckle, she ran her hands through his hair.

"You scared me then, because I'm not sure my dick would have ever spoken to me again, had I had to pull out."

As Hayley giggled, she felt him grow harder inside her and the sudden shock brought her back to business. "He talks to you, does he?" She asked coyly.

"Only when you're around. He's been like a deaf, dumb and blind kid since you left."

Hayley smiled at his stupid song reference and pulled his lips down to hers. "We best let him find his sense then," she winked, wrapping her legs around his back, pushing him further inside her.

As Jesse gasped, she giggled and Jesse allowed his urges to take over, knowing she was fully on board with this new development in this relationship. Pounding home, she clung on to him until all her energy had dissipated and they were exhausted and sweaty. Hayley couldn't remember ever coming so hard, but then hers and Jesse's sexual relationship was still incredibly new. Having only been together before her abduction, this was the only other time they'd given in to their primal urges. But the way they moved and gave each other what they needed was as though they were seasoned pros.

Everything felt right with him inside her, lifting her higher with each stroke.

Rolling off her, he laid down on his back and tried to take in some oxygen. Hayley curled herself around him and laid her head on his chest. Noticing a tattoo for the first time, she ran her fingers over it and smiled. Jesse took her fingers and kissed them, before she felt him suddenly relax and fall asleep beneath him. Wanting to ask him about the tattoo, she contemplated waking him, but he looked so peaceful asleep, so he left him and kissed his closed lips instead, before lying beside him and closing her eyes.

∼

IN THE MORNING Hayley opened her eyes. It was still dark, but she looked across and saw Jesse. Smiling, she shuffled across the bed to wrap her arms around his waist. They were back where they belonged, together. Closing her eyes, she could still feel him touch her bare skin, memories of him brushing his lips along her body, while he made love to her, made her skin flush. They had never connected like that, and it had been amazing.

"I like this," whispered Jesse in her hair, whilst wrapping his arms around her as she lay her head on his bare chest. Still smiling, she nodded before kissing his chest. "But I need to get to work," said Jesse immediately regretting his words when he felt her slump against him. "But I really don't want to leave this bed," he added, which seemed to abate her disappointment as she lifted her head to look him in the eyes. "Christ, don't look at me like that, or I'll definitely not be getting to work on time."

Broadening her smile, he grabbed her hips, lifting her further up his body, until she could feel how much he wanted her. Widening her eyes, she kissed his stubbled jaw. Laughing at what she was doing, he flipped her, so she was underneath and then crawled down her body, kissing every inch of her skin. Hearing her gasp, he smiled against her skin before hovering over her, looking down into her eyes. "Tell me what you want." Looking at him confused, he lowered himself enough to touch his lips to hers. "I want you to know that I'll do anything you want."

"I already know that," she whispered. "Just make me feel good," she smiled, watching him smile back at her.

"That I can do," he said, running a hand over her breast and taking her nipple in his mouth as he watched her eyes close and back arch.

CHAPTER 10

"Good night?" asked Martin with an eyebrow raised after entering Jesse's office, seeing him stare at the photo on his desk with a grin wider than Orion's belt.

"Could say that," smiled Jesse.

"Sounds ominous," Martin sighed, falling into the chair.

Jesse placed the photo back.

"We've just had the tox reports back, it's an interesting read." Martin threw it on the desk in front of Jesse. "The bloke was as high as a fucking kite!"

Jesse picked up the folder.

"I doubt he'd have even known he had a noose around his neck, and they injected it. He didn't do it himself." Jesse looked to him to confirm. "They plunged it into the back of his neck above his hairline; don't know many drug users who do it like that."

"Fuck! So, it's murder?"

"Thought you'd be happy," Martin rose from the chair and opened the office door. Before leaving, he turned to see Jesse rubbing his chin, no doubt thinking about the man's case and how he'd handle it now. "You might want to cover up those scratches on your neck before the DCI knows more about your love life than you'd want."

Jesse grimaced, smoothing his fingers down his neck to feel for scratches. When he felt only smooth skin, he heard Martin laughing down the corridor. "Arse hole," mumbled Jesse under his breath, before laughing.

Back at work, Hayley watched Rob move around the kitchen. The anxiety of speaking to him about what had happened between her and Jesse was eating away at her.

"What's up with you today?" Asked Ash, walking past her as she frantically tried to prepare moulds.

Hayley looked up, seeing that Rob had heard the question, and he was awaiting an explanation too. Shrugging, she just made the excuse that she'd been up all night, instantly regretting it and immediately interjecting because Daniel hadn't slept well. But the mistake wasn't lost on Rob. She could kick herself, she hadn't even meant it like that, and it was just the only thing that sprang to mind. In reality, she was a nervous wreck around Rob. She couldn't work out what angle he was coming from, and she felt like she was walking on eggshells.

"Up all night?" Asked Rob, entering the locker room at lunchtime.

Hayley turned to see he was behind her as she slipped out of her whites. "I didn't mean it like that, I just couldn't think of what to say," she answered, rolling her eyes as though he hadn't been the one, she was trying to deceive.

"So, what's the actual reason?" Hayley looked away. "Did he stop?"

This time when Hayley didn't answer, he grabbed her arm, and she pulled it back in pain.

"Did he stay?" There was fire behind his eyes and it alarmed her. He'd never spoken to her like that before.

"Rob, you're hurting me." She wasn't sure, he realised. But his hand tightening around her wrist felt as though it was cutting off the blood supply to her entire hand.

"And you're not answering me."

Looking him in the eyes, she tried to finally work out what he wanted from her, but he acknowledged her non response as a sign of guilt.

"So, what, you're back together?" He raged, flinging her wrist away from him.

Taking her wrist in the other hand, she rubbed away the pain. "He wants to try," admitted Hayley timidly, looking down to the floor, suddenly feeling tiny and unsure.

"And you just opened up your legs?" Snapped Rob.

"Fuck off," Hayley barked, turning back to her locker.

Before she knew it, Rob pushed her into the locker door. Her forehead hit the lock and sent a pain straight through her skull. "Get off," she said through clenched teeth, as he used his body weight to pin her to the locker. The realisation that he was much stronger than her was unsettling but familiar. With her face plastered against the cold metal, she tried to push herself back from it with her hands, but her body was in line with the locker and she couldn't put any weight behind herself. She hated being weaker, and she could feel herself panic.

"So, I'm gathering, I'm dumped for a golden boy?" He seethed, sending spittle flying to her face.

"Rob, please get off, you're hurting me," she pleaded. "Get off!"

"You said you'd never get back with Jesse." His face was as close to hers as he could get without touching, and she could almost feel the rage coming from him.

"I wasn't going to," she said weakly. "We talked."

"Well, maybe Jess needs to know what a prick tease his girlfriend has been, by putting out to his brother behind his back."

Hayley's face must have shown the hurt she felt, as his own expression changed a little. Or maybe it was shock about what he had just said. But he stepped back from her and she removed herself from the locker so she could stand up straight.

"I have not," said Hayley quietly, but she felt guilty even as the words left her mouth. She'd allowed him into her home, and she'd kept his advances secret. Guilt wasn't an unfamiliar experience for her, but it didn't make it feel any easier.

"So, you've told him about our kiss?" He asked, rubbing his chin, watching her chest rise and drop.

Hayley shook her head.

"What about Rachel?" He asked. "You're damaged goods to him, you know," said Rob, reading her face. "He won't ever want you on his arm."

Hayley suddenly wanted to cry, but she'd be damned if she would give Rob the satisfaction of seeing it.

"He's using you, can't you see that?" He stepped closer to her as he pushed his thumb into her neck. Stiffening, she felt him trace his thumb across her jaw line before letting go. "I'm sorry, I overreacted, I shouldn't have shouted at you."

He sounded genuine, like he was remorseful for losing his temper, but that she had never seen that side of him before and it scared her know she knew what he was capable of. "I just worry you don't see Jess for what he really is."

"What's that?" Asked Hayley, unable to stop the break in her voice from coming out, or the tears in her eyes from falling.

"He resents you Hales, you cost him his promotion and now they watch him like a hawk. He'll get no further up the ladder unless he takes out the whole of Gemini."

"What's Gemini?" Asked Hayley firmly, not wanting to think about the promotion she may have foiled.

"Never mind about that. Why do you think he's heading the investigation that he is? He's trying to prove himself. Trying to earn your trust back just so he can use you again. There's only one reason he wants you in his bed, and that's because you hold the secret to his investigation," seethed Rob. "I don't want to see you get used."

"I don't know anything," she answered shakily.

"Come on, you know more than you think." Stepping away, she watched him slam the door behind him as he left.

Realising she was shaking all over, she grabbed for the bench, falling down on to it. With her mind spinning, the tears flowed freely. Was that why Jesse had told her about the case? Was he pumping her for information? Did he think she knew more than she did? Did he blame her? Was this all about taking revenge?

Hayley exited the car, turning her face from the wind, but her hair still thrashed her face. Jesse watched her attempts to tame her hair, but the wind wasn't letting up, and she was struggling to stop from choking on the ends as they caught in her mouth. He couldn't help but smirk at her struggle.

Hayley knew he was watching her, she could feel him, and her temper increased.

He could put her out of her misery by turning away, but there was something enjoyable about watching her get pissed off with the elements with him observing.

"You just going to watch me struggle or do something useful?" She snapped.

"Wasn't sure you'd want me to hold your hair for you?"

Hayley gave him a look of 'really? That's where you're going with it?' She had barely spoken in the car, but he was aware she didn't really enjoy social gatherings, so he had let her travel quietly, but her temper was betraying her. It was more than just anxiety. She was furious at what he didn't know, and it wasn't the right time to find out. They hadn't seen each other for a couple of days because of work, but he wasn't sure if she had taken his absence as personal, and maybe he hadn't considered it from her point of view. They had slept together and today was the only other time they had seen each other. Maybe he should have attempted to get round, even if it was just to reassure her. Maybe she was viewing his absence from another perspective.

"I'll get the bags and Daniel then?" She asked sarcastically.

Jesse rolled his eyes, slamming the driver's door shut. Yep, he'd pissed her off.

Hayley watched him walk round the back of the car and lift the boot. Swallowing hard, she opened the back passenger door to retrieve Daniel, who was fast asleep in the car seat. They made their way to the hotel entrance to discover they were being watched by Jesse's Mum and Dad as Jesse opened the door to allow Hayley access.

She smiled courteously whilst walking towards them and Jesse watched her produce a fake smile.

"How are you?" Asked Marie, holding her arms out to embrace Hayley with a sleepy Daniel snuggled in her arms.

"Good, thanks," replied Hayley, smiling towards Michael as he looked on, watching their embrace.

"How was the drive?" Michael asked Jesse.

Hayley and Jesse shared a look, and then Jesse nodded.

"There's been an issue with the rooms we booked," started Marie looking suddenly apologetic and less confident.

Jesse glanced to Michael, but he just shook his head. He was too aware of how this would go down, and he didn't want any part of it. They all looked at Marie waiting and she gulped before wringing her hands in front of her and watching her fingers lace together.

"Seems they adjusted the rooms we'd booked, and they have given you a family room." Hayley nodded, still unsure why this would be an issue. "Apparently they needed to, so they could fit a travel cot in for Daniel and thought it would be best."

"OK." replied Hayley, looking back to Jesse for some kind of understanding why this was such an enormous deal.

"Yeah. But in doing so, they deleted the booking for Jesse's single. So, you two will be sharing." Hayley's eyes went wide and Jesse didn't like what they were reflecting. It was only a couple of days ago they'd shared a bed of their own accord. "We've asked, but there are no more room's available," she continued. "I'm so sorry."

"Don't be, it's fine," answered Jesse, watching Hayley look away. "Isn't it?"

Hayley glanced up at him before nodding timidly.

Jesse studied her, wondering what was going on in her head. Whatever it was, he was going to make sure he found out.

"OK, well you're both in room one-zero-two," said Marie, handing Jesse the key card.

Looking at the directions on the door was a list of rooms printed. Hayley noted they needed to turn left down the corridor, she did so while Jesse followed her with their bags.

"Well, that went better than expected," Marie mused, following them down the hall.

Michael just shook his head at her apparent ignorance of the tension between Hayley and Jesse. Nothing about that had gone down well.

∼

IN THE HOTEL ROOM, Jesse shut the door behind them and lowered the cases to the floor. Hayley stood near to the travel cot, gently turning round to survey the room.

"I'll sleep in the chair, then." Jesse nodded towards the winged armchair in the corner closest to the long window.

"We've slept in a bed before without jumping on each other, I'm sure we can make it one more night," she snapped.

"Have I pissed you off?" Asked Jesse, watching her lower Daniel into the travel cot who was now wide awake and staring at the lights.

"No," replied Hayley. "I'll unpack, you OK if I use the toilet?"

Jesse nodded, watching her walk into the en suit.

With the door shut, Hayley leant back on it and closed her eyes. How the hell was she supposed to get through the next twenty-four hours? Everything she ever wanted was in the next room, but he was unavailable to her. He was offering her everything she wanted, but she couldn't be sure he wasn't just using her to get more information for his investigation. He'd done it before. She needed to find more out about Rachel. If they were more than what he was telling her, then she would have her answer.

"Just you and me, little man," said Jesse, walking over to the cot holding his hands out. Daniel put his arms up, urging to be picked up, which Jesse did instinctively. Holding him in his arms, he rubbed his back, gazing at the door. "How we going to do this, huh?" Daniel made a gurgling noise, and Jesse lifted him so he was directly in front of his face. "No? Me neither. I think Daddy's done something to upset mummy."

∼

AFTER A FEW HOURS of television watching, and playing with Daniel on the bed, the tension had eased enough between them to feel comfortable lying on the bed watching Columbo whilst sharing a box of chocolates from the minibar, while Daniel napped between them.

"So, do you act like Columbo when you interview people?" Asked Hayley, not taking her eyes from the screen. She heard him laugh and reply that he did not. "I could imagine you in an old trench coat, with a cigar in your hands, asking roundabout questions. Knowing full well you'd figured it all out an hour before." She heard him laugh again, while she picked another chocolate from the box.

"They've not got my trusty sidekick on here though."

This time it was Hayley's chance to laugh. She knew he meant Martin. But the mention of him took her back to the time they'd both interviewed her. Nothing about that had been funny.

"Drink?" She asked, standing up, before walking over to the minibar.

Turning back, she looked over her shoulder when he still hadn't answered. "Well?" He looked like he was thinking about it, and then he gently nodded. Grabbing miniature bottles of brandy and a whiskey, she made her way back to the bed, holding them both up for him to choose from.

"The hard stuff," asked Jesse, raising his eyebrow. "Already?"

"Think I'm going to need it, and it only seems fair to share."

Jesse took the whiskey, smirking at her comment. "Is it that bad sharing a room with me?" asked Jesse, turning the miniature bottle around in his hands.

Hayley watched him until he raised his head to gain eye contact with her. She broke his gaze and cracked the bottle open in her hands, throwing the lid in the bin across the room. She silently congratulated herself for getting it in.

"Superb shot."

Hayley ignored him and gulped from the bottle, allowing the liquid to burn her throat and warm her stomach. She leant back on the headboard and closed her eyes. "No, it's not," she finally answered, peeking one eye open to see if her words had affected him.

He was looking straight at her, so she opened both eyes. They held their gaze for a few seconds longer than was comfortable before Jesse leant towards her. Hayley's eyes widened, and she leant back on impulse.

A loud bang came from the door. They both snapped towards it, realising someone was knocking.

Jesse swung his legs off the bed and moved towards the door, opening it on Rob, who took his time to look behind Jesse, Hayley smiled tightly.

"What is it? You doing room service now?" Jesse quipped.

"No, Mum just sent me to tell you we're going downstairs for a drink, if you want to join us." Jesse nodded. "But I can see the dude's asleep."

"Yep, we'll come down once he's woken up."

Rob nodded and turned on his heel. When Jesse turned back round after closing the door, Hayley wasn't on the bed, but the en suit door was closed. He swore under his breath. He needed to talk to her, and every time he came close something always jumped in the way. Dragging his right hand through his hair, he returned to his place on the bed, watching for the door to open.

Hayley clung to the sink, glancing at her face in the mirror, willing herself to get her emotions in check and stop being so bloody weak and pathetic. The tears came before she could do anything about it. Watching them roll down her face, she quickly wiped them away. Taking a few deep breaths in and out, until she felt they were even enough to risk exiting the bathroom, she straightened up. She couldn't hide in here forever.

Rob had made her feel unstable, as though everything around her was just a mirage, a trail of smoke that could be blown away. Just when she thought her life was starting to be rebuilt, he had come along and told her the foundations were hollow. That any pressure on them would make them crumble and leave her with nothing but a mess. Her heart craved Jesse, but she couldn't be sure he craved hers. If she gave her heart to him and then he crushed it, there would be nothing of her left to live. She was barely scraping by as it was. Daniel was the only thing that brought her joy, but he couldn't sustain her if she became any more damaged. It already felt as though people had taken pieces of her away. Chunks that could never be replaced or repaired.

"You OK?" Jesse asked once she walked out.

There was no getting away from his eyes. She felt like a deer in the headlights.

"You've been crying?"

Hayley's shoulders slumped, and she walked over to the bed, her eyes only on Daniel.

"Hayley?"

"Go downstairs. I'll come down once he's woken up." Still not looking at him, she stood still, attempting to make a point; it seemed to work after a few more seconds when she heard Jesse leave. Curling up on the bed, she sobbed quietly, so as not to wake Daniel.

∽

WALKING INTO THE BAR, Jesse scanned the room for his parents. He spied them sat beside a bay window, looking out over the golf course. Pulling an arm chair out from a low table, he sat down and picked up the pint he'd clearly been bought. Another glass remained untouched on the table. Knowing it was for Hayley made him think about how upset she looked before. He wanted to be in a position that enabled her to trust him but each time he made headway she resigned him to Groundhog Day.

"Rob, I still need to introduce you to Catherine's daughter," said Marie after a few minutes of silence.

"Mum, if you want me out of the way just say." Rob glanced from his Mum to his brother.

His father slapped him on the back and he took the hint to stand up and go somewhere with his mother so Michael and Jesse could speak alone. The action made him feel like a child, but he moved anyway, knowing they could be a lot more embarrassing if they chose to.

They were silent for a few minutes, just watching people pass by and wave at those that cared to be acknowledged.

"How's things?" Asked Michael once Rob and Marie had made their way to the other end of the room to more wedding guests.

"I'm guessing you mean with the room and not with my life?" Smirked Jesse placing his beer down on the coaster.

"You know what I mean."

Jesse leant back in the armchair, closing his eyes for a second. "It's going to be a long day," he admitted finally.

"Do you need me and your Mum to have the baby for a while?"

Jesse shook his head.

"Have you spoken with her?" Michael watched his son run his hands down his face.

"She won't talk," answered Jesse. "Every time I try, and I think we get somewhere-"

"Then make her listen instead."

Just then Jesse spied Hayley walking into the room. She'd changed, she was wearing a navy knee length dress with a sweetheart collar, she'd put her hair into a messy bun, and added a little makeup to her face which helped make her eyes shine brighter than they normally did, and probably enabled her to hide the fact she'd been crying to most people. She still took his breath away and watching her made his heart ache.

Michael turned to see her and lifted his arms up to catch her attention. It worked, and she walked over with Daniel in her arms. When she was a few feet away, Michael gestured to take her heavy burden, and she deposited him in his arms with a smile.

"Here," Michael handed Jesse a tenner and looked at Hayley. "Go with my son to the bar and get yourselves a drink."

Jesse knew what he was doing. They already had drinks. But they walked over to the bar anyway and waited for someone to serve them.

"What would you like?" Asked Jesse.

"Oh, err... diet coke." Jesse made a face. "I'll drink later, I've just downed a bottle of brandy and there's Daniel to think about."

He nodded.

"Where's Marie and Rob?" she asked, looking around. Jesse pointed to the far corner. She could see they were in deep conversation. "Who are they talking to?"

"I don't know, probably some aunt fourteen times removed."

She laughed, and he smiled at the sound of it. She had always been good at putting an act on. But he couldn't help it. When she didn't have her barriers up and was open and friendly, he liked it and until then she was a good faker to the rest of the world.

"Big wedding then?" She asked, noting the amount of people that seemed in attendance.

"Yeah," he said, still watching her, looking around at all the people. "If it's too much, we can always sneak out."

She glanced back at him, and he wasn't sure what emotions she was trying to hide. "I'll let you know."

After the barman had taken Jesse's order, he turned back to Hayley who had been pushed up against him by the bulging crowd, "Sorry."

"Don't be, least you can't run away this time." That comment earned him a scowl, and he instantly regretted it. Handing her her drink, he pushed his way through the crowd until they were free. "The weddings at four, so I thought we should-" but before Jesse could finish, someone cut in front of him and shouted his name in excitement.

Hayley turned to see a five-foot blond swooning over Jesse like she owned him. Rolling her eyes, she made her way back to the table, sitting on the seat that prevented her from watching, just in case she couldn't help it.

"It's his cousin. She'd always been quite.." Michael considered his next words, "Bold."

"Nothing to do with me," said Hayley, waving her hand dismissively.

"He's never really been into her," said Michael as if more to himself than anyone else, but Hayley knew what he was doing. "You look lovely, by the way."

She smiled politely.

"Jesse's eyes nearly fell out and rolled across the floor when you came in." When he looked back at her, she was holding an expression to say that she understood exactly what he was trying to do. "Your Mummy needs to give Daddy a chance," he said to Daniel, bouncing him on his knee.

"And Granddad needs to stop playing matchmaker," said Hayley, equally to Daniel. But it earned her a knowing wink from Michael. "Seriously, Michael. There's nothing to nurture. Me and Jesse are over."

Michael placed his hand on top of hers as he tried to find the right words. "You need to talk to each other before you do anything drastic."

Hayley let out a laugh, which took him back a bit. "Think the boats already sailed." She watched the confusion on his face, like he didn't quite understand her statement. "Jesse's already moved on. He's been seeing a fellow copper."

She downed the rest of her drink and made her way to the toilets, mad at herself for feeling so jealous, and leaving Michael stunned. The realisation that not only had Jesse slept with her to get Daniel back, but he had done so to re-investigate Demy Richards to get his promotion made her sick to the stomach. To think she had been so gullible was desperate.

After Jesse had made an escape from his overly enthusiastic cousin, he made his way back to his seat across from his father, who was singing nursery rhymes that made no sense. "I don't even think they're the right words," said Jesse laughing at his Dad's version of hickory dickory dock.

"When were you going to tell me, you'd moved on?" Asked Michael, turning serious.

"Thought I had," said Jesse, placing his drink on the table next to his other pint.

"You did, but I hadn't realised you'd actually *moved on*."

Jesse continued to watch his Dad play with Daniel on his knee. "What do you mean?" he asked, confused.

"Hayley just told me you've started seeing a colleague."

Jesse's eyes widened, and the shock on his face was clear for Michael to see. "Is that not true?"

Jesse sighed and ran his fingers through his hair. "Not totally."

The way his Dad held his gaze told him to continue.

"It was nothing, a one-time thing, but I explained that."

"Well, whatever it is or was, she's not happy."

Jesse looked in the direction she had left.

"Jesse." He turned to his Dad. "Don't do anything you'll regret." advised his dad, "Maybe we *should* get you another room."

"So, there was a choice?"

⁓

THAT AFTERNOON the wedding party dispersed to get ready for the nuptials to take place in the garden. As the amount of people at the bar lowered, Michael sat and watched the last of the party meandering. Marie had already gone back to their room to get changed, and Rob had left only a few minutes after.

Jesse held back, waiting for Hayley to get ready so they could pass over Daniel like a baton. Marie stepped back into the room first, so took Daniel and urged Jesse to go upstairs and get ready, otherwise he'd be late. Walking in, he saw Hayley curling her hair round the tongs, focusing her efforts on the mirror as she sat at the dresser. He watched her try to ignore him.

Hayley watched Jesse walk in and open the wardrobe door where he'd hung up his suit and shirt earlier. Sensing he was being watched, he turned his attention to the mirror, and she quickly went back to unravel her hair and wrapping another piece round the tongs.

"You look lovely," admitted Jesse.

"Thank you."

Dropping his gaze, he went back to the wardrobe, pulling out his shirt and laying it on the bed. After pulling his T-shirt off from over his head, he undid the top buttons of his shirt so he could slip it on the same way. Hayley watched as he pulled his jeans down and slipped out of them.

"Ow, shit!" looking up, he spotted her rubbing her head where the hot tongs had burnt her. "Hot," she said, embarrassed.

"Why thank you, ma'am," said Jesse in a southern American accent.

"Not you, the tongs. I burnt my head," explained Hayley.

"I know that too."

Hayley bit her lip, OK so he knew she'd been ogling him, great!

Jesse finished getting ready and Hayley reapplied make up, before spraying her hair to keep the curls in. Jesse searched for his cuff links and watched Hayley whiz round the room, putting everything that was hers away in her suitcase. "We are coming back, you know."

"I know, but I don't want Daniel picking something up that he shouldn't."

"Fair enough."

She continued, and he watched how she moved in that navy dress. It swished round her legs and pinched in at the waist, extenuating her curves. "I'll do the same in a minute."

"Struggling?" she asked after watching him for a few seconds, knowing full well he was.

"You know you could just help?" Jesse smirked.

"Yeah, but where would the fun be in that?" She said, smirking back.

He held out his wrists with the cuff links in his right hand. Walking towards him, she held his gaze. "What do you say?" she asked childishly, watching him roll his eyes.

"Please."

Laughing, she took both cuff links, stabbing them through the tight holes in his shirt wrists.

"I like it when it's like this."

She stopped on the second cuff link and looked up at him.

"When we're just laughing and joking."

She pursed her lips and went back to pushing the cuff link through the gap.

"Reminds me of when we first got together."

Stepping back once she'd finished, she turned round to find her shoes.

"We were good together."

"And then we weren't." Still looking for her shoes, she raised the side of the quilt to see if they were under the bed. When she looked up at Jesse, he was still staring at her. "What?"

"We could get back to what we were before you know."

"We tried, it didn't work, did it?" She snapped.

"Maybe we just didn't try hard enough?" Countered Jesse.

"Maybe," she answered, unconvinced.

Jesse lowered his gaze and then walked over to the en suit. "Are you looking for these?" He said, bending down and picking up some black high heels.

She sighed, walking over towards him with her hand outstretched, but he pulled them back. Looking at him to see what he was trying to achieve, he grabbed her waist with his free hand and pulled her into him. "It was never difficult loving you."

Hayley could feel all the tension melting away in his arms, and it scared her how quickly he obtained her. Pulling back quickly, she turned around so he couldn't see how much it hurt to do it.

"Hayley-"

"Jesse. Just go." She didn't turn to watch him leave. When she heard the door, she turned to see her shoes on the bed.

CHAPTER 11

THE SUN SHONE HIGH IN THE SKY. FLOWERS DRAPED AROUND THE ARCH, held a scent reminiscent of the wildflowers from Hayley's childhood. The bride wore a white elegant fitted satin slip, whilst holding a fresh flower bouquet of lilies and peach carnations. Her arm hooked around her father's, she slowly stepped towards her future husband. Hayley sat with Jesse to her left and Marie on her right with Daniel sat on her knee straining to be put down.

"Doesn't she look wonderful?" Asked Marie.

Hayley nodded and smiled. She was trying to be happy, but the thought of eventually walking down the aisle without her father present was gnawing at her. He'd died over a year ago, trying to protect her. The only time he ever had, and it had cost him his life. She felt guilty every day because she'd begged him to help her, not realising that a few short hours later he would be dead for his efforts. Whilst they'd never been close, the thought that one day his place by her side would be vacant was sobering.

Feeling Jesse's hand on her leg, she glanced to him. He smiled sympathetically, as though hearing her own inner monologue.

After the ceremony, all the guests had photos taken in front of the lavish hotel and then made their way into the reception room, which was decorated with more flowers with white seats, bearing peach bows and white tablecloths. Hosting bottles of wine in the centre. Everyone found their place settings and took their seats, awaiting the speeches that were being done first to allow everyone to relax with the meal. The best man was hilarious and everyone laughed and cheered before raising their glasses to toast the happy couple.

When the starters came out, the conversations were already flowing around the room. Hayley was enjoying listening to the chatter of people who knew each other so well.

"So, who's this little chappy?" Asked an elderly lady sitting opposite Hayley, with a blue rinse and a thin flowery dress on.

"This is Daniel," smiled Hayley, glancing to her son who was trying to force an entire petite pain into his mouth. Taking it off him, she pulled it open before tearing a piece off and giving it to him before the imminent scream came from having lost his food.

"Oh, isn't he beautiful? You must be very proud?" Hayley nodded and smiled again. "And he looks the spitting image of his father." Hayley said nothing, but she heard Jesse thank her, fully aware of the occupants at the table looking at her. "How long have you two been together?"

Before Hayley could answer and put the poor woman out of her misery, Jesse jumped in and said a "couple of years". Hayley's wide eyes were no surprise to him, but when he took her hand in his, she made sure he felt the pain her grip held, whilst smiling through gritted teeth.

"Oh well, I think it's wonderful. Young love. Are you married?"

"No," Hayley quickly interjected before Jesse could answer.

"Yet," said Jesse, smiling at her in a way that threatened challenge.

Hayley rolled her eyes. He could have his fun.

"Oh, wonderful. Make sure I get an invitation, won't you?" She winked, before tearing her roll open to spread the butter in.

Hayley looked at Jesse with eyes that asked him what the hell he was doing? He just shrugged, trying not to smile too wide.

After the meal and more talk about a relationship with Jesse that she wasn't in. The tables cleared and moved from the area to allow for access to the dance floor. They designed a crèche in the corner to accommodate all the young guests while older kids ran around causing a riot. Thankfully Marie had taken Daniel upstairs for another nap, but Hayley was sure the nap was more for her own benefit than Daniel's. She had looked exhausted.

Jesse handed her a glass of champagne from the serving waiter, making his way around the hall with a silver platter. Taking it, she sipped it tentatively while watching Jesse talk to another distant family member who had descended on them. Hayley smiled and nodded when needed, but other than that she took little notice. She scanned the room for people she might know or something to pique her interest. Seeing Rob staring back at her, he held up his glass, doing the same she timidly smiled back before glancing at Jesse who was still in deep conversation. She still hadn't told Jesse about Rob and she wasn't sure how to handle it, the last thing she wanted to do was cause conflict in the family but she no longer felt safe around Rob. She'd never have thought him capable of such violence but then she'd been wrong before, maybe she was just a lousy judge of character.

"You look about as enthralled to be here, as I do," whispered Rob from behind her a few minutes later.

"Is it that obvious?" She asked, taking another sip of champagne, while glancing to Jesse who was in full flow of explaining a childhood mishap that his uncle had told everyone in their small gathering.

"Fraid so," he smiled, placing his hand at the bottom of her back. Stepping forward slightly, she relaxed when his hand dropped away.

"Great. And there was me thinking I could find a career in acting," she answered.

He laughed loudly, and it took her by surprise. Looking around, she noticed Jesse was watching them whilst still conversing with the group.

"Did you like the meal?" He asked, whispering in her ear, having stepped closer to her again.

"It was OK," she answered.

Rob was like a regular Jekyll and Hyde. This version was fine, but she no longer trusted him not to turn.

"Come on, you know you can tell me the truth," he winked.

Hayley smiled awkwardly, glancing to Jesse now and then. "Beef was over-done, the gravy was like piss water and the dessert wasn't even set."

"Put your claws back in," she whispered in his ear. "They could have always asked you to do it?"

"Could have asked us both, we'd have done a better job," grumbled Rob, putting his hand on her waist. "Can we go outside, we need to talk?" Whispered Rob in her ear.

Swallowing hard, she looked back to Jesse, who was tilting his head. Looking at her as though to ask if she was OK? Slightly nodding, she walked away with Rob behind her. Everything told her it was a bad idea to go anywhere with Rob alone, but she couldn't risk causing a scene either.

The cool breeze was refreshing after the heat of the dining room. Noticing her shiver, Rob took his suit jacket off before wrapping it round her shoulders.

"Thanks."

"Can't have you dying of pneumonia," he smiled.

Placing a hand at the bottom of her back as he guided her towards the trees that helped shadow the immaculate lawn that she knew from earlier led to the lake. Continuing to walk, Hayley grew more nervous the further away she got from Jesse. Pulling the blazer across her chest, she tried to comfort herself. Once they were out of site of the wedding party, Rob looked around as though to check they were on their own before placing his hands in his pockets and lowering his head. Waiting for him to say something, she scanned the area. It was beautiful. The sun was hitting the lake at just the right angle to let it shimmer and illuminate the lilies that floated carefree on top.

"So, how are you?" Asked Rob, stepping in line with her as she tried to stop her heels sinking into the soft soil. Leaning up against a tree so she could rest her feet on the bracken beneath, she looked up at the branches, trying to control her nerves without showing them. Rob leant his hand on the same trunk watching her.

"I'm OK, today's been nice," she responded absently.

"Nice?" Asked Rob.

Intrigued, Hayley nodded warily.

"You and Jesse seem close."

"I'm just his plus one," answered Hayley, wondering why she was justifying herself to him once again.

"You just look closer," said Rob, straightening up. "Why is that?"

"No idea," answered Hayley pushing herself away from the tree, but before she could move Rob was in front of her with his hands on her stomach pushing her back against it. "Rob, what are you doing?" Fear flooded her system, and her legs stiffened and felt as though someone had poured lead into them.

"You look stunning," he said, moving her wavy hair from her right shoulder, gliding his finger along her shoulder blade.

Hayley watched Rob glance over her shoulder, but before she could look, he moved in. Pushing his body against hers, forcing her backwards, imprinting her back with the bark of the tree. Suddenly he covered his mouth with hers. Trying to push him away felt fruitless until she finally broke free and stared straight at him.

"What the hell…?" Turning at the familiar voice, Hayley saw Jesse looking at them both like they'd just killed his dog.

"Jesse?" When Jesse's eyes caught hers, she saw only hatred, and she took a step back at the shock of it.

"Oh Jesse, shit! We were going to tell you. I didn't want you to find out like this," explained Rob taking Hayley's hand in his.

Tugging it away, she looked at him in horror.

"It just happened."

"What?!" Hayley screeched.

"How could you?" Asked Jesse, his face filled with sadness and betrayal. He wasn't even looking at Rob, he directed his anger solely on her.

"Don't blame her, Jesse. We just got close," said Rob calmly, watching his brother stare at Hayley as though he wasn't sure whether his eyes were deceiving him.

"Jesse, it's not true. I swear it wasn't what it looked like," pleaded Hayley, realising at how cliché she sounded. "He kissed me, I tried to-"

"Hales darling, there's no reason to lie now. He needs to know the truth."

Looking at Rob in shock, she shook her head as if to rid herself of the scene unfolding before her.

"We've been sleeping together for weeks. We love each other."

While Hayley tried to defend herself and make Jesse see reason, she watched his face disintegrate into confusion. Tears welled as his face contorted into something that she could only describe as disgust. Walking away from her, she watched him leave and dropped to her knees in despair. Tears rolling down her face, her entire body shook, realising the only man she had ever truly loved was walking away from her, thinking she had done something she hadn't and never would.

"How could you?!" Screamed Hayley looking up at Rob.

Rob shrugged his shoulders nonchalantly. "Now he knows how it feels to have someone take away the thing you love the most," he answered coolly.

"You did this to get revenge for Caitlyn?" She asked, wiping away her tears.

"Does it matter?"

"But why?"

Walking over to her, he lowered himself to her crouched height, taking his time to look at every mark and line on her face. "You. Destroyed. My. family," he said calmly but forcefully.

"I didn't ask to me abducted Rob," she cried.

"No. But you had a job to do. A job that you thought you could walk away from."

"What the hell are you talking about?" She cried.

"All you had to do was marry Demy and have his child. That was all that was being asked of you. But you got my family involved and had my child killed."

"What? I don't know what you're talking about. What child?"

"Caitlyn was having my baby. Till you came along and destroyed us. She lost our baby, because of you."

"Oh, my God! Rob, I didn't know, I swear I didn't know."

Grabbing her jaw and pushing his fingers into her cheeks, he contorted her lips out. "You destroyed my life, and now I am going to destroy yours."

The rage in his eyes shook Hayley to the core, and she froze.

"I will take everything away from you and you'll wish you were dead."

∽

When Jesse got back to the hall, the disco was in full swing. Different coloured lights darting around the room. He couldn't see any of it. He wasn't even sure how he'd made it back. He couldn't think of anything other than the body lock his brother and Hayley had been in. Jesse felt sick, but he didn't even have the energy to expel the bile swirling around in his gut. Standing still near the door, he swayed on his feet before he felt arms wrap around his shoulders.

"Are you OK lad, you look like you've seen a ghost?" It was his uncle Harry but he couldn't even acknowledge him, he just felt himself being pushed across the room until they forced him down into a tub chair. "Do you need a drink, lad?"

"What's wrong?" His mother's voice filtered in as she pushed her way through the gathering crowd.

"Get back, give him room." His Dad's voice.

Feeling a little coolness on his face, he realised people were backing up.

"Come on, move back, I'll see to him." Once they were on their own, Jesse dumped his head in his hands. "Son, what's wrong?"

Jesse shook his head. He couldn't say it, but he also couldn't get them out of his mind.

"Jesse, you're scaring me, what's wrong, are you hurt?" Shaking his head, he sobbed.

"What is it then sweetheart, what's wrong?" Asked his mum, taking his hand from his head to hold.

"Hayley and Rob," answered Jesse.

Marie and Michael both looked at one another and drew their brows together. Looking back to Jesse, they waited for an explanation.

"I saw them together." The shock was obvious on their faces and he'd have laughed at the sight had it not been about his life.

"That can't be true," answered Michael after a few minutes. "She wouldn't do that."

"Well, she has," said Jesse, wiping his face on his hands. "Where's Daniel?" He asked, realising he was no longer in his Mum's arms.

"He's upstairs, Annie is watching over him." Annie was one of his older aunties and was quite possibly sleeping on the job. "He's fine."

"No," said Jesse, standing up. "I'm taking him home."

Nodding, his parents backed up while having a silent conversation between themselves.

When Jesse reached the room, he knocked gently before using his key to open the door. Annie was indeed a sleep on the bed, while 'murder she wrote' played out on the television set. Walking over to the travel cot, he looked down to see the blankets and cuddly rabbit toy he sleeps with. Taking the blanket out, he confirmed his suspicions he wasn't hiding beneath them. Dumping them back in the cot, he raced into the en suit, but nothing with brown hair and blue eyes shone back. Rushing back into the bedroom, he gently nudged Annie until she stirred.

"Annie, where's Daniel?"

"Daniel?" watching her wake up and get her bearing was painstaking, but he knew he wouldn't get a coherent response without allowing her time to properly wake up. "He's in the cot," explained Annie.

"Shit!" He must have missed her. She had got to Daniel first. Pulling her cupboards open, he noted everything was still in its place. Glancing round the side of the bed, he noticed her suitcase was on the floor. That's when the sickening feeling in his stomach intensified. Feeling his phone vibrate in his pocket he pulled it out, it was Martin.

"Mart."

"Is Hayley with you?" Asked Martin.

"No, yes, no, not really," answered Jesse. "Why?"

"Well, that was conclusive," said Martin dryly. "Demy's out."

"What? how?" asked Jesse, astounded.

"He broke out. I've not got the details yet, but they organised it. We have eight dead guards and prison out of control. They have drawn in armed response to control the situation, but Demy's visible, leaving on CCTV. The car's dumped and torched, leads gone cold, they had damaged seems all the CCTV in that area over the last few weeks and its let them get away without a trace."

"So, you've no idea where he is?"

"None what so ever. That's why I'm calling. I know you're both at a wedding today, but I wanted to give you the head's up. Be vigilant, and I advise you stay as close to Hayley as possible." Jesse rolled his eyes at that. He didn't want to be anywhere near her, but he could keep his feelings at bay if it meant keeping her safe. At least that's what he was trying to tell himself.

"When did he escape?" Asked Jesse.

"About two hours ago."

"Shit. OK, leave it with me. I need to find Daniel and Hayley."

"Why? You lost them?" Laughed Martin.

"We had a row. I'll call you back." Putting his phone away he thanked Annie who was now fully awake, and a little confused. Rushing downstairs, he noticed his Mum and Dad still sat where he'd left them. "He's not there. Have you seen Hayley?"

"No, son," answered Michael. Spinning around on the spot, he scanned the area, but he couldn't see Daniel or Hayley. "He must be here somewhere."

"Demy's escaped," answered Jesse.

With no other explanation needed, both his parents stood up and started walking round the dining room in search. Realising neither Daniel nor Hayley was there, Jesse removed his mobile from his pocket and contemplated ringing her, but he couldn't bring himself to talk to her. Too hurt and too angry.

Glancing back up, he noticed Rob rushing over to him. He appraised his clothes. His jacket arm was ripped, his pocket torn and his shirt underneath covered in dirt and grass stains. Looking back at his brother's face, he noted how guilty he looked. "What the hell happened to you?"

"Nothing," answered Rob.

Not wanting to care whether his brother was in trouble or whether they just liked it rough in the woods, he shook his head to rid himself of the notion before asking where Hayley was. Rob shrugged before walking away from him. Taking a deep breath, Jesse made his way back outside. He had to find her.

∼

Jesse stopped at the lake, watching the moonlight filter onto the surface, wobbling with every ripple from every stone he threw. He was distraught. How could she have betrayed him like that? He thought they'd finally come together, sorted out their differences. But to find that out, he wasn't sure he could get past that.

Jesse had been sat out for a while, it was getting chilly and no doubt his parents were wondering where he was. He'd have to answer a barrage of questions. He wasn't in the bloody mood for that. Maybe he could slip upstairs, lay down, and wait for Hayley. She'd have to come back for hers and Daniel's stuff, then they could talk about it. He wasn't sure what would come of it, but they had to talk. They had Daniel to consider, if nothing else. He'd be damned if he would watch his brother marry the love of his life, though. Picking up a broken stick, he lobbed it into the water, watching the ripple effect before straightening his legs and making his way back.

The music came to his ears after a few minutes and got louder the closer he got. Looking at the patch of grass he'd recently walked away from, the memories of Rob's confession came flooding back in full techno colour. Glancing around, he couldn't see any evidence of Hayley, so he started walking back to the dining hall. He'd have to phone her. She needed to know about Demy. Hating her didn't mean he'd want her to come to any harm. Looking up, he could see people dancing on the inside of the glass. He really wasn't ready to talk to anyone. Rubbing his jaw, he side stepped just to give himself an extra few minutes to compose himself through the shadows the trees cast.

Walking towards the outside of the woods for the shade, he carried on walking around until he saw a lone, black strappy shoe on the floor. Bending down and picking it up, he noticed it was the same as Hayley's.

What the fuck was going on? Throwing the shoe on the ground with much more force than required, he made his way deeper into the wood, before seeing bare legs on the floor. Rushing over with a dark feeling in his stomach, he noticed how high her dress sat, gathered around her waist, revealing dark navy underwear. Her wavy hair covered most of her face. Skin as pale as snow, apart from a set of purple handprints round her neck.

"Holy fucking Christ" Jesse stepped back, falling on his backside. Covering his mouth with his hand, he fought to keep the tears and stomach contents in as they threatened exodus.

"Hayley, oh my God, Hayley."

Crawling towards her, he felt for a pulse, but couldn't feel one in her wrists. Realising his hands were shaking, he needed to steady them. Gently touching her neck, he pressed to feel a pressure point. Anything that could tell him he hadn't just lost the love of his life.

There, he found it; it was weak, but it was there. Scrambling for the phone in his pocket, he rang dispatch, giving them his name and rank, where he was and what he knew.

Not being able to see her chest moving, he covered his mouth over hers, stifling a cry as he did so. Please don't let this be the last time he kissed her, he thought, pinching her nose and raising her head back as he blew into her mouth, watching her chest rise and then fall twice before starting chest compressions.

"Come on, Baby, fight. Fight. Baby. Fight."

After thirty, he pinched her nose again and breathed for her. Only to repeat the process until the blue lights illuminated the sky and the paramedics took over.

When he looked around after watching the paramedics transfer her to a stretcher with an oxygen mask covering her face, he realised his Mum and Dad with half of the wedding party were behind him, white as sheets and in shock. His Mum cradled a crying Daniel.

"Go Son, we've got Daniel. Go be with Hayley," said his father, pushing him towards the stretcher that was being wheeled to the parking lot, past the large window to the hall.

∼

JESSE WAITED in the hospital corridor. He didn't know what to do; he felt helpless just sat there waiting, but he knew he'd be more harm than good. The professionals had her in their care, and they'd promised to do their best. He'd have to trust them like he asked victims of crime to do with him. But being the one without answers and far more questions than he could voice, he was quickly losing his mind.

Martin wandered down the corridor in his jeans and t-shirt whilst holding two polystyrene cups. "Someone from the office called me. Told me you were here."

Jesse nodded. Thankful he was there, but he didn't have a lot to say. He wasn't sure his voice would hold out, anyway.

"What happened?" Asked Martin, handing him a cup while he sipped his own.

"No idea," he answered, shaking his head. Taking the seat next to him, he tucked his feet under the chair.

"They must get their coffee at the same place we do. Tastes like elephant dung."

Jesse just smiled slightly; he knew what Martin was trying to do.

"Heard you got to try out your CPR skills."

Again, Jesse nodded, taking a sip of his coffee. It burnt his lip, but he didn't care.

"Any idea who did it?" He asked finally.

"The last person to see her was Rob."

Martin stared at him for a few seconds before looking away. "You don't think-"

"I've no idea, Mart," he sighed. Taking another sip, still fucking hot, but still didn't care.

Silence ensued and Martin read the posters on the wall while Jesse counted the squares on the floor.

"They were sleeping together," volunteered Jesse finally.

When Martin had said nothing, he turned to him, Martin was just staring down at him wondering what the hell was going on in his head.

"Do you believe that?" He asked after a while of silence.

"She didn't exactly look innocent."

After what felt like an hour, Martin shook his head. "No fucking way," said Martin, shaking his head. "I just can't see it."

"Neither could I, but you didn't see her face," answered Jesse.

Martin took a sip of coffee, trying to process the information.

"They were getting all up and personal with each other outside."

Martin shook his head in disbelief. "How's she doing?" Asked Martin a few minutes later.

Jesse was struggling with whatever he'd had to face before finding her, but he was still here, worrying, which told Martin more than he needed to know.

"The nurse said she's being treated, they'll come and let me know when they have news."

Martin didn't know what to say. What could he say? So, he just sat there, next to his friend, offering unwavering silent support. A few minutes later Martin slapped his shoulder and nodded towards the approaching nurse.

"Mr Hallam, Hayley's in ICU, she's sedated, and on ventilation as it damaged her wind pipe. So, if you hear wheezing, don't panic. We're aware and we're monitoring it. It should repair itself with plenty of rest, and then we'll remove the ventilator. When she wakes, please don't let her speak. Let us know and we'll run some tests. She must take it easy and rest to help regain strength in her throat. She will feel rough, to say the least. But I thought you'd appreciate being able to sit with her."

Jesse nodded, following her down the hall as she spoke, with

Martin on his heels. When the curtain was drawn back, he saw her. Even though he'd seen plenty of people in the hospital before, it still took his breath away. Taking a seat by her bed, Martin stood by the window, looking out, allowing them some privacy.

Jesse took her hand in his and brought it up to his cheek. "Hayley, sweetheart, I'm here."

Hayley's eyes fluttered but remained shut.

"I'm not going anywhere. Jesus Hayley, I'm so fucking sorry." Jesse felt a hand on his shoulder, squeezing. Trying to pull himself together, he held her hand, rubbing his face free from tears. "Every time we get it together, something happens."

"You got together again?"

"Yeah, we actually talked," Jesse said, trying not to laugh as he imagined the smug look on his friend's face.

"Told you communication was king," laughed Martin sadly.

"Then I found Rob and her-"

"Leave all that till she's woken up, mate," advised Martin.

Jesse nodded absently.

"Where is he anyway?"

"I've not seen him since the reception." Martin walked back to the window. "He looked like he'd been in a fight. His jacket was torn, and he was covered in dirt."

"You don't think?-" Martin couldn't even finish that sentence. He couldn't believe for a second that Hayley would betray Jesse like that, but then what did he really know? But Rob being in a mess before they found Hayley injured didn't sound good. "Shit, I don't know, I just can't see them together." sighed Martin "especially after he blamed her so much about Caitlyn."

Suddenly Jesse's back iced up, leaving him stood ramrod straight. The gut feelings, the looks, the questions, they all made sense. Someone had been sabotaging his efforts and been dripping poison in her ear.

"Oh, my God," whispered Jesse a few seconds later.

Martin turned to his friend at the same time he turned round to him.

"She kept saying it wasn't what it looked like."

"Maybe it wasn't," Martin shrugged.

"He kept touching her all day. Hand on her hip, on her back, and she kept looking at me and moving away from him. I thought after, that she'd been trying to hide it from me, but maybe he was making her feel uncomfortable for another reason."

"You think he's been trying to get between you?" Asked Martin.

"I don't know, but he came round asking if she was on the market. Reckoned he was just checking in case a delivery driver or someone took a liking to her. Wanted to know if I wanted him to step in," said Jesse, relaying what he could remember.

"What has she said about him?" Asked Martin.

"Just that he was OK at work, but she looked like she was keeping something back. I thought maybe he'd been saying something then, but after today I just assumed, she was trying to hide a relationship."

"You will have to have this conversation when she wakes up," warned Martin.

Jesse spent hours bent over her bed. Watching her eyes flicker, holding her hand, smoothing her hairline, anything that allowed him to touch her just to ensure she was still with him. Martin left after an hour of exhaustive conversation, but promised to come back the day after. The nurse popped in now and then to check vitals, even bringing him a coffee now and then, as he refused to budge. His phone sat silently in his pocket, knowing he had a hundred or more texts before he pulled it out. Holding Hayley's hand with his left, he scrolled down with his right. Plenty of messages from his Mum and Dad, they'd packed everything up and headed home, asking for news of Hayley, talking about Daniel. Other messages were from friends and family that had seen the ambulance arrive at the hotel, wishing him their best and hoping all was OK.

Then there was one from Rob, tapping on it to open it up, it read. Sorry.

Glancing to Hayley, he saw she was watching him. Tears leaking from her eyes. Filing the message away for later, he slipped his phone back into his pocket.

"Hey, sweetheart. How you feeling?" Hayley's eyes widen once she realised she had a massive tube stuck down her throat. "Hey don't panic, it's helping you breathe. Calm down, OK?"

Watching her trust him warmed his heart. He'd get the nurse, he just wanted to stay with her a second longer.

"Don't speak, I've got you a pen and paper you can use, the nurse says you need to rest your throat, it'll take time to heal."

Watching her watch him with fear in her eyes lanced his heart. "Hayley. I love you, that will never change. I don't care what you've done. I just need you to know that OK?"

Walking over to the windowsill, he picked up the paper and pen Martin had left for him and carried it to the bed. Placing the pen in her right hand, he angled the clean paper underneath it. "Do you want to know anything before I find a nurse?"

Where's Daniel?

"He's with Mum and Dad," answered Jesse, reading her message.

R U Sure?

"Yes, they were there when the ambulance arrived, they've packed up and taken him home."

Rob.

Jesse stared at the pad, feeling the bottom of his world fall out. She was asking for him. "I'm sure he'll be here soon." He said sitting back in the chair letting go of her hand. "I'll get a nurse; they need to run some tests before they take the pipe out."

Watching Jesse leave, she picked up the pad and wrote furiously.

The nurses and doctors all came in, checking her vitals and telling her what they were doing. She looked around the room for Jesse, but he was nowhere. Unable to stop the tears, the doctor asked if she was in any pain.

They then went on to explain how they would take the tube out and how she had to help by coughing and staying calm. Deciding that they were ready to take out the tube, one nurse held her down to maintain the correct angle while the doctor gently pulled it away. Coughing and spluttering, they handed her a cup of water while they explained how she was likely to progress and what to expect and watch out for.

Once they were done, he explained what medication she was on and how it would affect her, detailing what she would be looking at as far as recovery was concerned.

CHAPTER 12

WHILE DRIVING HIS DAD AND DANIEL TO THE HOSPITAL, JESSE TOLD Michael about Demy's escape. Since Martin had stayed with him at the hospital, they'd naturally progressed to discussing the break out and he needed to tell someone he could trust to keep it to himself. He hadn't properly had time to process, and his Dad always had a level head about these things.

"Your mum's been trying to get hold of Rob, but he's not picking up."

Jesse listened, but he had nothing to say about him. His priority right now was making sure Hayley was OK. They'd have to deal with what happened after she was out of the hospital, but right now he needed to focus on getting her better. Especially as it seemed Rob had done a bunk after blowing his life apart.

"Your Great Uncle Jeff said he saw him having an argument with some men just before the ambulance pulled up."

"What men?"

"He didn't know them. They were in bike leathers. Had helmets on. But he could hear raised voices, that's what made him look," answered Michael.

"What happened after that?"

"He said Rob stormed off in his car."

Jesse nodded, watching the traffic around him as he tried to pull safely into the left-hand lane. "How's Daniel been?"

"Good as gold. A bit upset last night, but he's been full of beans this morning."

Jesse smiled, thankful that his son wasn't feeling as low as he was.

"Jesse, I don't believe for a second something was going on between Hayley and Rob. Are you sure you've not misunderstood?"

"Misunderstood? No, I'm sure. I saw them with my own two eyes. He had his hands all over her, and they were kissing. Not much to misunderstand," snapped Jesse.

The car fell silent again, and he flipped the radio on to ease the tension. "A young man has been found dead. Close to the river Trent in Newark. Police have not identified the individual yet but say that his death is suspicious so are asking for anyone in the area who might have seen something between 10pm last night and 9am this morning to contact the incident room on…." As the broadcaster drooled out the number, Jesse wondered what had happened.

"Doesn't sound good, does it?" Said his Dad.

Jesse shook his head, while he pressed the pre-set buttons on his stereo for another station.

"Where was Daniel last night?" Asked Jesse, remembering how he'd been missing from his room when his Aunt Annie had been babysitting.

"Oh, your uncle Leonard went to check on Annie and when he realised she'd dosed off he checked on Daniel and he was wide awake so he brought him to us so as not to wake her. You must have missed him on your way down."

Nodding, Jesse finally found a station that was calm enough for his nerves to handle, and they drove the rest of the way to the hospital in relative silence. When he reached the room, she was asleep. Turning back to his Dad, he asked him to get himself and Daniel something from the cafeteria before she woke. Turning around, they left Jesse to stand and stare at her as her chest moved up and down. Spying the paper in her hand, he walked closer and read his name scrawled on the top. Slipping it from her delicate fingers, he peeled it open.

Jesse, you need to know that I did not sleep with Rob. He's been strange recently, been trying to pressure me to go out with him, but I wouldn't. He pushed me back and lunged at me; I didn't have time to stop him before he kissed me. I'm so sorry. Some men came, said things I don't understand. Thought I was going to die. I love you, always. X

Jesse read the note again, hoping he'd read it wrong. He wanted to wake her up and talk to her but he knew she needed her rest, so exiting the room he ran after his Dad. Spying him at a table with Daniel, he watched Michael split a cheese sandwich in half before offering Daniel one.

As soon as he reached the table, he placed the note in his dad's hands. When he finished reading, he looked up to meet his son's worried expression.

"She wrote it while I was gone. It was in her hand."

"Do you think it's true?"

"Why would she lie?"

Michael looked towards Daniel as he peeled open his sandwich, taking out the grated cheese one bit at a time before eating it.

"Who are the men she's talking about?" asked Michael.

"I've no idea. What if they were the men Jeff saw?" Asked Jesse. "Are you sure you've heard nothing from him?"

"No, you're Mum's going out of her mind. Trust me, if he gets in contact, I'll tell you." Jesse nodded. "Go be with her, I'll keep m'laddo, company."

Smiling, Jesse left the table after giving Daniel a kiss on his head.

Walking back in the room, he saw that Hayley's eyes were still closed. Sitting at her bedside waiting for contact from the outside world felt like hours had passed when in reality the clock was barely moving. He needed to know what was going on. He'd barely spoken to the detective in charge, at the time his mind had been elsewhere. Opening his eyes, he realised he must have drifted off.

Looking at Hayley, he smiled to see she was awake and staring at him. "Hey, you should have woken me up."

She tapped the notepad; it read, **How?**

He laughed. "Fair point, I'll get you a bell."

She smiled.

"Daniel's in the canteen with Dad, or at least he was before I fell asleep." Nodding, she touched her sore throat. "You want anything to eat or drink?"

Watching Hayley write **Nurse bought water and jelly, urrggh**, he laughed. **No solid food for a while, sucks, literally**.

"I see you've not lost your sense of humour," said Jesse.

I'm so sorry.

"Hey, not now, OK? Let's get you better. Besides, I feel like I'm having a conversation with an etch sketch, so it can wait." She smiled and he could see she was trying not to laugh. "I love you." Grabbing her hand, he squeezed it before kissing her forehead.

"You two really need to get a room," said Martin, pulling the curtain across to enter.

"What's happening?"

"Not a lot at the moment. We've got people out, scanning footage, but it looks like he's hiding at the minute. No one's seen or heard from him." Hayley looked at both of them confused and then the penny dropped for them. She didn't know.

"Hayley, I meant to tell you, but then I found you on the floor half dead."

Looking at Martin, she recognised how sheepish he looked before looking back to Jesse. "D-"

"Rob's nowhere to be seen," jumped in Martin.

When Jesse glanced back to Martin to ask him why he'd stopped him telling her about Demy, Martin flicked his head to one side to ask to speak outside the room away from her.

"Jesse, I need to tell you something else," said Martin solemnly, both looking towards Hayley for her to agree, which she did not; they left her room to talk outside in the corridor.

She could see the news wasn't good from Jesse's reaction, and then whatever he returned made Martin run off down the corridor. Opening the door again, Jesse walked in looking paler than before. Waiting for him to respond took all the patience she had left.

CHAPTER 13

Five days later Hayley was out of hospital and resting at Jesse's house. Daniel was stopping at his Marie and Michael's as much as possible while he was at work so she could get the rest she required, but she was struggling to let him go.

Rob was still out there somewhere, and no one had any idea what he planned to do next. They had updated the police with the note and the information that Jeff could give them, but so far Rob was in the wind.

Demy seemed to have completely disappeared too. Ports and airports were notified, but with his type of connections it wasn't above the realm of possibility that he could get out of the country some other way. Hayley couldn't settle knowing he was free. While he was being held captive, she was sure she was safe. But when no one knew where he was, he could pop up anytime and take away her freedom once again, or worse.

Hayley entered the house, gently raising the wheels of the pushchair over the rim of the door. She could hear Elvis Presley singing from the front room. Smiling to herself, she tapped on the front room door to signal she was there. Hearing a familiar voice beckon her, she walked in. Michael sat in his armchair, with nothing in his hands. Usually, he'd have a cross word or a Sudoku puzzle to complete, but it seemed the music was enough to captivate his interest.

"Hi sweetheart, to what do I owe this pleasure?" Hayley smiled and leant forward to kiss him on the forehead.

"See you," she croaked, smiling as she took a seat on the sofa.

"You sound like you've been on fifty a day," remarked Michael playfully. "But it's good to see you, where's the little monster?" Michael watched her as she pointed to the kitchen to save her voice. "Marie's just popped to the shops, she's the Elvis fan." announced Michael. "How did you get here?"

"Taxi, don't worry, I know not to be out on my own," she whispered. She couldn't imagine how he was feeling about everything. Knowing his son was capable of something like that must have come as quite a shock. Having to see the evidence of his crime must have to feel like a punch to the stomach, so she pulled the collar of her blouse up, wishing she'd worn a scarf. "Needed some company," she smiled.

"Sweetheart, I hate seeing you in so much pain. And to think it was one of my own, well. Words can't express my regret."

As tears welled in her eyes at all the heartache she had caused this family, who had taken her in when she had nothing. Regret and sympathy dripped from the man who she had found comfort in, on more than one occasion. Sometimes in hers and Jesse's relationship that she had found it hard to speak, but somehow Micheal had always known what to say. He always had a quote or an anecdote that would hit home just when it was most needed. He was one of the most perceptive men she knew, and the most caring. The love she had for this man was all-encompassing and made her feel valued.

"It's not your fault," she croaked.

"Aye, a father is neither an anchor to hold you back, nor a sail to take you there. But a light to guide the way. Maybe the batteries in that particular torch ran out, duck."

MARTIN LOOKED up at Rosa hovering over his desk, looking from her back to his screen he waited and when she remained silent, he clicked on the keypad to pause the image, "What's up?" he asked watching her struggle with something was on her mind.

"Is the D.I around?" She asked quietly.

"Somewhere, why?" Looking around herself, she passed him the file she'd been hiding behind her back, "What's this?" he asked curiously.

"Open it," she nodded, looking around again.

Feeling somewhat cautious, as though he would find some kind of banned substance, he peeled back the gummed opening. Peering in, he saw only sheets of paper. Looking back to her to ensure she had indeed just given him some paperwork and acted as though it was state secrets, she urged him to look. Taking the paper out slowly, he scanned the information, before flicking through to the one underneath and then the one underneath that.

"This isn't early retirement shit is it, cus I've got three kids to feed," he laughed. "What am I looking at?" He asked as confusion marred his face while glancing at the paperwork in his hands.

"DNA samples."

"Ok Poirot. Why am I looking at DNA samples, who do they belong to?" Grabbing the sheets as if he was annoying her, she flicked through until she came to the pages that held the identification and findings report. Passing it back to him, she watched his eyes widen and then look at her in disbelief. "When did you run these?"

"About a week ago."

"Holy fucking shit," exclaimed Martin, pushing back on his chair as though the results had sparked in front of him and he was backing away from a fire.

"Yeah, pretty much what I said," explained Rosa smirking.

Martin picked the paperwork back up, flicking through the sheets. "What gave you the hunch?" asked Martin, wondering why she had picked up on this and not him. Was he losing his touch?

"I went back to Robert's mum to take a statement and notify her. She didn't want to go through the ID process, so she opened her jewellery box to retrieve a lock of hair. A pendant was hanging in it, after the vine case I always note jewellery now. It caught my eye and when I asked her about it, she lied, said she couldn't remember where she got it. It suddenly hit me about the whole seed and fruit thing they got going on. What if her kid had come from that, then I thought it could be a common denominator? Seems I was right to be curious because then you told me about what the tests had brought up on the boys, so I pressed for these tests. As you can see, they all come back fairly conclusive."

"If this case has anything to do with the Vine Cross, then Daniel and Hayley are in trouble," said Martin, staring at the results in front of him.

"Yep, I don't think we can afford to discount this," Rosa concurred. "If we genuinely believe that they are going down the route of destroying all participants of the sect, then they could be next?"

"But why? They want nothing to do with it?" Asked Martin, standing up to which Rosa shrugged.

"Maybe they haven't got a choice; if this is blood driven, she could be the only living relative to who's doing this."

"No, that makes no sense. That would make her too important to take out, surely? Unless someone else was trying to remove it?" Said Martin, tapping his chin with the folder for some much-needed clarity.

"You think someone's trying to take over, getting rid of the old lot?"

"Crap, I have no idea how these people's minds work. It's like explaining the inner workings of a group of psychopaths."

Taking a deep breath, he sat back down and leant back in his chair while he tried to catalogue everything they knew. "OK, we have two boys killed. One with wings attached for Christ knows what reason. They're both related. You found evidence to suggest that their fathers are those we incarcerated, pending trial for crimes done in the name of the Vine Cross. And now we have this!" Waving the file in his hands. "And I've absolutely no idea what it tells us other than our boss is about to have his nuts put in the blender."

"So, do we bury it?" Asked Rosa.

Standing in silence, she waited for the cogs to turn in Martin's mind about how they would go forward with the information she had garnered. "Jesus Christ, I've no idea."

Rosa leant back on her heels, deflated. She hadn't had a clue either, and she was hoping Martin could talk her into doing something one way or the other. "Do you think she knows?"

"I suppose there's really only one way to find out," answered Martin. "You're going to ask her."

"Me? Why me?"

"You went digging around and found this, and if I go, she's unlikely to tell me the truth because of my relationship with Jesse. Plus, if she did admit it to me then I would have to tell Jesse. And if he finds out I know, I'll be taken off his Christmas card list and, in another nick, before you could say bring out the mine pies."

"Great, so I'm off his Christmas card list instead?" Mumbled Rosa.

"It won't get to that. When you find out, we'll both work out how to proceed."

"So, I'm telling her what? That I just fell upon this information and now I want her to spill her guts? What if she doesn't know? It will devastate her," answered Rosa.

"Then you have your answer," pointed out Martin.

"And if she knows, and she's been keeping this quiet?"

"That's when we have to work out why and how much she's involved. Keep schtum, and we'll work on that part together."

"You know she could go to Jesse and just tell him I accused her though, right?" Asked Rosa, taking the paperwork from Martin's hand.

"Use your feminine skills," winked Martin.

"Mention feminine anything to me again, and I'll break your masculine appendage," she smiled animatedly, whipping the paperwork from his hands before storming off.

"Sir!" Martin laughed. He loved winding her up.

THE VINE TREE

AN HOUR later Martin looked up to see Jesse coming towards him and scanned him for any signs of irritation. There was none, so relaxed a little.

"They've found a body at Cotham tip; grab your jacket, looks like we've got another."

Rosa and Martin shared a look as she entered the incident room with three coffees, a look that didn't go unnoticed by Jesse.

"Rosa join us, and then you two can explain the awkward glances while I decide whether to discipline the pair of you for having the lousiest poker faces, I've ever seen."

"It's fine, I'll explain in the car," admitted Martin, leaving Rosa to physically relax in front of them, while she handed them each their coffee.

"Jesus, what have you two been getting up to?" He asked warily, looking from one to the other. "Car, come on," he said, flipping the car keys in Martin's direction.

Rosa gave Martin a thankful look before watching him disappear behind the door.

"So, what's going on?" Asked Jesse, placing his drink in the cup holder and clicking his seat belt in, whilst wrestling with the paperwork piled on his knee.

Martin bit his bottom lip, watching for vehicles as he headed out of the car park. Pulling across the traffic, he made his way towards the traffic lights that would undoubtedly turn red as soon as he got there. Martin felt Jesse's eyes bore into the side of his head before he'd pieced together how he would pass the information on without getting himself or Rosa into any trouble, but no matter how he phrased it in his head it always ended in the same way. She'd broken protocol and breached confidentiality. But there was no way he would let her take the flack for that. Without it, they'd still be scratching their arses, although with it wasn't much different. It only led more weight to the argument that Jesse would have to leave the case, again.

Taking a deep breath in, he glanced to Jesse, confirming he had been staring at him, waiting impatiently for him to explain.

"You two shagging?" Asked Jesse.

"What? No! Jesus." Martin sighed. "We might have broken procedure," explained Martin cautiously. "Which may have confirmed that this case relates to the sect."

"How?" Jesse asked, intrigued.

"We ran some tests, DNA to be exact."

"OK," answered Jesse warily.

"Oh shit! There's no easy way to say this," admitted Martin on a sigh.

"Mart, just spit it out."

"Hayley is Frank's daughter." Stopping at the second set of traffic lights, he glanced at Jesse who looked like he'd taken a punch to the stomach and simultaneously taken a swift knee to the groin.

Giving him a few seconds to process, he pulled away and turned the car along the roundabout, taking him past the castle grounds that loomed over the old market town like a derelict wall. It was once important but now just invited eager tourists to reminisce over the reign of King Charles the second and the Civil war. The council had recently placed a bronze statue in the middle of the roundabout to show case the cavaliers and the round heads that had fought there in the sixteen hundreds. The statue caused much controversy in the town, especially when there seemed little money available to provide descent amenities to the local population.

Martin's head had wondered while he gave Jesse time to reflect on what he'd just told him. Making his way past the superstore and to another set of traffic lights he positioned himself in the left-hand lane to go forward and make his way out of town towards Cotham.

"So, Demy's her brother?" Asked Jesse absently as he watched the buildings fly by the passenger window. "Just when I didn't think that bunch of bastards couldn't get any worse," he said, shaking his head despondently.

"Technically, he's her half-brother," answered Martin. "Do you think she knows?" He asked cautiously.

"Christ, I don't know," he said shaking his head further as he ran his hand through his hair loosening knots. "If you knew that, would you want to admit to it?"

"No, but it leaves us with a bigger problem."

"What?" Asked Jesse, unsure he could take anything else on right now.

"Daniel."

"What about him?"

"Do we know the tests are correct? Do they? And how does that place him in their little sect thing?" Offered Martin looking to him as they waited for the lights to change.

"Daniel's mine," argued Jesse defiantly.

"Christ, I know that. The sprog couldn't look any more like you unless you did a Dolly the sheep, but that doesn't mean they believe it. Or if they do, that he's not still important to them," admitted Martin solemnly.

"You think he's a target?"

"It's a possibility. I mean, from what Hayley told us, it sounded like Rob might actually work on their behalf, and he threatened Daniel. Whether or not he did that to scare the crap out of her, we'll never know, I suppose. Unless we find him. But this sect doesn't look like it's giving up soon. This is about more than revenge. They want something. I just can't figure out what," mused Martin.

"Hayley, that's what they want," answered Jesse, feeling a little queasy.

"Yeah." Martin said, shaking his head as though he unconvinced. "I think it's something about Hayley." Flicking his gaze back to Jesse again, he realised he was listening intently so he carried on. "Rosa found a necklace at Robert's house. His Mum said she couldn't remember where she had got it, but Rosa says she was lying. Seemed uncomfortable talking about it. The necklace was the same as Hayley's. These kids are connected to this sect somehow. From what Rosa's dug up, she thinks they channel blood lines, to purify, maybe even to sacrifice. But Hayley could have been sacrificed ages ago, they've had her in their grips too many times to count and it's never been about killing her. So, it makes you wonder what it is about?"

"You think they set her up to carry a child for them, don't you?"

"It would make sense. Although why is beyond me," said Martin shaking his head in frustration. "Who's her mum?"

"They reported Helena Cartwright missing two thousand and seven, but Hayley said she saw her die. She came down one night from a particularly nasty argument when all had gone quiet and her dad, Baxter." clarified Jesse. "Was stood over her. Her mum was slumped up the wall with blood trickling down her face."

"So, Baxter had someone move her body. I can't see him having done that himself."

"Who knows, a lot could have changed before we set eyes on him," said Jesse, recalling Baxter's dishevelled appearance in his dilapidated house when they'd been there to question him over Hayley's disappearance over a year ago.

He didn't look like someone capable of premeditated murder and disposal of a body, he could barely dispose of the rubbish that had littered his house. But having allowed Hayley to be abused by Demy and the sect for years he'd finally come through in helping her escape and getting her to the police station, why? He'd never find out because when they went back to check on him, they had removed his body, leaving a pool of his blood in the living room.

The crime scene investigators had determined he was shot in the head, possibly from the back, as he sat and watched the sports channel. Whoever had done it took his body with them. They hadn't attempted to clean up, so forensics wasn't a concern for them, but maybe proving they'd delivered on orders was.

"Don't take this the wrong way, but do you think Hayley might be holding out on us?"

Jesse didn't answer, but the thought had crossed his mind before. But why would she lie to him? What could she possibly gain or was she just afraid? "What's happening with Rob?"

"Rob's gone dark. He took out all his cash from ATMs over the course of the last week and we found his car at East Midlands airport. He had tickets booked for Italy and had already landed before Hayley woke up."

"So, he knew what he was doing, he planned it."

"Looks that way."

"I don't get why he would try to get me to think they were together. If he was going to kill her, anyway." Martin shrugged. "I mean, what's the point? He could have just killed her."

"Maybe he just wanted to cause maximum damage. If you thought she'd cheated when she died, maybe he thought it would eat you up."

"I thought we'd sorted things out," admitted Jesse. "We seemed to be back to normal. How could I miss something like that?"

"Doesn't sound like there was much to miss. Besides, Hayley hadn't confided in you about what Rob was doing. Had you known, you might have been able to see the bigger picture quicker."

Jesse nodded contemplatively.

"How's your Mum and Dad?"

"Not good, they're putting on a brave face. Mum feels guilty, as though she somehow made him bad," answered Jesse.

"Joy of having kids, you feel responsible."

"Don't I know it," said Jesse, thinking of Daniel.

CHAPTER 14

That afternoon Hayley took Daniel outside. It was a pleasant day; the sun was shining, and it was warm enough to be out in a T-shirt, so she took to the back garden to hang the washing out. Feeling almost better and having Daniel sat on an old rug playing with his toys while she was the queen of domesticity felt calming. She couldn't get over how many clothes Daniel got through, but she quite enjoyed seeing them hanging from the line in Jesse's back garden. It felt nostalgic, but better. She and Jesse were working on things, mainly themselves. Since the attack she had opened up to him a lot more and the fear of telling him about Rob had been unfounded. He hadn't blamed her, which is what she'd assumed he'd do. He had comforted her, apologised for not seeing things clearer and promised to always be by her side no matter what, and something he said or did made her believe him.

"Long time no see!" Hayley looked to the fence.

A familiar figure stood in front of her, hanging over, perched on something as the fence stood up to six feet tall. The woman wore a tight-fitting pink blouse with her jet-black hair scooped into a pony tail. Hayley's eyes widened as she remembered who she was seeing.

"Oh, my god! Jemma!" Jemma smiled, glancing over to Daniel bashing plastic shapes together. "How are you?"

"Good. Good, you?" Asked Jemma watching Daniel. "He yours?"

Hayley laughed. "No, I kidnapped him, set a ransom for a Belgian bun before I hand him back."

"I'll take that as a hint; want to bring him over for some cake?"

Hayley shook her head, her smile waning as she realised Jesse wouldn't want her leaving the house. "Oh, come on, I've just iced a coffee cake. You'll be saving me from getting fat. Seems like an age since we caught up."

Hayley contemplated leaving the garden. It was only next door. Surely, he wouldn't mind if she just visited his neighbour for a cup of tea and a slice of cake? "Come on, I've only got an hour before I have to pick the kids up from school, I could do with some adult company."

Hayley laughed, she knew how that felt.

"OK," nodded Hayley. "Give me five minutes, I'll put another load on and be straight round."

"Good, see you in a minute," she called, stepping down from whatever equipment she'd used as a step. Hayley heard the conservatory door creak shut.

Knocking on the door with Daniel clinging to her like a monkey, she balanced her handbag on her shoulder. Jemma opened the door wide and led her through to the kitchen at the back of the house which overlooked the conservatory and garden revealing a football net and a patch of muck that was dug up from penalty practice.

"Bloody kids," muttered Jemma, seeing where Hayley's eyes had stopped. "Doesn't matter how many times I tell them, they have to slide, tackle, and dig up all the grass." Hayley couldn't help but smile, wondering if she'd be having the same conversation in a few years.

Placing Daniel on the floor, he gingerly stepped into the conservatory, holding himself up with the door frame and a wooden toy box as he peered round to investigate. "Oh my God, look at him. When did he start walking?"

"Recently, couple of weeks; he's still a little wobbly."

"Tea or coffee?" Asked Jemma, waving a cup in the air.

"Coffee please."

Taking a seat at the table, she eyed the coffee cake sat in the middle of the table. Jemma was always baking and then complaining about how much weight she put on because she was the only one in the house that ate. It amused Hayley; she was sure Jemma had picked it up somewhere that to be a good mother meant baking every day, and so she did. She was the type who looked content at housework and childcare, but Hayley recognised she was super smart too and wondered how she was content in such a mundane environment. Hayley loved Daniel to bits and whilst she enjoyed her days off from work with him; she loved being her own person too; she was unsure she could cope being stuck indoors every day.

"You look well," admired Jemma as she squeezed her own tea bag between two teaspoons to get the strength out.

"Thank you, so do you." Hayley fidgeted with turtleneck collar, hoping it was high enough to hide the marks she still sported, and avoid a conversation she didn't want to get into. Whilst her throat was still a little scratchy, it was now passable as a simple sore throat.

"I heard what happened," said Jemma.

Hayley's smile faltered.

"I'm sorry, are you OK now?" Hayley nodded. "I couldn't believe it when Jesse told me."

Hayley took a sip of coffee, feeling vulnerable. It wasn't like Jesse to disclose things about her, but then she presumed he'd asked her to keep an eye out for him.

~

"THERE'S MORE," said Mike begrudgingly as he walked around the stainless-steel table to a tall square table on wheels that held the implements to do his job. "We found these at the scene," he said, handing over a plastic evidence bag with what looked like playing cards inside.

"A Playing card?"

"That's what we thought at first, but there's a message on it."

"Where?" Asked Jesse, flipping it over and looking through the bag.

"Under UV light it says The Vine Cross will rule."

"Where was this?"

"Back pocket of his jeans," admitted the pathologist.

"The Vine Cross," answered Martin disbelievingly. The card, covered in Fleur de lis, sat with a vine cross in the centre. It was the brand on Hayley's back, the label on the drugs they'd recovered and the reason they kidnapped Hayley. "Well, that's just sealed the deal."

"Do you think it's them?" Asked Mike, watching the two faces in front of him pale.

"That cross is as synonymous to them as the swastika is to the Nazi's," said Jesse. "So yeah, it's them." Handing the evidence bag back to Mike, he stormed out the lab.

"I'm sorry it's not better news," spoke Mike sadly as Martin turned back towards him.

"It's not your fault. Besides, we've never found a calling card before. Maybe this will help," said Martin, picking it up from the table Jesse had left it on.

"I'm afraid to say there's no forensics on it."

"I figured as much," admitted Martin. Mike raised an eyebrow. "You would have led with it."

∽

"WHAT ARE YOU THINKING?" Asked Martin, catching up with him once he'd thanked Mike and picked up the paperwork detailing the blood work and the injuries sustained.

"That we need to find these bastards before they pull another family apart," answered Jesse, hoping he wasn't describing his own.

"Who first?"

"You take the swan, boy. I'll go to the second set of parents, they need an update anyway and Rosa can take the last one. Make sure you both take someone with you. I will pull Hancock out of recovering CCTV, and he's probably got square eyes by now, anyway."

"OK, sure, I'll let you know when I find anything," said Martin, pushing through a set of swing doors in search of Rosa.

"Martin!" Turning back, he waited while Jesse thought. "Keep the card to yourself, just for the moment."

"OK, what about Rosa?" Asked Martin, knowing she'd need to be as informed as them if she was interviewing next of kin.

"Just Rosa," confirmed Jesse before leaving Martin to continue.

∽

"To think evil sects are an actual thing, and only up the road, oh! It gives me shivers," said Jemma, shaking her shoulders for effect. "How did you get out?"

Deciding this was a bad idea, Hayley wasn't sure how to respond, so she looked around the kitchen awkwardly. Something didn't feel right, but she couldn't put her finger on why. The fact Jesse had told their neighbour more than she felt comfortable with wasn't helping her anxiety. She didn't do pitiful and sympathetic looks well, and she was getting her fill with Jemma across from her. She wished she'd asked for something stronger to drink.

"Oh, I'm sorry, that's vulgar of me, and it must be horrible to think about."

Hayley smiled politely and looked in Daniel's bag for his juice bottle. Anything to give her a distraction.

"I can't imagine having to stop with someone who treated me like that. It must have been terrifying," pried Jemma again.

Hayley smiled tightly, hoping she was giving the impression that she should move on from the subject.

"Do you have to give evidence?"

Hayley swallowed hard, she'd been attempting to keep all those worries to the back of her mind. She had enough going on in the present without worrying about the future.

"I'm sorry, I've not seen you in ages and here I go raking up all that for you, I'm being insensitive." said Jemma, finally understanding the atmosphere she was creating.

Moving towards Daniel, who had found some cars to play with. She placed his juice cup between his legs, glimpsing it, he snatched it up hastily before guzzling its contents.

"I think its best I don't talk about it, especially since the court case hasn't taken place yet," remarked Hayley, hoping she was coming across as polite but assertive enough to end the prying, as she sat back down on the chair watching Daniel.

"Are you working now?" Asked Jemma, taking a sip of her drink.

"No, well yes… I was. Till this last time, but I'll hopefully be going back again soon," said Hayley, glancing towards Jemma.

"I can't imagine that. Working with little uns, it's bad enough trying to get them out the door for school, never mind doing a full-time job."

Hayley nodded, taking a sip of coffee.

"I get six hours a day to tidy this place up and I swear it's still not enough."

Hayley looked around the place. It was spotless.

"So, are you and Jesse back together then?" Smiled Jemma, with stars in her eyes, eagerly waiting for gossip.

"I'm staying with him whilst I recuperate. We're taking it slowly, so we'll see," smiled Hayley. Before taking another sip of coffee, willing the drink to finish so she could escape the Spanish inquisition.

"You've got your own place now, haven't you?" Asked Jemma, taking a tin of biscuits down from the top shelf of the cupboard.

"Yeah, it's just a little flat. But it's nice enough," answered Hayley, twiddling her fingers in front of the cup she held.

"Want one?" Offered Jemma as she prized the top off, snatching a pink wafer off the top, holding it between her front teeth as she held the tin out to Hayley.

Hayley shook her head, then glanced at Daniel who had spied the tin and was shuffling on his bum to get closer, she smiled. "Maybe I'll get one for him," she laughed. Thanking Jemma as she opted for a none chocolate version before handing it to Daniel, who let out an excited squeal before shoving it in his mouth and sucking the life out of it.

"You ever thought about getting married?" Asked Jemma.

Hayley felt her throat dry out again and lifted the drink to her lips before replying that she hadn't. She wasn't about to tell her she'd had enough of marriages to last a lifetime.

"How long have you been together?" she asked, slicing a good wedge of cake from the immaculately decorated trophy in the middle of the table. Handing her the wedge on a clean white plate, she cut herself a piece half the size and Hayley hoped she would not expect her to eat the enormous slice she had offered her.

"We weren't together long before Daniel came about," answered Hayley evasively.

"Was it a one-night stand thing?" Asked Jemma. Flicking the forks, she grabbed from the cutlery draw, seemingly more interested in their relationship than Hayley liked.

"Err… no, not really. We just lost contact," Hayley answered diplomatically.

"Oh, that's a shame, so how long were you on your own?" Asked Jemma, taking a large bite of cake from her fork she'd shovelled into it earlier.

"six months," answered Hayley.

"You poor thing, must have been awful," continued Jemma, taking another bite of cake and savouring the coffee frosting. "I can't imagine being on my own. If nothing else, who would run out and get the gherkins?" Jemma laughed.

Hayley managed a humourless smile, but her mind wandered back to the time Demy used her as a punch bag and donation incubator. She still had nightmares of lying on the floor curled up freezing whilst her latest bruises came out, or the blood turning black enough to peel off. The shame of cutting her hair and disguising herself with blond hair dye, so that anyone who could offer help wouldn't recognise her from the pamphlets the police had doled out.

"Long story," answered Hayley. There was no way she would share those six months of her life with anyone. Those were her burdens to bare, no one else's, and no one could make her feel any worse about her involvement in them. Jemma raised her eyebrow.

"Might we need a hard liquor license for that conversation?" Asked Jemma.

Hayley laughed but didn't answer. No amount of liquor would ease that conversation, but she got the feeling that if she denied the opportunity, Jemma would dig her heels in more. She evidently saw her as some kind of project, just what she needed.

"We will have to get going. He needs a nap," said Hayley light heartedly, hoping he'd show some sign of tiredness to back her up.

"Nonsense, there's a cot upstairs. He can rest there," said Jemma, standing back up and pulling a bottle of white wine down with two glasses.

"Oh no, I don't think I can have that. I'm still on tablets from the hospital," said Hayley, watching Jemma twist the cap off.

"Oh, come on! One, that's it, don't make me drink on my own," whined Jemma.

Casting a look at Daniel who was not feigning tiredness in the slightest, she looked back up to Jemma's smiling, expectant face.

"One!" she replied, holding her index finger up while she watched the triumphant smile stretch across her face as she poured a full glass of wine. Hayley gave her a look of 'really?' whilst Jemma gave one back of 'it's still only one glass.'

"So, knight in shining armour, was it?" Asked Jemma, sitting comfortably on the dining chair as if she was getting ready for a bed-time story.

"Not exactly," Hayley took another sip of the strong dry white wine and then watched Daniel fumble with his wafer that held more moisture than the foam scouring pad from the sink. He'd made more crumbs out of it than seemed to hold it together, whilst resembling a lint wheel after a brush down over a sofa.

"Did you meet through his job?" Asked Jemma, taking another large mouthful of cake.

"No." His brother, thought Hayley, and didn't that come with a whole other part of the story she didn't want to repeat. Was her life always going to be this complicated? "We met at a party."

"So, what drew you to him?"

Hayley thought about it. She could answer this honestly and wanted to be congruent for a change, so she thought long before answering. "He was kind. Looked at me when he spoke to me, not just at me, but in my eyes. Like he was having a conversation with my soul." Not knowing where that had come from, she shook it away and laughed at her poetic explanation.

"Wow, don't be embarrassed that sounds amazing," said Jemma dreamily.

"Yeah, well, he was," Hayley cut a piece of her cake using the side of her fork, thinking maybe it was better if her mouth was working on food rather than speech. "Is."

"Can you remember what he was wearing?"

"Yep. He had a dark blue shirt, black jeans, brown boots and a leather jacket on," giggled Hayley realising how childish she sounded. "But it was his eyes. They pierce you. Hold you in the present."

"Wow, Tom's eyes are just this mucky blue colour," explained Jemma in a rather scornful tone.

Hayley laughed before taking a sip of wine again.

"You sound like you really love him."

"He's a good man," answered Hayley, nodding with a sinking feeling that maybe he was too good for her. "The best."

"Sounds to me like you should send out 'save the date cards,'" said Jemma.

"I don't think so, he's a divorcee and I'm really not into the whole marriage thing," answered Hayley.

"Shame, you'd look lovely in white," Hayley smiled before taking another sip.

∽

"DI Hallam." Jesse picked up his office phone and handed Martin a report from one constable who had been speaking to witnesses earlier in the day. Martin looked down to read while Jesse took the call.

"What, when?"

Martin lifted his head to the urgency in Jesse's voice.

"Is she OK?"

Martin put the paper on the desk, shooting Jesse a worried, questioning look.

"Where's Daniel?"

Martin grabbed his jacket off the chair slipping it on, not that it was cold it just held everything he needed in it; it was easier than emptying the pockets.

"I'm on my way." Jesse slammed the phone down. Grabbing his own blazer, he rushed for the door, opening it. "Hayley's in the hospital, someone's stabbed her." Running outside, they jumped into Martin's car.

~

JESSE AND MARTIN rushed into the hospital entrance, giving theirs and Hayley's names at the desk. After waiting a few tortuous minutes, they were shown down a corridor where a nurse came over to them.

"The Doctor will be with you shortly, if you'd like to wait in this room, I'll make sure he comes to see you as soon as possible," said the nurse gently as she walked them to a separate room away from the desk in the middle of the corridor.

On opening the door, Jesse saw Jemma holding on to Daniel who was crying uncontrollably. Standing up, she passed him over before wiping the stray hairs from her face. In doing so, Jesse noted the dried blood covering them and down her silk top.

"It looks worse than it is, I swear," said Jemma, watching his eyes take her attire in.

"What happened?" Asked Martin, watching Jesse struggle to calm Daniel down, as he bounced him while rubbing his back, and making soothing sounds in his ear.

"She went back to fetch a nappy and wipes and she was gone a while. I thought I best check on her. That was when I noticed the front door wide open. So, I stepped in just to see that she was all right and I found her in the kitchen on the floor. She was out cold. When I tried to wake her, that was when I saw the blood and called an ambulance."

"Where was Daniel?"

"With me. Like I said, she only nipped back. I said I'd watch him," answered Jemma.

"Thank you… sorry, what's your name?" Asked Martin.

"Jemma Radcliffe."

"Well, Jemma sounds like you did all you could."

Jemma stood slightly taller at that and smiled nervously. "Well, I best get back; I need to pick the kids up. Will you let me know how she gets on?" She asked Jesse. Nodding, she thanked him and walked to the door, turning back round she said. "I changed his nappy, hope that was OK?"

"Of course," laughed Jesse. "Thank you."

Nodding, she left, gently closing the door behind her.

"I'll pop round later, see if she remembers anything else. How you doing?" Jesse looked at him skeptically. "Sorry, stupid question." Watching Jesse sit down with a now much calmer Daniel. Martin glossed over the posters on the wall.

"Do you think it was him?" Asked Jesse after an age of silence.

"Too early to tell," answered Martin, walking over to the window. Looking out, he could see the wind had got up, as the trees swayed violently. "But I think we should start there."

"I will put a bullet in his head when I find him," admitted Jesse, laying his cheek softly on top of Daniel's head, looking at Martin with fire in his eyes.

"I won't argue with you on that one. But we've got to find him first," said Martin, leaning on the window with crossed arms and ankles. "Your gun license come through yet?"

"Yep," answered Jesse. "I can now legally carry and fire."

"Within reason," reminded Martin.

"I'll have reason soon enough, don't worry about that."

Just then the door swung open and Jesse turned to face it while Martin stood up from the window, placing his hands in his pockets to wait.

"I'm sorry for the delay. I'm doctor Nanniakara. I presume you're Hayley's partner?"

"Yes," answered Jesse, standing up whilst supporting Daniel's weight in his arms. "DI Jesse Hallam, this is DS Martin Wells."

"Police?" Asked the doctor. "But you are Hayley's partner?"

Nodding, Jesse walked closer to him as he scanned them both as if to check their credibility.

"OK. Well, Hayley sustained a bang to the head which knocked her unconscious. The cut to her abdomen was fairly superficial, in that it didn't go deeper enough to cause injury to any organs, and thankfully didn't hit any major blood vessels. But it has caused some muscle damage which will take time to heal. We have stitched her up, but because of her head injury we'd like to keep her in overnight just to be absolutely sure. She is resting, but I can show you to her now."

Jesse and Martin let out deep breaths of relief and followed the doctor out.

∼

LAID on the bed and hooked up to a drip, she was feeling like a freight train had hit her. Still weak but not as sleepy, she waited for the doctor to return. Seeing Jesse walk into her room, she let out a sob of relief at seeing him there. Quickening his pace, he was at her side in seconds, holding her hand in his with Daniel clenched to his chest with his free arm.

"What happened?" Asked Jesse, his words laced with concern.

"I don't know. I got home and someone came at me," answered Hayley.

"Did you see them?" Asked Martin.

"No. They were behind the door. I walked through to the kitchen and that's the last I remember until I woke up here."

Martin and Jesse shared a look, but Hayley was too busy smiling at Daniel to see it.

"How you feeling?" Asked Jesse, sitting on the side of the bed.

"Ask me something that means I don't have to curse in front of our son," she smiled before leaning back on the pillow.

Jesse noticed how tired she looked and if he didn't know better, she was trying to hide how much the whole thing had affected her by putting on a front. "Ok, I'm going to call Dad, see if he minds picking Daniel up, so I can stay with you."

"No. Don't be silly. I'm fine, honestly," said Hayley.

"You're not fine," argued Jesse. "Someone stabbed you." Standing up, he handed Daniel over to Martin, who took him awkwardly without pre-warning and walked out of the room while pressing on his phone screen.

"He's just worried," said Martin.

"I know," smiled Hayley tightly. "He just walks round with the weight of the world on his shoulders, and now I'm adding to it, again."

"You didn't ask to be stabbed," reminded Martin.

"I think it was a woman," said Hayley, watching Martin walk closer to her. "I smelt perfume like candy floss. Before I walked in the kitchen. I remember thinking Jesse must have bought a new air freshener, but I'd not noticed it before, and then everything went black."

"OK, that's good to know," nodded Martin. "Was the door unlocked when you popped back?"

"No, it was still locked."

"What about the back door?"

"I didn't get that far, but I'm sure I locked it before I went to Jemma's," answered Hayley.

"And there were no windows open?" Asked Martin.

"Not that I can remember."

"OK, we'll check it out when we get back. Have you heard anything from Darren?" He asked conspicuously.

"No. Why?"

"OK, Dad's on his way," said Jesse, walking back into the room.

CHAPTER 15

Jesse had sat with Hayley for almost an hour, and she'd been asleep for half that time before his Dad arrived to take Daniel home with him. Not wanting to wake her, he left to get a coffee and a cold drink from the vending machine along the corridor.

Martin had left soon after the call, saying that he'd call round his house to see how the police were getting on there, with a promise to call and update later, on his way back he saw a woman wondering the corridor as if she was looking for someone. When she spied him, she quickly shuffled off in the opposite direction. Watching her turn the corner, he entered Hayley's room to see that she was stirring.

"What happens now?" Asked Hayley, taking the offered fruit drink.

"An officer will no doubt come and take your statement soon."

"Is Daniel OK?" Asked Hayley, worrying about what he might have seen.

"Dad's feeding him chocolate buttons outside."

"He splitting them in half again?" Asked Hayley, trying not to laugh. "I keep telling them they'd melt before they choke him."

"You and me both, but it keeps him occupied," admitted Jesse, smiling before taking a sip of his coffee and grimacing.

"You look like shit," said Hayley observing his face and dishevelled shirt.

"Thanks," he chuckled, watching her smile return to her face. "Can't say you look much better." Then he held up her hand and kissed her knuckles. "You scared the crap out of me. I'm sick of seeing the inside of this hospital."

"Sorry, I wasn't planning on having any more nights in here either," she said, smiling sympathetically. "They told me last time they'd start charging me board for the amount of coffee they made you."

Jesse laughed, "That's because this coffee tastes like shit." He remembered how they'd looked after him. "How you feeling?"

"Do you really want me to answer that?" She asked sarcastically. Hayley could tell he was fighting back tears. "Hey, I'm fine, it's just a scratch," she soothed him. She hadn't realised how much he had been holding in whilst he had been waiting for her to come round, but it had shaken him. "I'll be fine, they've fixed it," hoping she looked more positive than she felt, she added. "Just a nick."

Just then Martin walked in, offering Jesse a coffee before realising he already had one. He wandered over to the windowsill and placed it there. Turning, he offered Hayley a smile before placing a box of a milk tray on the table that hung over the side of the bed. "Thought you might want cheering up and grapes don't really fit the bill," laughing, she thanked him before ripping the cellophane off the box. "Can I have a word?" Nodding, Jesse walked out of the room to stand with Martin in the corridor.

"What do you know?" Asked Jesse. Martin pulled out his phone, scrolling down he found what he was looking for and then showed Jesse. "A card?"

"It was in the kitchen."

"Does it have a message?"

"It says The Vine Cross will prevail." Jesse ran his hand through his hair, pulling at the roots. "So now we know."

Hayley sat watching Jesse pace with anguish coating his face.

Spying her, Martin took Jesse's arm, steering him out of Hayley's view further along the corridor. "He's trying to panic you."

"Well, it's working," snapped Jesse. "He's circling."

"Yep, he could have taken her today. Why didn't he?" mused Martin. "Jesse, I think we have to face facts that this could be more about Daniel than you'd like to think."

"But why? It makes no sense." Martin just shook his head. He didn't understand either. Suddenly Jesse's phone rang, and he lifted it out of his pocket, seeing it was his Dad he accepted whilst frowning at the video app, his Dad never video called him.

∼

WATCHING Martin and Jesse race past her window made her sit up, wincing at the pain, but only concerned with how threatened they looked. Just then a woman with tied back, dark brown hair in a bun entered with a surgical mask over her mouth and nose, dressed in pale green scrubs, holding a clipboard in her hand.

"I'm here to take you into surgery," said the lady, slightly muffled by the mask.

"No, I'm fine. They told me I just need to rest," answered Hayley absently, wondering where Jesse had run to.

"I'm afraid that's not the case," said the nurse, taking a syringe from her pocket with a bottle of clear liquid. Placing the needle in the bottle, she tipped it and pulled the liquid into the syringe. Once satisfied, she took Hayley's arm and plunged the needle in.

"What are you doing?" Shouted Hayley, snatching her arm away. But when the nurse pulled her mask down, she was even more confused. "Lynnie?" suddenly feeling cool then drowsy, Hayley felt all her muscles relax and her eyelids close under their own weight.

∼

Jesse knelt on the floor crying. Blood coated his trousers and pooled on his shirt, but that was the least of his worries as he held his father's head, watching the life seep from the wound opening his throat.

When Jesse had got the call, it was a video showing Daniel in the back of a car with his Dad on the outside being pinned up against it. Daniel was screaming and his Dad was looking at the person behind the phone, terrified, before Jesse had to watch a knife slice across his own father's throat. By the time they reached the carpark Michael was already bleeding out. Dumped on the ground as though he was nothing more than unwanted litter.

Martin was immediately on the phone calling for assistance while passersby gathered and paramedics from a returning ambulance, rushed over with a stretcher and first response kit. But one look at the man covered in blood told them nothing they could do would help. Whilst they checked for a pulse, Jesse grabbed onto his Dad as if pure will power would heal the wound.

∽

SITTING IN A ROOM, silently replaying the slaughter of his father in his head as though it was on a continuous loop, Jesse stared into space.

Martin hadn't left his side, but noticing how many minutes had passed he realised he would have to inform Hayley about Daniel and Michael as Jesse was in no fit state to do anything. Once the tap on the door came, Martin opened it and ushered the police officers in. Telling them he'd be back as soon as he'd informed Hayley. When he reached her room, he took in a deep steady breath before blowing it back out, and readjusting his neck on his shoulders. Walking in, he noted the bed was no longer in the middle of the room. Spinning back round, he walked over to the reception. "Hi, where's Hayley Timpson."

"sorry I can't-" Taking out his I.D she scanned it before telling him she was in the room he'd just vacated.

"She's not there, there's no bed," answered Martin.

Looking unsure, she nervously tapped on the keys and scrolled through the data on her screen.

"No, she should be in there, there's nothing logged," answered the sweet but slightly dopey young receptionist.

"OK, we will try this again," said Martin, leaning his arms on the top of the high desk. "She's not there, so, where is she?"

"I've no idea, there's nothing logged in the system," she answered politely but sternly.

Slapping his hand on the desk, she jumped. "Get me the CCTV that covers that room, now!"

Unsure of what to do. She looked back down the corridor.

"Now!" shouted Martin. Quickly picking up the handset, she tapped away before saying a quick hello and relaying Martin's message in a more measured tone.

∼

TWENTY MINUTES LATER, the commotion outside made Jesse wander over to the door. Looking through the slim line window, he noted four officers in uniform walking around, talking to staff. Pulling on the door Jesse entered the active corridor, uniforms were taking notes and asking questions while nurses tried to overhear without being too obvious about it, but failing.

Wandering over to a uniform, who was writing information down on his notepad, Jesse took his identification out of his inside pocket, holding it up ready for when the man turned. "Excuse me, what's with all the uniforms?" Hoping it was because of his Dad but with a sickening belief it wasn't.

Turning, Jesse could tell he was about to deliver a line of the no comment variety, but then on seeing his identification he lowered his head before looking around. "Are you not here for the same reason?" Asked the officer.

"No, I was just in the visitor's room. I saw all the uniforms," admitted Jesse.

Nodding, the officer seemed to consider once again whether he should tell him.

"Look, I'm not on the clock, but if they need me to be, I'd rather know what's going on."

"Apparently a woman's gone missing from upstairs. They're trying to find her. It seems she must be important because we arrived in force about ten minutes ago."

Nodding, Jesse thanked the officer before watching him leave. When a feeling in his stomach told him that the officer was talking about Hayley, he rushed to the elevator before punching the number furiously. Inside, he noted the dried blood under his fingernails. He needed to wash them. Tears sprayed from his eyes as he stumbled back, using the wall for support. Visions of his dad lying on the floor in a pool of red liquid battled for space in his head over seeing his son screaming and imagining Hayley's hospital room empty.

∼

"Jesse." Raising his head, he watched a pale Martin walk towards the open elevator. "She's gone."

Already thinking it did nothing to prepare him for the information he'd hoped he was only imagining. Dropping to the floor, his legs finally gave way. Feeling Martin try to move him from the lift; he stumbled to exit before slumping up against the reception desk.

"Hayley's not in her room," admitted Martin. "I requested the CCTV. Jesse, a woman, went in dressed as part of the surgical team. She took Hayley in the lift and exited out by the morgue on the ground floor at the back. Two men took her off the gurney and placed her in the back of their Tranny van."

If Jesse thought he'd gone through every emotion already, he was sadly mistaken. The shock took him a second or two to wade through, but when he did, it flooded his body with adrenalin and anger.

"Are you fucking kidding me!" Shouted Jesse.

Martin unconsciously took a step back. As much as he'd done to locate Hayley, he knew Jesse wasn't in his right mind. "It was a diversion." stated Martin. "I think they got us out the way so they could take Hayley."

"They have them both," warned Jesse. "Jesus Christ Mart, they have them both!" Cried Jesse, cradling his head whilst on his knees.

~

Hayley could hear voices, but her head was pounding too loudly to translate. Shifting her heavy head, she attempted to prise her eyes open, but they wouldn't budge. The fog in her head was making it difficult to get her bearings.

"What was I supposed to do?" Hissed a female voice.

Hayley froze, recognising the well-spoken but shrill voice.

"Not cause her such injury; she needed to be in good health. He will go ape shit," warned the man's voice.

"How was I supposed to get her to the bloody hospital? If I just cracked her over the head, she'd have come round and just taken Paracetamol," whined the girl.

"We will have to cover it up."

"How?" Asked the girl.

When there was no response, she tried again to open her eyes. Squinting at the bright light shining over her, she scrunched her eyes up and tried to shade them with her arm, but on trying to lift her arm she realised she couldn't move it, looking down, noting they tied her to the bed frame with gaffer tape. Attempting to move her legs, she noted they were free, but dull in feeling. Still being blinded, she attempted to scan the room she was in. It felt small, confined, but still the light blinded her.

Suddenly the door opened and someone came in, but the light prevented her from seeing the person's face.

"Ah, you're awake." It was the man from earlier. "We need to get you dressed, he's waiting."

Without warning, he ripped open her hospital gown with a pair of scissors. Once the cool air hit her bare skin, she shivered. "Get off!" She shouted, thrashing her legs as her wrists remained pinned to the bed. "Get off me!"

"Lynnie, get in here!" Shouted the man. "Your sisters waking up, give me a bloody hand!"

Hayley momentarily stilled, working out if the voice she'd heard earlier indeed belonged to her sister.

"Where's the corset?" Asked Lynnie on entering the room.

Hayley wanted to see her to confirm, but the light was blinding and she wanted to beat the shit out of it.

"I left it on the couch,"

Realising Lynnie had left, Hayley took a breath before swallowing; her heart was thudding like a herd of elephants charging.

"That'll be the drugs." said the man, as if reading her mind.

"What am I doing here?" She asked once Lynnie had reentered.

"I'm getting you dressed for your performance," answered Lynnie.

She felt Lynnie slip a patch of fabric under her back. Once she brought the pieces together, she heard them being click. Getting tighter as she continued down. Next, Lynnie pulled a thong up her legs, and over her hips, once in place a suspender belt was put in place and then she rolled stocking up her legs clipping them to the belt evenly around the tops of her thighs. Lastly Lynnie pushed a belt around the back of Hayley's throat. Once it was in place, she tightened it so it was snug, before clipping on a metal chain. All the while Lynnie hummed a familiar tune as though she was just fulfilling a hobby or a chore. Once she finished, she stood. Turning the lamp away, Hayley could finally see once her eyes adjusted.

"Ok, I will release your wrists, but if you try anything funny, we'll make you pay," warned Lynnie. "Do you understand?"

Nodding furiously, she watched Lynnie cut the tape. Bringing her wrists to her now tightly bound chest, she rubbed at them, trying to gain feeling back into her fingers.

"OK. Stand up," commanded Lynnie.

Watching both the man and Lynnie, she gently swung her legs over to one side of the bed and pushed herself to stand. But once she stood, her balance shifted, and she fell forward, taking a breath as she tried again and wavered.

THE VINE TREE

"OK, shoes." Lynnie placed two red stilettos on the floor in front of her. "Put them on."

Hayley already knew there was no way she'd be able to walk in them.

"They won't be on long."

Hayley wasn't sure whether she should feel relieved at that. As she slipped her feet into them and gained an extra four inches in height. Tightening around her feet, she felt ready to topple.

"OK, there's a mirror here, walk round and stand in front of it."

The mirror was on the opposite side of the door to her stood full length. Glancing to the man, she could see he was enjoying seeing her dressed up like a Moulin rouge extra. Deciding to do as she was told while she could, she tiptoed round to the mirror unsteadily. Now she knew how Bambi felt.

Standing in front of the mirror she could see the red and black laced corset, the black lace stockings and suspenders, and the heavy black belt collar that a heavy thick looking chain hung from being held by the man, who was examining her like a piece of meat he wanted to devour. Just then Hayley felt her stomach tugged in even tighter from her sister pulling fiercely on the corset laces at the back. Once she was sure she'd pass out from lack of oxygen, or from the sharp pain in her side, Lynnie stopped pulling and tied the ends up to keep the shape. Her stomach was now wafer thin and her boobs hung over the top precariously, making them seem four times bigger.

Hayley glanced in the mirror to see if she could see anything else in the room without turning around and making it too obvious. But it was just her, him, her sister, the lamp and the bed they had tied her to.

Pulling out a radio from her underneath her top at the back of her jeans, Lynnie put it to her lips, static followed before she relayed a message, they were ready and to set the room up. Placing the radio back behind her, she grabbed a lipstick from her front pocket, taking it out. She swivelled the stick up before layering it onto Hayley's lips. Satisfied, she told Hayley to purse her lips and then she brushed black eye shadow on her lids, before taking out a black pencil. Not wanting to be poked in the eye, Hayley took it from her and drew a grim line under her eyes.

"Much better." smiled Lynnie.

Walking to the door, she opened it back up and waltzed out. The man did the same, tugging the chain with him so Hayley had to follow. Once they were outside the room, Lynnie tapped three times on another door before opening it up. Once Hayley entered, she saw the throne-like chair in the middle of the darkened room and a nasty feeling sat in the pit of her stomach. Darting her eyes around the room, she noticed all the paraphernalia. Whips, belts, chains, toys, paddles, and an insurmountable treasure chest of things that didn't look entirely familiar, but drew fear into her, anyway.

"Sit in the chair." Demanded a voice.

When she turned, she saw Frank, and a rush of fear shook her body from head to toe. As soon as he saw the look on her face, he smiled, pleased with himself. Knowing he terrified her worked for him. The chain tugged. They led her to the chair. Sitting down, she defiantly kept her eyes on Frank.

Watching Frank crouch down in front of her, she reared back. Frank didn't kneel for anyone, and he'd never allow her to have more height on him. It was a sign of power he never gave away. Watching the others leave, she heard the door lock but dared not take her eyes from his.

"You look stunning, my child." Hayley swallowed. "We have Daniel."

Her breathing became erratic, and he seemed to get turned on by watching her chest rise and fall.

"Michael is dead and if you don't do as I demand, Jesse will be next." said Frank calmly and evenly. "So, you need to tell me where she is?"

"Who?" Asked Hayley, confused.

Frank watched her intently as he tutted.

"I don't know who you mean."

"Did you really think you could keep something like that from me forever?"

Hayley tried to breathe, but the corset was hurting her, digging into her offended side.

"The baby didn't die, did it?" Frank chided.

Hayley couldn't stop the tear falling down her face, and there was no point. He was looking straight at her and he knew the truth. "Where is she?"

"I don't know," answered Hayley, watching him grow agitated. "I don't know, I swear."

Seeing Frank stand up, she watched him walking around the room, touching implements that hung from the wall.

"I believe you." Frank finally admitted.

But Hayley's relief was short-lived.

"But that leaves us, or mainly you, with a gigantic problem."

Turning back to her, he walked over to her holding a horse whip, twisting it in his fingers like a majorette. "That son of mine is an idiot, but he's also the only reason you're still alive."

"I don't know what you mean," admitted Hayley.

"No. You don't do you?"

Rubbing his thumb down the side of her face, she pulled away from him, but the lash to her thigh was unexpected and she screamed. Looking down, she watched as the welt grew in size and stung.

"You had one job," said Frank. "All you had to do was to carry *his* child."

"He threw me down the stairs," cried Hayley. "I tried to do my job," she answered through gritted teeth.

"So why tell us she died?" Whispered Frank in her ear.

"Because you would kill her," answered Hayley. "I heard you."

"And what made you think, that was a choice you could make?" Asked Frank, moving her shoulder length hair behind her ear.

"I was her mum," she mumbled, knowing full well that that held no weight with him. For her in meant everything, her blood, her responsibility, her love, her child.

"And I was her father," answered Frank.

Hayley shivered at the memory. "You lost me a lot of money, Hayley, more than you can imagine."

Hayley didn't understand, but she would not ask him what he meant. She wasn't sure she wanted to know.

"Do you know how much people pay for thoroughbred horses these days?"

Hayley shook her head, keeping her gaze forward while he circled her.

"Not nearly as much as a child."

"I don't know where she is," cried Hayley desperately.

"No, I know. Darren said." With the mention of his name, she flipped round to see his eyes. "Before I finally plunged that ornate knife, he liked to experiment with so much into his heart."

Hayley's stomach lurched, but she swallowed the acid down as tears welled in her eyes.

"I tortured him. He squealed like a pig. But he was brave, a tough kid. You'd have been proud of him," Hayley couldn't stop the sob from leaving her throat. "But him like you. Cost me money."

Walking so he was in front of her, he placed his hands on the top of her thighs as he weighted down on them so that his nose was touching hers. "So, you'll pay me back some of what you stole and give me back the respect I deserve."

"I can't. I have no money," she answered.

"No, my darling. But you have this," he said, watching his own hands sweep down her body, holding onto her tiny waist as he pulled her towards him, so he stood between her legs. "This body will be for my pleasure and my pay back and then when we're finished, you'll carry my child once again and finish the deal we made all those years ago."

"But Demy's supposed to be the father, and he's in prison. How am I supposed to pretend it's his when he's behind bars?" Frank laughed at that and stepped back.

"Oh, my dear child, your cop friend hasn't been very honest with you, has he? Demy escaped, and he's here." Hayley wanted to pass out. "And we will record it for the evidence that the counsel requires."

Shaking uncontrollably, she cursed her body for betraying her.

"After that you'll be mine to have, and I have every intension of getting what's owed."

Hayley could feel her stomach wanting to expel, but held her mouth closed, willing it to relent. "And just in case you get any grand ideas of escaping again, I have Daniel. So, unless you want him to come to any harm, you'll do exactly what I say."

"You can't keep him for all that time," she cried. "Take him home, I'll do it. I swear."

"Unfortunately, the past dictates otherwise, and besides, he can stay with you once you've taken part in our brief presentation."

"What presentation?"

Smiling, Frank pulled a black curtain across from right to left, revealing behind it, three cameras positioned in a way that pointed to her from slightly different angles. Behind that was a screen with live footage of Daniel playing with some cars, and a bottle of milk beside him. On seeing him, she pressed her lips together, trying to stem the flow of tears that threatened. Frank was watching her face intently and as she turned to him, he pressed a button on the screen that got rid of Daniel and brought up a list of details with amounts next to each item, and a vote count.

"So, this is a voting system. We give the subscribers a list of things they can watch. They vote and pay. If they win the vote, they get to watch it. Whilst all others are momentarily blocked. It ensures those that want to see something pay the most. Each vote amounts to around a thousand pounds each, so our job is to make sure they get what they pay for. If they don't, then my clientele would look elsewhere."

Hayley watched him detail what he had planned for her as though he was offering produce at a supermarket.

"I have turned off anything that could stop your chances of conception, and of course we have taken out the snuff button."

Hayley closed her eyes, trying to breathe through her mouth slowly to control her growing anxiety.

"So, they have six hours to place their votes, starting when I leave this room. We will record you throughout the vote casting, so don't do anything you wouldn't want people to see." laughed Frank, watching her glare at him with hatred. "If you even think about doing anything silly, I'll take it out on that little boy."

Walking closer to her, he grasped her chin, so she had to stare right at him. "I know men who'd pay good money for him, he's a cute kid," sneered Frank. "And I have to admit, I can't wait to get back inside you. I will make sure you don't even remember your pig friend's name."

Letting go of her chin, he tapped on the door before they opened it for him. Once it was closed again with a lock clicking into place, the three cameras flashed with bright red lights. Looking back at the screen, she watched the amounts rise and messages scroll along the bottom that she couldn't read as they were too small from such a distance. Knowing she was being watched when all she wanted to do was cry had her looking around the room, for anything that could take her mind off why she was there. But everything in that room was for only one reason, and that was to deprive her of any self-respect, worth or humanity. They would finally destroy her and it would be in this room in front of hundreds of depraved individuals.

CHAPTER 16

Jesse sat with his head in his hands, waiting. They had brought him back to the station and were sitting in DCI Walkers office awaiting a meeting, whilst trying to not go out of his mind with worry. Having watched his hero murdered, cradling his head in his lap while his life seeped into his clothes and the concrete beneath them. He'd then had to endure hearing that not only had his son gone, but they had abducted Hayley too. Having undergone questioning and put up with well-wishers providing their thoughts, they exhausted Jesse. The last thing he needed was a meeting, but he understood the DCI needed to be abreast of his case, especially now that he was unlikely to be on it while his own family took up all his thoughts and resources.

"I'm sorry to keep you waiting, Jesse," said the DCI as he walked into the office and sat behind his desk.

"It's fine," said Jesse, noticing the blood that sat under his fingernails; he needed to get them washed.

"No, it's not. But needs must I'm afraid," admitted DCI Walker. "I'm sorry for what's happened today, I can't imagine-" But he didn't finish his sentence when he noticed Jesse fighting the wobble of his bottom lip. "Anyway, I need to know where you are with the swan case." Jesse nodded heavily. Just then the door opened again, letting in Martin and Rosa.

Martin took the seat next to Jesse while Rosa leant up against the door as if to prohibit anyone entering or leaving.

Jesse instantly felt better knowing they were there to help him get through this. "Sir, we had a suspect. DNA on the boy's clothing and confirmation from parents that the boys were with the same man. Problem is, he later allegedly took his own life. Later it became apparent that someone had injected him with heroin and we believe while he was high, they tied him up, to make it look like a suicide attempt. Unfortunately, we have no suspects who might have done that or why unless directly linked to the boys' deaths and someone found out, taking the law into their own hands. We have identified the twine used to strap the wings to the boy, but regrettably it's nothing special. Regular garden twine and a nightmare to track. We know they kept both boys refrigerated prior to dumping, and as of now we still don't have a reason for that. The second boy had a brand on his back and it's almost identical to the one used last year." Jesse took a breath to gather his wits. Any mention of the sect right now was like a dagger to his already brutalised heart.

"Plus, a message cut into the torso on the man found near the Trent, which identifies association with the sect. We recently recovered another body, who we are yet to identify. There was another card associating this back to the sect. We believe at this point that all these deaths are related to the sect, especially as we found a pendant at one boy's houses and his mother refused to tell us where she got it from."

"Sir," spoke Martin, glancing to Jesse as if apologising. "We have identified the man found at Cotham tip, as Darren Baxter."

"Hayley's brother?" Asked Jesse.

Martin nodded solemnly.

"Sir, we also have reason to believe that Hayley is Frank's daughter," said Rosa quietly. "DNA confirms a match."

"Who authorised a DNA check?" asked DCI Walker.

"I did, sir, with Hayley's permission," lied Jesse. "Demy's was already on the database."

"You should have come to me with that," stated DCI Walker on a steady breath. "OK, so we have nothing on the boy's death?"

"Not much sir, no, it's almost like they've disappeared into thin air. If it hadn't been for their bodies being displayed, we might have never known they were missing," answered Martin.

"Families?"

"Dodgy as fuck. But so far, they have alibis. Unfortunately, their timescales aren't too reliable though," answered Martin.

"The families are definitely hiding something, sir. But we've been unable to determine what," admitted Rosa.

"How far have you pushed that?"

"As far as we can. Medical reports, school, nurseries, neighbours, but there's nothing conclusive coming back. Just a lot of nothing," answered Jesse. "We've checked finances and there's nothing untoward there either."

"So, we have no motive and no weapon. Witnesses or leads of any kind?" All three looked at him shaking their heads defeated.

Jesse was all too aware that had today not been the worst day of his life, his boss would rip him a new one. Clearly, he was trying to keep his temper in check as he breathed out through his mouth and in through his nose. "OK, well, as I'm sure you're aware I will have to pass this case on to another team. So, if you'll make sure that happens immediately and as smoothly as possible, I'd appreciate it, Martin and Rosa. Jesse, I won't be expecting you in the office for the foreseeable future for obvious reasons and you have my sincerest sympathy."

"Thank you, sir," said Jesse.

"I'm going to do something incredibly unusual, and that's come clean about something from the other year."

When all three of them exchanged looks, they leant forward and waited for the DCI to continue.

Taking a deep breath in, he scanned their eager faces and almost wanted to laugh at their expectant faces. "Over a year ago, I had Dave in here bleating on about how Jesse might be tied up in the abduction of Hayley."

They all nodded. This wasn't news to them. He'd been a dirty cop and had obviously been trying to set Jesse up. They had sacked him for not following procedure. There had been a lot more that he'd done, but evidence of the facts and his handling hadn't been forthcoming. So, the only road they could go down was termination of employment due to not following procedure and protocol.

"I called his old DCI to get some background. What he told me was enough to consider that he was involved in the coverup and potential set up."

"We already know this sir," explained Jesse, not wanting to sound irritated.

But while he was in this office, he wasn't out there looking for his son and Hayley.

"I know, but what you don't know is that Dave's old DI is under suspicion of taking back handers. It seems DI Templeton wasn't being as careful as he thought, because once IA got involved, they ripped his team apart."

"What's this got to do with today?" asked Martin, sensing Jesse's struggle.

"On that same team was a guy who now goes by the name of DCI Mansfield."

"He was the guy who arrested me," answered Jesse.

"Yes, and in doing so, I decided to do a little digging. It seems this man might not be as squeaky clean as we first thought."

Unlocking the top drawer of his desk, he rifled through some paperwork until he came to a blue manila folder. Placing it on the desk, he opened it up to pictures of DCI Mansfield at different places from some distance.

"I spoke with an old friend of mine who offered to help, he's a PI. With a bit of information, he was able to find out what the DCI has been getting up to, and yesterday he posted this to me."

Finding the correct photo, he handed it to Jesse, who angled it so Rosa and Martin could see.

"Demy Richards," said Rosa, glancing to DCI Walker as if he'd confirm what she was seeing.

"Why's he speaking with Demy Richards?" Asked Martin.

"I'll get to that. My friend thinks he had something to do with the escape. The only other police official in the gaol when the truck hit, was DCI Mansfield. Supposedly visiting an inmate for information on the case he is investigating. When I spoke to his chief, he couldn't understand why he'd be there or who he was speaking with and not only that, but he'd never reported being there."

"I'm not sure I completely understand what you're saying," said Jesse warily.

"I'm saying I strongly believe that not only was Mansfield working for Demy and his cronies when he was in the same team as Dave, but that when they cleared him, he continued in his own team. It always bothered me how swiftly they arrested you once they took the statement from Lynnie. It was as though it was already pre-planned, and of course at the same time the shipment was being moved. Creating a hell of a diversion that might have worked had it not been for the information garnered from the surveillance Martin installed. Look, right now, I have no conclusive evidence, which is why I mentioned nothing before and have been trying to gain information on the quiet so as not to raise too many red flags. It's quite plausible that he could cause damage to us and our case if he saw we were attacking, so I needed to make a watertight case, but with the predicament we're all now in, I think we need to get to Mansfield before Demy."

"You think he's in danger?" Asked Rosa.

"It depends what Demy wanted him to do. If he's completed his role, then I don't think it's out of the realm of possibility."

"Sir, I'm sorry if this sounds tactless, but how the hell is this supposed to help us?" Asked Jesse.

"Because I now have leverage on Mansfield. Maybe we can use it to get Hayley and Daniel back. I have a complete dossier on him and his back handed deals, but we can use it as blackmail to get to Demy. If Mansfield believes he's about to be spun over, and then we come in with the proof, he'll need to believe they have set him up. I'm hoping he'll flip on Demy and at least get us to Hayley and Daniel."

"But that would require handing everything over," answered Martin.

"Exactly. What we gain with one hand, we lose in another. It's going to take a lot of subterfuge, but I'm willing to play the part of someone who's been working for Demy, if you lot can back me up if the shit hits the fan."

"Are we going undercover, sir?" Asked Rosa, concerned.

"We're on our own."

When all four looked at each other, they knew they'd be going into territory that could not only be dangerous but illegal. Checking they were all on board, they nodded before Martin slapped his hands together.

"OK, what do we do?"

∽

A few hours later, Adam Hancock entered the room they had commandeered at the police station. All turning from the table they were leaning over, they watched him approach. "They've got divers checking the Devon where they found the van, and they're scouring the park. CCTV is still being checked, but so far they have nothing," said the Adam shaking his head with frustration.

Jesse bowed his head, hoping he would see them alive soon and not identifying their corpse.

"I can't see them using the Devon, it's too close to home," said Martin.

"I agree," nodded DCI Walker. "This is far too thought out. They're prepared and trying to throw as many red herrings our way as possible."

"Which means they need time," stated Rosa.

"Time for what?" Asked Adam.

"Something they can't do straight away," shrugged Rosa. "If they're buying time, then it means we have time," admitted Rosa, looking straight at Jesse as though to offer comfort.

"Wasn't Demy involved in sex trafficking?" Asked Adam.

Martin shot him a look to shut up. None of them needed reminding of how depraved the son of a bitch was, least of all Jesse.

"I'm just saying if that's his business, then maybe we need to look at how he transports them. Maybe he's waiting for a boat to get her out of the country."

"His dads in marketing," said Rosa quietly. All eyes on her, she realised they required her to expand on her comment. "OK, hear me out. With his credentials, I'd bet my life savings that he could sell ice to an Eskimo."

"So?" Asked Martin.

"So, what if he's selling something on the dark web?"

"You think he's waiting for bids?" Asked DCI Walker.

"It would make sense why they took them earlier than needed. They'd need to be secured in order for bids to take place. I heard from Dana in vice that it works much like any selling page. The highest bidder gets the goods. Of course, with it being the dark web it can be anything, drugs, weapons, women, children." As she finished, she watched Jesse drop into his chair. "I'm not saying that that is what's going on," she countered. "But it's an option."

"But it makes sense, and he is a sick bastard," remarked Martin, laying his hand on Jesse's shoulder. "Can you get someone to look into that?"

Rosa nodded before leaving the room to make a call.

Silence filled the room, and all minds wandered to the horrors that could befall Hayley and Daniel as they stood around the table contemplating a plan.

"I still think this is more than just sex," said Martin finally.

When the DCI, Jesse and Adam looked at him, he shuffled on his feet.

"Do you know something?" Asked Jesse.

Martin glanced to the DCI. Seeing him nod, Jesse caught the air change and stood back up, glancing from one to the other, impatiently waiting.

"Last week someone sent us a USB. It had no letter, and I had no idea who it was from, but they addressed it to me. When I put it in the computer, I realised they'd heavily encrypted it, so I took it down to Jeff, one of the techie's downstairs, a bit of a whizz kid."

"Martin, get to the fucking point before I die of old age," snapped Jesse.

"He found a video. It was Darren informing us of what to expect, and he said there was going to be a war over the leadership of the vine cross. He said Hayley was pivotal in the right person gaining the crown and that we should keep her safe at all times."

"And you're only just telling me this now?"

"I only found out this morning. Like I said, he encrypted it. By the time I'd got the message, she was already in hospital. I was coming back to let you both know when the call came through."

"But he informed me, and I've been working with Jeff all morning," answered the DCI. "From what Darren says, it sounds like her betrothal came with a life plan designed even before her own mother was born," continuing on a sigh. "He also listed the many people responsible for the trafficking connected with the vine cross."

"We had that before," said Jesse, unconvinced.

"No, they gave us the names of the people who ran things for *them*; *these* are the people who dictate those moves. These people are MPs, business tycoons and presidents. This thing is huge and fraught with potholes. We make one wrong move with this information and not only will we be waking up with a horses' head in our bed, but we'll more than likely have our families shot dead quicker than we can shout Goodfellas." stated Martin.

"You know that was the Godfather, right?" asked DCI walker.

When both Jesse and Martin looked at him like he'd grown two heads, he shook his head and apologised.

"Did you know it was Darren, when we arrived?" Asked Jesse, wondering if he'd recognised what they had left of him when they'd visited his resting place at Cotham tip, but kept it to himself.

"No, he was a mess remember, and I only met him once," answered Martin thinking what information to divulge about the injuries he'd sustained before death. It had been obvious when they had seen him laid out that they had tortured him. Nothing was going to come as that much of a shock. "They removed his tongue before slitting his throat."

Just the word throat had him thinking of his dad's body on the video, and Jesse sat down on the nearest chair before his legs gave out. He had no time to think about his Dad things were heating up and he still had to find Hayley and Daniel before they received the same fate. The news that they'd tortured Darren so badly before death did nothing to allay his fears about those, he loved most being in the hands of such nefarious people.

"I don't think I can take anymore Mart, they're fucking animals," said Jesse as he lifted his head to look at them both. "Who else knows?"

"The team. They're under strict instructions not to let this information go any further," answered DCI Walker.

Jesse nodded, he knew how important it was to keep that information to themselves, especially when it seemed like they couldn't trust too many people around them. His team had been infiltrated before, and the feeling that someone on his team might put both his child and Hayley in danger ate away at him. Working down his team members in his mind, he tried to remember anything he may have missed, but he was coming up blank. Maybe he was just overreacting once you had a mole it was difficult to genuinely trust those around you.

"They must have found out he talked, that would explain the tongue," said the DCI.

"How did you know he talked?" Asked Martin, as far as he knew he, Hayley and Jesse were the only ones to know. He'd never divulged his source or that he had even had one.

Jesse watched DCI Walker smirk under their sharp gazes.

"He sent you a USB with more data on an organisation then I've ever seen in my entire career, and he said on the video that the information from before wasn't complete. There's a reason I do this Job, and that's because I listen to evidence and come to the correct conclusion. Admittedly, I didn't have to be some Jedi mind master, I just watched the bloody video with you," answered DCI Walker.

"Shit, sorry sir," answered Martin, feeling rather foolish.

"We're all on high alert, I get it. But you ever insinuate me being dirty again and you fuck off!"

"Sir," said Martin, bowing his head ashamed.

"It also means they don't care about us knowing they did it," answered Jesse, trying to get back to the point.

"He was at Cotham tip, the whole idea could have been that we never found him," answered Martin, making sure not to create eye contact with his DCI.

Jesse squeezed his shoulder to offer some support. They had a strong bond, worked together for many years, and been there for one another when things had gone sideways. Laughed over a beer when they needed the humour to cut through the tension, taken coffee breaks away from the station to digest information or tear it apart to start again, they'd cheered each other on with their accomplishments, personal or professional.

Martin had worked tirelessly to bring Hayley home safely the first time, albeit in circumstances Jesse hadn't been entirely comfortable with. But always with the foresight that she would be well protected and back where she needed to be as soon as possible.

Jesse had equally bent over backwards to ensure Martin had been on time to each of his children's births and covered workloads when he was suffering from exhaustion. They had done their bit as friends and colleagues to support each other, but Martin couldn't shake off the feeling that something monumental was about to happen.

Nothing about Daniel's abduction seemed right, if that was the correct word to use, there was an undercurrent and he realised Jesse felt it too. There were too many pieces to pin down, too much going on in the dark.

CHAPTER 17

BLOODY CLOTHES ARRIVED IN PLASTIC EVIDENCE BAGS, AND JESSE looked at them, knowing they were Daniel's before he took them in his hands. Crinkling the plastic under his fingertips as though he could feel through the plastic and connect with his son, he felt tears drip down his nose before he was conscious of crying. Pale and gut punched, he stumbled back, losing his balance before falling on the cold hard floor of the station.

The officer who had handed them to him looked around nervously before trying to lend a hand, to enable Jesse to stand. Once he firmly planted his feet, and could stop staring at the clothes, he wandered over to the plant pot near the elevator and threw up. His body convulsed as his brain pounded in his head. He couldn't speak, and he could barely take in air as he choked on the remnants of his stomach contents. As his stomach finally emptied, his chest tightened and his wind pipe burned. Slumping down on the floor he cried, great big, hollow sobs of desperation.

After a while he felt Martin grip his shoulder. Jesse didn't have the energy to stand or even look up. His entire world had collapsed around him and he could feel himself being crushed within the wreckage.

Martin knelt down and tugged Jesse into his arms, trying to offer some comfort as despair set in. But the longer he held on, the more he absorbed the pain, and it wasn't long before tears were falling from his own eyes. Selfishly thinking of what he had lost on top of how he would feel if it were his own son. Seeing his friend in such anguish was soul destroying, and he had no clue how he was ever going to come back from this.

∼

DCI F*ryer* *sat* at Jesse's desk across from him while he tried to compose himself and become lucid.

"How can I help you?" asked Jesse, wiping his face of tears and snot.

Sympathetically smiling, the DCI sat watching Jesse for a second as if to make an assessment or find the right words. "I need to talk to you to gain any relevant information. You know how this works, but we're also working in the critical time frame. I need a quick but thorough outline from you and then I can get back out there, where you want us most." Jesse nodded. "So, tell me what happened and what you know?"

"Hayley is a witness to the Dmitri Richards' case. He kidnapped her last year and when she escaped, she gave birth to Daniel." DCI Fryer nodded as more tears fell from Jesse's eyes.

He hadn't told him anything he didn't know already, but he had to let Jesse speak in his own way, but trying to distance himself. "He's mine, but since she came back things have been difficult. I'm sure you'd understand. Things don't just go away when the bad man gets put behind bars."

"Of course," nodded DCI Fryer.

"We separated. We were getting close again until Rob tried to get between us."

"Your brother?" Asked DCI Fryer reading from the notes in front of him.

Jesse nodded.

"Go on."

"We were at the wedding and when I went back outside. She was lying there..." the memory of Hayley laid out on the floor flashed in his mind and he pushed his hand to his mouth to stop his lip from quivering. He'd thought he had lost her then, but this was so much worse. Swallowing hard and removing his hand, he took in a breath, while DCI Fryer waited patiently. "She recovered and was stopping with me; we thought it best, especially with Daniel. He was going to my mum and... Mum's every day just so Hayley had time to recuperate. She hated it, so he was at home with her when they stabbed her. She'd been to our neighbours for a drink and had gone back to get her change bag, when they hit her from behind."

"OK, what happened at the hospital?"

Jesse bit down on his hand again as it shook and looked at the floor.

"Jesse, I'm really sorry to have to make you live this all again, but I need to know what happened."

Nodding, Jesse wiped the rogue tears and clasped his hands together.

"Mart came over and wanted to tell me something. When we were outside the room, I got a video call, which was unusual because he never video calls me."

"Your dad?" Asked DCI Fryer.

Jesse nodded.

"Dan-" coughing to clear his throat of emotion, he looked up to the DCI's face and silently begged him not to continue. "He was in a car." Taking a breath, he stood up and paced the room, breathing slowly as he ran his hand through his hair, trying not to fall apart any more. "You know what happened next," said Jesse finally.

"What happened when you got back inside?"

"Mart went upstairs to inform Hayley and when he got there, she was gone. That's when he got hold of the CCTV and saw her being wheeled out."

"The mortuary?"

Jesse nodded as he watched the DCI take notes.

"Do you remember anything about the car Daniel was in?"

"It wasn't that clear a picture," answered Jesse.

DCI Fryer nodded while he thought about what to say.

"Do you think it's possible that your brother has done this?" asked DCI Fryer after a few moments.

Jesse leaned back in his chair for support, and bit his bottom lip as he thought.

"I don't know what's going through Rob's head at the minute. Revenge, jealousy, anger, they're all motives but I can't see him doing this. He's a conniving bastard, but he's not an organised criminal."

"What Did Martin come to tell you at the hospital?" Asked DCI Fryer.

"He'd found a-" standing back up, he walked over to the window to look out. He couldn't tell him about the card. It would open up too many other avenues, and he'd have to explain why he'd kept them quiet.

"Found what, Jesse?"

"He'd found a coffee machine that made decent coffee. He knows I hate that shit in there."

Jesse didn't turn round to see his disbelieving face. The excuse was about as bad as it could get. But his mind wasn't working right now. His brain was fried and barely operating. Coming up with a reasonable lie was beyond his capabilities.

"And that was all he came to say?"

Jesse nodded.

∽

OPENING HER EYES, she momentarily wondered if she was blind as everything was in complete darkness. Glancing around gave nothing away, only that she was in a stiflingly hot room. Sweat pooled on her forehead and between her breasts that they'd forced together through the corset. But it was the dampness on her side that concerned her. Having only just had stitches, she was sure Lynnie had burst them when she'd tightened the corset. Focusing her eyes so they grew accustomed to the darkness.

They blinded her once again when the overhead lights beamed on. Screwing her eyes tightly closed to stop her retinas from burning, she attempted to calm her breathing when she realised no one was coming in the room with her. Placing her hand where it hurt, she touched wetness and when she looked down, she could see the red liquid. She couldn't worry about that right now. A cut to her stomach was nothing compared to the pain she'd be in if they used any of the sex paraphernalia coating the sides of the room.

Looking around, she could see items that looked like they'd be more at home in an abattoir or an operating room. Feeling her anxiety kick up another notch, she pulled her face away. This was all about fear, she told herself. They just want to scare me.

Looking back up to the screen, she could see the vote count go up and messages of what they'd like to do to her swipe across the bottom of the screen. Swallowing, she decided the only safe place to look was her feet, so she put her head down and hummed to a song she wishes she was dancing to instead.

∼

WALKING BACK into their make shift command centre, Jesse slumped into a chair whilst scanning the maps and paperwork sprawled out on the table before him.

"You look like shit," pronounced Martin.

"I feel like shit. What we got and please tell me we have something because Fryer has fuck all," said Jesse hopelessly.

"That bad?" Asked DCI Walker.

"He's just acting within the guidelines. Local paedophiles, convicts, shifting through CCTV all that bollocks," answered Jesse, taking one of the cups from the middle of the table and sipping it. Lukewarm tea, disgusting. Not finishing it, he placed it back on the table. "They've sent the clothes over to the lab."

"OK, I have something," said Rosa entering the room with Jeff the technician close behind her. "Jeff room, room computer genius," introduced Rosa, walking over to the computer behind the DCI. Turning it on, she beckoned Jeff over as he puffed his chest out at her introduction. Pushing him down in the swivel chair, she tapped on the monitor while he tapped on the keyboard. After a few minutes he was in, and a dark screen came up. Comments ran along the bottom and bids ran up the side.

"What is this?" Asked Martin, disgusted as he read a grotesque description of foreplay.

"This is the site currently in progress. It's called the Vineyard. Subscribers are to vote on certain aspects of tonight's presentation," explained Rosa.

Tapping on the digital clock in the corner, he saw the stop watch counting down from three hours, ten minutes and thirty-seven seconds.

"How did you get into this?" Asked the DCI.

"She said I didn't have to tell you as long as I do my job," said Jeff, pointing to Rosa. "But the only reason I'm in this is to keep my job," pointed out Jeff before anyone jumped down his throat.

"Just tell me you weren't a subscriber?" asked DCI Walker, hopefully.

"No, I wasn't a subscriber, but I'm friends with people on the dark web who were. Otherwise, I never would have got in. That's the trouble with the dark web, no one trusts anyone. I have had to make sure I have people's names I can use to get me on certain sites, and that's taken a long time," answered Jeff. "Hence, why I'm on these sites to begin with. Trust me, I can do without the nightmares."

"Why are you even on it?" Asked DCI Walker.

Jeff went to open his mouth to respond, but Jesse cut him off when he saw something move on screen.

"What's that?" Asked Jesse, pointing to the screen.

"Hold on, I'll lighten the screen." Once Jeff hovered over the brightness tab in the settings, the screen became lighter and Jesse saw her instantly. Sat in the middle of the screen on a throne, wearing a corset with a belt strapped around her neck, bright red stilettos making her look like something out of a BDSM porn movie, was Hayley. Her eyes were closed and her lips were parted slightly, no doubt taking in deep breaths as her chest heaved up and down.

"I think she's singing," said Jeff absently.

"What's she singing?" Asked DCI Walker. "Can you get sound?"

"Yep. Hold on." Tapping away, he brought up an atmospheric sound, proof enough that they did indeed have ears in the room.

"I can't hear her," pointed out Walker.

"No, it's too low."

"Turn it up, she may give us a clue," demanded Walker.

"She's a chef, not a member of the secret service. Unless she's turned into Gerry and the Pacemakers, I'm not sure what she's singing will bloody help," snapped Martin.

Just then the sound got louder, clear from the buzzing, and then a tune came through lightly.

"… you're my… my begin… I… I'm win…" sang Hayley quietly.

"All of me," whispered Jesse while a tear ran down his face.

"Does that mean something to you?" Asked Walker sympathetically.

Casting a look at Walker to shut the hell up while he got himself under control. He walked away, pacing the floor near the door, while the other all shared looks and waited.

"Does it tell you anything?" Asked Martin once Jesse had wiped his face on his hand. Drawing his chin up, while his eyes glistened with unshed tears, Jesse swallowed down his emotion.

"She's singing our song," answered Jesse with a croaky throat.

"So, it's not anything important?"

Martin saw the rage ignite in Jesse's eyes before anyone else and dived forward to get between the techie and Jesse, who looked ready to pulverise the computer geek.

"No, you're right, nothing fucking noteworthy at all, you little prick! Only that she's singing the fucking song we first danced to, which means she's wishing I was fucking there! Which I'm not cus I'm with you bunch of fucking idiots!" Grabbing the chair closest, Jesse slung it across the room before almost pulling the doors off its hinges and storming out.

"Shit! I didn't mean-" stuttered Jeff.

"I know. Don't worry. He's stressed. Let him calm down," said Martin, placing his hand on his shoulder. "He's just witnessed his girlfriend being sold on the internet and discovered his son's dead; I think he's allowed an outburst."

"Now you're in, what can you find?" Asked DCI Walker.

"I can try to work out where the original address is, but normally with these things it pings them all over the place. So, this could take a while," answered Jeff honestly.

"You get us the addresses and we'll determine how likely they are," said Martin helpfully.

"Are we talking UK?" Asked Jeff as his fingers flew over the keys.

"I bloody hope so," answered Martin, looking back at the wide-open door.

The minutes ticked by, as did the hours. With not much time to spare, Jeff let out a triumphant yelp.

"Have you found something?" Asked Rosa, watching Jeff put his arms above his head to straighten out his back.

"They don't call me a genius for nothing," remarked Jeff proudly.

"Where?" Rushed out Martin as he made his way back behind Jeff's seat.

"Somewhere in this area, I'm sure of it," said Jeff, circling the map on screen. "It keeps kicking me out when I get any closer, so this is your target area."

"How big is that?"

"It's around a five miles radius," answered Jeff.

"Can't you get any closer?" Asked Martin.

"It depends?"

"On what?"

"On whether you want me to break through their firewall?"

"What would it mean if you did?"

"That they'd know someone was trying to get in and potentially kick me out. Create a virus kick back or worse," answered Jeff eyeing

Jesse who sat by the door. As if distance alone would stop him from understanding what he meant.

"OK, so we need to work out what is in this area. They'd need somewhere fairly obscure, or at least out of view. So, we span out from the middle, which is Sconce Park by the look of it." said Rosa looking on maps placed haphazardly on the table. "We look for anything unmarked, dilapidated, or uninhabited. Jeff can tell us what they are and we'll visit them one by one."

"That's going to take too long," said Jesse despondently, spying the stopwatch on screen. According to that, they had less than thirty minutes and were pinning all their hopes on it. With nowhere else to go, they were desperately running out of options.

"No, it isn't. Adam can use one car, and the DCI can use another. That leaves you, me and DS Wells in our own."

"So, we can hit five places at once," confirmed Walker.

"Exactly. Fanning us out will cut time by a fifth. The further out we go, the more ground we must cover, but if we're right, they'll be closer rather than further away," explained Martin.

Looking at one another, they all nodded before leaving Jeff to forward addresses as he found them.

Jumping in their prospective cars, they piled out of the parking lot and made their way towards Sconce Park where the river Devon was situated. Once they were all given their prospective haunts, they divided themselves and went in search of the spot hiding Hayley.

"We've all got our places. Be thorough, but be quick. Good luck, everyone," said DCI Walker through the radio.

"Copy that!" rang out the control panel simultaneously.

On arriving at the allotments, Jesse realised why he'd been told to cover east. It was fairly unlikely to garner results, and his boss was attempting to keep him out of the action. Deciding to check just in case, he stepped out and made his way to the locked gates. He retrieved his identification from his inner pocket for the approaching gardener.

Martin walked through the boat yard looking for anything out of the ordinary. There was no one around to ask, but that meant there were no noises to distract him either. Listening as he walked steadily along the path, he turned back towards the car, glancing towards the reception office he headed toward it before leaving.

Rosa opened the heavy metal door, flicking her flashlight on as she entered. Looking around her, all she could see were metal beams and dry dirt covering the floor. The entire space was cold and empty.

Adam stepped out and walked up to the padlocks on the huge heavy solid doors. Attempting to move them, he relented when they wouldn't budge. Deciding to scan the area, he walked around the outside of the old metal corrugated walls of the warehouse.

"This is DCI Walker, there's nothing at the old museum. Does anyone have anything yet?"

"Negative," said Jesse.

"Me neither," spoke Martin.

"Nothing, Sir," answered Rosa.

"Hancock?"

When no answer came back, they all stood waiting.

"Hancock, come in?"

Waiting, but growing more apprehensive by the second, they each held the radios out, willing it to speak back.

"I'm in the car now," shouted Jesse, throwing his radio on the passenger seat as he gunned the engine. Spinning out of the allotment towards the roundabout that would lead him onto Bowbridge road, near the warehouse Adam was searching, Jesse prayed he'd found something.

On arriving he could see Hancock's car sitting idly by the side of the road. Taking the radio, he held it up to his lips. "Hancock's car is empty, the place looks locked up. I'm going to take a walk around the perimeter."

"Hallam you stay there. I'm on my way!" Bellowed DCI Walker.

"Sorry sir, I can't hear you," answered Jesse. "It's breaking up."

"Don't you give me that bollocks," answered Walker.

But Jesse was already out of the car and skulking towards the warehouse.

"Shit!"

Martin chuckled to himself as he heard the conversation unfold between his boss and his friend. Having heard the non-response from Adam, he'd thrown himself in the car also and was minutes behind Jesse. Pulling up, he parked next to Jesse's car before informing the DCI that he too had arrived and the signal was poor so he'd do a walk around.

When Martin stepped round the back, he flashed his torchlight towards the floor and saw drag marks leading into the warehouse through a smaller service door. Deciding to step around, he kept moving until he came to the opposite side he'd started. Walking the length of the warehouse he listened out for any noises, but all he could hear was the train line less than a mile away and someone playing loud music from a far. When he reached the front, his DCI was just pulling in.

"Have you seen anything?"

"There are drag marks at the back, leading inside. I've not seen Jesse or Adam."

"Shit. You know the damn fool ignored me, right?"

"I think it's the signal, sir," lied Martin.

"Bollocks Wells and don't you start," he warned, taking out his radio. "Jeff, I need blueprints for the warehouse on Bowbridge road. Also, I need you to tell me if anything changes on screen. If we're at the right place, they may try something."

"Yes, sir," replied Jeff instantly.

Looking at Martin, he scratched his head.

"How are we handling this, sir?" Asked Martin.

"I have no fucking idea."

"Great," nodded Martin sarcastically, looking back at the warehouse.

CHAPTER 18

❦

Once inside, Jesse looked around, but it was pitch black. With no sunlight to lend a hand and no bulbs on to guide the way he kept to the walls. Feeling around gingerly until he arrived at a door. Taking a deep breath, Jesse felt into the back of his trousers and secured his fingers around the gun he'd placed there at the station away from prying eyes. If this would be his only chance, he would make sure he took it. Pulling it out and holding it in his left hand, he nuzzled the door open, thanking a higher entity for the silent admission he slipped in. Looking around again, he noted lock ups lining the inside of the worn-out warehouse. Feeling exposed, he glided along the corridor until the shade covered him where the fluorescent strip lights above him couldn't quite reach. Stopping to take in the roof and any hidden spots he hadn't noticed before, he steadied his breathing to stop the rushing sound the adrenalin was making in his ears.

"Put him in there and we'll deal with him later," said a voice far off.

Glancing round the edge of the first lock up, he saw two men. One was locking the door they'd just exited while the other pulled his phone out from his pocket.

"Boss, we have the canary. It's dealt with."

Jesse ducked back as the man turned on the spot.

"Yes, sir. We'll be there in ten."

Just as Jesse was making his way back silently towards the door, he heard the man talk again. "Do you want the boy picking up?" Jesse stilled, waiting for a response he would not hear. "Yep, I'll inform her to get him ready."

So that was it. Neither Daniel nor Hayley was here, but they'd panicked enough to neutralise Adam. Had he seen something?

Making it outside, he silently ran towards the cars. On seeing Martin and DCI Walker, he urged them to get in. Deciding to ask questions later, they pulled away and drove up the road, pulling into a transport car park further along.

Parking up a few seconds later further down the road, shaded by the trees that stuck out from an alley, they each got out walking to the centre.

"So, what happened?" Asked Walker.

"I think Adam's inside, but neither Hayley nor Daniel are there. The man I heard said he was on his way to get Daniel."

"So, one of us follows him," said the DCI.

"You, I'm going after Hayley," said Jesse.

"What makes you think they're not together?" Asked Martin.

"They're not," answered Jesse.

Walking back to where the trees stopped. He poked his head round to look further down the road outside the warehouse. "He's getting in the car."

Rushing back to their own, they all jumped in.

∼

THE INCIDENT ROOM WAS BUZZING. Calls were coming in from every phone. Tactical response delivered messages, confirming and validating progress. Stab vests were being handed out, comms checked. All while Jesse sat in a dirty alleyway trying not to lose his shit. He had no reason to believe Daniel was still alive, but as long as Hayley remained in that chair, he still had a chance.

After following the car for five miles, he had waited there until the driver got back in the car. Signalling for Martin to stay, he drove behind the car close enough not to lose him but far enough away not to be spotted. Ten minutes later they pulled into a large warehouse off the A1. Giving the man five minutes to get comfortable, he called the command centre, letting them know where he was and what he was planning on doing. Jeff let him know Hayley was still on screen, alone.

"What's happened?" Asked Jesse, answering the phone once he saw Martin's name flash up.

"He's not here," answered Martin.

"Shit!" Hissed Jesse, trying to keep his voice down. "What's there?"

"Not a lot. It's just boxes of shit, and I mean shit. I can see absolutely no reason for him stopping here."

"Do you think he saw us?" Asked Jesse, cursing his own eagerness.

"It's possible," admitted Martin.

"They've planted decoys before, and CCTV wasn't extensive enough to keep up. Maybe they've led us on a wild goose chase." Jesse mused. "What-"

"Fuck!"

"Mart?!.. Mart-"

Pulling the phone away from his ear, he realised someone had disconnected them. Suddenly feeling a lot more alone and unsure of himself, he crouched down. Peeking out around the corner at a low level so as not to be detected.

That was when he saw Demy. Putting a hand on his gun to check its proximity, he watched as Demy laughed with the other four men as though they were firm friends. All dressed in black leathers, he wondered if they were the ones who'd been with Rob or had broken Demy out of prison.

Slipping back round, he contemplated how to get inside. If he knew Hayley was definitely in there, he'd go in Rambo style and take his chances, but without having a clue whether or not he was close, he needed to make sure he was undetected long enough to find out.

Sneaking his head round he saw them high five each other like the morons they were and clash beer bottles together.

"Demy! What the fuck are you doing?"

Glancing to the person who'd just walked out, he recognised him as Frank. The son of a bitch who shared DNA with Hayley. The thought stuck in his throat. He had no right being her father. Wondering if Hayley knew, he shook his head. He had no time for thinking like that. They could talk later. He hoped.

"I'm celebrating freedom!" Shouted Demy with his arms outstretched, his gaggle of merry men laughed.

"Well sober up, you've got a job to do. Try not fucking it up this time," warned Frank.

"Jesus, all I've gotta to do is shove this in," laughed Demy, throwing his pelvis forward while holding his crotch as the other men jeered.

"If that was all we you had to do, we wouldn't be in this mess," Frank sneered.

Demy stumbled back, seemingly thoroughly chastised.

Jesse fingered the trigger, wondering how long it would take for them to realise he'd smashed a bullet into his skull. Not long enough.

"Inside."

Watching the men trail their boss inside, he looked around at the cars and bikes haphazardly parked up. Keeping low to the ground, he scuttled over to the closest car. Peering in the window, he noted there were no keys in the ignition, so slipped the car door open, quickly flipping the visor down to check for a key. Nothing. Chancing a look in the glove compartment, he noticed a flip blade. Taking it, he shoved it in his sock, pushing it down as far as he could inside his shoe. Walking with it would be uncomfortable, but at least he'd remember it was there if he needed it.

∼

"THEY'RE GEARING UP. Tactical's been called in. They think they've an idea where they're being held," said Rosa at the operations door.

DCI Walker and Jeff shared a look.

"Where?" Asked DCI Walker.

After allowing Martin to follow the suspect, he'd made his way back to the control centre to see what they had and if any more information was coming in. Both Martin and Jesse were in contact, but it was just a case of tracking them and waiting for the call to go in. He needed everyone on board and with having kept so much about the case to himself; he wasn't relishing offering it in the eleventh hour.

"A1, old peel warehouse."

Sharing another look before rushing over to the maps on the table, they shuffled papers around until they found what they needed.

"Shall I get DS Wells?" Asked Rosa.

"Text him and pray to God that he has that phone on silent," warned DCI Walker.

∽

Martin woke up with a banging headache. Rubbing the back of his head, his hand met with blood. Gradually sitting up, he squinted from the pain in his head before fully opening his eyes to survey his surroundings.

"Glad you could join us," said Adam.

Martin rubbed his head. He couldn't think straight. The ringing in his ears was causing hallucinations.

"I'm sorry we had to hit you, but it seems you enjoy going into places you have no business getting involved in."

Martin looked back up towards the figure; they'd sat him on a wooden chair, watching him with a gun strapped to his chest.

"Adam?"

"Yours truly," smiled Adam, sitting back in his chair, proudly.

"Why?" Asked Martin.

"Why do you think?"

Martin had no clue, and the banging going on his head wasn't helping him join any dots. In fact, his entire head comprised more dots than the solar system, but just like astrology they made no sense to him.

"That prick thinks the world revolves around him."

Martin looked around, but all he could see was a concrete cell with bars on one end. Where the hell was he?

"Rachel's too bloody good for him."

"Rachel?" asked Martin, who the hell was Rachel?

"She's beautiful, intelligent, charismatic, funny…"

Martin rolled his eyes, instantly regretting it when his head spun.

"OK, I get it. This Rachel chick has a golden muff. What the hell's that got to do with me?" Asked Martin.

"Don't talk about her like that!" Shouted Adam.

The sudden noise brought Martin up short, and it was then he realised he was in serious trouble. His colleague was a nutter.

"He used her!"

"Adam, I've no idea what you're talking about, mate. Whose Rachel and what has this got to do with me?" Asked Martin calmly with his palms out.

"I love her."

Martin bit his tongue. Why did he always get the psychopaths? Why hadn't he chosen a job that was safer? Maybe driven a bus or sat at a desk telling people to turn it off and on again? That had to be better than facing a nutter with a loaded gun.

"I'm sure you do."

Adam nodded sombrely.

"But Adam, I need to go. Daniel's out there somewhere, and he's hurt."

"He's not, he's fine," answered Adam.

"How do you know?" Asked Martin warily.

"Because I wouldn't let anyone hurt him. I'm not an animal," defended Adam. "It was pig blood."

"Cause you're not, very Carrie like," said Martin, hoping his voice didn't relay his sarcasm. Martin wasn't entirely sure how to respond to that, so shuffled back until his back hit the icy wall, so he could lean on it.

"I won't hurt you as long as you do as you're told."

Martin looked at him and kept quiet. Adam was tall, but not as tall as him. He was thin, Martin had much more weight behind him, but

Adam had a gun and that was one hell of an advantage to have. Plus, the birds flapping their little wings around the inside of his skull didn't help his concentration any.

～

"We have visual confirmation, they're keeping Hayley and Daniel apart so we're having to move in on two different bases at the same time. We will go in as quietly as possible to get the best result. But now we know that we have two coppers acting as vigilantes we need to be careful when we take down targets."

DCI Fryer directed the last part at DCI Walker, but he held his gaze. He didn't want to be in the position of telling DCI Fryer that he may have added unnecessary complications to his extraction plan, but he wanted the guilt of having two officers killed by accident weighing down on him even less.

～

Jesse stood up and slammed his body against the wall. Easing the door open, he flicked his head round. Not seeing anything to cause him harm, he slipped through the doorway and tuned his ears into the silence, whilst trying to calm down the adrenalin in his system that was deafening him.

"We've got five minutes." Came the voice.

Looking along the corridor, he couldn't see anyone, but they were loud enough to be closer than he'd like.

"Then neutralise him."

That didn't sound good. Who was he talking about?

"The presentation will last about three hours; we need to give them a good show, especially after all the trouble it caused."

It was Frank, and he was getting closer. Looking for a place to hide he saw a door across the hallway. Stepping across he swiftly opened the door, tucking himself behind it, he realised he was in some kind of closet.

"The baby's inconsequential. But he's keeping her from freaking out, and right now I need her compliant. She can do what the fuck she likes after that."

Jesse bit his lip, he was sure that he was talking about his son.

"She has no idea. Where ever that baby went, it will be too difficult to get it back. I've got my people working on it."

What was he talking about? Feeling his phone vibrate in his pocket, he lifted it out. **Tac 10 mins.** Shit! If they came in too soon, everything could blow up too late and they'd be pointless.

"Do what you like with him."

Jesse clenched his hands together, forcing himself to stand where he was and not take out the man now, promising himself he'd get the chance.

Listening again until he was certain the corridor was empty, he slipped out. Rounding the top brought him to a selection of rooms, with all their doors closed. It would be like opening a macabre lucky dip. This was dangerous. One false move and he'd be handing over everything they needed. Seeing the door open ahead of him, he took a step to the right, so he was out of sight. Glancing round, he noticed a dark-haired woman lighting a Vape stick. The smell of candy floss filled the hall, and he almost gagged on it.

"Have you seen the amounts coming in?" Asked a man excitedly.

"Yeah, Frank's getting all wet," answered the woman, bored.

"I still don't get why she's this bloody important. I'm fairly sure if you doll any bird up like that, the money would have flown in. I'd do her."

"You'd do your grandma," said the girl sarcastically as she laughed at him.

"If she looked like that, I would," said the man joining in the laughter.

"You're disgusting," laughed the girl before inhaling her sweet vapour. "Besides, Hayley means more than just this show. She was born to do a job and instead got ideas above her station. They own her."

"How so?" laughed the man, intrigued.

"She was born because of a family contract between the two families. They had to procreate to get their hands on some kind of dowry they set up, but that dowry expires as soon as the bloodlines cut. This is their way of retying those threads. The baby she has will be sent away and saved for her suitor. Then the entire thing continues. It's fucked up, but not my problem." shrugged the girl.

"Wow, that's really old age medieval shit right there," laughed the guy.

"You have no idea," Lynnie sighed. "They have a set of rules they all have to follow. If they don't, then they can question their membership, and ultimately cancel. If it extricates them, then they lose out on all the benefits. They all toe the line, so to speak."

"What benefits?" Asked the man.

"Ruling the fucking world, Jax," answered the woman, passing the man her Vape. "Frank's family is the highest up because of how closely they follow the rules. The fact that Hayley broke away meant they questioned his dictatorship. And he now has a battle on his hands. If he doesn't regain control, then there will be an all-out war for leadership and he could lose," suddenly lowering her voice, Jesse leaned in closer. "From what I hear, there's another competitor with a lot of clout. The only way for this not to turn nasty is for Hayley to do as she was born to do."

"Wow, that's some heavy shit," said the man blowing out smoke, who Jesse now knew as Jax.

"That was why they made her marry him at fourteen, so no one else could get there first. They were supposed to marry officially at eighteen, but sounds like Demy got too handy and she ran."

"That's why Frank's pissed at him?" Asked Jax.

"Among other things," answered Lynnie, taking her Vape back.

"So why are *you* helping him?" Asked Jax.

"Simple. She ran and left me, so fuck her."

"Jesus, remind me never to get on your bad side," said Jax halfheartedly.

"I'll get what I'm deserved once I do this," smiled Lynnie.

Taking the door, she re-entered the room she'd only recently exited. Jesse just stood with his back to the wall, processing everything he'd just heard. There was so much that now made sense, but even more that didn't. He needed to find Hayley and get her out before the show started. But how was he going to find her without making them aware of his presence? Looking back to the message on his phone, he contemplated his next move.

∽

MARTIN SAT in the cell on his own but he knew people weren't far away as he kept catching parts of conversations. Nothing that made any sense but something he could rely on whilst he thought of a plan of escape. One thing he hadn't heard was a child, so he wasn't sure whether he was in the same place as Daniel or not and there was no telling how big the unit was whilst he sat in an eight-by-eight cell.

"Adam mate!" When he heard nothing, he shouted again.

A few seconds later Adam came into view. "What?"

"I need a waz mate."

Adam looked at him as though what did he expect him to do about it?

"There's no loo in here, just let me go for a piss before I embarrass myself?"

Adam looked around him, unsure, but then nodded. Taking the keys from his pocket, he slipped them into the lock.

"Thanks mate, you're a lifesaver," Martin sighed, stepping back as the door swung open.

Once through the door, he passed Adam and then swung back, punching him in the throat. Staggering back, Martin grabbed the keys from his hand and slammed the cell door shut, swiftly slipping the key in and locking it.

"Like I said, Life saver," said Martin, flipping the keys in the air before catching them.

"You'll not get away with this," croaked Adam, holding his throat.

"No. You won't. Because once they see you've failed, you're done for. You should've really learnt to pick your side's better." Walking away, Martin took the corner.

∽

"Whose stupid idea was it to use him as bait?" Asked DCI Fryer glancing from Rosa, Jeff, DCI Walker and the rest of his team as they watched Jesse being manhandled into the Vineyard room with Hayley.

"I think he might have done that one on his own," answered DCI Walker.

"Or they caught him," offered Rosa.

"He should never have been there in the first place!" Bellowed DCI Fryer. "What the bloody hell were you thinking?"

Normally DCI Walker wouldn't put up with such behaviour in front of his team, but he fully empathised with the predicament he'd unwillingly put DCI Fryer in, so kept his mouth shut. They could talk once the mission was over and he could be more open about what he knew.

∽

Watching the door close, Hayley looked at Jesse. His reddening cheek and left eyes proved someone had thumped him, and with his hands and legs bound she could see he wasn't there of his own free will.

"Jesse," whispered Hayley, not knowing if the recoding picked up on sound and visual.

"Jesse." Kneeling down beside him, she touched his face. Watching him sleep, knowing they'd knocked him out cold. "What have they done?"

Looking up to the screen, she saw an extra line of colour added to the thread. Squinting, she tried to read it, but it was still too far away. Deciding it was important, she walked over to the screen, and once she was almost touching the screen, she could read it.

New player, open to all elements as subject one, plus snuff video. Starting bid 1000.

Hayley's blood ran icy cold. They would kill him and get paid by people watching it. Stepping away, she realised she was shaking; she had to do something, but what?

"Jesse, wake up." She ran her hands through his hair, noting the dampness at the back; she pulled her hand away, inspecting it, seeing blood. Stifling a cry, she kissed his head.

"Jesse, please wake up. Please," she pleaded.

When he groaned, she moved back to see his face."Jesse."

Groaning again, he gingerly lifted his head, while trying to prise his smashed eye open.

"Oh, my God, Jesse. You're alive," she said, placing his head back on her buxom.

"You trying to smother me in those?" He groaned.

Unable to help herself, she laughed, pushing his head back up so she could see his face.

"What the hell are you doing here?" She asked.

"Saving you," Jesse grimaced, trying to show his smile.

"Well, you've done a shitty job," answered Hayley.

"Thanks." Looking around, he saw all the implements, the leather and the velvet coverings. "Is that a throne?"

"Yeah, well, they think they're fucking royalty, don't they?" She said whilst inspecting the back of his head. "You'll need stitches."

"I will ask nurse Ratchet outside."

"You've seen Lynnie then?" Asked Hayley.

"I didn't know that's who it was, but to be fair that makes sense, now," answered Jesse.

"I'm so sorry I got us involved in all this."

Jesse nodded, he didn't hold her responsible, but she clearly felt guilty and him arguing with her about it wouldn't help anyone.

"They have Daniel."

"I know. They killed Dad," admitted Jesse, watching Hayley's eyes water, stabbed him in the heart.

"I'm so sorry," she cried.

This time it was his turn to comfort her.

When her mouth was as close to his ear as she could get in their cuddle, she whispered, "How are we going to get out?" Hayley could smell the grime on his skin but she didn't care, his touch alone felt like coming home and she needed to feel him.

Covering his mouth in her hair below her ear, he whispered his plan.

"I love you so much, Jesse," whispered Hayley.

"I love you more."

"They've increased the time," whispered Hayley.

"I thought they might," smiled Jesse against her soft skin.

Stepping away, she sat back in the throne and glanced at the screen. They were still bidding, and they now set the time for an hour later, which meant they still had time to do something.

"You know my Dad did nothing wrong?" Looking at him, her eyes widened. "He didn't deserve to die!" Shouted Jesse.

"I know. I'm sorry," she cried.

"You know he died because of you, right?" Biting her lip, she nodded, every insecurity she had coming forward.

Jesse stood up and walked towards her. Stalking her to make her feel small. "What the fuck did I see in you, anyway?" He said, looking her over.

"I don't know?" Cried Hayley, unable to stop the tears from falling.

A whirling noise told them a camera had moved or zoomed in. Without checking Jesse grabbed her jaw, with both his bound hands, making her face him.

"All this trouble for what? This?" He lowered his hand down her body as if to emphasise it.

"I'm so sorry, Jesse. I never meant for this to happen," cried Hayley, wrapping her arms around him.

"It seems only fair to get what's mine before we both die," said Jesse, hovering over her.

Running his fingers down her left shoulder, Hayley couldn't help the shiver than ran down her spine at his touch, but she kept her eyes on his.

"I think they knew putting me in here with you dressed up like a whore would only lead to one thing." Jesse smirked. "One for the road?"

"You wouldn't dare!" Shouted Hayley, moving as far back into the throne as she could.

"Who will stop me?" Asked Jesse devilishly.

Grabbing the chain behind her neck, he tugged on it until her throat was open to him. Running his warm tongue down her throat and onto her breasts, she tried not to pant. Forcing her legs open, he trailed his fingers down the corset until they were between her legs. Feeling her heat, he decided the unclip each attachment on her stockings. Hayley stayed stock still, while twisting her hand around the chain. Going to his flies, Jesse popped the top button, but before he could get any lower, the door swung open.

"Get away from her!" Shouted Frank. "She's not yours to touch!"

Jesse glanced to Hayley, who coughed and spluttered.

"What... wha... did... wha.." Choking, she held her throat while Jesse stepped back, covering one camera with his back.

Frank rushed forward as her face turned red. Stepping in front of her, he checked her airway. Jesse watched Hayley's right hand swing up and catching the chain he wrapped it around Frank's neck, tightening it as Frank fell onto Hayley who couldn't move while still being attached to the other end.

Once he was still, Jesse fumbled with the belt and released it from round her neck. Right on cue, three men entered the room and Hayley and Jesse looked to one another. Still, being bound was an inconvenience, but it didn't make it impossible. Kicking Frank on the floor, Jesse swung with the chain as Hayley ducked. The chain hit the first one in the face and went down as the other two lunged forward.

Hayley turned around to find something heavy as they all wrestled on the floor. Seeing an opening, she smashed a metal ball attached to a strap into one man's heads, popping it like a spot. It splattered her and momentarily stunned her. Feeling her hand being grabbed, she saw Jesse, and they ran through the doorway. Hot on his heels as he manipulated his way around the corridors swiftly.

A cry from behind him pulled him up short as he glanced back. He flung her in the closet he'd occupied earlier. Closing the door quietly, he turned to Hayley as she bent over.

"Are you OK?" Whispered Jesse.

Pulling her hand away from her side, she showed her palm to him.

"Shit."

"I think Lynnie split my stitches," whispered Hayley, placing her hand back on her side to hold the pain in.

"Have you seen Daniel?" Asked Hayley as Jesse peeked out the door for a safe exit, closing it again before turning to face her.

"No, I don't know where he is. Martin was going after him while I came for you," answered Jesse.

"Why? You should have both gone for him, you'd have more of a chance."

"What? You think I'd leave you behind? Are you crazy?"

Hayley shrugged as she watched the shock flush across his face. Feeling embarrassed, she looked away.

"Hayley, I love you, more than anything. When are you going to realise that?"

When she didn't answer, he grabbed her hands and pulled her towards him so she'd look at him when he spoke. "I would rather die than let those freaks get hold of you. There's no way I would let you get hurt again."

Watching her face for any sign that she didn't believe him, she rewarded him with a slight smile before nodding.

"Good. Now do you have any idea where they're holding him? Did they mention anything?"

"No, but I heard him. They had him on a screen playing with some cars, but it was mute, and then they took it off when the bidding started. But when I was walking round the room, I heard a really distant cry. I'm sure it was Daniel."

Jesse stood thinking, working out what to do. He couldn't afford for them to be caught, but if Daniel was really here and he was still alive, he couldn't let them move him either. "How sure?"

"It was young. Unless my mind's playing tricks on me? It was him."

Taking in a heavy breath, Jesse looked around the small closet he'd tucked them in. "OK, we're going to need to get you out of those clothes," remarked Jesse, looking her up and down.

It was freezing outside, and they'd seen enough of her. Besides, it wasn't exactly practical for an escape.

"Jesus, Jesse, there's a time and a place."

When he looked back at her to explain what he meant, he caught her smirking. "Stop being cute and grab that mop head."

Twisting round Hayley snagged it, being careful to lift it over the metal top of the bucket and not tip it over to clatter and provide their whereabouts.

"I'm going to open the door. When they see you, I want you to nod."

Hayley looked at him as if he was crazy.

He kissed her lips. "Trust me."

Nodding, she watched him tuck himself behind the door with his hands on the handle. Taking his phone out with his other hand, he sent a text before slipping it back in his pocket.

"They let you keep your phone?" Asked Hayley.

"They took the radio," answered Jesse as if that answered everything. Lifting on his toes, he felt across the top of the racking until his fingertips caught what he was looking for. Pulling it down, he checked it over before taking the safety off.

"How did you know that was there?"

"I put it there. Now shush and step back," answered Jesse, waving his arms at her as if to push her back himself. "One... Two.... Three..." whispered Jesse before slowly opening the door.

When Hayley could see the corridor but no one there, she looked to Jesse, shaking her head, but he held his fingers out to her to stay. Just when she was feeling less tense, she saw a shadow cast across the hallway and darted her eyes to Jesse. He knew she'd seen something. Not long after, she was emphatically nodding while Jesse forced the broom handle into the guy's throat, pulling him backwards as they thrashed against the closed door.

Thinking Jesse was struggling Hayley grabbed the first thing she could reach and smashed it at the man's head, slumping forward Jesse let him drop. Looking up at her, he felt around in the guy's pockets, finding a set of keys he flicked through them. Nothing stood out as an appropriate key to one of the rooms. Feeling deflated, he ran his fingers down the guy's legs to check for any weapons, but he was clean.

Cursing, he went back to the door. "OK, we try again."

"Are you crazy, what happens if there's more than one?" Hissed Hayley.

"Then you grab another paint tin," smiled Jesse.

"No. Let me go out."

"What? No way!" Hissed Jesse.

"Jesse, we could be stuck in here all night and this room won't hold that many more people. Let me go out. Maybe they'll lead me to him?"

"Or they just shoot you?" Argued Jesse.

"They won't kill me, they can't."

With the last word Jesse straightened, looking at her confused as she looked to the man on the floor.

"Why can't they?" asked Jesse.

"They need me," said Hayley sheepishly. "I can't get into this now. We need to get Daniel. If anyone will be a target, it's you," answered Hayley.

Jesse stood stock still, watching her as though he could finally piece everything together. Suddenly Jesse's phone vibrated. Glancing to it, he dropped it back into his trouser pocket.

Realising he wasn't going to offer her an explanation for his face suddenly turning pale, she moved closer. "What did he say?" Asked Hayley warily.

Whatever it was, it hadn't been good. Watching emotions flit across his face and something stop him from opening his mouth, she waited, growing more concerned by the second.

"What. Does. It. Say?"

"He's on camera. They've just started a bid."

Grabbing the door quicker than Jesse could react, Hayley flew outside. Forgetting about the pain in her side and her bare feet that skidded on the floor from being covered in the thin material of the stocking, she took the route back to the room as if her life depended on it. Hayley crashed into the room and was instantly knocked out, hitting the floor with a thud.

When Jesse arrived a few seconds later, they thrust a gun into his face. Holding his hands to the side as they dragged him in the room before they kicked the door shut. Watching Hayley on the ground, he could see her chest still rising and falling, giving him some relief.

"Next time you strangle someone, make sure you do it properly," said Frank, rubbing his throat.

"Where's Daniel?"

"On a boat to a very horny man."

"Fuck you! Where's Daniel?" Shouted Jesse.

"Get me that baby and you can have yours," Frank sneered in Jesse's face.

"What the fuck are you talking about?"

"That bitch lied to you. To all of us. She didn't miscarry. She gave birth. Her and her brother palmed her off as someone else's."

Jesse flicked his gaze to Hayley, who was still unconscious on the floor. Was that what she had been hiding? Had she given her baby away to save its life?

"How am I supposed to find her?" Asked Jesse, looking back to watch Frank smile at how easily Jesse had agreed.

"Use your head, you're a copper. I'm sure you can find out if you really need to."

"And what happens if I do?" Asked Jesse.

"You get your son back," admitted Frank.

"And Hayley?"

"That bitch is none negotiable. She owes me," seethed Frank.

Jesse watched her for a few more seconds while thinking of a way to get them both out.

"Did you know she's your daughter?" Asked Jesse.

Watching Frank's face contort would have been pleasing if he thought he could get anything from it, but this man was as evil as they come and Jesse wasn't sure how the news would be taken and whether it was news to him at all. But the sudden shock betrayed him and Jesse stood taller, knowing he might have something to finally disarm him.

"What did you say?" Asked Frank, looking back from Hayley to Jesse.

"We did tests, she's your kid."

When the laughing started, Jesse wasn't sure if it was shock or hysteria. Watching him bend over and laugh with such force wasn't something he'd expected, and it threw him off balance. What had he said? Pulling the gun from the back of his jeans, he aimed it at Frank. "Get down on your knees with your hands above your head."

Looking up to Jesse, he saw the gun and smiled.

"You have no idea what you're getting yourself involved in, do you?" Asked Frank, laughing.

"I don't care. Hands above your head," warned Jesse.

"You won't stop this from happening."

"Hands behind your head or I'll shoot," continued Jesse.

"Did she tell you she hid *our* daughter?"

When Frank saw the flicker of doubt cross Jesse's face, he knew he had him where he wanted him.

"Didn't she tell you she carried my baby? That I came to her room every night until the job was complete."

"Hands above your fucking head!" Shouted Jesse.

"She gave her away, because she knows her destiny. She knew the buck would stop with her. She made this happen. She knew the rules and she still put your son in danger."

"You're testing what little patience I have left, so shut the fuck up and put your hands above your head, now!"

"She used you! She used you to get the money herself, and she's used you and your son to draw in the crowd. If she doesn't conceive our child, she'll be rewarded while our entire existence will come into question; you think she chose you because she loves you. She chose you because you'd fight for her."

"What the hell are you talking about?" Asked Jesse, glancing to Hayley who stirred slightly.

"She is the queen in all this. She owns all this. She's the most important playing piece on the board and she's going for check mate. She wants everything and she will do anything to gain it. She's sly, deceitful, and conniving. She makes a father proud."

"You slept with your own daughter?" Asked Jesse, disgusted.

"That's the problem Jesse, once your dick sees the goods, it doesn't matter what the brain tells you. She's a witch, and she's had me under her spell, and now she's turned her charms on you. Think about it. What do you actually know about her? What has she given you? Without you digging, what information has she volunteered?" Sneered Frank, watching his words have their desired effect.

Jesse knew he shouldn't allow him to get inside his head. But he couldn't help thinking back to things she had said or done things he'd found out and then confronted her with only to get a wall of silence or a lie in return. She kept things from him all the time; he didn't even know she had a daughter. Had no idea she'd slept with Frank, but then that didn't feel right. There was no telling what Frank had done. Before Jesse could focus properly, something hit him over the head and fell down like a sack of potatoes.

"Get her in the van," said Frank.

"Yes, sir," spoke Lynnie quietly as she placed the fire extinguisher on the floor.

"It seems we're going to Plan B," added Frank.

"What are you going to do with him?" asked Jax, entering behind Lynnie.

"Chuck him in the boiler room and set a match."

"What about the boy?" asked Lynnie.

"He comes with us. We can use him."

Lynnie glanced to Hayley who was still unconscious on the floor with a cut on her head. Grasping Hayley's wrists, she tugged her out of the room, pulling her along the floor, while her head lolled back.

~

JESSE WOKE to crackling and then coughing. His throat was on fire, fighting to open his eyes made them sting and on releasing them he was met with a wall of heat. Orange and red flickers scorched the wall, cracked the paint and filled the room so all moisture evaporated. Black smoke crawled up the walls, consuming the ceiling. Gasping, he realised his lungs weren't expanding but expelling much needed oxygen.

Dropping fully on the floor the heat burnt through his top, crawling along the floor whilst trying not to inhale he felt a draught, it had to be a door, but with the fire taking hold and the smoke making visibility almost zero he had to hope he was right as he lifted himself up, shoving his shoulder into the door he wanted to cry when it refused to budge.

Chest stinging, he leant forward trying to breathe while he looked around the gloomy room for another exit. He would die, there was no way he could get out of this, and he'd have happily gone if he knew Daniel and Hayley were free but the last time, he'd seen Hayley she was lying on the floor bleeding and Daniel had been screaming in the back of a car watching his granddads throat being cut. Tears stinging his eyes, he shoved the door again, but with absolutely no give he had to look for something that could force it, before he lost all energy and his lung collapsed in on themselves.

~

When Martin arrived, the smoke was billowing out of the back of the warehouse. Knowing instantly that that wasn't a good sign, he ran towards it. Without even touching it, he could feel the heat and tugged on his hair, hoping his worse fears weren't about to come true.

"Jesse! Hayley!"

When all he could hear was the sound of the fire exciting itself, he hoped the feeling in his stomach was just adrenalin, but when a sound came back, he knew.

"Jesse! Hayley!"

Hearing a bang, he looked around to see any gap in the wall that would allow access. With no windows he couldn't even see in, but there was no way that sound was just a rogue tin of paint falling. Someone was trying to get out.

Searching around himself he couldn't see anything that would be useful. Swearing he ran back to the car to check the boot. When he opened it, the DCI ran up behind him. "Found anything?"

"Someone's round the back in the fire, I can't get in!"

"I've got the fire brigade on the way."

"It's gunna be too late. Someone's getting cooked!" Called Martin as he ran round with a car jack in his hand.

"Shit."

Looking at one another as though one of them would suddenly have an idea, they jumped when the explosion sounded, ducking; they watched as debris fired off in every direction while other lighter things floated around them like confetti. Shocked faces searched each other before looking back at the warehouse as it tore itself apart.

"Holy shit!"

"Someone was in there!" Shouted Martin with tears in his eyes. "Oh my God, someone was in there!"

CHAPTER 19

Hayley opened her eyes slowly. Trying to take in where she was before anyone could observe, she was awake. Breathing slowly, she could feel she was on a mattress with her arms tied above her head. Her wrists were being cut into. The restraints felt like tie wraps. Hayley slid her feet along the mattress but couldn't feel restraints on those.

Peeking out of an eyelid, she could tell she was in a cell. Bars stood at a small window on the wall to her left. Light was shining into the room from past her feet, so she guessed that's where the door was. Deciding she was on her own, she fully opened her eyes. Shifting her bum up the bed, she pushed her arms up the headboard so she could almost sit; it was then she noticed the light was coming through a Perspex wall at the end of the bed. Seats lined up in front of it, as though they were getting ready to view a performance. So, this was the ceremony room.

A tear spilled from her eye and she cursed it for showing up. Pulling on her wrists only helped the wraps to dig into her skin deeper, so she stopped. Looking down her body, she noted they had taken the corset off, replacing it with a red lace cover up. Sighing, she relaxed onto the bed and looked around again. This time she noticed the television in the corner above where the Perspex stopped.

Closing her eyes again, she tried to calm her breathing and remember what Jesse had once told her about what to remember if they took her. Smell; she could smell damp, like an outside damp grass smell. She could also detect ash, as though something close by had burnt recently. Wood, she was sure, not food or rubber or anything too potent. But then another smell appeared, something sweet. It was familiar, but she couldn't pick out from where.

Deciding to abandon that for the moment, she thought about sound. OK, she could hear the wind. It was howling outside. She could hear a ticking noise, almost like when a radiator being turned on and heating, other than that there was nothing. Feel. She could feel the mattress. The tie wraps. The scratchy material they dressed her in. A chill in the air. Taste. Her mouth tasted dry but sweet, as though she had swallowed something recently that was sugary, but she couldn't remember eating anything.

It was then she realised how dry her mouth was; she needed a drink. Opening her eyes, she scanned the room again. She couldn't see anything any more useful than before. Sighing, she relaxed into the mattress. That was about as useful as a chocolate fireguard, thought Hayley.

Why hadn't he shown her something like martial arts, something that might have been fucking useful? Then, remembering she had been with Jesse, she tried to remember what had brought her here, but her head refused to work. Where was Jesse?

Laying on the bed, resigned to her fate and hoping she'd survive the ordeal, she finally heard chattering. Sounding as though it was coming from a hall or corridor, she realised the noise was getting louder and therefore closer. Her heart sped up and she could feel her body sweating as the footsteps sounded out around her.

Suddenly the television flashed on, blinding her for a few seconds in the darkened room. Once her sight came back and could focus, she saw in the centre of the television was Daniel. He was playing in a travel cot with mega blocks, lining them up, like he so often did.

More tears rolled down her cheeks, and she wished she could wipe them away, but she just let them fall watching her beautiful boy play contently. Looking away was no use. She could hear him, he was babbling. She couldn't break down, so she tried singing songs in her head to cover over his voice.

Just then she saw men taking seats, positioning themselves to watch her degradation. They didn't once look at her; they were too busy chatting amongst themselves as if this was a boardroom and they were getting ready to take a meeting.

A man appeared in the doorway and rolled a camera in. Plugging it in, he positioned it so it was directly on her. Then the light flashed red, and he left. Heart rate picking up. She realised she was about to go through something she'd never forget, and she silently prayed for Jesse to forgive her.

"We meet again."

Hayley knew that voice, but she closed her eyes. Willing herself to believe she was somewhere else. She could get through this if she took herself some place else.

"They have allowed us to carry on."

Hearing a sound, she opened her eyes to see Demy sliding his tie out from his collar.

"They can't hear you, so you can scream as much as you like, in fact I insist. I'll enjoy it so much more. They just like to watch."

Looking at the television screen, he looked back to her. "Thought you might need reminding of your options. I'd have put Jesse up there too, but he's a little dry n crispy."

"Where is he? What have you done?" Spat out Hayley through gritted teeth. "Just leave him alone, and I'll do whatever you want," she begged, trying to remain firm, as tears streaked her face.

"Jesse's not my concern anymore but him," he said, pointing to the television screen, "I'll keep my end up as long as you keep yours," he laughed, "No pun intended."

Hayley watched him pop the buttons on his shirt and tug the ends out of his trousers. Pulling his flies down, she watched him step out of them. He was already erect, and it made her stomach flip.

"Any false moves and they slit his throat."

Hayley watched as the victorious smile spread across his face. He had her exactly where he wanted her, and there wasn't a damn thing she could do about it. She also knew it wouldn't end with him, because unbeknown to him he was sterile and so to fulfil her prophecy, Frank would once again step in to deliver the goods. Her stomach twisted at the thought, but she had to do this. She had to protect Daniel.

"Last time was all a bit rushed. So, I will take my time. The doors locked. There's no place to go, so I will cut the ties off your wrists."

Hayley waited. Climbing over her body, he tugged on the wrists straps before slicing through them with the penknife from his pocket.

"Do you want a drink?"

Hayley looked at him, confused.

"No need to be uncivilised. If you'd like a drink, I can get you one brought in."

Hayley nodded, her throat was drier than sandpaper right now and maybe the liquor would help. With any luck, they'd add it to an intravenous drip.

"Brandy?"

Nodding again, she watched him snap his fingers and a man on the other side of the Perspex stood up and disappeared. Demy sat up before taking his socks off and slipping out of his shirt, before slipping his penknife back in his trouser pocket. Watching him, she noticed how well built he was. He must have used his time inside to build up in the gym.

Just then the door opened and Frank handed a bottle and two glasses over to his son, winking at Hayley before re-closing the door. Pouring the brandy into the crystal glasses, he handed them both to her, while he held the bottle in the other hand. Taking one, she contemplated smashing it into his skull.

"You wouldn't be quick enough," he answered, smirking as if reading her thoughts.

Sitting on the bed, holding his glass in both hands, he watched hers shake as she lifted the glass to her lips.

"You know, you'd have made an amazing Queen, if you could have just learned to be more submissive."

"I thought Queens were meant to be in charge," answered Hayley, feeling the burn of liquor in her throat.

"They are, of lesser beings. Not of their Master," said Demy, before taking a sip of Brandy while eyeing her over the glass.

"And you're supposed to be my Master, are you?" Scoffed Hayley. Immediately regretting her attitude when he turned to her with those steel eyes of his.

"I know you helped those women get their kids out."

Hayley swallowed another mouthful of Brandy.

"We found them."

Hayley had hoped she was wrong. That once again Jesse's case would have nothing to do with her. But when Demy looked to her, she knew that those boys' deaths were because of him. He'd constructed them, demanded them, and he had blood on his hands.

"And we found her," he whispered, moving her hair around her ear. "She's with us now, so all this will be inconsequential."

When Hayley's eyes widened in shock, he placed his hand around her neck, pinning her to the bed.

"I'm going to enjoy ripping you apart. While your little boy watches his mummy scream."

Looking towards the camera, they had wheeled in. They were going ahead with the film, but now they didn't need her, she'd die. She was about to have every shred of dignity, humanity and self-respect ripped away from her for all those deviants to witness. Bile expelled quicker than she could react to, and she choked as Demy watched her eyes ring in alarm at not being able to fill her lungs. Just as the spots appeared and her body shuck, he flipped her on her side to cough out the remnants in her mouth and throat burning. Her eyes teared up and her throat fought to remain open.

"Tutt tut tut. What a mess," said Demy, shaking his head, dissatisfied. "Now get on the bed and open your legs, I have some toys that need breaking in."

"I fucking hate you," seethed Hayley.

"Yeah, but once you loved me," answered Demy, watching her face pale as she looked to the floor. "There was once upon a time the little girl with the pigtails was begging for it."

Grabbing her chin, he tugged until she was looking straight at him. "I remember you watching me, smiling at me like I held the moon. Patching me up and pushing your breasts under my nose. I remember that sweet innocent girl throwing herself at me when she was just a kid. I remember our first time. The first time you allowed me in. That was all pleasure, babe, and you know it."

"And then you hit me," she cried. "If her conception was so important, why twist it into something horrid? You could have had it all. All you had to do was treat me right, treat me like-"

"Like a princess?" Asked Demy, laughing. "Oh, Hannah, baby. I didn't want a princess. I want you to be submissive."

Hayley cringed at the name he called her. He only ever called her that when he was trying to overpower her. It was as though if he completely rid her of her identity, he could gain complete control over her. "I want everything."

"You're sick," announced Hayley.

"You only just realised?"

Hayley looked at him, trying to work out what game he was playing.

"Thought you were quicker than that," he said, standing up and hovering over her, as she shifted back onto the bed to lie down and get ready to close her eyes.

Filling up her glass with brandy, he brought it to her lips. She swallowed the liquid quickly. Once she'd finished, he tucked both their glasses under the bed. Sitting on the bed next to her, he separated her legs and looked to her most private parts. Hayley gulped and stared up at the ceiling. Think of something else, anything else; just think of clouds and lambs...

"You remind me of your mother," he confessed.

That made her look at him.

"She was beautiful, strong, and compassionate."

"You knew my mother?" She asked.

Hayley's mum had died before they had moved to Averham; there was no way Demy could know her mum. He was lying; he had to be.

"I found her with my dad. She was shocked I'll give'r that, much like you are now." Laughed Demy. "They must have been having an affair. Thought they could keep it secret. Then, not long after they conceived you, she upped and left. I knew you were his and hers the second I saw you, Hannah. They may have called you Hayley when you came back, but I knew who you really were. You were my Dad's bastard. But with *that* blood running through your veins, I couldn't very well kill you, could I? so I had to have you instead. Make you kneel to me. Take my orders and serve me, and it was fucking beautiful."

Hayley could feel the alcohol work itself back up, but she forced it down again.

"You were so young when you arrived. So sweet and innocent and so utterly naïve. The second I told my dad I wanted you he said I had to earn you, so he sent me away to do his dirty work. I killed men for you, slit women's throats and lay with psychopaths just so I could learn how to tame you."

Standing at the foot of the bed she could feel his eyes on her, and after a few grunt noises that showed he was getting himself ready, she felt him straddle her body. Leaning over her he sniffed her hair whilst pushing the bra straps down her arms, revelling in the feel of her skin on his fingertips, and tracing the outline of her cups he flicked her breasts from them, exposing her nipples. Bending down, he ran his wet tongue along them, sitting back to watch them peak when he blew on them. Hayley flicked her eyes to the screen and then closed them. Willing herself to just go with it. Daniel needed her to do it.

"Have you any idea how hard you make me?" He whispered along her stomach, then as if to prove it, he thrust his still clothed penis into her thigh.

She couldn't stop the sob leaving her mouth, and she knew he'd heard it, as he chuckled while running his tongue down her left thigh. "I can smell you, I knew you wanted this."

Before she could answer, she heard shouting. Forcing her head up, she saw the men beyond the Perspex mid dress, trying to shuffle themselves back into their trousers. Looking down the corridor at the commotion.

Demy sat up, pinning her thighs to the bed, and waited for the imminent knock on the door. When it came, they swiftly opened it and Hayley saw the bloody figure hunching over being half carried, half dragged by two thugs wearing guns. Throwing the figure unceremoniously on the floor, they stepped back and shut the door before grinding the lock across. The figure groaned and then looked up, instantly connecting with Hayley's eyes. Smiling his crooked smile even through the blood, sweat and grime covering him, his teeth shone out like bright stars.

"Jesse!" Exclaimed Hayley, excitement quickly being taken over by concern when the smell of burning hit her nose.

"Well, well, well," said Demy, nodding at the dishevelled man on the ground. It was then she realised Jesse's wrists and ankles were bound with tie wraps.

"If it isn't the thorn in my side." Shifting from the bed, he moved over to Jesse, pulling his head by his hair. "Thought you'd come and enjoy the entertainment, did you?"

"Let her go," growled Jesse, before spitting out blood.

"What? When the fun's only just beginning? No chance."

Dropping Jesse's head, he looked to the Perspex window, clicking his fingers before swivelling them. Hayley watched as the man dressed in a blue pinstripe suit nodded before leaving. A few seconds later, the television flashed with black and white spots before a computer screen came up. Wondering what was going on, Hayley watched as its cursor navigated the documents on the screen before it opened up a live feed with comments running down the side of the video showing the room with her on the bed with Jesse still on the floor and Demy looming over him. Having a bad feeling deep in her stomach, she glanced at Jesse who had turned his head to the screen to watch. When he looked back to her, he looked a lot less satisfied than when he was thrown in.

"OK, looks like we're ready," said Demy. "And you two are the stars of the show."

Glancing to one another again, Hayley saw a flicker of fear. Whatever he had planned, it wasn't this, and that meant they were in real danger.

"So, now we have a live feed ready and waiting to be turned on. I suppose I best tell you the plan," said Demy, slamming his hands together and making Hayley jump a mile in the air. Demy laughed, and Hayley cursed herself for showing how scared she was.

"The camera in the corner," said Demy, pointing to it. "Will capture our home video. It will then live stream to all those who wish to take part. They will then vote on scenarios that they would like to see, and we will take part in them. We obviously need to give them a good show. They pay a lot of money for the privilege of watching a live action snuff film."

"A what film?" Asked Hayley.

"He's going to kill us," explained Jesse flatly.

Demy tutted, moving his index finger from one side to the other.

"No, no no no no, you're going to kill each other."

"I never agreed to this! Let him go!" Shouted Hayley. "You said Daniel would be safe. How can he be? If he's got neither one of us?" Asked Hayley, trying to compose herself.

"I keep my promises. I'll allow him to go home. But I didn't promise who to," reminded Demy. "I've left you Marie, and I'm sure Rob wouldn't mind being the white knight once you're not here to contradict his story."

"You fucking bastard!" She shouted again, tears streaming down her face. "You set him up, didn't you?"

"Hayley, it's OK," said Jesse trying to calm her down, but when she looked at him, she was anything but calm. "It's OK."

"How the hell is it OK?" She cried, not taking her eyes from his. Hoping he'd somehow let her know he had a plan. But she got nothing other than love, and that would not save them right now.

Demy moved over to the camera and fiddled with knobs and dials on the back. For what reason, neither Jesse nor Hayley was sure. They wanted to say so much, but with Demy being in the room neither said another word.

"OK, we have some requests," said Demy, as though he was making them aware of someone's drinks order. "Just waiting on those results now."

Looking down at the lingerie she was sporting, she felt as though she may as well be naked. It wasn't as though it was revealing everything already. But when she looked at Jesse, she realised just how vulnerable he was wearing a shirt, jeans, heavy boots that she didn't recognise and his ripped leather jacket. He looked as though he'd crawled through barbed wire. Kneeling up so he was leaning on his knees and ankles, he shuffled closer to her.

"Remember what I said at the beach," whispered Jesse.

Hayley nodded slowly, unsure how that would help their predicament.

"I love you."

Hayley nodded again, trying to force the quiver in her lip to stop as tears rolled down her face whilst she stared at Jesse.

"OK, we have our first one. Jesse, you will need to get out of your clothes."

"Fuck you!" Shouted Jesse through clenched teeth.

"No, that will be her job," said Demy, pointing to a shocked Hayley. "It will involve you two in some BDSM; we will start things off light." Hayley couldn't hide the look of pure shock written across her face. If *that* was light, what the hell were they going to be made to do? "Here, we have blind folds, whips, gags, handcuffs…" said Demy, reeling off what was in the black bag he was holding. Which he'd hidden behind the camera's tripod. "… dildo's, rings, anal tools, I mean just about anything. I've even been kind enough to supply lube."

Hayley couldn't stop the sudden shudder of fear trembling down her body. Throwing the bag on the bed he watched as the two people he had imprisoned sat with fear in their eyes, and he loved it. Picking up a control for the television from the floor, he pressed a button and Daniel came back up, sitting with his toy cars.

"Just in case you forgot what was at stake."

"I can't do this," said Hayley almost to herself. She could feel her chest tightening, and she was struggling to breathe. She had to calm down before a panic attack arrived, but she couldn't, everything was so overwhelming.

"Are you going to get these off then? How am I supposed to fuck her if I'm tied up?" Asked Jesse.

The sudden use of his voice in such a harsh way made her search his face, but he was giving nothing away.

"Good, I like your eagerness. But you'll not be fucking her, that's my job," admitted Demy with a devious smile.

"You said-"

"I said, I had a bag of toys," remarked Demy, raising his brow.

Jesse looked back to Hayley, the shock and the horror of their situation still painted on her face.

"Ever been fucked by a man before Jesse?"

Oh, hell no! Jesse shook his head ferociously.

"I'll take you then when I'm done; you'll watch me rip her apart." Hayley's eyes were as big as saucers as she stared at Jesse's. "When I say rip her apart. I mean, she will scream to die," whispered Demy in Jesse's ear.

"Jesse, I can't do this," whispered Hayley, as her face crumpled in fear.

Jesse turned back to Demy, watching him enjoying himself.

"Untie me then," said Jesse.

Demy pulled out the penknife from his trousers that remained crumpled on the floor. Staring into Hayley's eyes, Jesse mouthed to Hayley to trust him. She nodded, but felt far less confident than she hoped. Feeling his ankles free up. He waited until his wrists did too. Being far too aware that the man behind him had a flick knife in his hand, Jesse rubbed at his wrists as he freed them. Not taking his eyes from Hayley, he slipped his buttons from his shirt. Once they were free, he shuffled his shoulders out of his shirt and dropped it on the floor.

Gone was the hope of relief she would feel when she saw a wire taped to his chest. There was no wire, and she wanted to cry, especially when she saw her name tattooed over his heart. When had he got that? Why hadn't she asked him before now? Flicking the stud buttons open on his jeans, he then pushed them down his legs before realising he'd have to undo his boots. Bending down, he slowly untied his right boot before lifting his left foot out. Doing the same with the other before stepping out of his jeans, he retrieved the knife from his sock, hiding it in his palm as he stood up. Standing tall, he eyed Hayley and gently nodded.

"A fine specimen he is Hayley," said Demy. "You will need your boxers down too," said Demy in a fake whisper.

Rolling his eyes, Jesse slowly swept them down, still not taking his eyes from hers. Suddenly cold metal plunged into his kidney and Jesse cried out as warm blood flowed from the wound Demy had inflicted.

"Just in case you had any ideas about who was in charge here." whispered Demy close to his ear.

Jesse stifled any further reaction of the pain he felt so as not to give Demy the satisfaction but more importantly to ensure Hayley wasn't aware of the injury.

He needed her to be focused not panicked.

"OK Hayley, looks like you need to liven him up a bit. Best get your mouth round him."

"She doesn't need to do that," said Jesse stubbornly.

"It seems she does," explained Demy. Eyeing his package from over his shoulder. "Unless that's it?"

Deciding to ignore him, before he lashed out and cost them their only chance of escape. Jesse beckoned for Hayley to crawl down the bed to him. Flicking his eyes to the side of the bed, she glanced to Demy, who was watching his own hand run down Jesse's back. Sliding her finger into the edge of the glass, she brought it up between her fingers, hiding it down the side of the bed. Jesse smiling a little to say he was proud of her. She crawled further down the bed until she was millimetres from Jesse's manhood.

"That's it, Hannah. Open your mouth, let him in," soothed Demy from behind Jesse.

Looking up to Jesse, he took a breath before tapping his left peck three times. Nodding, she eyed his fingers.

"Come on Hannah, it's mine or his?" Taunted Demy. One tap, Two taps, Three taps.

Whipping to the right, Hayley swung the glass, smashing it into the side of Demy's head. While it disorientated him, Jesse lunged at him, forcing him to the floor as he rained blows to his head. Once Jesse was sure he was unconscious, he looked to the Perspex window where twelve men sat with their dicks in their hands, seemingly unfazed by the man on the floor. Shaking his head at the sight, he grabbed Hayley, holding her trembling frame in his arms. She held onto him with all her strength. Once he felt safe enough to let her go, he crouched down, picking up his jeans he slipped them on, buttoning and zipping the top she watched him crouch again for his shirt, seeing blood.

Suddenly Jesse's feet went from underneath him and he folded onto the floor like a scrap of paper. Holding his side, he looked up to see Hayley's eyes focus on what was behind him, before she screamed and lunged forward. Knocking Demy off his feet, she landed on him, smashing his wrist on the concrete floor repeatedly until his grip on the penknife finally gave way. Reaching for it, she felt his hands grip her neck, forcing the life from her. She extended her hand, but each time her fingertips hit the knife, it spun. Her vision blurred and she could feel her lungs tighten, screaming to open.

Jesse being able to see what she was trying to do shuffled across the floor. Barging into her, she moved over Demy's body an extra couple of inches, grasping the knife she swung and punctured Demy's carotid artery, spraying her in bright red warm fluid. Looking down, she screamed. When all her energy depleted, she slumped over Demy's body, delighted he didn't move.

"Baby."

Turning her head, she spied Jesse holding his side, but looking at her with more relief than pain. "He's gone."

Looking to her hand, she noticed it still gripped the handle of the knife. Looking to the Perspex, she noticed the men shuffling themselves away hurriedly. Knowing she wasn't even out of this horror show made her cry. She was exhausted and still men were outside, people who wanted to harm her.

"Baby, look."

Looking towards the screen that Jesse nodded towards, she saw a man in a stab suit with police written on the front lift her son from the gaze of the camera. Quickly looking back to Jesse, he smiled through the pain.

"We've got him."

Letting go of the knife, she scrambled towards Jesse. Taking his head in her hands, she kissed him with all the energy she possessed.

∽

"Upstairs sweetheart, look after your brother and sister, I'll be up shortly." rushed her mother, while glancing to the front door as if terrified.

"Mum, what's going on?" Asked Hayley flicking her gaze back to her Dad who looked shocked and in pain, as he held his head in his hands on the sofa. As though it was too heavy to lift, to simply tell them it was OK. They were alright, they were just going to bed early and that horrible swirling in her stomach was just from her meal not settling yet.

"Please baby, do as I say. Upstairs, pull the drawers across your bedroom door and stay until I get you."

Her mum had never asked her to do that before and she could see the beginning of tears in her eyes. Why was her mum trying not to cry? Deciding to do as she was told, she carried her sister upstairs while her brother lagged as though he was more bored that concerned, but that suited her fine. If they weren't scared, maybe she was just overreacting?

"I love you." On hearing her mother say those words she turned, but she was already gone.

Walking into their sparse bedroom, she helped her brother and sister into her bed, tucking the covers around them. Then turning to the chest of drawers she pushed on them to skid them across the carpet, but they were heavier than they looked. Leaning her back on them, she pushed all her strength down into her feet, until it finally budged and stopped behind the door. Their only way out. Looking at the window, she tiptoed to it and saw men coming towards the house. Not wanting to be caught, she ran back to the bed and slipped in, holding her brother and sister to her chest.

That's when the shooting started, the banging, and the voices that were unrecognisable but deep and loud. Hayley couldn't hear what they were saying, but they didn't sound happy and they scared her. Pulling the covers up higher, she settled in while telling her brother and sister that everything was going to be OK. But she didn't feel it and as the minutes went by, the noises got louder, the shouts more aggressive, the screams piercing and then a thud.

Silence.

Time passed in the silence and looking to her siblings she could see that they were both asleep. Creeping out from between them, she gently and ever so quietly slipped out from the warm confines of the blankets and pulled on the legs of the drawers. When there was gap enough to fit her slender body down the side between the wall and the drawers, she pushed with all her might until the door was free.

Stepping out she scoured the upstairs hoping to find her mum had already come to bed, but of course she wasn't. Tiptoeing downstairs, she opened the living room door gently, and lightly stepped to the kitchen door, which was already open. Looking through the gap where the hinges where she saw the back of her dad as he crouched over, with shaking shoulders. Biting her lip, she tried to see more of the room and then that's when she saw her Mother's foot lying close to her dad. Stepping out from behind the door, she stood resolutely in the doorway watching her Dad cry.

"Please forgive me, I'm so sorry." When he turned to see who was watching, his face crumpled. Over his shoulder she could see her Mother's pale face, with red trickling down her forehead and sliding down her face, making a river between her closed dull lips.

"Hayley, sweetheart. I'm so sorry." Looking to her father, she noticed the baseball bat in his hand. What had he done?

∽

POLICE FORCED their way into the room. Blood. So much blood. Someone was speaking to her but her head was under water, she couldn't make out the sounds.

"Hayley, you're safe" Finally she heard what they were saying, and she stared at the man she had killed. "Hayley, you need to come with us."

Letting the person lift her up, she grabbed at the jacket someone threw over her shoulders.

"Hayley, you're safe, Daniel's safe, we're taking you home," said the voice.

"Daniel," said Hayley absently.

The officer steered her down the corridor in to the fresh air, towards a car, "Daniel."

"He's safe, you'll see him real soon."

Hayley sat in the back of the car, numb. She was aware of people around her. Things moving, lights flashing. But she was numb. She couldn't move, but she couldn't stop shaking either. She couldn't hear, but it was too loud, and the blood in her hands grew darker.

Why was she shaking? Her teeth chattered, but she wasn't cold. She couldn't feel anything. Why had that memory come back? Why was it so vivid? Who were those men?

No, she knew who those men were, or at least two of them. It had been Demy and Frank. Why had they come to her home? Why had her mum died?

∽

SUDDENLY THE DOOR OPENED, letting in a cold draft. Turning, she saw Jesse. Standing up abruptly, she flung herself into his arms, causing him to stumble back and nearly lose his footing.

"Steady there."

Martin was behind him, but she didn't even see him as she clung on for dear life. Jesse could feel her trembling in his arms, but he couldn't let go. Once he knew Daniel was safe and relatively unhurt, he needed to make sure Hayley was alright.

"Are you OK?" Asked Jesse.

Nodding furiously, she grasped for Jesse once again until a throat clearing made her look up. DCI Fryer looked on, none too pleased about the situation.

"You're side?" Asked Hayley, watching his face smile as he looked her up and down.

"I will be fine, don't worry. If I forget to tell you later," whispered Jesse. "You look hot."

Laughing, she kissed Jesse as though she needed him to breathe. Yet more tears escaped.

"Hayley, I need you to get back in the car. We need to get you back to the station and processed," said DCI Fryer.

"Processed?" Asked Jesse. "You're not charging her, surely?"

"You know the procedure, Jesse. Backup, you can have her back as soon as we're finished."

Hayley looked at him wide-eyed, shock clear on her face at the thought of being charged for murder.

"And I need your report on my desk yesterday."

Shaking his head, Jesse tried to comfort her. "Don't worry, you'll be fine, I'll meet you at the station with Daniel, OK?" Nodding, she bent back down to take her seat back in the car, before DCI Fryer closed the door.

"I'll see you there, take care of her," warned Jesse.

Rolling his eyes, he opened the front door and climbed in.

∼

"Drink up; you need it for the shock."

Hayley took the offered tea, curling her fingers around the mug.

"They have processed you?"

She nodded.

"Jesse's been notified, he's on his way, he's bringing a change of clothes."

Nodding again, he wasn't sure if she was taking anything in. She'd stopped shaking, but the resolute numbness was a sure sign that this would not be easy to get over.

"We need to interview you while everything is still fresh in your mind. I know it's difficult, but we can stop as many times as you like. We'll record it, and you'll be in a soft room. Are you ready?"

"Daniel."

"He's with Jesse."

He'd already explained several times they had him and he was safe, but he supposed she was finding it difficult to believe. After all, the last time she had seen was when he was on that screen in that room.

"They have checked over him and he's well."

Nodding again, she stood up to follow DCI Fryer to the soft room. Walking in, she was shown a green sofa, with a coffee table separating it from an identical one opposite. The room had posters on the walls and a play table in the corner for young children. A bookcase sat to the side, and a plant lived behind the door, looking a little less well kept than it should have.

"Take a seat. Our resident psychologist will be with us shortly. She'll just be here to make sure you're taken care of."

CHAPTER 20

WALKING INTO THE STATION, JESSE STOPPED AT THE DESK TO IDENTIFY himself, and why he was there. From there he was led to a private room to fill in his statement and wait for news. Being unable to sit for long, he paced, watching the minutes tick by on his phone as there was purposely no clock in the room. Coffee after coffee sat on the small table untouched from well-wishing officers dropping in to see how he was holding up. He was feeling like the prize goldfish. Suddenly the door opened and in walked Martin holding two cups of coffee from the machine.

"Please don't tell me you've brought me another bloody coffee," Jesse sighed, eyeing Martin's hands.

Martin followed his eyes and poured the cup's contents into the nearby plant pot in the corner.

"That's plastic," noted Jesse.

Martin just shrugged.

"Well now, it's an air freshener. Eau de la fine roast," Jesse shook his head, being unable to hide the laugh. "Heard anything?"

"She's being interviewed, seems there's a lot to discuss."

"You've not seen her yet?"

Jesse shook his head.

Sitting down on the chair, Martin took the other. "How's your side?"

"Stinging like a bitch. But it can wait," said Jesse, rubbing his side.

"What, you've not seen a medic yet?"

"Unfortunately, they wouldn't take no for an answer, so I'm freshly stitched." answered Jesse.

"Good," answered Martin. "How's Daniel?"

"He's good, physically. But it took a long time to calm him down enough to stay with Mum."

"Your mum has him?"

"There is no one else," answered Jesse coolly.

He was still feeling raw over his father's brutal death and the days seemed to have stretched to months with most things. But the death of his father was still so raw and felt like only yesterday. Which made him morbidly laugh. It was only yesterday.

"To be honest, he's probably a good distraction. The hard bit will be getting him back home," admitted Jesse.

"Yeah," nodded Martin, noticing the darkness around Jesse's eyes. "How are you?"

"Battered, bruised and knackered," sighed Jesse.

"I can't say I'm surprised. It was a hell of a night."

Jesse looked down to the gaping hole in his shirt that had darkened with blood earlier. "How did you get out of that back room?"

"I managed to prise the door open with a metal rod. It was a good job, because by the time I made it to the other end of the warehouse it had gone up."

"Yeah, I know. I was on the outside trying to get in."

"Shit! So, you thought?.."

Martin just nodded.

"Can't get rid of me that easy." Jesse smirked. "I should have changed." Noted Jesse out loud, smelling the shirt and observing the stains.

If Hayley saw him looking as bad as he did, she might go into another panic attack. Besides, he stunk of smoke and sweat.

"When did you last eat?"

Jesse shrugged.

"Right well." said Martin "I'm going to grab you something, you look like shit on a stick."

Jesse watched Martin leave, feeling the vacuum of the room once again. Downing a couple more Paracetamol, he grimaced once they slipped down.

∽

Martin and Jesse sat across from one another, not speaking. Having offered few words and devoured a chicken sandwich and a packet of crisps, Jesse slumped back on the seat. "I didn't realise how hungry I was."

"I could tell. Thought I was going to have to pop out for some Gaviscon halfway through." Jesse smirked at Martin's gibe.

"Do you think she's eaten?"

"I'm sure they're taking good care of her." Jesse nodded, looking far off.

"Hey, she's safe," reminded Martin.

"Yeah, but…, it was sick. I don't know how the hell she's survived before now," said Jesse, holding his head in his hands.

Martin wished he could tell him some good news, but the officers on the case were all tight-lipped. He'd tried on numerous occasions, he wasn't sure if it was because they couldn't or wouldn't though.

"We've been digging into that USB stick and all the files contained on it this morning. Everyone is going in as we speak, they've handed us everything on a plate. The files will only corroborate anything that Hayley had been through, and there're thousands of them."

"I've heard this before," Jesse sighed, not wanting to get his hopes up.

"No, all we got before was all Demy and Paul's involvement, and anyone they cared not to protect. This time, when I say everyone, I mean everyone. There will be some huge arrests in the up-and-coming days. I mean lead business executives, politicians, diplomats, everything. This was huge, bigger than we ever could have imagined, and global."

Jesse sighed, he was so tired, but he needed to see Hayley and take her home.

"Darren knew he was close, says they've been watching him and that he didn't have long to live. But he wanted to expose them before he died, unfortunately he didn't get to see it. But he'd posted copies to all the major papers. Thank fully because of the encryption it's stalled them. The chiefs keeping them all at bay for now, while we sort through the files. But this will explode. It will disrupt the entire establishment."

"There's something I still don't understand," said Jesse, scratching his neck.

"What?"

"The boys, why kill the boys, how could they possibly be a threat?"

"Well, according to Darren, there was a war going onto between the leadership campaign of the crown. Four families were vying for the spot. One was Frank, one was some Italian and the other an American, but the fourth goes by the name of Castor, and that's all we have on him, he's invisible."

"How can he be going for a title if no one knows who he is?"

"According to the information he sent us, no one needs to. He just has to have enough money, power and a bigger army then the others. As long as deals are done, favours are paid and they make money no one cares who anyone is, anyway it seems Castor was out to destroy Frank's rein. Which meant taking out anyone who could resume his power through inheritance."

"But those kids weren't his."

"No, but they belonged to his army. We think he was taking out the next generation. Like a ruling class, if you take out the heads, then they go down the line and you're looking at cousins and aunts, etc."

"But they must know Daniel wasn't..." looking at Martin, Jesse realised what he was saying. "Hayley."

"Yeah, she was important to both roles. Frank wanted her to carry his heir, make him rightful king as she holds his blood, and her mother who was Queen."

"Apparently her mum married Alexi, Frank's brother. While he was in charge, being the older brother, she became Queen. She's the most important playing piece on the board until her daughter carries royal blood, by either Demy or Frank or another founding father. But with the Queen being dead, they only had Hayley to rely on. Much like Frank taking out Alexi, Frank held all the power. No one else can marry a Queen, it would bring out all-out war among the sect. That's why we believe Castor is in fact Alexi, and he set up his own death. Preparing for the day, he could kill Frank and take leadership back. Now what we don't know is whether Daniel is some kind of half-blood prince."

"What the fuck are you talking about?" Asked Jesse, unsure he hadn't fallen into a fantasy book. "If you start talking about magic hats in a minute, I'm having you sectioned."

"I know, it's bizarre and desperately out there, but I swear I'm not tugging your squirrel with this. I came here to get you and Hayley, Marie and Daniel into a safe house."

"You're telling me Hayley is some fucking princess in a royal war!"

"More like a mafia princess, but yeah. There's a war going on, and she's at the centre. This sect has been responsible for billions of pounds moving around the globe, and they've just had a leadership challenge and their lead competitor has just been arrested. When the new leader moves in, which he inevitably will, we do not know how that will affect Hayley or Daniel, at least not until we know who takes over."

"And if this Castor is Alexi, what then?" Asked Jesse.

"Then he either claims her or signs for her execution."

"This can't be real. I'm in a fucking nightmare," said Jesse, holding his head in his hands as he tugged at his hair.

"What Darren gave us, gives us a way in, to work with others around the world in bringing these people down. But you know as well as I do, not all countries will accommodate us or work alongside us to bring these people down. Especially if their government is involved in illegal gains."

"And where's Castor?" Asked Jesse.

"According to records that Darren got, we think he's in Russia."

"Then we might as well give up now," said Jesse, defeated. "We haven't got a prayer of collaborating with them."

"Which is why we hide you lot. New identities, new jobs, new life," answered Martin. "Do you think you can do that?"

Jesse held his praying hands to his forehead, breathing into them as if to warm them up.

"Hide until we find out what kind of threat, you're in."

"Jesus Christ Martin, what the hell I have walked into?" Asked Jesse desperately.

"Nothing I've ever seen, that's for sure."

Watching Jesse with his head in his hands, he was unsure whether to fill him in on the investigation of the boys or not. When silence enveloped them, Jesse looked back up to see the fraught look on his face.

"What is it?" Asked Jesse, watching Martin pull his tie from his throat.

"The swans. They can be a symbol of love or motherhood."

Jesse continued to listen.

"We know the boys were connected through the church. Their biological mothers were part of it. We think they killed the boys to send a message. That anyone involved in the vine would have their children cut out of it. Like I said, I think they're trying to take out the old allegiances."

"But there was only one boy with the swan's wings?"

"Yeah, that's because his mother was a founding member's wife." Martin swallowed before continuing. "We spoke with her, they assaulted her much like Hayley. She got rid of her offspring through an illegal adoption to protect him. They meant him to die. She said they believe the blood of the firstborn between the royal families is holy and as such is sacrificed for the good of the church. They believe that once the child's blood is spilt, they rein over all for their sacrifice.

She said the congregation pay handsomely for it, and their power over it, restored. It's the second child that lives and is married off."

"So, *this* is a war?" Asked Jesse, dumbfounded. "And Daniel is her second child."

Martin nodded.

"But we have no evidence that Hayley had an older sibling?"

"No, I think Hayley's mum found out what would happen to her and ran. I can only presume that she was too old to sacrifice when they got her back," answered Martin.

"That's why they need Hayley. If she's one of the last female blood lines, then she holds the key to the next ruler," spoke Jesse, not quite believing what he was saying.

"Only we have no idea how many more female blood lines there are, and it makes me wonder if that's what all those murders were about with Demy. Maybe he'd counted his chickens before they'd hatched. He thought he had the golden goose and took out the women responsible for any competition. It makes the way they died, make a lot more sense."

"The cuts and the bloodletting," said Jesse as if to himself. "He was ensuring he'd be crowned. You think those women were in Hayley's position of just carrying heirs?"

"We didn't know those women because they didn't exist. I think they're reared specifically for this one job, to bear fruit." explained Martin. "He wasn't as crazy as we thought, but he *was* a game-changer. I think he found these women who could help rival his campaign for leadership and took them out so that Hayley became the ultimate prize. But it meant she was also untouchable, as in, if she died their entire structure would fall apart."

"So that was why they never let her out?" Asked Jesse. "But by those rules they'd have needed her to give birth twice, one for the sacrifice and one for the heir?"

Martin nodded.

"They could play it that the first baby died already," answered Martin.

"Only it didn't," answered Jesse, watching his friend's face turn from confusion to shock.

Just then the door swung open and DCI Fryer stood in the doorway, glancing from Jesse to Martin as he entered the room and closed the door. "OK, she's been processed, cleaned up and interviewed. She'll have to come back, but we've got enough to be moving on with at the moment. The psychologist is just having a few moments with her, and then we'll take you to her."

"How is she?" Asked Martin, standing at the same time as Jesse.

"She's..." taking a breath, he wasn't sure how to continue. "She's had to deal with a lot. I don't think it's properly hit her yet, but she's lucid enough."

"Did they..?" Jesse hoped Fryer understood where he was going with that, because he couldn't form the words.

"No, you got there in time. Unfortunately, Demy wasn't so lucky, she killed him on site," answered DCI Fryer.

"She killed him?" asked Martin, astonished.

DCI Fryer and Jesse nodded solemnly. "She's not under arrest, she can go home, but as you can imagine, she's pretty shaken up."

"Can we go, I need to see her?"

DCI Fryer nodded, walking them to the lounge he'd just left. Tapping on the door, he poked his head through. "Hayley, Jesse's here to take you home. Can I let him in?" asked DCI Fryer softly

Hayley nodded, wringing paper tissue in her hands. The lady next to her patted her hand and moved to the door as it opened wider and Jesse rushed in.

Jesse stood staring at her, dressed in the clothes he had brought her earlier, hair dishevelled, eyes dark and red rimmed, face puffy from crying but pale from exhaustion. Hayley looked up into his light blue eyes. She wanted to run into his arms, but she couldn't move. All she could see was pain and anguish, fear and shock. Did she really look that bad? Finally, standing, she stood silently watching him digest what he saw. DCI Fryer and the psychologist called Marina stood by the door watching the exchange, or lack of, probably unsure whether to leave.

"I... I... k... killed... h... him," said Hayley starting to break down on the words, before she'd finished her knees gave way and she began to drop. Before hitting the floor, Jesse's arms had swept around her, forcing her to breathe in his cologne as he pinned her head to his chest.

DCI Fryer and Marina shared a look, then closed the door behind them.

"I killed him," she cried.

Jesse closed his eyes, absorbing every tremble of her body, his shirt soaking up every tear. Holding his eyes closed tight, he wished he could take away her agony.

"How's Daniel?"

"He'll be a lot better once he sees you," he answered, pulling away from her to see her teary eyes. "Come on. I'm taking you home."

Turning away from the room, they walked down the corridor to the exit. Jesse with his arm draped over Hayley's shoulder.

"Jesse, we need to get a move out. Officers are at Marie's now," said Martin, coming off the phone.

"What's going on?" Asked Hayley, tensing, stopping as she registered what Martin had said. Martin and Jesse shared a look, and Hayley looked from one to the other, waiting. "Well?"

"We need to get Hayley tested too. Know for sure," said Martin, as though Hayley wasn't stood right in front of him.

"What's going on? What don't I know?"

Sharing a glance again, both breathing out heavily before pursing their lips.

"Tested for what?"

CHAPTER 21

THEY WALKED INTO THE CLINICAL LOOKING, DISINFECTANT SMELLING house. The painted the walls were white, with no hooks or blemishes. The floors were wooden throughout, except for the tiled kitchen floor. The bathroom at the end of the corridor held a white suit with a roll top tub with a curtain rail and a white shower curtain surrounding it. Jesse opened the door to the master bedroom, and then a smaller room with a bed cot.

"Well, its white," said Hayley.

"I wish Mum was here," said Jesse.

Hayley rubbed her hand up and down his arm to offer comfort.

"You don't have to do this, you know, go be with her," she said.

"Hayley, there's no going back. Whether or not Mum needs me, I can't leave you and Daniel. And you know Daniel can't come with me,"

Hayley nodded, they'd been told everything. After realising the organisation was much bigger than expected, they could no longer be absolutely certain they had everyone involved as Hayley and Daniel seemingly playing important roles because of their heritage. They couldn't be sure of their safety until they had all the facts and all the perpetrators behind bars. Added to that, Hayley was the material witness to most of the case. So was now a witness in need of protection.

The role of Jesse's job had meant he was also in severe danger if anyone wanted to go through him to her or vice versa. So, they'd moved away from the area under an alias. Jesse had been informed it was highly probable he would need to retire from the force in order to live a civilian life and remain under the radar, something that had brought tears to Hayley's eyes knowing how much he loved his job, but he just nodded resolutely as though his entire world hadn't just changed.

Hayley had been on the run since she was sixteen and had come accustomed to moving around, having no ties but she had ties now. To a job and her colleagues as well as Jesse's family and as quickly as she had felt part of them, she was now being taken away from them. Not that there were many left now. Michael was dead and Rob was in the wind but it was a life she had felt safe in and now she was back to square one, living each day as though it might be her last.

"Jesse I-" Jesse stopped her from speaking by holding a finger to her lips. "What?" She whispered, watching him look around the room as if he was trying to find something whilst holding Daniel in his arms.

"Can you hear that?" Asked Jesse, stalking in front of her.

"What?" Whispered Hayley. "I can't hear anything."

"Exactly," smiled Jesse, watching her frown turn to a smile.

"Idiot," said Hayley, nudging him out of the way.

"Harsh. Let's get sorted out, have something to eat, and when Daniel goes to sleep, we'll have that chat."

"What chat?" Asked Hayley, spinning back round to face him.

"The one we've been putting off for over a year."

"OK," said Hayley, swallowing.

Picking up a suitcase from the floor, carrying it along the hallway until she faced a bedroom.

"Jesse!" calling out, she waited for Jesse to come back into view from the kitchen.

"What's up?"

THE VINE TREE

"There's only one bed."

"We only need one bed, Daniel's still in a cot, isn't he?"

"Well... yeah... but..." stammered Hayley, feeling her cheeks flush. "It's just... er... one..."

Smiling at her embarrassment, he decided to let her off the hook.

"Hey, don't worry about it, I'll take the couch, you take the bedroom, OK?"

Nodding foolishly, she rushed into the bedroom to unpack.

They had not discussed sleeping arrangements, and she'd just assumed they would put them in for accommodation that allowed for separate rooms, obviously not.

Jesse had cooked and sorted Daniel out after getting grumpy by giving him a bath and laying him down in his cot with his favourite blanket and toy. He joined Hayley at the small dining table in the kitchen. Having washed up and tidied the kitchen back up, she welcomed the taste of the wine Jesse had nipped out to buy earlier while she was still unpacking.

"So, come on we need to talk," said Jesse, having filled her empty glass with wine, hoping to loosen her up enough to talk freely.

They needed to be honest with each other and this was the ideal opportunity with a new home, a new relationship, an alternative life. Taking the glass, she took another sip before eyeing him over the glass. His stern but compassionate face told her there was no getting out of this.

"What do you want to know?" Asked Hayley, unsure where he wanted her to start.

"Start from the beginning," answered Jesse.

"I met Demy when I was nine. We were in a small village and while Dad drank himself silly, I had to look after Darren and Lyndsey. I didn't mind looking after them, of course, but some days it just got too much," she shrugged hopelessly.

"How do you mean?" Asked Jesse.

"I was running the home single-handed. In between school I made meals, washed, cleaned, tidied and shopped. I was exhausted, and they were tiring, especially when all they used to do was complain I wasn't their mum when I told them to tidy their shit up," answered Hayley taking another sip, remembering the times she'd cried on her bed from grief after face planting it from exhaustion.

"Kids, I suppose," remarked Jesse.

"Yeah, only it's the last thing you want to hear when you miss her like crazy and want to be just as good as her."

Jesse nodded sympathetically.

"That's when I met him. I was struggling with some shopping. One bag split and I lost it, kicked shit out of the tins in them, stubbed my toes then fell into a mess in the middle of the road. Apparently, he'd seen the whole thing, so he helped me. When we got back to mine, I offered to make him a drink. We got chatting, and he told me he was fourteen, said he was out working with his dad when he'd spotted me. Because it was the countryside, he could drive his dad's car. He seemed really nice and I think I fell a little in love with him then. He listened to me tell him about Mum and Dad, offered me a shoulder to cry on."

"Understandable," said Jesse, although the idea made him feel sick.

"Then my dad was furious one night, said they had cheated him out of everything. We'd already moved, and we didn't have a lot as it was, but after that night we had literally nothing but the clothes on our backs. That was when I started a Saturday job, I'd not had it long when they forced me to live with Mr Richards as a maid. Apparently, my work would pay off my dad's debts. My brother was handed a job, but I was never told what. My sister was too young, I suppose, so she stayed with Dad."

"Go on," urged Jesse softly.

"I used to see Frank beat the shit out of Demy and his mum, but he didn't touch me. When Frank saw how close I was getting with Demy, he asked me if I loved him. I nodded, and he asked me if I'd ever slept with a boy before. When I shook my head, he said he'd allow it, but only if we kept it a secret between the three of us."

"Shit," exhaled Jesse, rubbing his face.

He wasn't sure he could sit through this, but he had to if she was to feel safe with him. He could do it if he reminded himself this was more for her to unburden than him to have information.

"So, we would cuddle up and sleep with each other, but that was it, just sleep," said Hayley wanting him to know she hadn't been *that* easy.

"It was nice, he was warm, and he seemed to understand how much I missed Mum. We'd talk all night, and I felt safe with him. But then after a few months Frank came back to me and asked me if his son was any good. You know. I said we hadn't done that, we just cuddled. So, he got really angry and told Demy he had to go to some camp to learn how to be a proper man, and if he didn't come back and do the job better, he'd do it for him. I didn't understand what he meant at the time. Demy was my friend I wasn't sure how he could do better. He was good to me, I trusted him and I didn't want him to have to go somewhere because of me."

Taking Hayley's hand across the table, he gently entwined their fingers.

"When he came back, he was different, harsher, more abrupt, and colder, but now and then I'd see a glimmer of the boy I knew and so when he wanted to, you know, I let him. It was horrible, it hurt, and I was in pain for a while, but he told me that was normal, that I'd get used to it. But I told him I didn't want to do it again. He said he'd be more gentle next time, and I'd begin to like it. When my period finally came, he knew obviously and so he must have told his dad because that's when Frank set up the ceremony, by then I'd seen more of Demy's dark side than his good and I told my dad I didn't want to do it. I told him what me and Demy had done and that I didn't want to do it anymore. He said I should have thought about that before I whored myself out. I was heartbroken, not least because I didn't want Demy but because my dad wouldn't stop it. I felt like he blamed me, that I had done something dirty and wrong," taking another sip, she moistened her dry throat.

"I told you the rest before, but two years into the marriage there still wasn't a baby and his dad was going spare. Belittling Demy in front of others, saying he clearly wasn't man enough, not stacking enough of the goods. But when we'd get back, he'd take it out on me, say that I was the reason for us not conceiving and I was making a fool out of him. After a while his dad sent him away on business and I couldn't wait. I was so excited to just be left alone. Only, I wasn't. He turned up that first night and every night Demy was away. I was so relieved when he came home, I jumped on him, kissing him, I swear he must have thought I'd gone mad. But that night we made love, actual love, not just an attack, and I fell in love with him all over again.

I thought things would be different. I had my Demy back, and the month after we found out I was pregnant, he was over the moon and so was I. All I'd ever wanted was a family of my own and with Demy, things seemed to have sorted themselves out. It was perfect, and it was for a while until we went to a party where his dad drank too much and put the idea in his head that the baby might not be his, especially as he'd left me for a whole week on business the month before I had conceived. As soon as he said it, the bottom fell out of my world, because as much as I'd wanted to forget what he had made me do. I'd genuinely hoped it was Demy's and so I'd decided to believe that that's what had happened. That the minute he had treated me nicely we'd been rewarded with a child, but of course as soon as we got home, he laid into me. Asking me who I'd been with, I told him no one, I couldn't very well tell him the truth could I? So, I lied over and over, crying, screaming for him to believe me, but when I grabbed his arm for him to listen to me, he flung it back and slapped me across the face. The force sent me down the stairs, and when he stepped past me, he told me he was going to the pub and he'd see me when he was ready. I cried on that floor for everything I knew I wouldn't get back. He hated me, and I loved him. I loved him so much, Jesse, and I hate myself for it. How could I have loved him when he treated me so badly?" Cried Hayley.

Jesse tightened his grip on her hand.

"I felt a pain in my stomach the second I tried to get up, and I knew. I just knew something was wrong. I wasn't due for another month and the pain was unbearable. I slid myself across the floor to the landline in the room's corner. Thankfully, I knew Dad's home number, and

Darren picked it up. When I explained what had happened, he called an ambulance straight away. He met me there, and that's when I realised I was in labour. The baby was born, but I told Darren I didn't want it being brought into this life. I worried Demy would hurt it if he got angry like he did me, especially if he thought it was someone else's. Darren was only a kid himself, but he said he'd sort it. I was too tired to argue or to ask him how, but a couple of hours later he came back and told me he'd changed the system to show the child was deceased and that he had paid the midwife off. I assume he had help, but he never told me how or where from and I didn't want to know. Later the midwife came in to tell me she had placed the baby with its parents after their own child had died. I thanked her, and she just said at least it would be one family she didn't have to comfort. She told me to look after myself and, in her opinion, I should think about getting away as soon as possible. Then the social were called in and they wanted to know who the baby's father was. I wouldn't give them a name, but I assured them it was a boy from school. They were sympathetic and condescending, but after speaking with my father they left us to it."

"Why didn't you tell them it was Demy's or Frank's you could have put them in jail?"

"Because I would only have been able to get one of them in trouble. How would I have proved both of their involvement? If they needed proof, they'd want to the test the baby's DNA, of which they couldn't because she wasn't dead. Then they'd have known I had got rid of her. Besides, even if one of them got convicted the other one I'd still have to contend with and how much worse would that have been knowing I'd effectively put their son or father behind bars and you forget they knew everyone. They wouldn't have gone to jail, and I'd have become their prime target. So, I went back, distraught at losing my baby, just not in the way they thought. There was only me and Darren who knew except whoever helped him and the midwife, of course."

"You've never tried to find her?"

"No, why would I? I hope she's happy and safe and that her parents love her and have been able to give her everything I couldn't." Hayley wiped the tears from her cheeks. "She'd be six."

"Hayley none of this was ever your fault, you know that don't you?" Assured Jesse, making her look him in the eyes.

"Jesse, how can it not be? I fell for it. I fell for him. I tried to make it work, when I knew it wouldn't. I knew he wasn't a proper businessman. I knew he wasn't packing eggs for a living, but I ignored it."

"You chose not to poke your nose into things you knew would get you killed."

"Until I did. I thought I'd heard enough to get him arrested. I phoned the police with all the information I had put together, but I'd been wrong. I hadn't got out of the house in time. I heard him come back as I was searching for my things to run, and I hid in the wardrobe, with my knees pressed up to my head hoping he wouldn't find me, that he'd think I had already left but he didn't and he found me. He beat the living shit out of me because he knew what I'd done. I don't know how, but he knew exactly what I'd told them word for word. It was then I realised I couldn't go to the police ever again."

"So, when we got together..?" Asked Jesse, realisation dawning on him to her shocked face when he had told her what he did for a job.

"It scared the ever-loving crap out of me. I didn't want to trust you, or fall for you, or you to know anything about me that might make you change your mind about me. But I couldn't help it, you were everything I ever wanted. You were kind, patient, compassionate, loving and calm. You were the exact opposite of Demy and I fell for you but it scared me, because I thought if I love you, I won't be able to see you for what you really are and I'd be blinkered again," she cried, watching her words affect Jesse strangely as he smiled sympathetically towards her.

"Which I did by interviewing you," said Jesse, remembering that day with such regret.

"Yeah. I was so cross with myself for letting my feelings get in the way again. I thought you were using me to get your job done or worse, that you were setting me up for Demy."

"You thought I had something to do with that?" Asked Jesse, shocked.

"For a little while, yeah," admitted Hayley shyly, shrugging. "It was all too much of a coincidence, getting hauled into the cop shop then an hour later I'm in his hands again."

"Oh, Jesus Christ, Hayley. I'd never put you in harm's way, you're my life," admitted Jesse, leaning over to kiss her on the forehead.

"Daniel is your life. I'm just the girl who trapped you," reminded Hayley, looking to the table her arms still rested on.

"What are you talking about?" Asked Jesse, dumbfounded.

"Jesse, we both know you wouldn't be trying so hard to make this thing between us work, if it wasn't for Daniel, and I get it, I really do. You want the whole family package, wife, kid, house and job and now it looks like you've got it, I just wish it was what you truly wanted," said Hayley slipping her hands from his. "I wish I was what you wanted."

"Hayley, what makes you think I don't want you?" Grabbing her hands back, he enveloped them in his.

"Because you said so yourself, Daniel needs a stable home and you miss him," answered Hayley.

"I miss you too," said Jesse, bringing her hands to his mouth to kiss her knuckles.

"I'm sure you do. But I wanted a man to miss me without the added appendage of responsibility and guilt," said Hayley, wishing he'd let her go, so she could hide in her room. She'd never been this honest with anyone and she was feeling beyond vulnerable, but completely naked and raw.

"Why do I feel guilty?" Asked Jesse.

"For not finding me. I know it tore you apart and I know you feel responsible for me, and it's admirable. You're a good man, a decent man, and I love you for it. I just wished you felt the same way about me as I do about you. But it looks like you're stuck with me now, and I'm sorry."

"Right, let me get one thing straight, and can you bloody well listen to me for once in your life?"

When she raised her eyebrow to him, he continued before she interrupted him.

"Do I want Daniel in my life? Yes, without doubt, he's my son and I love him dearly. Do I feel trapped here in witness protection? Yes, of course I do, we're going to have to become different people to the outside world and make up a fake life and background, new identities and new friends. Do I want the nuclear family? Yes, I want a wife and children and a job to pay for them. Do I want any of that without you? No. No, I can't think of anything worse.

I'm not here with you just for Daniel's sake, although I'm not naïve enough to think I wouldn't do anything for that kid. But I'm also here for you, and not out of some misguided notion of loyalty or guilt or anything else you think I have going on in my head, but because I love you more than that anything in my life and yes that includes Daniel. I love you more than anyone I have ever known and I would do anything, go anywhere, be anyone in order to be by your side, and not just so I can protect you. But because you might one day give me the chance to love you, completely and without restraint. And I'll wait here for you to get to that moment where you not only trust me, but that you love me with everything that entails. I want to wake up with you every single day, make love to you, be there for you when you cry at sappy movies you've seen a hundred times, give you the cushion so you can hide behind it when there's a violent scene in a film. I want to be that lip you pinch between your teeth when you're worried. I want to be the clothes that hang on you all day, just so I'm close. Hayley, I want to be the only man you look at ever. I want us to be everything to each other. I've never known anyone get under my skin like you do. You're infuriating, flippant, controlling, dismissive, argumentative..."

"OK, I get it, you *were* doing well.." said Hayley trying to lighten the mood.

"Exactly, anyone can love the good things about someone, but only someone truly besotted can love the things that annoy the shit out of them."

Hayley couldn't help but laugh.

"and while I can't promise you'll not drive me mad or I'll not drive you mad. I hope we can both find home in each other. Because it doesn't matter where we are, or what people call us, or what story we make up. You and I will always know the truth and that is, that while my heart beats in my chest, you know that it only beats to enable me to be with you."

"Holy shit, Jesse, you been watching those Hallmark films?" Laughed Hayley, wiping tears from her face.

"I don't need to. I know how I feel. You are everything to me," answered Jesse firmly.

"What about your dad?" asked Hayley.

"What about him?" asked Jesse, confused.

"He died because of me. I brought all this to your door and now you have no brother, your father died and your mum's on her own."

"My brother can take a running jump off a very tall building for all I care; you didn't make him strangle you, that's on him. Mum knows I love her and I'll work something out so I can get a message to her. But I know as long as we are safe, she'll be as happy as she can be, plus Martin will not let her go without, no doubt he'll have his three kids driving her nuts soon, just so she's not lonely. I'm not sure she'll forgive me for that one actually. But Dad died trying to save Daniel's life and I know if he had to make the same decision again, he would without a doubt. I only wish he died knowing Daniel was safe but Dad wouldn't have had it any other way. He'd have protected that kid with every fibre in his body because he adored him, and he adored you. He loved you nearly as much as me, and don't for a second think I blame you in any way for him dying, because I don't. They did that, and you took him out. I'd say that if you had any fears about me resenting you in any way, it should have disappeared the moment you took that man's life to protect mine."

"I didn't mean to kill him," she said, wiping the tears that had started up again. "I mean I'm not sorry but I-"

"I know. It scared you. You reacted. You were trying to protect me, and not for the first time. But Hayley, please from now on and just for my own sanity and manhood, let me take care of you?" urged Jesse, trying his best to keep a straight face, until she understood what he was saying.

"I'll try," she smiled.

"We're on our own," said Jesse, looking around as if he was waiting for someone to pounce out. "Daniel is asleep and we're wasting time, when we could christen our new home."

Watching his face as if he was whispering secrets, she suddenly caught on to where he was going with it and couldn't help but smile wider. "I've waited too fucking long for this, and it's about time you realised you belong to me."

"Really?" She whispered back coyly. "I'm yours, am I?"

"If you have to ask that question, then I'd say we're long overdue being acquainted, wouldn't you?"

Hayley nodded before Jesse pulled her up to her feet, touching his lips to hers. Softly he whispered kisses on her lips before smiling, sensing her breathing change. What started out as gentle quickly turned frantic, and after shedding their clothes and bumping into many walls, they finally fell onto their new bed.

"If you're not ready, tell me now," whispered Jesse, kissing behind her ear and down her neck, inhaling her scent. "Because I'm not going to be able to stop in a minute. I've waited too damn long."

When she didn't answer, he pulled away, looking back down on her. "We don't have to do this, we can take as long as you like," said Jesse, realising the last thing she needed was to feel pressured.

"Jesse, if you don't get inside me in the next five seconds, I might actually explode," she argued.

Chuckling, he straddled her, lowering the collar of her shirt, he kissed her collar bone gently as she allowed herself to be consumed by his touch. Lifting her T-shirt over her head, he laid back down while he assessed her.

"What are you waiting for?" she asked watching his eyes glaze over every inch of her.

"Just committing everything to memeory."

"Well, you don't need to, so stop dragging this out." she whined, making him smile broader.

"Someone's a little eager for my dick?"

The blush that enveloped Hayley's chest and cheeks pushed him over the edge and he laid on top of her, only to roll her over so she was over him. "If you want him, so better tell him."

Laughing, Hayley pulled down his zipper, releasing his dick from his boxers she stared at it unsure, but equally mesmerised.

"Hey,"

Looking back up to him, she saw worry in his eyes.

"You don't have to do this, we've had a big day," said Jesse curling her fallen hair around her ear gently.

"I've never done this before, well, not willingly."

Realising what she meant, he leant up and pushed his aching apendage back in, before pulling up the zipper.

"What are you doing?" She cried.

"I didn't mean I wanted you to do that," admitted Jesse. "Shit! I'm so sorry, I didn't think how that would sound."

"Don't you want me to?" She frowned.

Jesse's eyes almost bugged out of his head. "Want you to? God, yes. But that doesn't mean you should."

"Why?"

"Why?" asked Jesse astonished. Choking on his tongue he tried to think of something that wasn't condescending or hurtful. Struggling he scratched his head in though, panicking she was about to run off at any point. "Why?... well because I... I have no idea what... what you were..."

Smiling at Jesse's obvious discomfort she couldn't help but toy with him.

"Why are you smiling?"

"Because I've never seen you so flustered before."

"I'm not flustered."

Hayley couldn't help but laugh as she took his lips with hers. Holding his hands in her hair, she groaned at the sheer joy of having him under her. Teasing his zipper down, she took him in her hands and he groaned, helplessly.

Bending she lowered her mouth to him and took him in.

"Holy fucking mother of shit!" gasped Jesse.

Chuckling at his outburst Hayley worked Jesse the best way she knew how. Having not done it before she had to rely solely on instinct and the noises he made while she ran her tongue along the length of him. When he placed his hand on her head she froze and he seemed to understand. Taking it away she continued until every last drop of pleasure had made its way down her throat.

Wiping her mouth, she looked back up to him with a self-satisfied smirk. Watching him pant made her feel powerful and she'd never felt like that before with a dick in her mouth.

"You didn't have to do that," he said running his thumb along her bottom lip.

"Yes, I did."

Leaning up, he kissed her thoroughly, uncaring of the tang he could detect on her tongue. If anything, he made him want to be inside her more.

"Now let me get these bloody jeans off you." Pulling them off her, he took her pants with them and threw them somewhere behind them, before pushing his further down and lining himself up with her entrance.

Gasping at the invasion, her eyes rolled to the back of her head. Stopping to check she was still OK, Hayley gave him a look to say he if stopped she might cut his balls off, so he forged ahead. Pushing himself further in and rubbing her clit with his fingers.

Seconds later, she was pulsing around him, with a pillow over her face to muffle the screams of pleasure tearing through her body as Jesse hammered home until they were both spent, sweaty and shaking.

"Still feel like you might explode?" Laughed Jesse, as he lay down beside her, watching her stare at the ceiling.

"Think I already did," she laughed, catching her breath.

"God, I've missed that sound." Hayley turned to him, with one eyebrow raised. "You laughing."

"And all it took was you getting naked," she said sarcastically.

Laughing, he bent over her to kiss her again. He didn't care what they had to get through, as long as they got through it together. "I didn't think I could ever have this."

"What amazing sex with a hot bloke?"

"Or that he'd be so modest," laughed Hayley.

"Have what baby?" Asked Jesse, growing serious, watching her chest rise and fall, as he traced the lines of her freshly sewn stitches in her side.

"This feeling of contentment. Even though I know the world's falling down all around us. Here in bed with you none of that matters, it's just you and me and I love it."

"Me too," said Jesse, kissing her mop of hair. "Hayley, you know you're not to blame, don't you?"

"I know *you* don't."

"*You* shouldn't either. You were a kid, you weren't mature enough to make those kinds of decisions, what they did was damn right wrong in every sense of the word, but you were innocent."

"They took that to remember," smiled Hayley sadly.

"Hayley, what they took from you wasn't yours to give. You're not responsible for it until you're old enough to understand it. They stole something from you. Then, like a burglar blames the home owner for not having better locks, they laid the blame at your door. It shouldn't have been up to you to decide or be persuaded because it should never have been spoken about until you were ready. You're not to blame for someone taking something that belonged to you. They did something horrendous, and that's all on them. Every bit is on them. I need you to understand that, OK?" He asked desperately.

"OK," she nodded as a single tear escaped down her cheek.

"Good. Because in this family we only apologise for our own faults," said Jesse, kissing her lips gently.

"Our family?" Mused Hayley, liking the sound from her own tongue.

"Damn right. And we're team Jayley."

"What?" Squawked Hayley before pushing at his chest laughing.

"Well, our kids are going to moan at us for ganging up on them and closing ranks, we need a name."

"Kids?" She asked, watching his face intently, while brushing her thumb along his bottom lip.

"Yeah, I was kind of hoping to give Daniel some siblings," admitted Jesse, watching for her reaction.

"Were you now?" She asked, unsure.

"Only if you want to, of course," added Jesse, alarmed.

"I think we should try to get settled here first," answered Hayley, looking around the vacant white room.

"Yeah, you're right." He admitted, laying his head on his crossed arms, staring at the ceiling.

"Hey, that wasn't a no," said Hayley, watching his face turn from playful to serious.

"I know," he smiled tightly.

"Then why do you look so glum?" She asked, leaning on her arm to watch him.

"We're going to have to name them something other than Hallam," he admitted despondently.

"I'm sorry, Jesse."

"Hey!" said Jesse sternly, turning towards her. Hayley smiled before pretending to zip her mouth. "Better. Now keep it zipped."

Leaning over her, he lowered himself down her body until he got to her stomach where he kissed it, while caressing her breasts.

"Does it hurt?" Looking up, he gazed into her eyes. "Knowing I carried Daniel, and you didn't witness it?" Asked Hayley.

"A little, OK, a lot. I missed it all. We didn't get to celebrate, or watch, or feel, or anything."

Watching a tear roll down her cheek, he quickly wiped it away. "We missed out, but next time we'll do it all together, I promise."

Nodding, she tried to smile while holding in more wayward tears.

"I want to see you blossom and glow, and carry my baby, knowing he'll be our world just like Daniel."

"Don't forget you got to see that little boy enter the world." She said through the tightening in her throat.

"I know, the most amazing time of my life, but if I'd have known at the time he was mine, it'd have been a completely different story," said Jesse, rolling his eyes as he laughed.

"Only because you'd have been going nuts, checking that the midwives were properly qualified or something," answered Hayley, running her hand through his hair.

"Probably, but I'd have told him there and then that I loved him."

"Jesse, he knows, trust me. That kid loves the ground you walk on. I may as well be invisible when you're around," answered Hayley, smoothing his hair.

"I'm sorry you went through all of that with Rob on top of everything else."

"What did we say about apologies?" She asked, raising her eyebrow to him, while resting his chin on her chest. "Truth is, I should have told you and trusted you to deal with it, I didn't. I just tried to hide it and not acknowledge what was going on."

"I can't argue with that. Do you trust me now?" He asked.

"With what? Cooking, cleaning, childcare?.."

"Ha ha, you know what I mean. Do you trust me with your heart?"

"You've had it since I met you," she answered, smiling at his glossy eyes.

"You can have something in return if you want?"

Giggling, Hayley squirmed underneath him as he tickled her. When he stopped, she took his head in her hands, kissing his lips before looking him in the eyes.

"Just your heart."

"Well, surely you want him too?"

Laughing, she opened her legs, wrapping them around him while he got comfortable.

"Make me a promise?" Asked Hayley.

"Anything."

"Promise to always love me. Be honest with me. Show me respect and honour this very wanton body of mine," she asked, trying not to blush at her own words and failing badly.

"Oh babe, you didn't even have to ask, always."

Taking her mouth, he devoured her, tasting her, absorbing every sound and imprinting his mark.

"Now let me show you how much," he remarked, watching her naked body join with his.

Just then a cry went out. Sighing, she pulled the covers that had wrapped themselves around her legs off her and pulled away from him. He watched her leave the room, hearing her laugh before cooing at Daniel as she soothed him from crying.

CHAPTER 22

ALTHOUGH THE INTERLUDE HAD BEEN NICE, THE REALITY SOON CAME crashing down around them when they were joined by a liaison officer who detailed what was going on, and how they were all going to proceed under cover. There was to be no contact with anyone, including Marie and Martin. They were not to go near their old lives in any way; they had to memorise their new identities, sign new signatures, and take new bank cards. The officers in charge had already taken their phones from them, so they gave them new ones. It took most of the day to work through their new lives, helping each other build up stories about how they'd met, how they had got married, where, when and how he proposed, and how Daniel was a happy surprise after only a year of marriage.

Looking at the ring on her finger, she twirled it around, whilst sitting on the sofa as Jesse dished up cottage pie from the oven.

"I had hoped there would be an engagement ring on their before a wedding ring," sighed Jesse, passing her plate from over her shoulder.

"Yeah, well, we saved a fortune on a reception," laughed Hayley, taking her plate and settling it on her knee, before taking the cutlery he offered her.

"True. But it would have been nice to ask you. I even went ring shopping," admitted Jesse, taking a seat next to her.

"When?"

"While you were in hospital after Rob-" he didn't finish the sentence as it was still painful for them both.

Hayley nodded understanding. "Well, just so you know. If you'd have asked, I'd have said yes," she said, lifting a forkful of mash to her lips, eyeing Jesse as she swallowed.

Eyes bulging, he placed his plate down on the coffee table before taking hers from her and doing the same. Holding her hands, she faced him as he stared into her eyes.

"If we ever get out of this and back to our own lives. I want you to know that the first thing I will do, is ask you to marry me," he said sincerely. He needed her to know this wasn't a chore being married. He wanted this. He just wanted it in his own name.

"Then be assured that if you do, I will always say yes."

Smiling, he kissed her.

"I love you, Jesse, more than anyone in the whole world."

"Good, because I'd follow you to the end of it."

"And in the meantime, we'll enjoy married life as Mr and Mrs Conners," said Hayley winking.

"We will," he smiled, kissing her again before passing her her plate back. "Call this a pre-run."

"You know we're not going to be able to go back, don't you?" Asked Hayley wearily. "This might be it."

"Then at least we're already together. I can live this life for as long as we need to, as long as you're both safe."

Hayley nodding hoping he meant it, because life would never be the same again.

That night Jesse laid awake staring at the ceiling. Being out of the loop was unsettling. Not having any idea on whether the case was getting any closer to ending, or whether they had detained suspects, stopped him from sleeping.

Hayley lay next to him, sleeping soundly, although he wondered how long that would last. She was still having nightmares, understandably, but they were wearing her out. She needed a full night's sleep to recharge, and those monsters had stripped her of it.

Deciding he'd only unsettle Hayley further, he crept out of the room in his boxers. Making his way to the kitchen, passing Daniels room, he popped his head in to check he was OK. Sleeping with his hands above his head as if in surrender, the notion made him laugh.

Taking a mug down from the cupboard, he filled the kettle and flicked it on, listening to the slow rumble as he pulled out a chair at the circular table and propped his head up on his hands. Thinking of his Mum and Dad only brought tears to his eyes. He'd not be able to go to the funeral if this was still going on, he wanted to pay his respects; the man deserved that, if nothing else, and he deserved a lot more.

Why had they had to take him away? It had devastated his Mum. She'd never recover, he knew that. Wondering how much longer she'd last without him by her side, he heard the kettle reach boiling point and flick itself off. Pulling himself up he reached for the coffee canister, opening it he pushed his spoon in and tipped it into the cup, before pouring the water and reached for the milk out of the fridge.

Suddenly his phone rumbled on the table. Picking it up, a text flashed up from a number he didn't recognise.

Room 4, Beverley Inn, Lairgate. 11am.

Taking a sip from his mug, he stared at the message. No one had this number other than the team who'd placed them in Yorkshire away from the investigation and their home. But someone had it. Who? And what did they want?

Opening up the browser on his phone, he typed in a website he knew from work. Finding the link, he made the request, and a message pinged back ten minutes later with a location. Pulling his wallet out from his jacket pocket that rested on the chair, he rifled through the paper. Taking out five hundred, he made his way to the safe in the bathroom and unlocked it, taking out another five in fifty-pound increments. Rolling it up, he flicked one of Hayley's hair bands from off the sink over the cash. Picking up jeans from the wash basket and a fairly damp t-shirt, he pushed his feet into his boots, locking the door on the way out.

Ten minutes later, he placed the money in the open storage box at an office block. Walking away, he made his way to the pickup across town. Twenty-five minutes later he sat on a bench, hoping he hadn't just lost a grand. They needed all the money they could get at the minute. They'd withdrawn their funds from their banks, to make it look like they were on the run to anyone who cared to look. But the money had to last them as long as possible.

As a crowd neared him on the bench, he stiffened, expecting an altercation, but they just carried on past him, fooling around with each other. Sighing, he relaxed back into the seat, moving his foot beneath him. As he did, he felt something. Looking down, someone had placed a brown paper bag beneath him. Looking around, he couldn't see anyone. Sliding his hand under the bench, he pulled it out. Peeking in, he saw what he had paid for. Tucking it into his inside jacket pocket he made his way back to Hayley hoping she hadn't woken up.

Placing it in the locker, he secured the combination lock and stripped out of his clothes, throwing them back in the laundry basket. Folding back into bed, Hayley curled herself around him.

On feeling his cool skin, she groaned. "Where have you been?"

"Just had a quick walk. Clear my head, couldn't sleep." He felt her nod and then draw circles on his chest with her finger close to where her name was tattooed on his chest.

"I'm awake now too." He made an hmm noise, and she looked up to catch his eyes. "Be a shame to waste a peaceful moment. Don't you think?" She said watching the smirk pull at his lips. "And I am awake now, and you feel really cold."

"Yeah, think I might need warming up."

"Exactly what I was thinking," she said, moving her body over his. She could feel him running his hands down her sides until they came together on her bottom. Lifting herself up onto her arms, she dipped down to kiss him on the nose, then his forehead, cheeks and finally his mouth. Grabbing her, he rolled her onto her back as she giggled and screeched as he ran his fingers lightly down her sides, tickling her.

"Stop, stop, I give in," she giggled trying to breathe.

Him now on top of her, he pinned her wrists down at the side of her head and swept his mouth down her neck, hearing her moan and feeling her relax sent chills down his spine.

"When did you tat?" She asked curiously.

"I might have got that when you were taken," answered Jesse, watching her eyes turn to saucers. "We didn't really spend a lot of time being close last year so you didn't see it."

When tears pooled in her eyes, he grasped the back of her head and pulled her to him, covering her mouth with kisses.

"But we've slept together since then."

"You didn't notice it then. You had your eyes closed for most of it."

"I'm sorry."

"It's how you deal, I get that."

"Not very flattering for you though."

"We're not doing this, remember. You don't apologise for the shit you've had to deal with."

As tears slipped from her eyes, Jesse kissed them away.

After an hour of warming up, Hayley and Jesse slept soundly wrapped around each other. They woke to Daniel crying for his morning bottle and cuddle.

"I'll get him," said Jesse, pulling the covers away.

Five minutes later Daniel was between them with his bottle, gulping as though they had not fed him in a week.

"Kid, slow down. You're going to get indigestion," urged Jesse.

"Takes after his Dad," remarked Hayley, smiling as she ran her fingers over Daniel's fringe.

"We're growing men. Need our fuel, don't we, kiddo?"

Hayley laughed.

"I can almost forget everything else when it's like this," said Jesse, watching Hayley watch Daniel intently.

"I know what you mean."

"This is everything I've always wanted. You, me, him."

"Just didn't bank on the entire world trying to take us out?" Asked Hayley.

"No, didn't prepare for that one." He said solemnly, remembering the message from last night. "I love you, you know that, don't you?"

Looking at him, she could see how serious he was and nodded.

"I just need you to know, in case anything happens; I'd do anything for you."

"Jesse has something happened?" She asked, worrying from his tone that something had changed; he knew something that she didn't.

"No, I just need you to know," he shrugged, but then looked back to Daniel, picking up his hand and kissing his podgy fingers.

∼

AT TEN TO eleven Jesse stood outside the Inn looking around. It was fairly quiet, apart from the rush of traffic on the road passing by. Opening the door, he stepped in gingerly. Looking around the empty room, he could smell the distant tang of cologne and coffee. So, someone had been here. Trying a few doors, he finally came to one that opened up to a corridor with numbers on. Finding number four, he twisted the knob and pushed open the door. Realising it was empty, he searched for a light switch. Flicking it on, he immediately saw the photographs displayed on the double bed. Walking over to them, he recognised them as being taken over the last week. They were all of Hayley and Daniel, outside their safe home, at the local corner shop and in the garden.

"Shit!" Throwing the ones in his hands on the floor, he bolted for the door. Launching into the street outside, he ran, pumping his legs and arms as fast as he could. The knowledge that they had set him up, to leave them unprotected, ate away at him. The weight in his jacket pocket rhythmically thumped against his chest as he ran. Giving him little hope if he was too late.

∼

THE VINE TREE

HAYLEY SPLASHED water onto Daniel's tummy as he chuckled and got excited. She made duck noises with the only bath toy they had while he tried to grab for it. Hearing the door, she called out that she was in the bathroom.

After a few more minutes, Hayley decided the water was getting too cool, so she grabbed a towel from the floor and held it across her chest as she awkwardly picked up Daniel. Placing him on top of the towel and wrapping it around him, she stood up, 'oof'ing at his weight. She emerged from the bathroom, walking past the living room and kitchen to his bedroom. Lowering him into the bed cot, she rummaged around in his chest of drawers for something to put on him.

"The blue dungarees are nice," said a voice.

Spinning round, she held up the clothes to her chest, unable to breathe. Her heart beat fiercely in her chest, drowning out all other senses as she stared at the man who wanted to hurt her most.

"Frank?"

"No," he said, shaking his head. Before walking towards the cot and peering over. "He's adorable."

"what... who... what... why... what do you want?" She said, reaching into the cot to retrieve Daniel quickly. Holding him to her chest, whilst staring at the stranger who looked far too familiar.

"I came to tell you it's over."

"What's over?" She asked, glancing round the room for a weapon.

"This fake life of yours," answered the man dressed in a charcoal suit, white shirt with slicked back salt and pepper hair. It was then she realised the differences in appearance, rather than the similarities. But she couldn't make sense of it.

"I'm not coming with you," she said defiantly, hoping her will was the only thing needed. Where was Jesse?

"That's a shame," he said, smiling. "But understandable," he nodded, looking almost sorry.

"Just tell me what you want," she said, hoping he'd get to the point. Daniel was squirming and was no doubt picking up on her anxiety.

"I believe you're due some answers," he said. "I'm not here to harm you."

Hayley took a step back, hitting her back on the chest of draws.

"Jesse will be back soon, so we haven't got long. Maybe we should sit down."

"What have you done to Jesse?" She panicked.

"Nothing. Shall we?" He said calmly, offering her the doorway.

Hayley watched him leave through it, and then tentatively followed. Realising she was still wrapped in only a towel, she prayed the knot at the top would hold.

He sat on the chair nearest the television, closest to the window. "Sit."

She sat down on the sofa as far away from him as possible with a still naked Daniel, who'd unravelled his towel earlier in the cot.

"I'm afraid I have some explaining to do."

Hayley waited, not taking her eyes from him.

"My name is Alexi, and I have been working on the inside of Gemini since I dramatised my suicide. There's only a handful of loyal subjects that know of my existence. Well, until your brother blew the operation apart."

Hayley stiffened.

"Don't panic. I told him to, it was time to become the face of Castor."

"I don't understand," admitted Hayley, confused.

"Well, you see, in Greek mythology Castor and Pollux were twins but had different fathers. Castor and Pollux fell in love with Phoebe and Hilaeira, nieces of Leucippus. The twins abducted them, thus starting a feud. Castor was mortally injured, while Pollux killed Lynceus. As Idas approached Pollux, Zeus threw a thunderbolt, thus saving his son's life. Pollux then asked his father to grant half his mortality to his brother, hence they transformed into the constellation Gemini, and able to travel back and forth to Hades."

"Great, thanks for the Greek mythology lesson. But what the hell has any of that got to do with me?"

"Your mum was Phoebe and her twin sister was Hilaeira."

Hayley still didn't get what he was talking about. How did any of this relate to her?

"Demy's mum is Hilaeira. That's why your DNA is so close," concluded Alexi.

"Demy's mum is Selina," countered Hayley.

But she watched him shake his head.

"I still don't understand," she answered, hugging Daniel closer.

"Our Father abducted Phoebe and Hilaeira for us. But Pollux, or Frank, was enraged and took what was rightfully mine. Then he killed their parents to make them vulnerable. Our father saved him from death by doing business with the Italians and as such Pollux, Frank, ensured I was brought with him to share the burden. Together we held a legitimate business and an illegal one. But Pollux grew envious. I was succeeding where he was not. Where he was more concerned with business, I wanted a family. So, he took what was mine, to father a child. He thought he could take away my hope and crush me. Knowing I'd destroy myself for allowing him to do it, but I decided to play him at his own game and while he was building the business, I was building a case. Finding everything I needed to pull him and the organisation down. I found a like-minded assistant in Darren, and with his tech skills we were able to salvage as much evidence as possible. It did not harm Darren, but he did owe me a favour. This was then emailed to your friend's office, where I believe they have as much material as they'll ever get to bring down a worldwide organisation. Now, all that comes with a heavy price and I'm afraid it's not one I care to pay. So, I will be leaving and you'll never see me again, unless you choose to come with me."

"Frank-"

"I know what he was trying to do, and I'm sorry I couldn't protect you. In all honesty, I needed to know who you were first. Rumours are no good to a man like me, in my position. I needed cold, hard facts before I could carry out a rescue mission. It could have had us both killed and then we'd have been no good to anyone."

"Who I am?" She asked incredulously.

Watching the shock flitter across her face, he realised she didn't know, and he sat back in the chair to get comfortable.

"I found out Frank tricked your mother into sleeping with him before they married us. What he didn't know was that we had already done so ourselves. We were very much in love Hannah."

"Hayley," she corrected.

"My apologies. She named you Hannah when you were born, she must have changed it."

"And now you know?" She asked, wondering how he had taken any tests that she wasn't aware of.

"Yes, you're mine and Phoebe's. Tests confirm it. You see, Identical twins have very close DNA, often thought to be identical. But it's not, and I've had my lab working on it to find out one way or the other. Without the police knowing they could have two almost identical candidates, they only saw the similarities between the bloods they had. It took my people closer inspection to reveal the truth."

"But the bloodline?" Asked Hayley, feeling as though finally all the pieces were coming together.

"It was made to create a bond between the founding sixteen families. As the generations continued, they would become much stronger. Those sixteen families turning into eight then four then two, finally there would be one ruling family and as long as they adhered to the rules they would remain in control. Unfortunately, if they stepped out or caused conflict it became a type of war to regain power and then the whole sixteen to one family would begin again with recent cousins or whoever could claim blood rule. You see, Frank was right up to the top. He needed you to be with Demy, and then your offspring would be the final person. If he could control that child, he would have full power over the entire organisation. But Frank initiated a splinter group, just so he could be as depraved as he wished with like-minded people. Call it a club and suddenly it becomes all high brow," answered Alexi staring at Hayley. "The splinter group was the vine cross, and it's that group I have helped you disband."

"Gemini?" Asked Hayley, still trying to marry what he was telling her with what she already knew. "Rob said that? Why would he say-?"

"That's the 'club' as you'd call it. Gemini is the ruling class, a prestigious club for wealthy men, unfortunately with every club comes a dark side, and that's where all the blood lines come in. Don't get me wrong, it's taken very seriously that certain families are married off together, to unite business and allegiances, but it was never meant to be used to help profit in sexual abuse. He made his branch of the club to make them feel somehow superior, but it didn't rule their businesses. Just their sick urges. Everyone at Gemini is aware of it, and while it didn't interfere with business, it was allowed to run. But Demy was stupid. He brought it to the table and used it to try to manipulate our clients and benefactors. The call was given out, and I accepted it. It was the justice I needed and with the full backing of Gemini. The information they have on file, leads to all businesses contained within his club. It does not affect investments in Gemini, nor will it. All allegiances with people within that club have been dissolved and no one will come to their aid unless they want the full weight coming down on their heads. I'm trusting you with this information because I feel I owe you it. I've already checked for surveillance and disconnected those in residence, so I'm asking you one last time, you can either come with me and build a life or stay here with Jesse and Daniel, but you need to decide quickly."

"I'm staying," she answered immediately.

There really was no contest. Nodding as though he expected it, he stood only to come face to face with a gun.

Hayley spun round to see Jesse holding it. "Jesse don't."

"Who are you?" Asked Jesse, ignoring Hayley while staring at Alexi and slipping in front of Hayley to shield her and Daniel.

Alexi lifted his arms up to show his empty hands. "I came to ask you to look after my little girl."

Turning quickly to Hayley, she nodded confirmation.

"You're a good man, Jesse Hallam, and I sincerely apologise about the death of your father."

Jesse straightened his gun, levelling it with his nose.

"It wasn't by my order, I assure you."

"Jesse, this is Alexi or Castor, or apparently my father," said Hayley.

"You sent me out to the Inn?" Asked Jesse.

"Yes, I needed time with my daughter; you being here would have caused conflict," he said, pointing to the gun. "I'd give it seventy-two hours before you can return to your old life."

Jesse gently lowered the gun.

"I'm sure my daughter will explain everything once I've gone."

Jesse turned to Hayley, who was now by his side.

"Not good enough, what's going on?" Asked Jesse, bringing the gun back up and pointing it at Alexi's face.

"The Vine Cross was a branch on a formidable tree, that's the best way for me to describe it."

Jesse carried on staring at him.

"The Tree is called Gemini, and it has strong rich roots that support the entire infrastructure, but like anything that's organic. It can become diseased, and when those branches start to become ill, they infect further up the branches until they rot the entire tree. The Vine Cross was a poison, but a shiny new toy, as with most toys it became useless. But the people who championed it wanted to grow it. Thus, causing the disease. Last year you managed to cut some of those branches, but you didn't cut far enough up the branch, and that's my fault. I had benefactors that I was trying to protect. Unfortunately, those benefactors turned out to be spoiled. So, I enlisted the help of Darren, and between us we designed a way in which to eliminate the disease without destroying the tree."

"And what part of the tree are you?" Asked Jesse.

"The trunk. I get the branches what they need. Feeding them with the nutrients from the ground, whilst preserving the roots."

"I'm loving the analogy, but what the fuck do you do exactly?" Asked Jesse, growing bored with the man's tale.

"I do what needs to be done to make the world go round. Politics is a greasy business and everyone wants something. I make sure everyone gets what they need, to keep balance, without one taking over the other," explained Alexi calmly.

"What are we talking? Drugs? Trafficking? Nuclear warheads?"

Alexi nodded his head to all three.

"How can you be party to that?" Gasped Hayley, holding Daniel to her protectively.

"I don't tell the sick fucks to do it, and I certainly don't condone it. But if I'm required to keep peace between two global giants, sometimes I have to step outside of my comfort zone. I don't make these people do anything. I just facilitate it and then charge the earth, which then gets invested into helping these people."

"A regular Robin Hood," snorted Hayley.

"No, and I don't pretend to be. I'm not a good man, I'm a businessman. A good one, but a businessman all the same," explained Alexi, watching Hayley flick her gaze from him to Jesse.

"Am I just supposed to let you walk out of here?" Asked Jesse.

"Yes. If you don't, you'll die before your finger pulls the trigger. I suggest you don't test that fact," he added calmly, looking from Hayley and Daniel to Jesse. "Can I ask you for one thing?"

"What?" Answered Jesse sternly.

"Can I hug my daughter and grandson?"

Jesse didn't move, still stood between them, he searched for Hayley's eyes as she stared at the man in front of her, resembling the man who had tried to destroy her. After a pause for thought and a lot of tension, Hayley nodded, stepping towards him. Wrapping his arms around her tears streaked his face, and it took Jesse back to see a man who hadn't shown any vulnerability in his stance since he'd thrust a gun in his face, cry. Lowering his gun, he placed it into the back of his jeans.

"I'm truly sorry your mother died, I loved her very much."

"What happened?" Asked Jesse.

"She and I had a falling out. I was horrible to her, and she ran. Once I found out she had slept with my brother, I was consumed with rage and I took it out on her. For which I'll never forgive myself, especially as later I found out he had tricked her. She thought he was me, and he had played her. When she ran, she saved Han- Hayley from that life and so married Baxter. He was a good man, but he had problems of his own and when Frank found him, he used his weaknesses against him. Her mother found out, but by then it was too late and

Frank had her killed. Of course they swore Baxter to secrecy and made the move to Averham, where Hayley would be reinstated as the heir. All Baxter had to do was let Frank do whatever he wanted and Frank would stop doctored evidence being leaked to the police of his involvement in her mother's murder."

Kissing Hayley on the forehead, he bent down to kiss Daniel too. "Protect them with your life, Jesse."

Holding out his hand, he shook Jesse's firmly. "Do a better job than I did."

"I will," he answered, watching Hayley wipe tears from her eyes and hiding her face in Daniel's neck.

"If you ever needed my blessing, you have it," said Alexi, eyeing Jesse meaningfully.

"Alexi?"

Turning, he watched Hayley's eyes flitter from his to Jesse's, unsure of herself. Straightening, he waited, as did Jesse.

"Do you know where she is?"

Jesse looked confused, and she hated knowing she'd have to explain later. But if he knew, she needed to know too.

Looking from Jesse to her, his shoulders drooped a little, and she took it as bad news, and a sob broke free.

"She's doing well."

When she heard the words, she looked at him with disbelief. She thought he was going to tell her they had killed her.

"She's thriving. They love her very much and I'll keep an eye on her for you. I promise. What you did was the most selfless thing anyone could do, and your mum would have been incredibly proud. As am I," answered Alexi.

"Thank you," she whispered, not wanting to look at Jesse's face just yet.

"I wasn't going to do this, but I have a picture if you'd like to see?"

Nodding, she stepped closer as he fumbled on his phone. Stretching the image out between his fingertips, he held it out to her.

"She looks just like you."

Nodding as tears fell, she scanned the child's face for similarities between her and Frank.

"I don't see him in her at all."

Nodding again, she was thankful that he had read her mind.

"She started school, doing well by all accounts."

"Is she loved?" She asked as her voice broke.

"More than anything."

"Was it you, who helped Darren place her with another family?" Asked Jesse, having seemingly tied it all together.

"He didn't know who I was. But yes, it was me. We'd crossed paths and I assume he thought he could trust me. Thankfully, he was right."

Taking her hand, Jesse wrapped it in his before Alexi gave Hayley and Daniel one last kiss on the head and walked out of their home.

"Where the hell did you get the gun?" Asked Hayley once Alexi was out of sight.

"Ah, long story," answered Jesse, scratching his neck.

CHAPTER 23

Watching the coffin make its way down the aisle of the church, Hayley tightened her grip on Jesse's hand. Feeling her offer comfort, he kissed the top of her head to reciprocate. Today was difficult for everyone, particularly his Mum who stood next to him watching her husband make his way to the front. Once everyone was seated, the priest started his sermon, while his mother wept quiet tears beside him. Hayley clung to him. He wasn't sure which of them she was trying to support most, but he appreciated her being there.

After the first hymn of 'Amazing Grace' Jesse stood and made his way over to the pulpit to deliver his reading. Unfolding his paper, he looked around at all the faces staring back at him and was pleased to see so many. His father had been a good man, one of the best, and he deserved a packed church.

"I just wanted to say a few words. Firstly, thank you to you all for coming today. It means a lot to see so many people come and see him off. Dad was a good man, one of the best, the best. He was always there for me to offer support, advice, help and a quip or two. Nothing was too much work for him. He always gave a hundred percent, and he always did it with strength and dignity. He was the person who told me how to be a man, how to protect those around us, cherish those dear to us, and be that shoulder of support. Dad never claimed to have the answers, but he would always listen. I have many fond memories of him from being a child to being an adult, and I can say with absolute certainty that the man I called Dad also became my best friend." Looking up from the paper, he scanned the crowd again.

"My mum and dad were married for nearly thirty years, and they had two sons. Me and Rob. Unfortunately, none of us know where he is today, but I hope that he's raising a glass somewhere. Before he died, he was looking after his grandson, who he loved dearly. If he wasn't breaking up chocolate buttons, he was stock piling treats by his chair, ready and waiting to hand them out when he returned. I know Daniel loves him very much, and it's going to be difficult watching him grow without his granddad there to show him how to get into mischief. Dad told me once that I was like him, in that when I fell in love, I would do so completely. Just like him, I want to do everything to make sure those close to me know that I love them and I know he loved my mum with all his heart."

Wiping an errant tear from his cheek, he looked to the back of the church and saw a shadow cross over the arch. Looking back to Hayley, he smiled and looked back down to his paper.

"My dad was my rock. He was always there to offer support. He never once condemned me for bad choices other than letting the love of my life slip through my fingers. He was pretty pissed with me for that." A few titters sounded out at that. "But Dad was a constant. He made me want to become the best version of myself. He pushed me to see my flaws and work on them. He never dismissed my insecurities, but he never allowed them to take over. He taught me to face my fears, because fear was only an imaginary foe. Once you saw it for the illusion, it was, you could work through it. Only he never taught me how to work through your worst fear when it actually happens and that was losing him."

Swallowing, he took a breath and screwed his eyes up while rubbing between his eyes to retain some composure. "He was my hero, and now he's Daniel's too. If I could have him back for five more minutes. I'd tell him that he made me who I am and that no matter what happens he'll not be forgotten and I'll never let him down ever again."

Wiping the tears from his face, he folded the paper and placed it back into his pocket. "I would just finally like to say that he'll not be forgotten. Nor will any of his stories die, he'll be with us always and we'd very much like to invite you back so we can celebrate Dad's life together, thank you."

After watching the coffin being lowered into the ground, and each mourner casting a red rose in. Jesse and Hayley stood watching while the last of the mourners departed. Hayley held onto his hand as he looked down at the coffin below. Rubbing his arm, she hoped he was doing OK, but he'd barely spoken since the reading. Having watched his mum hobble to their car to wait for them, she felt unbearably split. She wanted to offer Marie comfort, but she couldn't let go of Jesse. A few more minutes of silence and Hayley looked up to Jesse's stoic face.

"He was there," spoke Jesse.

"Who?" Asked Hayley, wondering to what he was referring.

"Rob,"

Hayley felt an icy tingle flow up her spine, before looking around to see if she could see anyone lingering.

"I was reading, and he was at the back."

Hayley swallowed, unsure what to think about that. The man had tried to kill her, but he was Michael's son. He belonged here.

"I don't understand how he could do it?"

Hayley wished she could say something, but what could she say?

"If I ever see him again, he'll be the one needing a box."

"Jesse, don't," said Hayley softly. "Let's get your mum back."

Nodding, he left his father's graveside, and they made their way to the car.

EPILOGUE

A YEAR LATER.

"You ready?" Asked Martin, nudging Jesse's arm.

Blowing air out from between his pursed lips, he straightened to the sound of the wedding music. Jason Mraz's I'm Yours sang out. Turning he saw Hayley dressed in a long white lacy dress with a flower band in her hair pinning her braided crown to her head, holding a bouquet of white and peach coloured roses with matching dahlias.

Watching her walk towards him on her own made his heart stop and his breathing seize. He knew how much it meant to her to walk down the aisle on her own, with her stepfather deceased and her real father unable to attend she was adamant she walking on her own. The only other man she would have wanted had died, and it warmed his heart to know she would have chosen his father.

Catching his eyes, she smiled that brilliant smile before wiggling her hips at the music as she got closer. Laughing as he laughed at her playfulness. Looking towards his mum, dressed in a rose-pink summer dress and matching blazer, held his youngest son on her knee, bouncing him to keep him from crying. Whilst Daniel swung his legs on the chair looking bored beside her. Fiddling with his white bow tie. He couldn't help but smile.

When Hayley caught where his gaze had gone. The love in her eyes for her family was clear for everyone to see. When they had found out that she was pregnant again, he had immediately lowered to one knee and asked her to spend the rest of her life with him.

"You look stunning," said Jesse, taking her hand.

Smiling, she thanked him before passing her bouquet to Sam. Her friend from work who had been thrilled to be asked to be her Matron of Honour.

After the registrar had welcomed everyone, explaining what they were all doing here today, she offered Jesse his chance to speak.

"Hayley, I promise to love you, cherish you, protect and honour you."

He winked, and she couldn't stop the blush from running up her neck.

"You are the first thing I think of when I open my eyes and the last thing on my mind when I close them. I knew a long time ago that you were the one for me, and a very smart man told me once to hold on to you tight and be the man you needed. Which I will always strive to be. I will always trust you, be loyal to you, be honest with you, and I'll forever respect you. I love you unconditionally and you have changed my life, bringing me so much happiness and blessing me with two sons who I adore, even if they do wake up earlier than the birds and crash on our love life."

Hayley laughed as tears flowed down her cheeks. Smiling, she sniffed and tried to dislodge the mound in her throat.

"You are my world and the only reason it turns. There would be no sunlight without you. You are my light on dark days and my peace in a storm."

Smiling, Hayley swiped more tears from her face.

"Jesse, I promise to love, honour and respect you. You came into my life like a knight in shining armour, saving me from a fate worse than death. You breathed life into my existence and gave me a family who saw me for me. We've had our fair share of threats and misfortune, but I'm the luckiest woman alive to have met you and be sharing my life with you. I trust you, will be loyal to you, and be honest even if I know you won't like it. I respect you because I know how much you love me and because of that I adore you. I watch you with our children and my heart sings each time I see you reflected in them. I'm so thankful that you came into my life and quite frankly you saved my life in more ways than one, and not only will I be eternally grateful, but I'm eternally yours."

Smiling, Jesse tightened his grip on her hand before turning to Martin for the rings. Hearing him sniffle he glanced up to his friend, witnessing him wiping his face on his hanker chief he turned back to Hayley who couldn't help the laugh that escaped.

"Bollox to the pair of you," grumbled Martin. "Took you long enough."

Jesse slapped him on the back, laughing before he took the rings from Martin. Pushing the ring onto her finger, Jesse repeated the words of the registrar, before Hayley did the same.

"It is my absolute pleasure to pronounce you husband and wife."

Everyone cheered, and Jesse grabbed Hayley, stating his claim. "I give you Mr and Mrs Hallam!"

∼

JOINING THEIR SONS, taking one each, they made their way through the garden that they'd booked for their ceremony and stood outside the orangery for photographs. Once the photos were done, they all headed inside to the restaurant for a sit-down meal. They had both decided on a small event but when they received a letter stating arrangements had been made for their wedding and he had bought and paid for it. They decided to take up the offer of their generous benefactor. Hayley only wished she could have seen him one last time to have thanked him.

After cutting the cake, Hayley decided to take the children for a nap until the evening was set up and ready. Carrying Michael and holding Daniel's hand, she escorted them to their room that they were sharing with Marie for the night. Only to open the door on a figure sitting by the window.

"What are you doing here?" She asked, holding onto Daniel's hand firmly. Jesse snaked his fingers round her waist, hoping to get a kiss before she disappeared inside, only to freeze when he saw who Hayley was looking at.

"Rob?"

∼

THE END

If you enjoyed this story, please leave a review, thank you. If you enjoyed this story and would like to read more about Hayley and Jesse, please check out The Vine Coda.

THE VINE CODA TEASER

CHAPTER 1

"Are you OK?" The whispered sign of concern caught his ears and before he knew it, he was looking up to find out where it had come from. "Are you okay?" asked the gentle voice once again.

Squinting as though that might help his eyesight, his eyes finally focused on a young woman with a heavy woollen coat and a brown handbag that she gripped tightly to her chest as though a gust of wind may blow it away; Peering down at him with concern reflected in her eyes, Rob couldn't help but feel visible once again.

Too many nights he had curled up with whatever material he could find to help keep him warm, or at least starve off the icing chill of the wind while he tried to get some shuteye. Not an easy feat when you had to keep one eye on your surroundings to ensure you weren't knifed in the back for the shoes on your feet, or the cardboard box you clung to.

After a few attempts to open his mouth speech failing him, he just nodded limply, before allowing the weight of his head to anchor his body. "I saw what happened. Do you want me to call the police or an ambulance?" On the word police he sharply looked up, jolting his neck from shaking it frantically. "You need to be seen, you're covered in cuts and bruises."

As if her words suddenly reminded him, they battered him, he looked down at himself. Half sat, half crouched on the dirty needle laden pathway under the bridge he'd been hoping to hide under.

"No," he scratched out of his throat. Seeming to weigh up her choices, she continued to stare at him as though he might change his mind if she hung around long enough. Finally, giving up any pretence of strength, he slumped onto the floor. Leaning up against the grimy graffiti ridden wall, he allowed his legs some relief by stretching them out along the path, becoming an obstruction for anyone who might choose to pass.

"I'm Freya," said the lady who was still watching him intently.

He nodded to acknowledge he'd heard but said nothing. If he ignored her long enough, she'd get the hint he didn't want to talk. "Why did they beat you up?"

Looking back up at her he saw her sparkly eyes, he couldn't tell which emotion was more prevalent, fear or concern but the fact she hadn't walked away already told him she was more concerned than scared. He'd seen those eyes before, or not those exact ones, but they had been blue and they haunted him every night when he closed his eyes, memories of what he had done. If the woman stood before him only knew what he was capable of, she would run for the hills not making sure he was all right.

Letting out a slightly gargled laugh, he watched her shrink as though he had made a fool of her.

"Because they could," he answered, wanting her to know he wasn't laughing at her more at what she might have expected him to say in response.

Watching her look around herself as if to check she wasn't being set up for a quick purse grab he grimaced at how untrusting she looked, he'd seen that look all too often before, it was the look Hayley had on her face right before she had realised he was going to end her life.

"Look, I don't normally do this, well… because it's too dangerous… but… but…" unsure what she was trying to say, he just sat and waited, trying to weigh her up.

The woman was of average height, slim with wavy chestnut hair, big blue eyes with a dainty elfin face and a delicate nose. She wore a long woollen coat over jeans, a turtleneck jumper and what looked like brown leather knee-high boots. She didn't look exactly well off, but she didn't look short of a bob or two either.

"Do you want to come back to mine? You can get cleaned up and you can use the first aid kit?" she asked while scanning his clothes, OK so she might have to incinerate his clothes and fumigate the house but she couldn't very well leave a man already down on his luck sitting on a dirty path after having been beaten up by a bunch of yobs for being just that.

"You want me to come to your house?" He asked, thinking his ears were definitely playing tricks on him. That couldn't have been what she said. That was crazy. What kind of person would willingly open their home to someone like him, looking and smelling the way he did, and a young woman to boot. Was she not concerned for her own safety?

Shuffling on her feet, she had another scan around to check they weren't being overheard. Looking back towards him, she worried her bottom lip between her teeth before checking her surroundings again.

"Sure. It's just a chance to grab a break." She answered as though she wasn't just offering her house, safety and sanity on a plate with all the trimmings.

She'd keep her bag with her at all times, she'd have easy access to a phone and her bank cards and cash were not something she wanted to willingly flaunt under his nose.

"Are you stupid?" He asked, frowning at her.

Taken aback, she opened her mouth to answer, only deciding to close it instead she stepped back. Glancing down to her own feet away from his scornful gaze, she suddenly felt embarrassed.

"You don't even know me," he answered, realising she was more insulted at being called stupid than grateful for the opportunity to withdraw her charity.

"Are you going to hurt me?" She asked, looking back to him, watching his dark eyes turn a shade lighter.

"No, but..."

"Then it's fine. I mean the offer's still there if you want it. No pressure," she said standing with her arms folded glaring down at him, which did everything to contradict what she was saying.

"How do you know you can trust me?" Asked Rob, amazed that a stranger was taking such a chance on him, no one had ever given him the benefit of the doubt before, even when he had done nice things for people, they had always thought he had an ulterior motive. Okay, sometimes he did, but he'd always thought it was best to spare the stick and use a carrot, at least until that fateful day that had changed his life forever. "Rob."

"Pardon?" Asked the woman, leaning closer to hear him.

"My name. It's Rob."

"Nice to meet you, Rob," smiled Freya, holding out her hand to him.

Taking it. He worried about where his hands had been but gently shook her hand anyway so as not to appear any ruder.

Gently heaving himself from the stench of the urine covered concrete floor, he brushed himself down as though that might do something to make himself more presentable. Which it did nothing of the sort; just highlighted how shabby his clothes were.

"It's not too far away; it'll take about 5 minutes."

He tried to smile, but he was sure it came across as more of a grimace. Turning, she stayed beside him as he hobbled forward. The kicking might not have been the first he'd received while living on the streets, but it didn't stop them from hurting his already battered body.

"Maybe 15." added Freya, watching his slow progress. When he chuckled, she couldn't help but laugh a little too. "Do you need to lean on me?" She asked, observing how his left leg appeared locked and unable to bend appropriately.

"No, I can manage. Thank you." She doubted it, but she knew when to leave well alone, so she just kept pace with him and carried on directing him to her home. All the time a little voice in her head was screaming at her that this was an awful idea, but she was sure the voice belonged to her oldest brother, so she shook it off and continued.

Reaching the door, she felt around in her handbag for the key, retrieving it she slipped the key in the lock, turning it before pushing the door open. The scent of spiced apple hit him in the nose the second the change in air caught him.

"Sorry, I was baking earlier. Stunk the whole house out."

"Smells amazing," said Rob, sniffing the air as if he could fill his stomach from scent alone.

"Are you hungry?" She asked, slipping her coat off before hanging it on the end of the banister in front of them. When he gave her a look, she reprimanded herself for the stupid question. Of course, he was hungry, he was homeless. "I'll get you something to eat after you've had a shower."

"A shower?" Asked Rob, shrugging off his filthy coat and laying it on the floor. It was too dirty to even contemplate placing on top of hers.

"There are some spare clothes in the bedroom first left off the bathroom, just wear whatever you like. Once you've cleaned up, I'll look at taking care of those cuts, but I don't want them to become infected, so you best clean up first."

"Oh." Rob was unsure what to say. The generosity she was showing him was astounding. He was fairly sure that she could knock him down with a feather if she wished.

"There're clippers in one of the bathroom cupboards too, if you fancy a trim."

"Wow, I'm not sure what to say," answered Rob, dumbfounded.

"Tea or coffee?" Frowning at her, she smiled that beautiful smile, the one that lit up her whole face. "Would you like tea or coffee?" she repeated as though she was talking to a five-year-old.

"Coffee, please."

"Righto. First door at the top of the stairs." She said before skipping off down the hallway without a care in the world. Watching after her, he shook his head. He couldn't work her out. Why was she being so nice to him, so trusting?

THE VINE CODA TEASER

Hearing the shower running upstairs, Freya pulled two cups down before spilling milk into them from a fresh carton. He'd looked a mess, and she had never seen someone take such a beating before. No one deserved that. There had been a gang of them against a lone homeless guy, she'd watched them rip the rucksack from his back, rifling through it as though it was their possession before punching him to the ground and cheering each other on as they all took turns putting their boots in. Knowing she wouldn't be able to stop them, she had had to wait until they had finished before she could go anywhere near the guy to offer help. He looked broken, his eyes told stories of visits to hell, and his clothes said he'd been on the streets for far too long. Normally if she saw the homeless, she could walk away, sure in the fact that they had somehow brought it upon themselves, bad choices, no economical background, drugs or alcohol abuse. But when she had witnessed six youths beating on one man, there was no scenario in her head that could allow her to just leave him.

Sitting the cups on the table, she sat down and waited, flicking through her phone on Facebook for something to do. When she heard the bottom step of the stairs, creak she knew he was downstairs, finishing a text to her friend to say she was at home and would phone her later as something had come up, she looked up in shock to see a freshly shaved, clean man wearing her brother's navy t-shirt and dark denim jeans.

"Wow, you look different," she said, lifting her jaw up from the floor.

"Thanks. Well, I hope it's a compliment, because I looked like shit before," he answered, trying to contain his smile.

"It was. Sit down, your coffee's getting cold." she said pulling out a chair. Grabbing it, he pulled it out further before sitting down. Wrapping his fingers around the cup, he brought it up to his lips, inhaling the scent before taking a sip. "Has it been that long?" she asked, eyeing him over her own drink.

"Too long," he answered, taking another sip, as the first warmed his empty stomach.

"How's the cuts?" She asked, pointing to his face.

"A little sore, especially as I caught them on the razor." Watching her wince, he laughed at her face. "But I've not been clean shaven for a while. I needed to see if I still looked like me."

"And do you?"

"Mostly," He answered sorely. Smiling, she stood before walking over to a cupboard to retrieve a small first aid kit. Coming back, she laid it open on the table taking her seat again she looked at his face trying to decide which cut to tackle first.

"Do you think anything's broken?" Freya asked, while opening a pack of sterilised wipes.

"No. It's just bruising."

Nodding, she dabbed the wipes to the cut on his nose. It was the longest and the scariest to look at, although it looked like his blood had done its job of coagulating. It still looked as though it wouldn't mind a couple of stitches just to support it. Every time he winced, she mirrored him and soon he was wincing just to get a reaction. When she cottoned on, she gave him a look to behave, before smirking and grabbing a bag of frozen peas.

"Here, put that wherever it hurts most." Taking it, he held them to his ribs, which had taken most of the force.

"Do they really hurt?" She asked, watching him try to get comfy.

"I think they were getting some penalty practice in, with my lungs," he answered.

"Yeah, they got a few good shots in," she said solemnly. "I'm sorry I didn't stop them, but I thought they might turn on me if I did," she explained. "That sounds awful, doesn't it?"

"Don't apologise Christ, if you hadn't turned up when you did, I would probably still be sitting in last night's kebab."

She smiled, silently thanking him for not being cross with her.

"Wouldn't usually mind, but it wasn't even my kebab."

When she looked back to him, she couldn't help laughing as he smirked at her.

"They're always best when you're drunk, anyway," she added.

"Totally," he laughed, moving the peas up a bit.

"So how come you ended up on the streets?"

"Long story," answered Rob.

"Sorry, I didn't mean to pry."

A memory suddenly struck him. He remembered saying the exact same thing to someone before, only he hadn't meant it as innocently as Freya did. He really had been prying and biding his time. The memory only brought him shame; he'd been an idiot and made a grave mistake, one that would never leave his nightmares and that wouldn't allow him to escape the streets.

"No. It's not that. It really is just hard to explain."

Nodding as though that was good enough, she popped the lid off the Germaline before smoothing it over his hands.

"I messed up."

"Don't we all?" She muttered, taking great care to cover each scrape and graze.

"Not like I did."

Looking up at him, she saw much sadness mixed in his eyes with great regret.

"I gather it's not something you can just apologise for?" she gently asked, while replacing the lid and depositing the tube back inside the first aid kit.

"It would take more than an apology," he confirmed, watching her watch him.

"Then I'm sorry," she murmured, looking away. Once again Rob stared at her. She was unique. Soft porcelain skin and full luscious lips, her long lashes dashed her cheeks, and was struck by how beautiful she was. "What do you fancy to eat?" Asked Freya, glancing back towards Rob.

Rob shrugged, he wasn't sure what she had said at first but when it finally sunk in; he was glad to have not put her out any more by answering with something she'd have to make or order in. "Okay, well if you're not eating regularly then your stomach is going to be quite sensitive so how about something light like toast or a sandwich?"

"Whatever. Honestly. Anything would be good right now," he smiled, watching her scan the full fridge, whilst worrying her bottom lip between her teeth again as she thought.

"Ham and cheese sandwich?" she asked, turning to him with a block of cheese and a pack of ham in her hands.

"Brilliant. Thank you."

Watching her take the bread out of the bread bin and slather the slices with butter, he couldn't help admiring her physique. She was trim but also seemed fairly contoured under her clothing; he wondered what she did for a living that could give her that body?

"What do you do for a job?" Asked Rob, giving in to curiosity.

"Oh. Me?" she asked. Rolling her eyes once, she realised of course he was talking to her. "Sorry. I'm a gym instructor."

That made sense, but if he said anything now, he'd come over as a creep, so he just nodded dutifully.

"Well, I do classes mainly, Pilates, yoga, that sort of thing."

"Wow." Again, he bit his tongue.

"Did you have a job before?" She asked, flicking the knife his way.

"Yeah, I was a chef," he answered.

"Oh wow, now that is amazing!" She cheered. "I'm a simple cook. Stir-fry, beans on toast. Anything that doesn't take much skill. I'd love to learn how to make a proper meal," she beamed.

"Maybe I can show you one day," Rob offered.

Once the words left his mouth, he regretted them, she'd allowed him to shower and eat, she wasn't offering anything more and he shouldn't be treating her as though she should.

"Sorry."

"No. That would be lovely," she smiled sheepishly.

"Not very practical though, since I'll be back on the street soon," he answered, wiping his hand down his face to rid himself of tiredness. The shower had helped clean him, relax his muscles, but the heat had dissipated and now he was cool enough to nod off.

"How will you get off the street?" She asked, going back to the sandwich.

"I won't. You can't very well go for a job interview stinking of piss and if by some miracle they were nose blind and well.. just bloody blind, then I have no address so they can't very well set up wages for a bank account without an address can they?"

"I didn't realise. How is anyone ever supposed to get back up then?" She asked, genuinely concerned.

"We don't. There's no safety net unless you're lucky enough to find a charity that will help. But honestly, they have limitations too."

"Gosh that's awful, how is anyone ever supposed to get back on their feet if they can't get a job to afford a home?" She asked as if appalled for him.

Rob just shrugged. His Mum had a home, but he knew he wouldn't be welcome. He had a home, if it hadn't been repossessed by the bank because of unpaid mortgage fees. But he couldn't go back. If anyone saw him, they would immediately arrest him and he would serve the rest of his life behind bars. With the prospect of bed and three meals a day it sounded enticing, but he'd pissed off the wrong people and he knew he wouldn't last a day in there.

Passing over the sandwich on a plain white plate, he took it before lowering it to the table as she made one for herself. Biting into it, it felt like heaven. Even when the ham stung his split lip, he couldn't stop from closing his eyes. His stomach had screamed for food for so long, he wasn't sure if it would know what to do with the foreign invasion.

"Slow down, you'll make yourself sick," Freya warned.

"Oh, my god it's so good," sighed Rob, suddenly realising he sounded like Sally in that film he'd watched once.

Chuckling, Freya sat across from him before biting into her own.

"I think this is the best ham and cheese sandwich I've ever eaten."

Freya blushed at the compliment, even though she knew realistically that it was only because he hadn't eaten in so long. She remembered being on a diet for so long once that when she finally ate chocolate; she thought she'd missed an entire era of new delicious recipes, but no, they'd been the same recipes and she was just acting like Augustus Gloop. Freya couldn't help laughing at Rob's sheer enjoyment made by her own fair hands.

"Would you like another?" She asked, eyeing his empty plate.

Rob shook his head, but apparently, he was unconvincing as she placed her second triangle on his plate.

"Eat it; I'll make us both more."

Deciding to take what was on offer, knowing he couldn't be sure where the next meal was coming from, he ate through it quickly.

After Lunch, Freya showed him through to the living room.

"Anything you want to watch?"

"I should really get going, leave you in peace."

"You can't go yet. I've not put your clothes in the wash yet, and I can't imagine you'll want to put them back on in that state."

"It'll not take long to ruin, I assure you," he answered.

"Well, I can't let you get them back on, so sit."

Smiling at her bossiness, he sat and when she handed him the control, he flicked the large flat screen on, and started scanning the TV guide. When Freya had left him to it to fill the washing machine, he laid his head back and closed his eyes.

Peeling his eyes open, he looked around, wondering where he was. Scanning the room, he could see it was comfortable and cosy. And then Freya came into his mind, his guardian angel. Looking around the room for a clock he noticed one on the fireplace, but being too far away and his focus not yet righted he stood up stiffly, walking over to read the dials. Realising he'd been asleep for a couple of hours, he walked out the room in search of Freya. Noting how dark it was outside he couldn't work out what was going on, everything was so quiet. Glancing to the digital clock of the cooker, he read 02.04. But that would make it..? Panicking, he rushed back to the front room. But she still wasn't anywhere to be found. Why had she left him sleeping? It was the early hours of the morning, and where was she? Looking upstairs, he tried to listen, blocking out any other noises like the ticking clock and the fridge's humming. But he couldn't hear a thing. If she was home and in bed, he couldn't very well just let himself in to say bye. She'd be terrified before she gave him a chance to explain. But the thought of just leaving felt wrong too, she'd done so much to put back his faith in humanity.

Suddenly his stomach grumbled, and he thought about feeding it from Freya's supply. But he had no idea what she usually ate, and so didn't have a clue what wouldn't be missed. He didn't want to take something that she'd bought specifically. That would just be rude and ungracious. Coffee, he could do that; trick his stomach into feeling full.

Walking back into the kitchen, he filled the kettle and turned it on. Staring outside the kitchen window, he looked up at the stars whilst wondering about what was going on at home. He missed them, even his brother. In fact, mainly his brother. He had spent the entire last year trying to get back at him, trying to relieve some stress and pent-up anger, but when he had finally exploded all, he felt was horror and shame and he just wanted to go back home. Feel the loving arms of his family. Put right their wrongs and start a fresh, but he'd killed his brother's ex-girlfriend and there was no coming back from an event such as that. Jesse would kill him. He knew how much she had meant to him, and he'd use it against him. He was no better than them. No better than the people who had put the idea in his head to make Jesse pay. Hearing the kettle flick off, he made his drink, sitting back down on the chair he'd occupied earlier.

"Thought I heard you," said a quiet voice.

Looking up at the door frame, he noticed Freya dressed in a long silk dressing gown. "Is there enough water in the kettle for another?"

"Of course," he answered, jumping up to make her a drink. "Sorry, I didn't mean to wake you, but I wasn't sure what time it was."

"You were shattered," she answered, taking the chair out and sitting across from him. "Thought it was best to let you sleep."

"You shouldn't have, but I appreciate it," smiling she took the offered drink and sipped. "I can't believe I slept so long, I'm so sorry."

"Don't be and stop apologising. If I'd have wanted you removed, I'd have phoned my brothers," she answered, laughing at the shock of fear in his eyes. "I didn't phone them."

Relaxing a little, he sipped his coffee.

"I have three brothers and then all their mates, and there are literally hundreds of them. So, I'm covered, trust me."

"Good to know," he smiled. "Especially when you invite waif and strays into your house."

Laughing, she took another sip as he smiled back at her.

"Would you like to stay?" She asked.

Rob almost choked on his coffee, setting it down before he spilt any more on her flooring, he tried to recover himself.

"It's just you were telling me about jobs and work yesterday, and I can't see how anyone can get back up when they need both at the same time. I've been thinking about it and I have a spare room. You could have that, get a job and then either leave or pay rent?"

"Why would you do that? You don't even know me?" He asked, watching her face intently as she tried to put together what she wanted to say.

"Look. I've seen people fall and not get the help they need, not because people don't care but because they don't always know how to care. I know what you need and I have that, it's not costing me anything, but it could be the stepping stone you need to get your life back together. Therefore, it makes the room priceless, but it also means that any rent you pay later on down the line will be extra. It won't be because I need it, and so if you turn into a twat, I can just call my brothers and get them to toss you outside. And I won't feel guilty because I would have done everything I could to help and it would be your fault for being a tool."

Unable to stop the spread of his smile, he laughed at her comments. "Wow, you really think this is a bad idea."

"Not necessarily, but I just wanted to get the worst-case scenario out there so we know we both understand," Freya advised.

"That's not the worst thing that could happen. You're putting a lot of trust in me when you don't even know me, what's stopping me murdering you in your sleep?" He asked, watching her flinch slightly at the word murder.

"Will you murder me?" She asked, raising her eyebrow.

"No. But anyone could say that. I'm sure Fred West didn't drive round telling women to get in the car because he had a nice patio to build."

"Do you want the room or not?" Asked Freya, exasperated.

"Yes. I do. Thank you," said Rob humbly.

"Well then, no more talk of serial murderers. Especially this late into the night. Gives me the Willies," she said, shaking her shoulders animatedly.

Laughing, he took another sip of coffee.

"Thank you, Freya."

Once her name left his mouth, her spine tingled, and she saw the deep pool of his eyes. There was something comforting inside them, but they were overshadowed with darkness. He was not in a good place, but he was trying to hide it, she could tell. Something inside of her wanted to be that person to help, encourage him to smile a genuine, unadulterated, spontaneous smile, where just happiness shone through. He was capable of it; she was sure. She just needed to get inside to work her magic.

"Okay, well it's late or early depending on how you see it. But I need my bed because I've got work tomorrow, but the spare bedroom is up the stairs, the second bedroom on the left. Mine is the first one on the left, don't get confused. I have a baseball bat under the bed and I know how to use it."

"I'm sure you do. Thanks, I'll finish this then head up."

"OK. See you at a more respectable hour and we'll go through some ground rules and chores."

Nodding he smiled watching her leave the kitchen.

How had he got so lucky to have fallen into her path?

ACKNOWLEDGMENTS

I would like to thank all those people in my life who have been there for me in my darkest moments, you know who you are, and I love you dearly.

Neil, I would not be who I am today without your unconditional love, devotion and support. So, you only have yourself to blame. It's not been an easy ride, but it's one I'll never regret.

You have my whole heart.

I would like to thank those who have helped me immensely in my writing career such as all those who have beta read this book and offered advice to those who received ARC's and given honest reviews.

Thank you to three authors who have also been on the other end of the computer offering encouragement, help and advice every time I've needed it.

C.R Riley, Julie Thorpe and Aubrey Brandon you are amazing authors and fond friends. I'm so thankful to have found you.

ALSO BY S. P. DAWES

The Vine Series

The Vine Cross

The Vine Tree

The Vine Coda

The Band of Brother's series includes some of the characters from The Vine series.

Path to Redemption

Thicker than Water

Fight for Me

All my books can be found on Amazon.

Printed in Great Britain
by Amazon